Praise for
BRENDA JOYCE
and her de Warenne dynasty

BRENDA

JOYCE

the *Prize*

HQN™

Recycling programs
for this product may
not exist in your area.

ISBN-13: 978-0-373-77363-3
ISBN-10:   0-373-77363-3

THE PRIZE

www.HQNBooks.com

Printed in U.S.A.

This one's for Aaron Priest and Lucy Childs

The best team in town! Thanks for getting me back on track and where I belong—writing about bygone times, alpha men and the women who dare to brave all to love them....

Also by *New York Times* bestselling author

BRENDA
JOYCE

PROLOGUE

July 5, 1798
The south of Ireland near Askeaton Castle

GERALD O'NEILL RUSHED INTO the manor house, his once-white shirt crimson, his tan britches and navy coat equally stained. Blood marred his cheek, matted his whiskers. An open gash on his head was bleeding and so were the cuts on his knuckles. His heart beat with alarming force and even now the sounds of battle, the cries of imminent death, rang in his eardrums. "Mary! Mary! Get into the cellar now!" he roared.

Devlin O'Neill could not move, stunned. His father had been gone for more than a month—since the middle of May. He had sent word, though, every few weeks, and while Devlin was only ten years old, he was acutely aware of the war at hand. Farmer and priest, shepherd and squire, peasant and gentry alike had risen up to fight the English devils once and for all, to take back all that was truly theirs—the rich Irish land that had been stolen from them a century ago. There was so much hope—and there was so much fear.

Now his heart seemed to simply stop and he stared at his father, relieved to finally see him again and terribly afraid. He was afraid that Gerald was hurt—and he was afraid of far worse. He started forward with a small cry, but

Gerald did not stop moving, going to the bottom of the stairs and bellowing for his wife again. His hand never left the scabbard that sheathed his cutlass, and he carried a musket as well.

Devlin had never seen his eyes so wild. Dear God.

"Is Father hurt?" a tiny voice whispered beside him, a small hand plucking at his torn linen sleeve.

Devlin didn't even look at his dark-haired younger brother. He could not take his eyes from his father, his mind spinning, racing. The rebels had taken Wexford town early in the rebellion and the entire county had rejoiced. Well, the papist part of it, at least. Other victories had followed— but so had other defeats. Now redcoats were everywhere; Devlin had spied thousands from a ridge just that morning, the most ominous sight he'd ever seen. He'd heard that Wexford had fallen, and a maid had said thousands had died at New Ross. He'd refused to believe it—until now. Now he thought that maybe the whispers of defeat and death were true. Because he saw fear in his father's eyes for the first time in his young life.

"Is Father hurt?" Sean asked again, a tremor in his tone.

Instantly Devlin turned to him. "I don't think so," he said, knowing he had to be brave, at least for Sean. But fear gripped him in a clawlike vise. And then his mother came rushing down the stairs, her infant daughter in her arms.

"Gerald! Thank God, I've been so worried about you," she cried, as pale as any ghost.

He seized her arm, releasing the scabbard of his sword to do so. "Take the boys and go down to the cellar," Gerald said harshly. "Now, Mary."

She cried out, her blue eyes filled with fear, riveted on his face. "Are you hurt?"

"Just do as I say," he cried, pulling her across the hall.

The baby, Meg, began to wail.

"And keep her quiet, for God's sake," he said as harshly. But now he was looking over his shoulder at the open doorway, as if expecting to see the British soldiers in pursuit.

Devlin followed his gaze. Smoke could be seen in the clear blue sky and suddenly the sounds of muskets firing could be heard.

Mary pushed the babe against her breast as she opened her blouse, never breaking stride. "What will happen to us, Gerald?" And then, lower, "What will happen to *you?*"

He opened the door to the cellar, the opening hidden by a centuries-old tapestry. "Everything will be fine," he said harshly. "You and the boys, the babe, all will be fine."

She stared up at him, her eyes filling with tears.

"I'm not hurt," he added thickly, and he kissed her briefly on the lips. "Now go downstairs and do not come out until I say so."

Mary nodded and went down. Devlin rushed forward as a cannon boomed, terribly close to the manor. "Father! Let me come with you—I can help. I can shoot—"

Gerald whirled, striking Devlin across the head, and he flew across the stone floor, landing on his rump. "Do as I say," he roared, and as he ran back through the hall, he added, "And take care of your mother, Devlin."

The front door slammed.

Devlin blinked back tears of despair and humiliation and found himself looking at Sean. There was a question in his younger brother's pale gray eyes, which remained wide with fear. Devlin got to his feet, shaking like a puny child. There was no question of what he had to do. He had never disobeyed his father before but he wasn't going to let his father face the redcoats he'd seen earlier alone.

If Father was going to die, then he'd die with him.

Fear made him feel faint. He faced his little brother,

breathing hard, willing himself to be a man. "Go down with Mother and Meg. Go now," he ordered quietly. Without waiting to see if he was being obeyed, Devlin rushed through the hall and into his father's library.

"You're going to fight, aren't you?" Sean cried, following him.

Devlin didn't answer. A purpose filled him now. He ran to the gun rack behind his father's massive desk and froze in dismay. It was empty. He stared in disbelief.

And then he heard the soldiers.

He heard men shouting and horses whinnying. He heard swords ringing. The cannon boomed again, somewhere close by. Shots from pistols punctuated the musket fire. He slowly turned to Sean and their gazes locked. Sean's face was pinched with fear—the same fear that was making Devlin's heart race so quickly that he could barely breathe.

Sean wet his lips. "They're close, Dev."

He could barely make his mouth form the words, "Go to the cellar." *He had to help his father. He couldn't let Father die alone.*

"I'm not leaving you alone."

"You need to take care of Mother and Meg," Devlin said, racing to the bench beneath the gun rack. He tore the pillows from the seat and hefted the lid open. He was disbelieving— Father always kept a spare pistol there, but there was nothing but a dagger. A single, stupid, useless prick of a dagger.

"I'm coming with you," Sean said, his voice broken with tears.

Devlin took the dagger, then reached into the drawer of his father's desk and took a sharp letter opener as well. He handed it to Sean. His brother smiled grimly at him— Devlin couldn't smile back.

And then he saw the rusty antique display of a knight in his armor in the corner of the room. It was said that an infamous ancestor, once favored by an English queen, had worn it. Devlin ran to the statue, Sean on his heels as if attached by a short string. There, he shimmied the sword free from the knight's gauntlet, knocking over the tarnished armor.

Devlin's spirits lifted. The sword was old and rusted, but it was a weapon, by God. He withdrew it from the hilt, touched the blade and gasped as blood spurted from his fingertip. Then he looked at Sean.

The brothers shared a grin.

The cannon boomed and this time the house shook, glass shattering in the hall outside. The boys blinked at each other, wide-eyed, their fear renewed.

Devlin wet his lips. "Sean. You have to stay with Mother and Meg."

"No."

He felt like whacking his brother on the head the way Gerald had struck him. But he was also secretly relieved not to have to face the red hordes alone. "Then let's go," Devlin said.

THE BATTLE WAS RAGING just behind the cornfields that swept up to the ruined outer walls of Askeaton Castle. The boys raced through the tall plants, hidden by the stalks, until they had reached the last row of corn. Crouching, Devlin felt ill as he finally viewed the bloody panorama.

There seemed to be hundreds—no, thousands—of soldiers in red, by far outnumbering the ragged hordes of Irishmen. The British soldiers were heavily armed with muskets and swords. Most of the Irishmen had pikes. Devlin watched his countrymen being massacred, not one by one, but in waves, five by five, six by six, and more. His stomach churned violently. He was only ten but he knew a slaughter when he saw one.

"Father," Sean whispered.

Devlin jerked and followed his brother's gaze. Instantly, he saw a madman on a gray horse, swinging his sword wildly, miraculously slaying first one redcoat and then another. "Come on!" Devlin leapt up, sword raised, and rushed toward the battle.

A British soldier was aiming his musket at a farmer with a pike and dagger. Other soldiers and peasants were intently battling one another. There was so much blood, so much death, the stench of it everywhere. Devlin heaved his sword at the soldier. To his surprise, the blade cleaved through the man completely.

Devlin froze, shocked, as the farmer quickly finished the soldier off. "Thanks, boyo," he said, dropping the dead soldier in the dirt.

A musket fired and the farmer's eyes popped in surprise, blood blossoming on his chest.

"Dev!" Sean shouted in warning.

Devlin turned wildly to face the barrel of a musket, aimed right at him. Instantly he lifted his sword in response. He wondered if he was about to die, as his blade was no match for the gun. Then Sean, the musket in his hands clearly taken from the dead, whacked the soldier from behind, right in the knees. The soldier lost his balance as he fired, missing Devlin by a long shot. Sean hit him over the head, and the man lay still, apparently unconscious.

Devlin straightened, breathing hard, an image of the soldier boy he'd just helped kill in his mind. Sean looked wildly at him.

"We need to go to Father," Devlin decided.

Sean nodded, perilously close to tears.

Devlin turned, searching the mass of struggling humanity, trying to spot his father on the gray horse. It was impossible now.

And suddenly he realized that the violent struggling was slowing.

He stilled, glancing around wide-eyed, and now he saw hundreds of men in beige and brown tunics, lying still and lifeless across the battlefield. Interspersed among them were dozens of British soldiers, also lifeless, and a few horses. Here and there, someone moaned or cried out weakly for help.

An Englishman was shouting out a command to his company.

Devlin's gaze swept the entire scene again. The battle-field had spread to the banks of the river on one side, the cornfield behind and the manor house in the south. And now the British soldiers were falling into line.

"Quick," Devlin said, and he and Sean darted over dead corpses, racing hard and fast for an edge of the cornfield and the invisibility it would give them. Sean tripped on a bloody body. Devlin lifted him to his feet and dragged him behind the first stalk of corn. Panting, they both sank to a crouch. And now, from the slight rise where the cornfield was, he could see that the battle was truly over.

There were so many dead.

Sean huddled close.

Devlin knew his brother was close to crying. He put his arm around him but did not take his gaze from the battle-field. The manor was to his right, perhaps a pasture away, and there were dead littering the courtyard. His gaze shot back to the left. Ahead, not far from where they hid, he saw his father's gray stallion.

Devlin stiffened. The horse was being held by a soldier. His father was not mounted on it.

And suddenly, several mounted British officers appeared, moving toward the gray steed. And Gerald O'Neill, his hands bound, was being shoved forward on foot.

"Father," Sean breathed.

Devlin was afraid to hope.

"Gerald O'Neill, I presume?" the mounted commanding officer asked, his tone filled with mockery and condescension.

"And to whom do I have the honor of this acquaintance?" Gerald said, as mocking, as condescending.

"Lord Captain Harold Hughes, ever His Majesty's noble servant," the officer returned, smiling coldly. He had a handsome face, blue-black hair and ice-cold blue eyes. "Have you not heard, O'Neill? The Defenders are beaten into a bloody pulp. General Lake has successfully stormed your puny headquarters at Vinegar Hill. I do believe the number of rebel dead has been tallied at fifteen thousand. You and your men are a futile lot."

"Damn Lake and Cornwallis, too," Gerald spat, the latter being the viceroy of Ireland. "We fight until every one of us is dead, Hughes. Or until we have won our land and our freedom."

Devlin wished desperately that his father would not speak so with the British captain. But Hughes merely shrugged indifferently. "Burn everything," he said, as if he were speaking about the weather.

Sean cried out. Devlin froze in shocked dismay.

"Captain, sir," a junior officer said. "Burn everything?"

Hughes smiled at Gerald, who had turned as white as a ghost. "Everything, Smith. Every field, every pasture, every crop, the stable, the livestock—the house."

The lieutenant turned, the orders quickly given. Devlin and Sean exchanged horrified glances. Their mother and Meg remained in the manor house. He didn't know what to do. The urge to shout, "No!" and rush the soldiers was all-consuming.

"Hughes!" Gerald said fiercely, his tone a command. "My wife and my children are inside."

"Really?" Hughes didn't seem impressed. "Maybe their deaths will make others think twice about committing treason," he said.

Gerald's eyes widened.

"Burn everything," Hughes snapped. "And I do mean everything."

Gerald lunged for the mounted captain, but was restrained. Devlin didn't stop to think—he whirled, about to run from the cornfield to the manor. But he had taken only a step or two when he halted in his tracks. For his mother, Mary, stood in the open front door of the house, the baby cradled in her arms. Relief made him stumble. He reached for Sean's hand, daring to breathe. Then he looked back at his father and Captain Hughes.

Hughes's expression had changed. His brows had lifted with interest and he was staring across the several dozen yards separating him and his prisoner from the manor. "Your wife, I presume?"

Gerald heaved violently at his bonds and the three men holding him. "You bastard. You touch her and I'll kill you, one way or another, I swear."

Hughes smiled, his gaze on Mary. As if he hadn't heard Gerald, he murmured, "Well, well. This is a pretty turn of events. Bring the woman to my quarters."

"Yes, sir." Lieutenant Smith whirled his mount toward the manor.

"Hughes! You touch a hair on my wife's head and I'll cut your balls off one by one," Gerald ground out.

"Really? And this from a man fated to hang—or worse." And he calmly unsheathed his sword. An instant later, one solid blow struck Gerald, severing his head.

Devlin stared—beyond shock—as his father's headless body collapsed slowly to the ground—as his head rolled there, both gray eyes open and still filled with rage.

He turned, still in absolute denial, and watched his mother fall in a swoon. Meg wailed loudly, kicking and flailing, on the ground by Mary.

"Take the woman," Hughes said. "Bring her to my quarters and burn down the damned house." He spurred his mount around and galloped off.

And as two soldiers started toward the manor—toward his unconscious mother, Meg wailing on the ground beside her—the reality of his father's brutal murder hit Devlin with stunning force. *Father was dead. He'd been murdered, savagely murdered, in cold blood. By that damned English captain, Hughes.*

He'd left the sword behind in the battle; now he raised the silly little dagger. A scream emanated from somewhere, a monstrous sound, high-pitched, filled with rage and grief. He vaguely realized the sound came from himself. He started forward unsteadily, determined to kill anyone that he could, anyone who was British.

A soldier blinked at him in wild surprise as Devlin raced toward him, dagger raised.

A blow from behind took him on the back of his head and mercifully, after the first moment of blinding pain, there was blackness—and blessed relief.

DEVLIN AWOKE SLOWLY, with difficulty, aware of a sharp pain in his head, of cold and dampness and a vague sense of dread.

"Dev?" Sean whispered. "Dev, are you waking?"

He became aware now of his brother's thin arms wrapped tightly around him. An odd smell pervaded the air, acrid and bitter. He wondered where he was, what was happening—then he saw his father standing shackled between the redcoats; he saw Captain Hughes raise his sword and sever his head.

Devlin gasped, eyes flying open.

Sean hugged him harder, once.

Full recollection made him struggle to his knees. They were in the woods and it had rained some time ago, leaving everything cold and wet. Devlin lurched aside and wretched dryly, clinging to the dark Irish earth.

Finally it was over. He sat back on his haunches, meeting Sean's gaze. His brother had made a small fire, just enough to see by, not enough for warmth. "Mother? Meg?" he asked hoarsely.

"I don't know where Mother is," Sean said, his tiny face pinched. "The soldiers took her away before she even woke up. I wanted to go get Meg, but after you went berserk and that soldier whacked you, I dragged you here, to be safe. Then they started the fires, Devlin." His eyes filled with tears. He began to pant harshly. "It's all gone, everything."

Devlin stared, for one moment as frightened as his brother, but then he came to his senses. Everything was up to him now. He could not cry—he had to lead. "Stop blubbering like a baby," he said sharply. "We need to rescue Mother and find Meg."

Instantly, Sean stopped sobbing. His eyes wide and riveted on his brother, he slowly nodded.

Devlin stood, not bothering to brush off his britches, which were filthy. They hurried through the glade. At its edge, Devlin stumbled.

Even in the moonlight, the land had always been soft with meadows and tall with stalks. Now a vast flatness stretched before him, and where the manor once was, he saw a shell of stone walls and two desolate chimneys. The acrid odor was immediately identifiable—it was smoke and ash.

"We'll starve this winter," Sean whispered, gripping his hand.

"Did they go back to the garrison at Kilmallock?" Devlin asked sharply, grimly. Determination had replaced the icy fear, the nauseating dread.

Sean nodded. "Dev? How will we rescue her? I mean, they've got thousands.... We're just two—and boys, at that."

That exact question was haunting him. "We'll find a way," he said. "I promise you, Sean. We will find a way."

IT WAS HIGH NOON WHEN THEY arrived atop a ridge that overlooked the British fort at Kilmallock. Devlin's spirits faltered as he looked past the wood stockades and over a sea of white tents and redcoats. Flags marked the commanding officer's quarters, well in the midst of the fort. Immediately, Devlin thought about how he and Sean, two young boys, could enter the fort. Had he been taller, he would have killed a soldier for his uniform. However, now he considered the possibility that they could simply walk through those open front gates with a wagon, a convoy or a group of soldiers, as they were both so small and unthreatening.

"Do you think she's all right?" Sean whispered. His color had not returned, not even once, since they saw their father so gruesomely murdered. He remained frighteningly pale, his lips chewed raw, his eyes filled with fear. Devlin worried that he would become sick.

Devlin put his arm around him. "We're going to save her and make everything right again," he said firmly. But somehow, deep in his sickened heart, he knew his words were a terrible lie—nothing would ever be right again.

And what had become of little Meg? He was afraid to even think of the possibility that she had burned in the fire.

Devlin screwed his eyes shut. A terrible stillness slid over him. His breathing, for the first time, calmed. The churning in his insides steadied. Something dark began to form in his mind. Something dark, grim and hard—something terrible and unyielding.

Sean started to cry. "What if he hurt her? What if...what if he...he did to her...what he did to Father?"

Devlin blinked and found himself staring coldly down at the fort. For one moment, he continued to stare, ignoring his brother, aware of the huge change that had just affected him. The ten-year-old boy had vanished forever. A man had appeared in his place, a man cold and purposeful, a man whose anger simmered far below the surface, fueling vast intent. The strength of his resolve astonished him.

The fear was gone. He wasn't afraid of the British and he wasn't afraid of death.

And he knew what he had to do—even if it took years.

Devlin turned to Sean, who was watching him with huge, tearful eyes. "He didn't hurt Mother," he heard himself say calmly, his tone as commanding as their father's had once been.

Sean blinked in surprise, and then he nodded.

"Let's go," Devlin said firmly. They scrambled down the hill and found a boulder to hide behind just off of the road. After an hour or so, four supply wagons led by a dozen mounted troops appeared. "Pretend we want to welcome them," he whispered softly. He had seen so many peasants waving and obsequiously greeting the British troops, and fools that the redcoats were, they never knew that after they had passed, the smiles were replaced by leers and taunts.

The boys stepped onto the road, the sun high now, warm and bright, to smile and wave at the troops as they approached. Some of the soldiers waved back, and one tossed them a piece of bread. As the wagons passed, the brothers continued to wave, their smiles fixed. And then Devlin dug his elbow in Sean's ribs and they took off, racing after the last wagon. Devlin leapt onto it, then turned and held out his hand. Sean leapt up and caught it and Devlin pulled his brother up. They both dove behind sacks of meal and potatoes and then they huddled closely, looking at each other.

Devlin felt a small, savage satisfaction. He smiled at Sean.

"Now what?" Sean whispered.

"We wait," Devlin said. Oddly, he was coldly confident.

Once the wagon was safely inside the front gates of the fort, Devlin peered out from their hiding place. He saw no one looking and he nudged Sean. They jumped to the ground and dashed around the side of the closest tent.

Five minutes later they were lurking outside the captain's tent, hiding behind two water barrels, mostly out of sight and, for the moment, safe.

"What are we going to do now?" Sean asked, wiping sweat from his brow. The weather remained pleasant, although the gray clouds far on the horizon threatened more rain.

"Shh," Devlin said, trying to think of how to free their mother. It seemed hopeless. But surely there had to be a way. He had not come this far to let her fall into Captain Hughes's clutches. Father would want him to rescue her— and he would not let him down again.

The ghastly memory returned—his father's severed head upon the ground, in a pool of his own blood, his eyes wide and still enraged, although lifeless.

Some of his newfound confidence wavered but his resolve hardened imperceptibly.

Voices were raised. Horses approaching at a fast gait could be heard. Devlin and Sean got to their knees and peered around the barrels. Hughes had stepped outside of the tent, looking quite content, a snifter of brandy in his hand, apparently also interested in the commotion.

Devlin followed the direction of the captain's gaze, looking south through the open front gates of the fort, the way he and Sean had come. He started in surprise. A horde of riders was approaching at a hard gallop, and the banner waving above the outrider was cobalt, silver and black, its colors painfully familiar. Beside him, Sean inhaled sharply, and he and Devlin exchanged a look.

"It's the Earl of Adare," Sean whispered with excitement.

Devlin clapped his hand over his brother's mouth. "He must have come to help. Quiet."

"Damn the bloody Irish, even the English ones," Hughes said to another officer. "It's the Earl of Adare." He tossed the brandy, snifter and all, onto the ground, obviously annoyed.

"Shall we close the gates, sir?"

"Unfortunately the man is well acquainted with Lord Castlereagh, and he has held a seat on the Irish Privy Council. He was at a dinner of state, I heard, with Cornwallis. If I close the gates, there will be bloody hell to pay." Hughes scowled now, and red blotches had appeared on his neck above the black-and-gold collar of his red military jacket.

Devlin tried to contain his excitement. Edward de Warenne, the Earl of Adare, was their landlord. And although Gerald had leased his own ancestral lands from Adare, the two men were, in fact, far more than lord and tenant. At times, they had attended the same country suppers and balls, the same fox hunts and steeplechases. Adare had dined a dozen times at the manor at Askeaton. Unlike other landlords, he had been fair in his dealings with the O'Neill family, never rack-renting them, never demanding more than his share.

Devlin realized that he and Sean were holding hands. He watched breathlessly as the earl and his men cantered toward the captain's tent. They never slowed and soldiers ran to get out of their way. Finally, abruptly, the riders halted before Hughes and his men. Instantly a dozen redcoats armed with muskets formed a circle around the newcomers.

The earl spurred his black mount forward. He was tall and dark, his appearance distinct and formidable, his presence emanating power and authority. But his face was a mask of rage. "Where is Mary O'Neill?" he demanded tersely. A navy-blue cloak swirled about his shoulders.

Hughes smiled tightly. "I take it you've heard of O'Neill's untimely demise?"

"Untimely demise?" The Earl of Adare launched himself to the ground and strode forward. "Murder is more like it. You've murdered one of my tenants, Hughes."

"So now you are a papist? He was fated for the gallows, Adare, and you know it."

Adare stared, trembling with fury, and finally he breathed low. "You bastard. There was always the chance of exile and a royal pardon. I would have moved heaven and earth to make it so. You arrogant son of a bitch." His hand moved to the hilt of his sword.

Hughes shrugged indifferently. "As I said, a papist and a Jacobin. These are dangerous times, my friend. Even Lord Castlereagh would not want to be associated with a Jacobin."

For a moment, Adare did not speak, clearly fighting for self-control. "I want the woman. Where is she?"

Hughes hesitated, his jaw flexing, more red color blotching his features.

"Do not make me do something I dearly wish to do—which is choke the very life out of you," Adare said coldly.

"Fine. An Irish bitch hardly enthralls me. They're a dozen a penny."

Devlin was so stunned by the gross insult that he reeled. He would have rushed forward to kill Hughes, but he didn't have to. Adare strode the brief distance separating him from Hughes and shoved his face up against the captain's. "Do not underestimate the power of Adare. I suggest you cease with any further slanders before you find yourself in command of redskins in Upper Canada. I dine with Cornwallis on the fifteenth, and there is nothing I would prefer to do than whisper some very unpleasant facts in his ears. Do you understand me, Captain?"

Hughes couldn't speak. His face had turned crimson.

Adare released him. He strode into the tent, his dark cloak billowing about him.

Devlin exchanged glances with Sean—and then he ran past the red-faced Hughes with his brother in hand and into the tent behind the earl. Instantly he saw his mother sitting in a small chair and he knew at once that she had been weeping.

"Mary!" the earl cried, halting in his tracks. "Are you all right?"

Mary stood, her blue eyes wide, her blond curls in disarray. Their gazes locked. "I thought you would come," she said unevenly.

Adare hurried forward, gripping her shoulders, his dark blue eyes wide. "Are you hurt?" he asked more softly.

It was a moment before she could speak. "Not in the manner you are thinking, my lord." She hesitated, staring at him, and her eyes filled with tears. "He murdered Gerald. He murdered my husband before my very eyes."

"I know," Adare responded with anguish. "I am sorry. I am so sorry."

Mary was undone; she looked away, close to weeping again.

He turned her face forward again and their eyes met another time. "Where's Meg? Where are the boys?"

Tears spilled then. "I don't know where Meg is. She was in my arms when I fainted and—" She could not continue.

"We'll find her." He smiled a little then. "I will find her."

Mary nodded and it was clear that she believed he might succeed against all hope. And then she saw her sons standing by the tent's front flap, as still as statues, watching her and the powerful Protestant earl. "Devlin! Sean! Thank God you're alive—you're unhurt!" She rushed to them, hugging them both at once.

Devlin closed his eyes, almost incapable of believing that he had found his mother and she was safe, for he knew the earl would take care of her now. "We're fine, Mother," he said softly, pulling away from her embrace.

Adare joined them, putting one arm possessively around Mary. His assessing gaze quickly moved over both boys and Devlin met his gaze. A part of him wished to rebel, though they desperately needed the earl's help now. But Gerald was not yet buried, and he knew Adare's real inclinations—he had sensed them for some time.

"Devlin, Sean, listen closely," Adare instructed. "You will ride back to Adare with my men and myself. When we leave this tent, mount up quickly, behind my men. Do you understand me?"

Devlin nodded, but he could not help looking quickly back and forth between Adare and his mother. He had seen the way Adare looked at his mother in the past, but then, many men had admired her from afar. Before Gerald's death, it had been so easy to tell himself that Adare admired her the way any man would. Now he knew he had lied to himself. He was relieved that the powerful earl was coming to their aid, but he was also resentful. The earl was a widower and he loved Mary. Devlin was certain of it. But what about Father, who was not yet even properly buried? Not yet even cold in his grave?

"Devlin!" Adare's words were a whip, his gaze as sharp. "Move."

Devlin quickly obeyed, he and Sean falling into line behind Adare and Mary. And the foursome left the relative safety of the tent.

Outside, the sun was higher, hotter, brighter. An unearthly silence had fallen over the camp and the mountains beyond where more ominous clouds gathered. Dozens of armed British soldiers had formed in banded rows about Adare's two dozen mounted and armed men. Clearly, if Hughes wished it, there would be another massacre that day.

Devlin glanced at the earl, but if Adare was afraid, he did not show it. Devlin's respect for him increased. Adare was very much like Gerald, and he must be as brave. He tamped down any fear that was trying to rise.

Adare never faltered as he crossed the ground between the tent and his men. He lifted Mary onto his mount. Hughes was watching, his face rigid with tension and hatred. Devlin pushed Sean at a knight, and as he leapt up behind another rider, Sean was hauled up onto the back of a horse, as well.

Adare was already in the saddle, behind Mary. His gaze swept over the boys, then the rows of armed British soldiers, and finally, Hughes. "You have trespassed upon what is mine," he said, his words ringing. "Never do so again."

Hughes smiled grimly. "I had no idea you and the lady were...involved."

"Do not twist my words, Captain," Adare cried. "You murdered my liege, you burned my land, and that is an affront to me and mine. Now let us pass."

Devlin looked from Adare to Hughes as the two men locked gazes. He was aware of sweat gathering between his shoulder blades and trickling down his back. For one moment, the fort was so quiet that had a leaf rustled, it would have been heard.

And finally, Hughes spoke. "Stand aside," he barked. "Let them go."

And the line of soldiers parted.

Adare raised his hand, spurring his horse into a canter, leading his men through the British troops and out of the fort.

Devlin held on to the soldier he was riding behind. But he looked back.

Right into the captain's pale blue eyes.

And the burning began.

It began somewhere deep inside his soul, emanating in huge, hard, dark waves, creeping into his very blood, until it consumed him, bitterly acrid, red hot.

One day he would have his revenge. One day, when the time was right. Captain Harold Hughes would be made to pay the price of Gerald O'Neill's murder.

Part One

The Captive

CHAPTER ONE

April 5, 1812
Richmond, Virginia

"SHE DOESN'T EVEN KNOW how to dance," one of the young ladies snickered.

Her cheeks burning, Virginia Hughes was acutely aware of the dozen young women standing queued behind her in the ballroom. She had been singled out by the dance master and was now being given a lecture on the *sissonne ballotté,* one of the steps used in the quadrille. Not only did she not comprehend the step, she didn't care. She had no interest in dancing, none whatsoever—she only wished to go home to Sweet Briar.

"But you must never cease with polite conversation, Miss Hughes, even in the execution of a step. Otherwise you will be severely misconstrued," the dark, slim master was admonishing.

Virginia really didn't hear him. She closed her eyes and it was as if she had been swept away to another time and place, one far better than the formidable walls of the Marmott School for Genteel Young Ladies.

Virginia breathed deeply and was consumed with the heady scent of honeysuckle; it was followed by the far stronger and more potent scent of the black Virginia earth, turned up now for the spring burning. She could picture the dark fields, stretching away as far as her eye dared see, parallel lines of slaves made white by their clothes as they spread the coals, and closer, the sweeping lawns, rose gardens and ancient oaks and elms surrounding the handsome brick house that her father had built. "She could have been built in England," he'd said proudly, many times, "a hundred years ago. No one can take a look at her and know any differently."

Virginia missed Sweet Briar, but not half as much as she missed her parents. A wave of grief crashed over her, so much so her eyes flew open and she found herself standing back in the damnable ballroom of the school she had been sent to, the dance master looking extremely put out, his hands on his slim hips, a grim expression on his dark Italian face.

"What's she doing with her eyes screwed up like that?" someone whispered.

"She's crying, that's what she's doing," came a haughty reply.

Virginia knew it was the blond beauty, Sarah Lewis— who was, according to Sarah, the most coveted debutante in Richmond. Or would be, when she came out at the end of the year. Virginia turned, fury overcoming her, and strode toward Sarah. Virginia was very petite and far too thin, with a small triangular face that held sharp cheekbones and brilliant violet eyes; her dark hair, waist long, was forced painfully up, as she refused to cut it, and appeared in danger of crushing her with its massive weight. Sarah was a good three inches taller than Virginia, not to mention a stone heavier. Virginia didn't care.

She'd been in her first fight when she was six, a fisticuffs, and when her father had broken up the match, she'd learned she was fighting like a girl. Instruction in how to throw a solid punch—like a boy—had followed, much to her mother's dismay. Virginia could not only throw a solid punch, she could shoot the top off a bottle at fifty feet with a hunting rifle. She didn't stop until she was nose to nose with Sarah—which required standing on her tiptoes.

"Dancing is for fools like you," she cried, "and your name should be Dancing Fool Sarah."

Sarah gasped, stepping back, her eyes wide—and then the anger came. "Signor Rossini! Did you hear what the *country bumpkin* said to me?"

Virginia held her head impossibly higher. "This country bumpkin owns an entire plantation—all five thousand acres of it. And if I know my math—which I do—then that makes me one hell of a lot richer than you, Miss Dancing *Fool*."

"You're jealous," Sarah hissed, "because you're skinny and ugly and no one wants you...which is why you are here!"

Virginia landed hard on her heels. Something cracked open inside of her, and it was painful and sharp. Because Sarah had spoken the truth. No one wanted her, she was alone, and dear God, how awfully it hurt.

Sarah saw that her barb had hit home. She smiled. "Everyone knows. Everyone knows you've been sent here until your majority! That's three years, Miss Hughes. You will be old and wrinkled before you ever go home to your *farm!*"

"That's enough," Signor Rossini said. "Both of you ladies step over to—"

Virginia didn't wait to hear the rest. She turned and ran from the ballroom, certain there were more titters behind her, hating Sarah, hating the other girls, the dance master, the whole school and even her parents... How could they have left her? *How?*

In the hallway she collapsed to the floor, hugging her

thin knees to her breasts, praying the pain would go away.
And she even hated God, because He had taken her parents
away from her in one terrible blow, on that awful rainy
night last fall. "Oh, Papa," she whispered against her bony
knee. "I miss you so."

She knew she must not cry. She would die before letting
anyone see her cry. But she had never felt so lost and alone
before. In fact, she had never been lost and alone before.
There had been sunny days spent riding across the plantation with her father and evenings in front of the hearth
while Mama embroidered and Papa read. There had been
a house full of slaves, each and every one of whom she had
known since the very day of her birth. There had been
Tillie, her best friend in the entire world, never mind that
she was a house slave two years older than Virginia. She
hugged her knees harder, inhaling deeply and blinking furiously. It was a long moment before she regained her composure.

And when she did, she sat up straighter. What had Sarah
said? That she was to remain at the school until her
majority? But that was impossible! She had just turned
eighteen and that meant she would be stuck in this awful
prison for another three years.

Virginia stood up, not bothering to brush any dust from
her black skirts, which she wore in mourning. It had been
six months since the tragic carriage accident that had taken
her parents' lives and while the headmistress had expressed
an interest in Virginia giving up mourning, she had solidly
refused. She intended to mourn her parents forever. She
still could not understand why God had let them die.

But surely that witch Sarah Lewis did not know what
she was speaking about.

Very disturbed, Virginia hurried down the wood-paneled
hall. Her only relative was an uncle, Harold Hughes, the

Earl of Eastleigh. After her parents had died, he had sent his condolences and instructions for her to proceed to the Marmott School in Richmond, as he was now her official guardian. Virginia barely recalled any of this; her life then had been reduced to a blur of pain and grief. One day she had found herself in the school, not quite recalling how she had gotten there, only vaguely remembering being in Tillie's arms one last time, the two girls sobbing goodbyes. Once the initial grief had lessened, she and Tillie had ex- changed a series of letters—Sweet Briar was eighty miles south of Richmond and just a few miles from Norfolk. Virginia had learned that the earl was trustee of her estate and that he had ordered everything to continue to be managed as it had been before his brother's death. Surely, if Sarah was correct, Tillie would have told her of such a terrible and cruel intention on the part of her guardian. Unless she herself did not know of it....

Thinking of Tillie and Sweet Briar always made her homesick. The urge to return home was suddenly over- whelming. She was eighteen, and many young women her age were affianced or even married with their own house- holds. Before their deaths her parents hadn't raised the subject of marriage, for which Virginia had been grateful. She wasn't quite sure what was wrong with her, but marriage —and young men—had never occupied her mind. Instead, since the age of five, when Randall Hughes had mounted her on his horse in front of him, she had worked side by side with her father every single day. She knew every inch of Sweet Briar, every tree, every leaf, every flower. (The plantation was a hundred acres, not five thousand, but Sarah Lewis had needed to be taken down a peg or two.) She knew all about tobacco, the crop that was Sweet Briar. She knew the best ways to transplant the seedling crop, the best way to cure the harvested leaves, the best auction houses. Like her father, she had followed the price per bale with avid interest—and fervent hope. Every summer she and her father would dismount and walk through the tobacco fields, fingering the leafy plants in dirty hands, inhaling their succulent aroma, judging the quality of their harvest.

She had had other duties and responsibilities as well. No one was kinder than her mother, and no one knew herbs and healing better. No one cared more about their slaves. Virginia had attended dozens of fevers and flux, right by her mother's side. She was never afraid to walk into the slave quarters when someone was ill—in fact, she packed a darn good poultice. Although Mama had not allowed her to attend any birthings, Virginia could birth foals, too, and had spent many a night waiting for a pregnant mare to deliver. Why shouldn't she be at home now, running Sweet Briar with their foreman, James MacGregor? Was there any point in being at this damnable school? She'd been born to run the plantation. Sweet Briar was in her blood, her soul.

Virginia knew she wasn't a lady. She'd been wearing britches from the moment she had figured out that there *were* britches, and she liked them better than skirts. Papa hadn't cared—he'd been proud of her outspoken ways, her natural horsemanship, her keen eye. He had thought her beautiful, too—he'd always called her his little wild rose— but every father thought so of a daughter. Virginia knew that wasn't true. She was too thin and she had too much hair to ever be considered fair. Not that she cared. She was far too smart to want to be a lady.

Mama had been tolerant of her husband and her daughter. Both of Virginia's brothers had died at birth, first Todd and then little Charles when she was six. That was when Mama had first looked the other way about the britches, the horses, the hunting. She had cried for weeks, prayed in the family chapel and, somehow, found peace. After that, her smiles and sunny warmth had returned—but there had been no more pregnancies, as if she and Papa had made a silent pact.

Virginia couldn't comprehend why any woman would even want to be a lady. A lady had to follow rules. Most of the rules were annoying, but some were downright oppressive. Being a lady was like being a slave who didn't have the fine home of Sweet Briar. Being a lady was no different from being in shackles.

Virginia paused before the headmistress's office, the decision already made. Whether Sarah Lewis had spoken the truth or not, it no longer mattered. It was time to go home. In fact, making the decision felt good. For the first time since her parents had died, she felt strong—and brave. It was a wonderful way to feel. It was the way she had felt right up until the minister had come to their door to tell her that her parents were dead.

She knocked on the fine mahogany door.

Mrs. Towne, a plump, pleasant lady, gestured her inside. Her kind eyes held Virginia's, solemn now, when usually they held dancing lights. "I'm afraid you will have to learn to dance sooner or later, Miss Hughes."

Virginia grimaced. The one person she almost liked at the school was the headmistress. "Why?"

Mrs. Towne was briefly surprised. "Do sit down, my dear."

Virginia sat, then realized her knees were apart, her hands dangling off the arms of the chair, and quickly rearranged herself, not because she wished to be proper, but because she did not want to antagonize the headmistress now. She clamped her knees together, clasped her hands and thought about how fine it would be to be in her britches and astride her horse.

Mrs. Towne smiled. "It isn't that difficult to cooperate, dear."

"Actually, it is." Virginia was also very stubborn. That trait her mother *had* bemoaned.

"Virginia, ladies must dance. How else will you attend a proper party and enjoy yourself?"

Virginia didn't hesitate. "I have no use for parties, ma'am. I have no use for dancing. Frankly, it's time for me to go home."

Mrs. Towne stared in mild surprise.

Virginia forgot about sitting properly. "It's not true, is it? What that wicked Sarah Lewis said? Surely I am not to remain here—forgotten—a prisoner—for another *three* years?"

Mrs. Towne was grim. "Miss Lewis must have overheard me speaking privately with Mrs. Blakely. My dear, we did receive such instructions from your uncle."

Virginia was shocked speechless and she could only stare. It was a moment before she could even think.

For a while, she had been afraid that Eastleigh would send for her, forcing her to go to England, where she had no wish to go. That, at least, was one dilemma she did not have to face. But he would lock her up in this school for three more years? She'd already been here six months and she hated it! Virginia would not have it. Oh, no. She was going *home*.

Mrs. Towne was speaking. "I know that three years seems like a very long time, but actually, considering the way you were raised, it is probably the amount of time we need to fully instruct you in all the social graces you shall need to succeed in society, my dear. And there is good news. Your uncle intends to see you wed upon your majority."

Virginia was on her feet, beyond shock. *"What?"*

Mrs. Towne blinked. "I should have known you would be dismayed by the proposal. Every well-born young lady marries, and you are no exception. He intends to find a suitable husband for you—"

"Absolutely not!"

Mrs. Towne was now the one speechless.

Anger consumed Virginia. "First he sends me here? Then he thinks to lock me away for three years? Then he will send me to another prison—a marriage with a stranger? No, I think not!"

"Sit down."

"No, Mrs. Towne. You see, I will marry one day, but I will marry for love and only love. A grand passion—like my parents had." Tears blurred her vision. There would be no compromise. One day she would find a man like her father, the kind of love her parents had so obviously shared. There would be—could be—no compromise.

"Virginia, sit down," Mrs. Towne said firmly.

Virginia shook her head and Mrs. Towne stood. "I know you have suffered a terrible tragedy, and we all feel for you, we do. But you do not control your fate, child, your uncle does. If he wishes you to stay here until your majority, then so it shall be. And I am sure you will come to be fond of your future husband, whoever he may be."

Virginia couldn't speak. Panic consumed her. A stranger thought himself to be in control of her life! She felt trapped, as if in a cage with iron bars, worse, the cage being immersed in the sea and she was drowning!

"My dear, you must make an effort to become a part of the community here. You are the one who has chosen to be disdainful of the other fine young women here. You have not tried, even once, to be friendly or amusing. You have set yourself apart from the moment you arrived and we allowed that, being respectful of your grief. I know why you held your head so high, my dear, but the others, why, they think you prideful and vain! It is time for you to make amends—and friends. I expect you to make friends, Virginia. And I expect you to excel in your studies, as well."

Virginia hugged herself. Had the others really thought her too proud and vain? She didn't believe it. They all despised her because she was from the country, because she was so different.

"You are so clever, Virginia. You could do so well here if you bothered to try." Mrs. Towne smiled at her.

Virginia swallowed hard. "I can't stay here. And they don't like me because I am different! I'm not fancy and coy and I don't faint at the sight of a handsome man!"

"You have chosen to be different, but you are a beautiful girl from a good family, and in truth, that makes you no different at all. You must cease being so independent, Virginia, and you will be very happy here, I promise you." Mrs. Towne walked over to her and clasped her thin shoulder. "I am sure of this, Virginia. I want nothing more than for you to become a successful graduate of this school—and a very happy young lady."

Virginia forced a brittle smile. There was nothing more to say. She was not going to stay at the school, and she was not going to let her uncle the earl choose a husband for her—and that was that.

Mrs. Towne smiled at her warmly. "Do give up your rebellious nature, my dear. The rewards will be great if you do."

Virginia managed to nod. A moment later, the interview was over and she fled. As soon as she was alone on her cot in the dormitory, Virginia began to plan her escape.

TWO DAYS LATER, VIRGINIA performed her morning ablutions as slowly as she could. The other young ladies were filing out of the dormitory while she continued to wash her hands. Early morning light was filtering through the dormitory's skylights. From the corner of her eye, Virginia watched the last of the young ladies leaving the long, rectangular room. Miss Fern paused at the door. "Miss Hughes? Are you unwell?"

Virginia managed a weak smile. "I'm sorry, Miss Fern, but I am so dizzy and light-headed today." She hung on to the bureau beside the washstand.

Miss Fern returned to her, touching her forehead lightly. "Well, you do not have a fever. But I suppose you should go to Dr. Mills directly."

"I think you are right. I must be coming down with influenza. I need a moment, please," Virginia said, sitting down on the edge of her narrow bed.

"Take a moment, then." Miss Fern smiled, walked down the aisle between the twenty beds and finally left the room.

Virginia waited, silently counting, "One-two-three," then she leapt to her feet. She hurried across the aisle to the fourth bed. She went right to the bureau there and began rummaging through contents that did not belong to her. Guilt assailed her, but she ignored it.

Sarah Lewis always had pin money, and Virginia quickly found twelve dollars and thirty-five cents. She took every penny, leaving an unsigned note instead. In it, she explained that she would pay the sum back as soon as possible. Still, it felt terrible being reduced to thievery and she could almost feel her mother's disapproval as she watched over her daughter from heaven.

"I will pay Sarah back, Mama, every darned penny," she whispered guiltily. But there was just no choice. She needed fare for a coach and an inn. As brave as she was, she didn't think she could walk the entire eighty miles to Sweet Briar without several nights' rest and a few good meals.

Virginia then reached under her bunk. In her cloak—despite the spring weather, the nights remained cool—she had wrapped her few precious personal belongings: her mother's cameo necklace, her father's pipe and a horsehair bracelet Tillie had made for her when she was eight. She also had an extra shirtwaist, gloves and bonnet. The entire cloak was bundled up and tied with string. Virginia went to a window at one end of the room, heaved it open and dropped the bundle to the sidewalk below.

Virginia somehow slowed her eager legs and walked demurely downstairs, passing two of the school's staff as she did so. Finally she reached the end of the hall. Ahead lay the gracious, high-ceilinged foyer of the building. There, marble floors vied with dark wood columns and even darker wood paneling. The front door wasn't kept locked during the day, as no student ever walked out. Virginia looked carefully around. This was her chance to escape, but if someone saw her now, it was over before her journey had even begun.

Footsteps sounded from a different hall. Virginia darted back around the corner, not daring to breathe, hearing two voices and recognizing them as belonging to the music master and the French professor. She assumed they would cross the foyer and come her way—all of the classrooms lay behind her. Virginia looked around and slipped into the janitor's closet.

The pair of instructors passed.

Virginia was sweating. She had also lost all patience. She cracked open the door and saw that the hallway was empty. She slipped out, peered into the foyer and found that empty, too. She inhaled hard for courage and rushed across, flinging open the huge and heavy front door. She stepped outside into bright spring sunlight and she smelled and even tasted freedom. God, it was good!

She ran down the walk and out the wrought-iron front gates, down the public sidewalk, around the corner, and found her bundled cloak. Virginia seized it and ran again.

"I'M SO HAPPY WE COULD see you most of your way, my dear," Mrs. Cantwell said, smiling and clasping Virginia's hands.

Three days had passed. Virginia had spent most of the first morning on foot until she had left the bustling city of Richmond behind. At a country inn she had eaten a hearty lunch, famished from her long walk. There, she had stumbled across the Cantwell family.

A matronly wife, three proper children, a plump, bespectacled husband—all traveling in a pretty private coach. Virginia had overheard their conversation, learning that they had been to Richmond to visit the husband's ailing parents. Now they were on their way home to Norfolk. Which meant they would pass within miles of Sweet Briar.

Virginia had helped one of the small children blow his nose and had quickly become the interest of Mrs. Cantwell. She had lied about her age and marital status, claiming that she was returning home to her husband after visiting her ailing mother in Richmond. She had quickly slipped her mother's ring to her left hand to corroborate her story. Mrs. Cantwell, upon learning of her destination, had quickly offered her a ride, clearly desperate for company and help with the children.

Now Virginia hardly heard the pleasant lady. They were at a crossroads, one sign reading Norfolk, the other reading Land's End, Four Corners and Sweet Briar. Her heart beat so hard that she felt faint. Five miles down the road was her home. Five simple miles...

"You must miss your husband so much," Mrs. Cantwell added.

Virginia came to life. She turned and clasped the blond woman's hands. "Thank you so much for the ride, Lilly. I cannot thank you enough."

"You have been so wonderful with the children!" Lilly Cantwell exclaimed. "And if we weren't so close to home, I would insist we take you all the way to Sweet Briar so we might meet your wonderful husband."

Virginia flushed with guilt—she'd become an adept liar as well as a thief in a very short time, and how she hated it! "May I write you?" she asked impulsively. She instantly decided she would write Lilly Cantwell and tell her the entire truth, while thanking her once again for her kindness.

"I should love to hear from you and remain friends," Lilly cried, beaming.

The two women hugged. Virginia then hugged tiny Charlotte, tugged Master William's ear and winked at little Thomas. She thanked Mr. Cantwell as well, and as their carriage pulled away, she thought she heard him remarking, "There's something odd about that young lady and I still don't think she's old enough to be married!"

Virginia grinned. Then she spread her arms wide and laughed loudly, spinning around and around, until her feet hurt and her ankle twisted and she was so dizzy she had to drop to the ground. Lying there, she laughed again. She was home!

She quickly got up, adjusted her bundle and began running down the dirt road. The five miles passed endlessly, but every gentle field, every spring-green hill, every gushing stream only made her hurry even more. She was breathless and hot when she first spied the beautifully engraved wood sign hanging between two stately brick pillars: SWEET BRIAR. A long dirt drive wound from the entrance up a hill all the way to the house, and surrounding it were the red curing barns, the whitewashed slave quarters and the fields and fields of rich brown sandy earth.

Her heart hammered like a drum. Virginia dropped her bundle and lifted her skirts and ran up the dirt drive. "Tillie!" she screamed at the top of her lungs. "Tillie! Tillie! Tillie! It's me, I'm home, Tillie!"

Frank, Tillie's husband, was hitching up a wagon not far from the front of the house and he saw her first. His mouth dropped open and he gaped. "Miz Virginia? Is that you?"

Behind him, his little twin boys were wide-eyed. Then, from the corner of her eye, Virginia saw the front door of the house open as Tillie stepped onto the veranda. But it was too late, she was already in Frank's arms. "Have you lost your wits?" she cried, hugging him so hard he choked. "Of course it's me! Who else would it be!" She stepped back, laughing up at the big young man.

"God Almighty, that fine an' fancy school sure ain't made you a lady," Frank said, grinning, his teeth stunningly white against his dark skin.

"You do mean 'thank God,' don't you?" Virginia teased. "Rufus, Ray, get over here and give me hugs, or don't you remember your mistress?"

The boys, both just shy of seven, rushed forward, grabbing her around her thighs. Virginia finally felt the tears rising in her eyes as she tried to bend down and hug them both.

Then she felt Tillie behind her, and slowly, she turned.

Tillie smiled, tears staining her coffee-and-cream complexion. She was as tall as Virginia was short, as voluptuous as she was thin, and very beautiful. "I knew you'd come home," she whispered.

Virginia moved into her arms. The two young women clung.

When she could control her tears, she stepped back,

smiling. "My feet hurt like hell," she said. "And I'm starving to death! How did the burning go? Did we find rot? And what do the seedlings look like?" She grinned as she wiped her eyes with her sleeve.

But Tillie didn't smile back. Her golden eyes were frighteningly solemn.

"Tillie?" Virginia asked, not liking the look she was receiving. Dread began. "Please tell me everything is all right." For something seemed terribly wrong and she was so scared to learn what it was.

She'd had enough of misfortune. She couldn't stand one more stroke of bad luck.

Tillie gripped her arms. "They're selling the plantation—and everything and everyone on it."

Virginia didn't understand. "What did you just say?"

"Your daddy's in debt. Beg pardon—Master Hughes *was* in debt—and now your uncle has an agent here and he's started selling off everything...the land, the house, the slaves, the horses, he's selling it all."

Virginia cried out. A huge pain stabbed through her chest, so vast that she reeled. Tillie caught her around the waist.

"What's wrong with me! Here you are, skinnier than ever, as hungry as a winter wolf, and I'm telling you our troubles! C'mon, Virginia, you need some hot food and a hot bath and then we can talk. You can tell me all about what it's like to be a fine lady!"

Virginia couldn't respond. This had to be a nightmare, an awful dream—it couldn't be reality. Sweet Briar could not be up for sale.

But it was.

SHE WAS WEARING HER MOTHER'S Sunday best. Virginia smiled bravely at Frank, who had driven her into Norfolk, smoothing down her blue skirts, adjusting the bodice of her fitted blue pelisse and then her matching bonnet. Her mother's clothes were loose upon her small frame, but Tillie and two other slaves had been sewing madly all night to make everything fit perfectly. Now Frank tried to smile back and failed. Virginia knew why—he was heartsick, afraid his wife and children would be sold off to some distant owner and that he'd never see them again.

But that wasn't going to happen. Virginia intended to move heaven and earth—and more specifically, her father's good friend Charles King, the president of the First Bank of Virginia—in order to prevent Sweet Briar from being sold. She swallowed hard, her entire body covered with perspiration. The stakes were so damned high. She was so deathly afraid. But Charles King had been a good family friend and now he'd see her not as a child but a capable lady. Surely, surely, he'd loan her the funds necessary to pay off her father's debts and save Sweet Briar.

Virginia closed her eyes tightly against the glaring sun, her smile faltering. God, she hated her uncle, the Earl of Eastleigh, a man she'd never met. He hadn't even discussed the state of the plantation with her! Yet it belonged to her!

Or it would, if it hadn't been sold off by the time she turned twenty-one.

Now the three years between the present and her majority loomed as an eternity.

"Miz Virginia," Frank suddenly said, restraining her from entering the imposing facade of the brick-and-limestone bank.

Virginia paused, her stomach churning with fear and dread. She managed a small smile. "I may be long—but I hope not."

"It's not that," he said roughly. He was very tall, perhaps

five inches over six feet, and dangerously handsome. Tillie had fallen in love with him at first sight, almost five years ago, not that anyone would have known it, with the way she'd snubbed him and put on airs. Apparently it had been mutual—not six months later he'd asked Randall Hughes for permission to marry her, and that permission had been instantly given. "I'm afraid, Miz Virginia, afraid of what will happen to Tillie and my boys if you don't get this loan today."

Virginia had been acutely aware of her responsibility to save Sweet Briar and her people, but now it crashed over her with stunning force. Fifty-two slaves were depending on her, many of them children. Tillie, her best friend, was depending on her, and so was Frank. "I will get this loan, Frank. You have nothing to worry about." She must have sounded forceful and confident, because his eyes widened instantly and he doffed his hat to her.

Virginia gave him another reassuring smile, silently begged God for a little help and entered the bank.

Inside, it was blessedly cool, oddly reverent and as quiet as a church. Two customers were at the teller's queue and one clerk was at a front desk. At a desk in the back sat Charles King. He looked up then and saw her, his eyes widening in surprise.

This was it, she thought, lifting her chin to an impossible height. Her smile felt odd and brittle, fixed, as she marched forward through the lobby and the spacious back area of the bank.

King stood, a fat man neatly and well dressed, his old-fashioned wig powdered and tied back. "Virginia! My dear, for one awful moment, I thought you were your mother, God rest her beloved soul!"

Her father had told her many times that she looked just like her mother, but Virginia hadn't ever believed it because

Mama was so beautiful, although they shared the same nearly black hair and the same oddly violet eyes. She held out her hand as Charles took it firmly, clearly pleased to see her. "An illusion of light, I suppose," she said, impressed with her own grace and bearing. But she had to convince Charles that she was a fine and capable lady now.

"Yes, I suppose. I thought you were at school in Richmond. Do come in—have you come to see me?" he asked, leading her back to his desk and the high chairs facing it.

"Yes, frankly, I have," Virginia said, gripping her mother's elegant black velvet reticule tightly.

Charles smiled, offering her a chair and some tea. Virginia declined. "So how have you found the big city, Virginia?" he asked, taking his seat behind his desk. His gaze held hers, with some concern. Virginia knew he was finally noticing how peaked she was, due to the terrible strain of her grief and now her worry over the state of her father's finances.

Virginia shrugged. "I suppose it is fine enough. But you know I adore Sweet Briar—there is no place I would rather be."

For one moment Charles stared and then he was grim. "I know you are a clever young lady, so may I assume you realize your uncle is selling the plantation?"

She wanted to lean forward and shout that the earl had no right. She didn't move—she didn't even dare to breathe—not until her temper had passed. But even then she said, "He has no right."

"I am afraid he has every right. After all, he is your guardian."

Virginia sat impossibly stiff and straight. "Mr. King, I have come here to secure a loan, so that I may pay off my father's debts and save Sweet Briar from sale and even possible dissolution."

He blinked.

She smiled bleakly at him. " I have helped Father manage the plantation since I was a child. No one knows how to plant and harvest, ship and sell tobacco better than I. I assure you, sir, that I would repay your loan in full, with any necessary interest, as soon as was possible. I—"

"Virginia," Charles King began, too kindly.

Panic began. She leapt to her feet. "I may be a woman and I may be eighteen but I do know how to run Sweet Briar! No one except my father knows how better than I do! I swear to you, sir, I would repay every penny! How much do I need to pay off Father's debts?" she cried desperately.

Charles regarded her with pity. "My dear child, his debts amount to a staggering twenty-two thousand dollars."

The shock was so great that her heart stopped and her knees gave way and somehow, she was sitting down. *"No."*

"I have spoken with your uncle's agent at great length. His name is Roger Blount and I do believe he is on his way back to Britain in the next few days after seeing to your affairs here. Sweet Briar is not a lucrative plantation, Virginia," he continued gently. "Your father had loss after loss, year after year. Even if I were foolish enough to lend a young and untried girl such a sum of money, there is simply no way you could ever repay me—not from the plantation. I am sorry. Selling Sweet Briar is the only intelligent and viable option."

She stood, sick in her heart, in her soul. "No. I can't let it be sold. *It's mine.*"

He also stood. "I know how upsetting this is for you. Virginia, I'm not sure why you are not in school, but that is where you should be—although if you wish, I could try to arrange a match for you, a good one, and speak with your uncle about it. That would certainly solve your problems—"

"Unless you think to marry me to a very wealthy man, then that solves nothing," Virginia cried. "I cannot allow Sweet Briar to be sold! Why won't you help me? I would pay you back, somehow, one day! I have never broken my word, sir! Why can't you see that this is all I have left in the entire world?"

He stared. "You have a glorious future, my dear. I promise you that."

She closed her eyes and trembled violently. Then she looked him in the eye. "Please lend me the funds. If you loved my father, my mother, at all, then please, help me now."

"I'm sorry. I cannot. I simply cannot lend an impossible sum to a young girl who will never in an entire lifetime pay the bank back."

She could not give up. "Then lend me the funds personally," she cried.

He blinked. "Virginia, I do not have that kind of wealth. I *am* sorry."

She was in disbelief. He started to say something about a fresh start, and she turned and ran wildly through the bank and outside. There she collapsed against a hitching post, panting hard, shaking wildly, tears of panic and desperation trying to rise. This could not be happening, she thought. There had to be a way!

"Miz Virginia? Are you all right?" Frank had her by the elbow. His tone was concerned and anxious.

She met his black eyes but did not respond—because an idea had struck her so forcefully that she could not respond.

Her uncle was an earl.

Earls were wealthy.

She would borrow the money from him.

"Miz Virginia?" Frank was asking again, this time with a slight pressure on her elbow.

Virginia pulled free of his grasp and stared blindly across the busy street. She did not see a single wagon, carriage or pedestrian.

She had not a doubt that her uncle had the funds to save Sweet Briar. He was her only hope.

But clearly he didn't wish to save the plantation, or he would have already done so. That meant she had to confront him directly—personally. A letter would not do. The stakes were far too high. Somehow, she would find the means to cross the Atlantic Ocean, even if it meant selling some of her mother's precious jewelry, and she would meet her uncle and convince him to save Sweet Briar rather than sell it. She'd beg, rationalize, argue, debate, she'd do whatever she had to, even marry a perfect stranger, as long as he agreed to pay off her father's debts. Virginia realized she had to make plans and quickly, because she was on her way to England.

She knew she could do this. As her father was so fond of saying, where there was a will there was a way.

She'd always had plenty of will. Now she'd find a way.

CHAPTER TWO

May 1, 1812
London, England

WORD HAD SPREAD OF HIS arrival. Cheering throngs lined the banks of the Thames as his ship, the *Defiance*, proudly edged her way toward the naval docks.

Devlin O'Neill stood square on the quarterdeck, unsmiling, his arms folded across his chest, a tall, powerful figure as still as a statue. For the occasion of this homecoming—if it could be called such—he was in his formal naval attire. A blue jacket with tails, gold epaulets adorning each shoulder, pale white britches and stockings, highly polished shoes. His black felt bicorn was worn with the points facing out, as only admirals had the privilege of wearing the points front to back. His hair, a brilliant gold, was too long and pulled back in a queue. The crowd—men, women and children, agile and infirm, all London's poorest classes—raced up the riverbanks alongside his ship. Some of the women threw flowers at it.

A hero's welcome, he thought with no mirth at all. A hero's welcome for the man one and all called "His Majesty's pirate."

He had not set foot in Great Britain for an entire year. He would not be setting foot there now, had he a choice, but it had become impossible to ignore this last summons from the Admiralty, their fourth. His mouth twisted coldly. What he wanted was a steady bed and a pox-free woman who was not a whore, but his needs would have to wait. He did not wonder what the admirals wanted—he had disobeyed so many orders and broken so many rules in the past year that they could be asking for his head on any number of counts. He also knew he would be receiving new orders, which he looked forward to. He never lingered in any port for more than a few days or perhaps a week.

His glance swept over his ship. The *Defiance* was a thirty-eight-gun frigate known for her speed and her agility, but mostly for her captain's outrageous and unconventional daring. He was well aware that the sight of his ship caused other ships to turn tail and run, hence his preference for pursuit at night. Now top men were high on both the fore and main masts, reefing sails. Fifty marines in their red coats stood stiffly at attendance, muskets in their arms, as the frigate cruised toward its berth. Other sailors stood with them, eager for the liberty he would soon grant. Forecastle men readied the ship's huge anchors. All in all, three hundred men stood upon the frigate's decks. Beyond the docks, where two state-of-the-line three deckers, several sloops, a schooner and two gunships were at birth, the spires and rooftops of London gleamed in the bright blue sky.

The past year had been a very lucrative one. A year of cruising from the Strait of Gibraltar to Algiers, from the Bay of Biscayne to the Portuguese coast. There'd been forty-eight prizes and more than five hundred captured crewmen. His duties had been routine—escorting supply convoys, patrolling coastal shorelines, enforcing the blockade of France. Nights had been spent swooping upon unsuspecting French privateers, days lolling upon the high seas. He had been rather wealthy before this past year, but now, with this last prize, an American ship loaded with gold bullion, he was a very wealthy man, indeed.

And finally, a smile touched his lips.

But the boy trembled and remained afraid. The boy refused to go away. No amount of wealth, no amount of power, could be enough. And the boy had only to close his eyes to see his father's eyes, enraged and sightless in his severed head, there upon the Irish ground in a pool of his own blood.

Devlin had gone to sea three years after the Wexford uprising, with the Earl of Adare's permission and patronage. Adare had married his mother within the year, although his baby sister, Meg, had never been found. The earl had fabricated a naval history for Devlin, enabling him to start his career as a midshipman and not as the lowliest sailor far below decks. Devlin had quickly risen to the rank of lieutenant. Briefly he'd served on Nelson's flagship. At the Battle of Trafalgar, the captain of the sloop he was serving on had taken an unlucky hit and been killed instantly; Devlin had as quickly assumed command. The small vessel had only had ten guns, but she was terribly quick, and Devlin had snuck the *Gazelle* in under the leeward hull of a French frigate. With the French ship sitting so high above them, her every broadside had sailed right over the *Gazelle.* His own guns, at point-blank range, had torn apart the decks and rigging, crippling the bigger, faster ship immediately. He'd towed his prize proudly into Leghorn and shortly after had received a promotion to captain, his own command and a fast schooner, the *Loretta.*

He had only been eighteen.

There had been so many battles and so many prizes since then. But the biggest prize of all yet remained to be taken, and it did not exist upon the high seas of the world.

The heat of highly controlled rage, always broiling deep

within him, simmered a bit more. Devlin ignored it. Instead of thinking of the future reckoning that would one day come with Harold Hughes, now the Earl of Eastleigh, he watched as the *Defiance* eased into its berth between a schooner and a gunship. Devlin nodded at his second in command, a brawny red-haired Scot, Lieutenant MacDonnell. Mac used the horn to announce a week's liberty. Devlin smiled a little as his men cheered and hollered, then watched his decks clear as if the signal to jump ship had been given. He didn't mind. His crew was top-notch. Some fifty of his men had been with him since he'd been given his first ship; half of his crew had been with him since the collapse of the Treaty of Tilsit. They were good men, brave and daring. His crew was so well-honed that no one hesitated even when his commands seemed suicidal. The *Defiance* had become the scourge of the seas because of their loyalty, faith and discipline.

He was proud of his crew.

Mac fell into step with him, looking uncomfortable in his naval uniform, which he seemed to have outgrown. Mac was Devlin's own age, twenty-four, and this past year he had bulked out. Devlin thought they made an odd duo— the short, broad Scot with the flaming hair, the tall, blond Irishman with the cold silver eyes.

"Ach, got to find me land legs," Mac growled.

Devlin smiled as the land heaved under them as high and hard as any storm swell. He clapped his shoulder. "Give it a day."

"That I shall, a day and seven, if you don't mind." Mac grinned. He had all his teeth and only one was rotten. "Got plans, Cap? I'm achin' meself for a lusty whore. Me first stop, I tell you that." His laughter was bawdy.

Devlin was lenient with the men—like most ships' commanders, he allowed them their whores in port, but he preferred them to bring the women aboard, so the ship's surgeon could take a good look at them. He wanted his crew pox-free. "We were in Lisbon a week ago," he said mildly.

"Feels like a year," Mac grunted.

Devlin saw the post chaise waiting for him—he'd sent word to Sean by mail packet that he was on his way back. "Can I offer you a ride, Mac?"

Mac flushed. "Not goin' to town," he said, referring to the West End.

Devlin nodded, reminding him that he was expected back aboard the *Defiance* in a week's time to set sail at noon, with all three hundred of his men. His rate of desertion was almost zero, an astonishing fact that no one in the British navy could understand. But then, with so many spoils taken and shared, his crew were all well off.

Thirty minutes later the chaise was clipping smartly over London Bridge. Devlin stared at the familiar sights. After days spent in the wind and on the sea, or at exotic, sultry ports in the Mediterranean, North Africa and Portugal, the city looked dark and dirty, unclean. Still, he was a man who liked a beautiful woman and refused a common whore, and his wandering eye took in more than his fair share of elegant ladies in chaises, carriages and on foot, shopping in the specialty stores. His loins stirred. He had sent several letters ahead and one was to his English mistress. He fully expected to be entertained that night and all the week long.

The London offices of the Admiralty were on Brook Street in an imposing limestone building built half a century before. Officers, aides and adjutants were coming and going. Here and there, groups of officers paused in conversation. As Devlin pushed open the heavy wood doors and entered a vast circular lobby with a high-domed ceiling, heads began to turn his way. Portraits of the greatest admirals in British history adorned the walls, as did paintings of the greatest ships and battles. His mistress had once said his portrait would soon hang there, too. The conversation began to diminish. An eerie quiet settled over the lobby; Devlin was amused. He heard his name being whispered about.

"Captain O'Neill, sir?" A young lieutenant with crimson cheeks saluted him smartly from the bottom of the marble staircase.

Devlin saluted him rather casually back.

"I am to escort you to Admiral St. John, sir," the freckle-faced youth said. His flush had somehow deepened.

"Please do," Devlin remarked, unable to restrain a sigh. St. John was not quite the enemy—he disliked insubordination, but he knew the value of his best fighting captain. It was Admiral Farnham who wanted nothing more than to court-martial him and publicly disgrace him, and these days, he was egged on by Captain Thomas Hughes, the Earl of Eastleigh's son.

Admiral St. John was waiting for him. He was a slender man with a shock of white hair, and he was not alone. Farnham was with him—at once bulkier and taller, with far less hair—and so was the Earl of Liverpool, the minister of war.

Devlin entered the office, saluting. He was intrigued, as he could not recall ever seeing Liverpool at West Square.

The door was solidly shut behind him. Liverpool, slim, short and dark-haired, smiled at him. "It's been some time, Devlin. Do sit. Would you like a Scotch whiskey or a brandy?"

Devlin sat in a plush chair, removing his felt. "Is the brandy French?"

The earl was amused. "I'm afraid so."

"The brandy," Devlin said, stretching out his long legs in front of him.

Farnham appeared annoyed. St. John sat down behind his desk. "It has been some time since we have had the privilege of your appearance here."

Devlin shrugged dismissively. "The Straits are a busy place, my lord."

Liverpool poured the brandies from a crystal decanter, handing one over to Devlin and passing the others around.

"Yes, very busy," Farnham said. "Which is why deserting the *Lady Anne* is an exceedingly serious offense."

Devlin took a long sip, tasting the brandy carefully, and decided his own stock was far superior, both on his ship and at home.

"Do you have anything to say for yourself?" St. John asked.

"Not really," Devlin said, then added, "she was in no danger."

"No danger?" Farnham choked on his brandy.

Liverpool shook his head. "Admiral Farnham is asking for your head, my boy. Was it really necessary to leave the *Lady Anne* in order to chase that American merchantman?"

Devlin smiled slightly. "The *Independence* was loaded with gold, my lord."

"And you knew that when you spotted her off the coast of Tripoli?" St. John asked.

Devlin murmured, "Money, my lord, buys anything."

"I know of no other commander as audacious as you. Who is your spy and where is he?" St. John demanded.

"Perhaps it's a she," he murmured. And in fact, the wench in Malta who ran an inn often used by the Americans was just that. "And if I do employ spies, I am afraid that is my affair entirely—and as it does aid me in the execution of my orders, we should lay the question to rest."

"You do not follow orders!" Farnham said. "Your orders were to convey the *Lady Anne* to Lisbon. You are lucky she was not seized by enemy ships—"

He was finally annoyed, but he remained slouched. "Luck has naught to do with anything. *I control the Straits.* And that means I control the Mediterranean—as no one can enter her without getting past me. There was no danger to the *Lady Anne* and her safe conveyance to Lisbon has proved it."

"And now you are rather rich," Liverpool murmured.

"The prize is with our agent at the Rock," he said, referring to Gibraltar. He'd towed the *Independence* to the British prize agent there. His share of the plunder was three-eighths of the total sum, and a quick estimation of that figure came to one hundred thousand pounds. He was wealthier than anyone would ever guess, and he had far exceeded his own expectations some time ago.

"But I do not care about the fate of the *Lady Anne,* a single ship," Liverpool said. "And while you directly disobeyed your orders, we are all prepared to ignore the matter. Is that not right, gentlemen?"

St. John's nod was firm, but Devlin knew it killed Henry Farnham to agree, and he was amused.

"I care about finishing this bloody war, and finishing it soon." Liverpool was standing and orating as if before the House. "There is another war on the horizon, one that must be avoided at all costs."

"Which is why you are here," St. John added.

Devlin straightened in his chair. "War with the Americans is a mistake," he said.

Farnham made a sound. "You are Irish, your sympathies remain Jacobin."

Devlin itched to strangle him. He did not move or speak until the desire had passed. "Indeed they are. America is a sister nation, just as Ireland is. It would be shameful to war with her over any issue."

Liverpool said bluntly, "We must retain absolute control of the seas, Devlin, surely you know that."

"His loyalties remain selfish ones. He cares not a whit for England—he cares only about the wealth his naval career has afforded him," Farnham said with heat.

"We are not here to question Devlin's loyalties," Liverpool said sharply. "No one in our navy has served His Majesty with more loyalty and more perseverance and more effect."

"Thank you," Devlin murmured wryly. But it was true. His battle record was unrivaled at sea.

"The war is not over yet, and you know it, Devlin, as you have spent more time than anyone patrolling the Straits of Gibraltar and the Mediterranean, as well. Still, our control there is without dispute. You will leave this room with your new orders, if I can be assured that you will effect them appropriately."

His brows lifted with real interest. Where was Liverpool leading? "Do continue," he said.

"Your reputation precedes you," St. John pointed out. "In the Mediterranean and off these shores, every enemy and privateer knows your naval tactics are superior, if unorthodox, and that if you think to board, you carry fighting men, men who think nothing of carrying a second cutlass in their teeth. They fear you—that is why no one battles you anymore."

It was true more often than not. Devlin usually fired a single warning shot before boarding with his marines. There was rarely resistance—and he had become bored with it all.

"I believe your reputation is so great that even near American shores, the enemy will flee upon the sight of your ship."

"I am truly flattered," he murmured.

Liverpool spoke. "We are trying to *avoid* war with the Americans." He gave Devlin a look. "Sending you there could be like releasing a wolf in a henhouse and then expecting healthy, happy hens and chicks. If you are sent westward, my boy, I want your word that you will follow your orders—that you will scare the bloody hell out of the enemy but that you will not engage her ships. Your country needs you, Devlin, but there is no room for pirate antics."

Did they truly expect him to sail west and play nanny of sorts to the American merchants and navy? "I am to chase them about, threaten them, turn them back—and retreat?" He could scarcely believe it.

"Yes, that is basically what we wish for you to do. No American goods can be allowed to enter Europe, that has not changed. What has changed are the rules of engagement. We do not want another ship seized or destroyed, another American life accountable to our hands."

Devlin stood. "Find someone else," he said. "I am not the man for this tour."

Farnham snorted, at once satisfied and disbelieving. "He refuses direct orders! And when do we decide to hang him for his insubordination?"

Devlin felt like telling the old fool to shut up. "It is a mistake, my lord," he said softly to Liverpool, "to send a rogue like myself to such a duty."

Liverpool studied him. And then he smiled, rather coldly. "I do not believe that, actually. Because I know you far better than you think I do." He turned to the two admirals present. "Would you excuse us, gentlemen?"

Both men were surprised, but they both nodded and slipped from the room.

Liverpool smiled. "Now we can get down to business, eh, Devlin?"

Devlin turned the corners of his mouth up in response, but he waited, unsure of whether he was to receive a blow or a gift.

"I have understood your game for some time now, Devlin." He paused to pour them both fresh drinks. "The blood of Irish kings runs in your veins, and when you joined the navy you were as poor as any Irish pauper. Now you have a mansion on the Thames, you have bought your ancestral home from Adare, and I could only estimate the amount of gold you keep in the banks—and in your own private vaults. You are so rich now that you have no more use for us." His brows lifted.

"You make me seem so very unpatriotic," Devlin murmured. Liverpool was right—almost.

"Still, a fine man like yourself, from a fine family, always at sea, always seizing a prize, always at battle— never on land, never at home before a warm hearth." He stared.

Devlin became uneasy. He sipped his brandy to disguise this.

"I wonder what it is that motivates you to sail so fast, so far, so often?" His dark brows lifted.

"I fear you romanticize me. I am merely a seaman, my lord."

"I think not. I think there are deep, grave, complex reasons for your actions—but then, I suppose I will never know what those reasons are?" He smiled and sipped his own brandy now.

The boy trembled with real fear. How could this stranger know so much?

"You have fanciful imaginings, my lord." Devlin smiled coolly.

"You have yet to win a knighthood, Captain O'Neill," Liverpool said.

Devlin stiffened in surprise. So it was to be a gift—after a blow, he thought.

Once, his ancestors had been kings, but a century of theft had reduced them to a life of tenant-farmers. He had changed that. His stepfather had happily sold him Askeaton when he had come forward with the bullion to pay for it. His grand home on the River Thames had been purchased two years ago when the Earl of Eastleigh had been forced by financial circumstances to put it up for sale. Liverpool knew Devlin had used the navy to attain the security that comes with wealth. What he did not know—could not know—was the reason why.

"Do continue," he said softly, but he had begun to sweat.

"You know that a knighthood is a distinct possibility—you need only follow your orders."

The ten-year-old boy wanted the title. The boy who had watched his father fall in an act of cold-blooded murder wanted the title as much as he wanted the wealth, because the added power made him safer than ever before.

Devlin hated the boy and did not want to feel his presence. "Knight me now," he said, "and barring any unforeseen and extenuating circumstance, I will sail to America and threaten her shores without inflicting any real harm."

"Damn you, O'Neill." But Liverpool was smiling. "Done," he then said. "You will be Sir Captain O'Neill before you set sail next week."

Devlin could not contain a real smile. He was jubilant now, thinking about the knighthood soon to be his. His heart raced with a savage pleasure and he thought of his mortal enemy, the Earl of Eastleigh—the man who had murdered his father.

"Where would you like your country estate?" Liverpool was asking amiably.

"In the south of Hampshire," he said. For then his newly

acquired country estate would be within an hour of East-leigh, at the most.

And Devlin smiled. His vengeance had been years in the making. He had known from the tender age of ten that in order to defeat his enemy, he would have to become wealthy and powerful enough to do so. He had joined the navy to gain such wealth and power, never dreaming that one day he would be ten times wealthier than the man he planned to destroy. A title added more ammunition to his stores, not that it truly mattered now. Eastleigh was already on the verge of destitution, as Devlin had been slowly ruining the man for years.

From time to time their paths crossed at various London affairs. Eastleigh knew him well. He had somehow recognized him the first time they met in London, when Devlin was sixteen and dueling his youngest son, Tom Hughes, over the fate of a whore. The wench's disposition was just an excuse to prick at his mortal enemy by wounding his son, but the duel had been broken up. That had only been the beginning of the deadly game Devlin played.

His agents had sabotaged Hughes's lead mines, instigated a series of strikes in his mill and had even encouraged his tenants to demand lower rents en masse, forcing Eastleigh to agree. The earl's financial position had become seriously eroded, until he teetered on the verge of having to sell off his ancestral estate. Devlin looked forward to that day; he intended to be the one to buy it directly. In the interim, he now owned the earl's best stud, his favorite champion wolfhounds and his Greenwich home. But the coup de grâce was the earl's second wife, the Countess of Eastleigh, Elizabeth Sinclair Hughes.

For, during the past six years, Elizabeth had been the woman so eagerly sharing his bed.

And even now, she was undoubtedly waiting for him. It was time to go.

WAVERLY HALL HAD BEEN in the possession of the earls of
Eastleigh for almost a hundred years—until two years ago,
when a cycle of misfortune had caused the earl to put it up
for sale. The huge limestone house had two towers, three
floors, a gazebo, tennis courts and gardens that swept right
down to the river's banks. Devlin arrived at his home in an
Italian yacht, a prize he had captured early in his career.
He strolled up the gently floating dock, his gaze taking in
the perfectly manicured lawns, the carefully designed
gardens and the blossoming roses that crawled up against
the dark stone walls of the house. It was so very English.

Unimpressed, he started up the stone path that led to the
back of the house, where a terrace offered spectacular views
of the river and the city. A man rose from a lawn chair.
Devlin recognized him instantly and his pace quickened.
"Tyrell!"

Tyrell de Warenne, heir to the earldom of Adare and
Devlin's stepbrother, strode down the path to meet him.
Like his father, Ty was tall and swarthy with midnight-
black hair and extremely dark blue eyes. The two men, as
different as night and day, embraced.

"This is a very pleasant surprise," Devlin said, pleased
to see his stepbrother. It made the homecoming to which
he was so indifferent suddenly inviting.

"Sean told me you were on your way home, and as I
have had some affairs to see to in town, I decided to stop
by the mansion to see if you were here yet. My timing is
impeccable, I see." Tyrell grinned. He was darkly, dangerously handsome and had had many love affairs to prove it.

"For once," Devlin retorted as they strolled up to the
terrace. "How is my mother? The earl?"

"They are fine, as usual, and wondering when you will
come home," Tyrell said with a pointed glance.

Devlin pushed open French doors and entered a huge

and elegantly appointed salon, choosing to ignore that particular subject. "I have just accepted a tour of duty in the North Atlantic," he said. "It is unofficial, of course, as I have yet to receive my orders."

Tyrell gripped his shoulder and Devlin had to face him. "Admiral Farnham is in a rage over the *Lady Anne,* Dev. Everywhere I go, I am hearing about it. In fact, even Father has heard that Farnham plots against you. I thought this was your last tour." His gaze was dark and frankly accusing.

Devlin moved to a bell pull, but his butler had already materialized, smiling as if pleased to see him. Devlin knew the Englishman detested having an Irishman as his overlord; it amused him, enough so that he had kept Eastleigh's staff when he had bought the mansion. "Benson, my good man, do bring us some refreshments and a fine bottle of red wine."

Then Devlin turned back to his stepbrother. Like the rest of his family, Tyrell thought he spent far too much time at sea and there was a general effort being made to convince him to resign his commission. "I am being offered a knighthood, Ty."

Briefly Tyrell stared in surprise; then he was smiling, smacking Devlin's back. "That is fine news," he said. "Damned fine!"

"Materialist that I am, I could not refuse the opportunity."

Tyrell studied him for a moment. "A storm gathers behind your back. You need to take care, Dev. I don't think Eastleigh has forgiven you for your purchase of this house. Tom Hughes has been lobbying around the Admiralty for a general court-martial," he said. "And he spreads nasty rumors about you."

Devlin raised a brow. "I really don't care what he says."

"I have heard it said that he has accused you of using vast discretion with French privateers—that is, allowing some to slip through your net for a hefty sum. That kind of gossip could hurt your career—and you, personally," Tyrell warned.

"If I'm not worried, why should you be?" Devlin asked calmly, but he thought of Thomas Hughes, who had never even been to sea, except on a fancy flagship where he and the admiral and other officers lived in state. Nonetheless, Hughes held the very same rank as Devlin, though Devlin knew the man could not sail a toy boat on a park lake. In fact, Lord Captain Hughes spent all of his time fawning over and playing up to the various admirals with whom he served. Devlin was well aware of the fact that Tom despised him, and it amused him to no end. He did wish he had wounded him that one time when they had dueled over the whore. "I am not afraid of Tom Hughes," he said dryly.

Tyrell sighed as Benson returned with two manservants, each bearing a silver tray with refreshments. Both men were quiet as a small table overlooking the grounds and the river was quickly set. Benson bowed. "Is there anything else, Captain?"

"No, thank you," Devlin said. When the servants had left, he handed his stepbrother a glass of wine and walked over to the windows overlooking the terrace. He stared out the window, not particularly enjoying the view.

It was impossible not to think about Askeaton.

Tyrell followed him to the picture window. As if reading Devlin's mind, he said, "You haven't been home in six years."

Devlin knew the last time he had been home, he knew it to the day and hour, but he smiled and feigned surprise. "Has it been that long?"

"Why? Why do you avoid your own home, Dev? Damn

it, everyone misses you. And while Sean does a fine job of managing Askeaton, we both know you would do even better."

"I am hardly at liberty to cruise up to Ireland whenever the urge overtakes me," Devlin murmured. It wasn't exactly a lie, but he was avoiding the question and they both knew it. The truth was he could sail up the Irish coast almost any time he chose.

"You are a strange man," Tyrell said sharply. "And I am not the only one who worries about you."

"Tell Mother I am more than fine. I captured an American merchantman carrying gold to a Barbary prince, a ransom for their hostages," Devlin said smoothly. "With my share of the booty, I could ransom a hostage or two myself."

"You should tell her yourself," Tyrell said flatly.

Devlin turned away. He missed Askeaton terribly, but he had learned in the past years that his home was a place to be avoided at all costs. For there, the memories were too volatile; there, they threatened to consume him; there, the boy still lived.

A FEW HOURS LATER, pleasantly relaxed from an abundance of wine, Devlin started upstairs, Tyrell having gone to the Adare town home in Mayfair. His private rooms took up an entire wing of the second floor; upon possession of the house, he had gutted the master suite completely, as if gutting the Earl of Eastleigh himself. He strolled through one pretty parlor after another, past vases and artwork others had chosen, past a piano that was never played, aware that not one item in the house—other than his books—gave him pleasure. But he hadn't bought the house for pleasure. He had bought it for a single purpose—revenge.

A maid met him on the threshold of his bedroom. She was flushed and perspiring, a pretty thing with brown hair and pale skin, and briefly Devlin thought of inviting her into his bed. But she turned a brighter shade of crimson upon espying him and then fled past him and down the hall with a gasp.

Devlin glanced after her, amused and wondering what had caused such a swift retreat. Had his intentions been that obvious? He was horny, certainly, but not aroused.

And then he entered the master bedroom and understood.

A blond Venus arose from the midst of his massive bed, a sheer undergarment caressing and revealing full, billowy breasts with large dusky nipples, round, lush hips, plump thighs and a dark ruby-red delta between.

Elizabeth Sinclair Hughes smiled at him. "I received your message and came as soon as I could."

His loins filled as he looked at her. She belonged to his mortal enemy, a man he was slowly but surely wreaking his vengeance upon, and she aroused him as no other woman could.

Elizabeth was very pretty, and now her green eyes moved directly to his swollen groin. "You are in need of attention, Captain," she murmured.

He moved forward, red-hot blood filling his brain, removing his shirt as he did so. With the raging blood came raging lust—blood lust—savage and uncontrolled. The beast always chose this moment to walk the earth. Devlin mounted her as he mounted the bed, pushing her down, unfastening his britches, thrusting his massive hardness inside.

Elizabeth cried out in pleasure, already hot and wet. He moved as hard and fast as he could, images of Eastleigh filling his mind, gray of hair, fatter and fifty now, and then fourteen years ago, slimmer, younger, crueler. His hatred knew no bounds. It mingled with the lust. His mouth found hers and he thrust there deeply, hurtfully, grinding against her, until he had become the beast itself. Elizabeth never knew. She gripped his sweat-slickened back, keening wildly in her ecstasy.

He wanted to release himself, too, but the hatred, the pleasure and the lust were so great and so satisfying that he refused, pounding deeper, harder, but ugly memories rode him now as he rode her...ugly, bloody glimpses of a dark and terrible past, rising fast and furious—a small boy, a headless man, a severed head, sightless eyes, a pool of blood.

He forgot the woman he rode as the wave preceding his climax, a wave of intense, growing pleasure, turned into one of anger and pain, and he was swept forward, against all will, a wave that now unfurled like a topsail, hard and fast. Behind that wave the memories chased him. *His father's furious, sightless eyes accused him now. You let me die, you let me die.* Devlin sought now only to escape, and when he climaxed, he did just that.

There was no moment of peace, no moment of relief. Instantly he was conscious, aware of the woman he lay upon, aware of the man he was cuckolding—aware of the gruesome memories that he now must bury, at all cost. Devlin flipped over, away from the countess, breathing harshly. In that instant a painfully familiar emptiness emanated from deep within him and consumed him entirely. It was so huge, so hollow, so vast.

Devlin leapt to his feet.

"Good Lord, one would think you'd been without for an entire year," Elizabeth murmured with a satisfied sigh. Then she eyed him with a small, pleased smile, her gaze lingering on his narrow hips and muscled thighs.

Naked, Devlin hurried across the bedroom, hardly aware of her words, quickly pouring a glass of wine. He downed it in a gulp, shaken, as always, by the memories he had vowed never to forget. He drained the glass and fought the beast until it finally returned to its lair.

"Nothing ever changes, does it, Devlin?" the countess asked, sitting up.

He poured another glass of wine and approached her, aware of his manhood stirring. Her gaze moved to his groin and she smiled. "You are becoming terribly predictable, Devlin."

"I could change that easily enough," he remarked casually, handing her the wine. As he did, he paused to admire her breasts. "You haven't changed," he added.

"And you remain a gentleman, in spite of your reputation," she said, but she was smiling and pleased. "I'm a year older, a bit fatter and lustier than ever."

"You haven't changed," he said firmly, but now he noticed the slight wrinkles at her eyes and the equally slight thickening of her waist. Elizabeth was several years his senior, although he wasn't really certain of her age—he had never cared enough to learn what it might be. She had two adolescent daughters, and he thought, but wasn't sure, that the eldest was fourteen or fifteen. Neither daughter belonged to Eastleigh.

"Darling, would it ever be possible for you to lie quietly by my side?" she asked, setting her glass down and stroking his inner thigh.

He hardened like a shot. "I have never pretended to be anything but what I am with you. I am not a quiet man."

"No, you are His Majesty's Pirate, for that is what I hear you called from time to time, when your exploits become dinner conversation." Her hand drifted upward, its back brushing his phallus as she toyed with his thigh.

"How boring those dinners must be." He couldn't care less what he was called, but he didn't bother to say so. The countess loved to chat idly after their various bouts of love-making. She had been the source of much of his information about Eastleigh for the past six years, so he usually encouraged her chatter.

Now she murmured, "I have missed you, Dev."

There was simply nothing to be said; he took her hand and placed it firmly on his swollen shaft. "Show me," he said.

"Spoken like a true commander," she said hoarsely, lowering her head.

He hadn't meant to give an order, but it was his nature now. He didn't move, waiting patiently for her to nibble and lick him, watching her dispassionately as she did so. One day Eastleigh would learn of their affair—he had only to decide which moment to choose.

Suddenly she lifted her head and smiled up at him. "Will you ever tell me that you have missed me, too?"

Devlin tensed. "Elizabeth, there is a better time for discussion."

"Is there? The only time we are together is in moments like these. I wonder what beats beneath your chest? Sometimes, Dev, I do think your heart is cast of stone."

His erection had been complete for some time, and talking was actually painful. But he said, "Have I ever made you any promises, Elizabeth?"

"No, you have not." She sat up, facing him. "But it's been six years, and oddly, I have become quite fond of you."

He did not respond. He did not know what to say, for once in his life at a loss.

"I may be in love with you, Dev," she said, her gaze riveted to his.

Devlin stared at her attractive face, a face as enticing as

her body. He carefully considered his words. He felt nothing for her, not even friendship; she was a means to an end. But he didn't dislike her—it was her husband whom he hated, not Elizabeth Hughes. He preferred for things to remain exactly as they were—he did not wish for her to be hurt, and not out of compassion. He was not a compassionate man. The world was a battlefield, and in battle, compassion was a prelude to death. He did not want to hurt Elizabeth only because she remained so useful to him; he wanted her at his disposal, on his terms, not hurt and angry and spiteful.

"That would not be wise," he finally said.

"Can't you just pretend?" she asked wistfully. "Lie to me, just once?"

He didn't hesitate. He rubbed his thumb over her lips, ignoring the tear he had just glimpsed forming in her eye, and then he rubbed it lower, over her throat, her chest and, finally, a swelling nipple. His mouth followed in the path of his finger. Several moments later, they were once again entwined in frenzy, with Devlin pounding deeply and forcefully inside her.

Several hours later, Devlin tested the water in his hip bath and found it warm enough. Elizabeth was dressing; he climbed into the claw-footed tub and sank down into the tepid water. After months at sea, the temperature was very pleasant. He'd had enough climaxes so that now, finally, his mind remained a blessed blank and there were no monsters to defeat.

"Darling?"

Devlin jerked—he had dozed off in his bath. Elizabeth smiled at him, elegantly dressed in a sapphire-blue gown with black velvet trim. "I'm sorry, I shouldn't have awoken you!" she exclaimed. "Devlin, you look so enticing in that bath, I could jump right in with you."

He raised a brow. "Isn't Eastleigh expecting you?"

She frowned. "We have supper plans, so yes, he is. I just wanted to tell you that I will be in town for another two weeks."

He understood. She wished to see him again before he shipped out, but that was perfectly fine with him. "I haven't received my official orders yet," he said carefully, "so I do not know when my next tour begins."

Her eyes brightened. "Tomorrow? Tomorrow afternoon?"

He smiled a little at her. "That would be fine, Elizabeth. Will Eastleigh also remain in town?" he asked. The question would seem innocent enough to her. After all, any lover would ask such a question.

"Fortunately, the answer to that is no, so perhaps we could even spend the night together."

He chose not to respond to that. He had never allowed any woman to spend a night in his bed and he never would.

Her expression changed; she appeared annoyed. "I have been ordered to remain in London for a fortnight! It's a miracle that you are here, too, so I should not be so put out, really."

"Why?" he asked mildly.

"Eastleigh's American niece is on her way to London. She is aboard the *Americana* and we expect her in the next ten days."

He was mildly surprised. He hadn't even known that there was a niece, much less an American one. He was very thoughtful. "You have never mentioned a distant relation before," he said calmly.

Elizabeth shrugged. "I suppose there was no reason to do so, but now she is an orphan and she is coming here. Eastleigh intended for her to remain in a ladies' school over *there,* but I imagine she thinks to latch on to our coattails. Oh, this is just what I do not need! Some uncouth colonial!

And what if she is beautiful? She is eighteen, and Lydia is only sixteen! I have no interest in having an American orphan compete with my daughter for a husband, and by all rights, the colonial is the one who should be married off first!"

Well, now he knew how old Elizabeth's eldest daughter was. He smiled slightly, wry. "I doubt she will outshine your daughters, Elizabeth, not if they are as beautiful as you." His reply was an automatic one, as he was thinking now, hard and fast.

Eastleigh's niece was on her way to Britain aboard an American ship. He was about to be given very specific orders to sail west to interfere with American trade there but not to harm any American ships. The niece was clearly unwanted and just as clearly she would soon be in his path.

Could he use this bit of information? Could he use *her*?

"Well, thank you for that!" Elizabeth said. "I am just annoyed at having to take her in. You know how pinched we've become these past few years. It has been one thing after another. We cannot afford to bring her out properly, Dev, and that is that!"

Devlin nodded. There was no guilt. He remained very thoughtful and it became obvious what he must do.

Eastleigh might not want the girl, but he wanted scandal even less. Oh, how he would enjoy pricking the fat earl one more time! He would seize the ship and take the girl and force Eastleigh to pay a ransom he could ill afford for a young woman he did not even want.

Devlin began to smile. His heart raced with excitement. This was a stroke of fortune too good to be true—and too good to be ignored.

CHAPTER THREE

Late May, 1812
The High Seas

THEY WERE BEING ATTACKED!

Virginia knelt upon her berth, her gaze glued to the cabin's only porthole, gripping a strap for balance as the ship bucked wildly in response to the boom of more cannons than she could count. She was in shock.

It had all begun several hours ago. Virginia had been told that they were but a day away from the British coastline, and that, at any time, she might soon see a gull wheeling in the cloudy blue skies overhead. Soon afterward, a ship had appeared upon the horizon, just a dark, inauspicious speck.

That speck had grown larger. She was racing the wind— the *Americana* was tacking slowly across it—and it appeared that the two ships would soon cross paths.

Virginia had been taking sun on the ship's single deck and had quickly become aware of a new tension in the American crew. The ship's commander, an older man once a naval captain, had trained his binoculars upon the approaching vessel. It hadn't taken Virginia long to realize they were worried about the identity of the approaching ship.

"Send up the blue-and-white signal flags," Captain Horatio had said tersely.

"Sir? She's flying the Stars and Stripes," the young first officer had said.

"Good," the captain had muttered. "She's one of ours, then."

But she wasn't. The frigate had sailed within fifty yards of them, maneuvering herself to the leeward side so she rode below the *Americana,* when the red, white and blue American flag had disappeared, replaced by nothing at all. Virginia had been ordered below. The crew had scrambled to the ship's ten guns. But Virginia hadn't even made it to the ladder when a cannon had boomed once, loudly but harmlessly, the ball falling off to the side of the stern.

"Americana," a voice boomed over the foghorn. "Close your gun ports and prepare to be boarded. This is the *Defiance* speaking."

Virginia froze, clinging to the dark hatch that would take her below, glancing back at the other ship, a huge, dark, multimasted affair. Her gaze instantly found the treacherous captain. He stood on a higher, smaller deck, holding the horn, his hair blindingly bright, as gold as the sun, a tall, strong figure clad in white britches, Hessian boots and a loose white shirt. She stared at him, briefly mesmerized, unable to tear her gaze away, and for one moment she had a very peculiar feeling, indeed.

It was indescribable.

As if nothing would ever be sane or right again.

Time was suspended. She stared at the captain, a creature of the high seas, and then she blinked and there was only her wildly racing heart, filled with panic and fear.

"Hold your fire," Captain Horatio cried. "Do not close the gun ports!"

"Captain!" the first officer cried with panic. "That's O'Neill, the scourge of the seas. We can't fight him!"

"I intend to try," Horatio snapped.

Virginia realized there would be no surrender. *She needed a gun.*

She glanced wildly around as the captain of the *Defiance* repeated his demands that they surrender to be boarded. An interminable moment followed as the crew of the *Americana* hastily prepared to fire. And suddenly the sea changed. A huge blast of too many cannons to count sounded, the *Defiance* firing upon them. The placid seas swelled violently as the ship bucked and heaved, hit once or many times—Virginia could not know—and as someone screamed, she heard a terrible groaning above her.

She turned and glanced upward and cried out.

Horatio was yelling, "Fire!" but Virginia watched one of the *Americana*'s three masts and all its rigging toppling slowly over before crashing down on several gunners. Several cannons now fired again from the *Defiance*, but not in unison. Virginia didn't hesitate. Lifting her skirts, she raced to the fallen men. Three were crushed and alive, one was apparently dead. She tried to heave the mast, but it was useless. She grabbed a pistol from the murdered sailor and ran back to the hatch that led below.

She could not breathe. She scrambled down and into the tiny cabin that she shared with the merchantman's only passengers, a middle-aged couple. In the small, cramped and dark space below, Mrs. Davis was clutching her Bible, muttering soundlessly, her face stark with terror. Virginia had glimpsed Mr. Davis on deck, trying to help the wounded.

Virginia gripped her arm. "Are you all right?" she demanded.

The woman gazed at her with wild terror, clearly unable to hear her or respond.

More cannons boomed and Virginia heard wood being

ripped apart as they were clearly hit again. Virginia leapt onto her narrow berth, grabbing a hanging strap for balance, and stared at the attacking ship through the porthole. The *Americana* lurched wildly, and she was almost tossed from the bunk.

How could this be happening? she wondered wildly, aghast. Who would attack an innocent, barely armed and neutral ship?

Mrs. Davis began to sob. Virginia listened to familiar prayers and wished the woman had remained silent.

What would happen next? What did that terrible captain want? Did he intend to sink the ship? But that would not make sense!

Her gaze moved instinctively back to the quarterdeck where he stood so motionlessly that he could have been a statue. He was staring, she knew, at the *Americana*, as intent as a hawk. What kind of man could be so merciless, so ruthless? Virginia shivered. Officer Grier had referred to him as the scourge of the seas.

Then she stiffened with real fear. The *Defiance*'s decks, a moment ago, had been frenzied with activity. Now the gunners at the cannons and the men in the masts were still. The only activity was a number of sailors climbing down into two rowboats that were tied to the frigate's hull. Her gaze flew back to the captain with real horror; he was sending a boarding party.

Now the *Americana* had become eerily quiet. Virginia already thought that Captain Horatio would not surrender, and nor would she, if she were in command. She checked the pistol to find it primed and loaded.

"Dear Father who art in Heaven," Mrs. Davis suddenly cried. "Have mercy on us all!"

Virginia could not stand it. She turned and seized the other woman's arm savagely, shaking her hard. "God isn't here today," she cried. "And he sure as hell isn't going to help us! We're being boarded. They must be pirates. We are losing this battle, Mrs. Davis, and we had better hide."

Mrs. Davis clutched her Bible to her bosom, clearly paralyzed with fear. Her mouth moved wildly now, forming words, but no sounds came.

"Come," Virginia said more kindly. "We'll hide down below." She knew there were lower decks and hoped they could find some small cranny to hide in. She tugged on the other woman. But it was useless.

Virginia gave up. Pistol in hand, she climbed back to the main deck and saw the first of the rowboats approaching. O'Neill stood in the bow behind his men, his legs widely braced against the seas. Virginia hesitated. Why the hell wasn't anyone shooting at him?

If she had a musket, he'd now be dead.

Her fingers itched, her palms grew clammy. She didn't know what range the pistol she held carried, but she did know it wasn't much. Still, he was getting closer and closer and why wasn't Horatio firing upon him?

Virginia could not stand it. She rushed to the rail and very carefully, very deliberately, took aim.

With some finely honed instinct, perhaps, he turned his head and looked right at her.

Good, she thought savagely, and she fired.

The shot fell short, plopping into the sea directly before the rowboat's hull. And she realized had she waited another minute or two for him to travel closer, she would have got him after all.

He stared at her.

Virginia turned and ran around the first hatch to the one that the seamen used. She scrambled down the ladder, realized she was in the sailors' cramped, malodorous quarters—she was briefly appalled at how horrid they were—when she saw another hatch at the far end of the space. She lifted that and found herself descending even lower below the sea.

She didn't like being below the ocean. Virginia couldn't breathe and panic began, but she fought it and she fought for air. Not far from the bottom of this ladder was an open doorway, through which was utter darkness. Virginia wished she'd had the wit to bring a candle. She went cautiously forward and found herself in a small hold filled with crates and barrels. Virginia crouched down at the far end and realized she still held her pistol, now useless, because in the midst of battle she hadn't thought to grab any powder and shot.

She didn't toss it aside. Her eyes adjusting to the darkness, she reversed it, holding the barrel now in her right hand.

Then her knees gave way. *He had seen her take a shot at him.*

She felt certain of it. She felt certain that the expression on his face had been one of utter surprise.

Of course, she hadn't been able to make out his features, so she was guessing as to his reaction to her sniper attempt, and if she were very lucky, he hadn't seen that miserable shot.

What would happen now?

Just as Virginia realized that the puddle of water she had been standing in was slightly higher—and she prayed it was her imagination—she heard shots begin: musket fire. Swords also clashed and rang. Her gut churned. The pirates had clearly boarded. Were they now murdering the crew?

And what was her fate to be?

She was seized with fear. Her first thought was that she might be raped.

She knew what the act entailed. She'd seen horses bred,

she'd seen slaves naked as children, and she could imagine the gruesome act. She shivered and realized the water was ankle deep.

Then she stiffened. The gunfire and sound of swords had stopped. The decks above were eerily silent now. Good God, could the battle already be over? Could his men so quickly subdue the American ship? Virginia estimated the *Americana* held about a hundred sailors. The deathly silence continued.

If he hadn't seen her, maybe he would loot the ship and sail straight back to the hellish place he had come from.

But what would he do if he had seen her attempt to shoot him?

Virginia realized she was trembling, but she told herself it was from the frigidly cold water, which was almost calf deep.

Would he kill her?

She told herself that murdering an innocent eighteen-year-old woman made no sense, although if one were a ruthless, mercenary pirate, she supposed that attacking a trading ship that was carrying cotton, rice and other merchandise was rational, indeed. So maybe there was hope.

For once, Virginia gloried in the fact that she was so skinny she was often mistaken for someone about fourteen, and that her face was too small, too pale, her hair utterly unruly. Thank God she did not look like Sarah Lewis.

Virginia froze.

Footsteps sounded directly above and to the right of her head. Virginia began to shake. Someone was traversing the hold where the sailors slept, just as she had in order to find her hiding place. Trembling again, unable to stop it, she glanced at the hatch she had come through. Her eyes had adjusted to the darkness, but still there was nothing she could see on the other side where the ladder from the upper deck was.

Wood creaked.

Virginia closed her eyes. After all the days she had been at sea, Virginia had become accustomed to the sounds of the ship—its moans and groans, the soft sigh and slap of the sea. She did not have to debate to know that this sound was not a natural one and that someone was coming down that ladder.

Sweat trickled between her breasts.

She gripped the pistol more tightly, holding it in the folds of her skirts.

He was coming down that ladder, she simply knew it.

On the other side of the hatch, light flickered from a candle.

Virginia blinked, sweat now blurring her vision, and made out a white form on the other side of the hatch, holding up the candle, turning slowly and thoroughly assessing the space there. She couldn't breathe and she feared suffocation.

He stepped through the hatch.

Virginia didn't move because she could not. He held up the candle, saw her instantly and their gazes locked.

Virginia could not look away. This man was the ruthless monster responsible for numerous deaths; she was not prepared for the sight of him. He had the face of a Greek god come down from Mount Olympus—dangerously, disturbingly handsome—high planes, hard angles, piercing silver eyes. But that face—the face of an angel—was carved in granite—and it was the face of a sea devil instead.

He was also far taller than she had assumed—she knew her head would just reach his chest—and broad-shouldered, his hips lean. His legs, while impossibly muscular from the days he spent riding the sea, were encased in bloody britches. Blood covered his white linen shirt as well. He wore a sheathed sword, a dagger was in his belt, but otherwise, she saw no other weapon.

Virginia bit her lip, finally breathing, the sound loud and harsh in the small space they now shared. She did not have to know anything else about this man to know that he was cruel and ruthless and incapable of kindness or mercy.

He broke the tense silence. "Come here."

She remained standing beside a number of piled-up crates. She wasn't sure she could obey even if she wished to—she wasn't sure that she could move. Virginia finally understood Mrs. Davis's paralyzing fear.

"I am not going to hurt you. Come out."

His tone was one of authority—she sensed he was never disobeyed. Virginia continued to stare into his cold eyes—she was incapable of looking away—as if hypnotized. He looked angry. She saw it now, because he was glancing at all of her—her mouth, her hair, her small waist, her sodden skirts—and his eyes were turning stormy gray, his jaw was flexed, his temples ticking visibly. It was very clear he did not care for the sight of her.

She took another huge breath, seeking courage, her hand holding the pistol behind her back, in the folds of her navy-blue skirts. Virginia wet her lips. "What—what do you want?"

"I want you to come here, as I never give an order twice, and this is the third time." Impatience edged his voice.

Virginia realized there was no choice. But stubbornly, childishly, she wanted reassurance from the least reassuring human being she had ever had the misfortune to meet. "What are you going to do with me?" she asked hoarsely.

"I am taking you to my ship," he said flatly.

He was going to abuse her—rape her. Virginia willed herself to stop shaking, but the trembling refused to cease.

"You have just attacked an innocent ship," she managed to say hoarsely. "But I am a young, defenseless woman, and I ask mercy of you now."

His mouth curved into a smile at once mirthless and merciless. "You will not be harmed," he said.

She started. "What?"

"Does that disappoint you?" he asked.

She stared, stunned, trying to determine whether to believe him or not. Then she realized she should not believe him, because he was a murderer, which meant he must be a liar as well. "I am not going to your ship of my own free will," she heard herself say.

His eyes widened in real surprise. "I beg your pardon?"

She tried to back up, but there was nowhere to go, and the wood crates dug into her back and her hand as it held the pistol.

Suddenly he laughed. The sound was raw, as if laughter was hard for him. "You dare to disobey me, the captain of this ship?"

"You are not—" she began, and bit her lip, hard. *Do shut up,* she told herself.

His smile was hard, his eyes colder than a block of ice. "I beg to differ with you. I am the captain of the *Americana,* as I have seized her and she has surrendered to me." And then he started for her. "I also have no patience. We have a fine nor'easter," he said, as if that explained everything.

Virginia didn't move, planning to strike him over the head with the pistol when he reached her side. But he was so tall, she would never succeed in wielding that blow. She glanced between his legs and decided to strike him there.

The space was so small in the hold that two of his hard strides closed the distance between them. Virginia's heart was banging so rapidly in her chest that it hurt. She stiffened as he reached for her, and as his large hand closed over her left arm, she swung the pistol at him.

He had the reflexes of a wild beast. He leapt aside, the butt of the gun grazing one rock-hard thigh, which it actually bounced off. His grip tightened on her arm and she cried out.

"That, *mademoiselle,* was distinctly unladylike."

Tears filled her gaze in a rush.

"But should I expect more from a vixen who thinks to shoot me?" he demanded.

She blinked and looked into pale, opaque eyes. *So he knew.* The adage was that the eyes were a window to the soul. If that was so, this man was soulless. "What are you going to do with me?" she whispered roughly.

"I told you. You will be transferred aboard my ship." He removed the pistol from her grip, tossing it aside. He gestured at the ladder in the other hold, never releasing her arm.

Virginia didn't move. "Why? I'm not pretty."

He started, then his gaze narrowed with comprehension. "Why? Because you shall be my *guest,* Miss Hughes."

She gasped at the sound of her name and real fear flooded within her. An instant later, her shrewd wit saved her—he had surely just learned her name from the captain or his crew. "My guest? Or your victim?" she whispered.

"God, you are defiant for such a little wench!" He moved her forward and her feet had no choice but to rise and fall, the one after the other. Her sodden skirts quickly tangled, making it hard to keep her balance. "Can you climb the ladder or do I have to throw you over my shoulder?" he asked.

But she had no intention of being manhandled by him until there was no other choice. Still, she heard herself say, "Captain, sir! I am on my way to London—my business is most urgent—you must let me continue on!"

He reached for her, clearly intending to hoist her into his arms, obviously devoid of any more vestiges of patience.

Virginia whirled, grabbed the ladder, gripped her skirts and scrambled upward. But she heard no movement behind her and suddenly she had an awful notion. On one of the top rungs, she paused and glanced down.

He was studying her calves and ankles, fully revealed in her frilly pantalettes. There was an odd look in his eyes and it made her heart skip wildly in fear.

His gaze lifted. "I haven't seen a woman in pantalettes in years."

Her color increased and a cruel comment made by Sarah Lewis when she had been in school in Richmond flashed through her mind: "Virginia, I hate to be the one to tell you, but those things are not in fashion anymore!"

The heat in her cheeks increased. She realized he had begun to climb up and she scrambled out of the hatch and into the hold where the ship's crew slept.

She gagged as she hurried through, acutely aware of her captor an inch behind her, giving her no chance to escape. But she would have to escape, and soon, wouldn't she? It was that or become reduced to being his whore.

Another ladder faced them. Virginia did not want to climb up first. The pirate lightly pressed her forward. "Go up, Miss Hughes."

She dared to face him. "It is clear you are no gentleman, sir, but keep your eyes to yourself."

An incredulous look crossed his face, followed by amusement, and for one moment, Virginia expected him to chuckle. "Miss Hughes, I am not interested in your charms."

"Good," she snapped, as her temper suddenly reared. "Then you can leave me on this ship and let me continue on my way while you rape someone else."

He stared at her for a long, tense moment. "I told you that you would be my guest."

"And I am to believe a murderer?"

His jaw flexed. "You may believe as you will, but I am not in the habit of raping my guests. Frankly, I am not in the habit of rape at all. Go up the ladder."

"Then why?" she asked, confused.

"I am very tired of your insolence, Miss Hughes."

Virginia saw that here, at least, was the unfettered truth. She hoisted her skirts and scrambled up, and this time she made certain she did not look back.

Above, clouds were scudding in the blue sky and the stench of death was everywhere. Virginia choked upon seeing five corpses of American sailors laid out neatly in a row, clearly about to be tossed out to sea. One of them was dear Captain Horatio. She fought genuine tears. He had been more than kind to her—he had, in an odd way, reminded her of her own father.

The rest of the American crew was shackled. Then she saw Mr. and Mrs. Davis, holding each other. She turned abruptly, suddenly furious.

"What will you do with Mr. and Mrs. Davis? Are they to be your *guests,* as well?" Her tone was filled with loathing and sarcasm.

"No." He wasn't even looking at her now. "Mac! Gus!"

A brawny seaman armed with two pistols, each tucked into his belt, two daggers and a sword hurried forward, followed by a slender blond lad, also heavily armed. Both men bore their share of blood, not their own. "Cap?" the redhead asked quickly.

"Gus will take Miss Hughes to the *Defiance.* Make certain that her bags accompany her. Issue the following orders—no one is to speak to her, look at her or acknowledge her in any way. She is my personal property, and as far as the crew is concerned, she does not exist. Am I clear?"

Mac nodded. "Yes, sir."

Gus nodded grimly as well. Neither man looked her way, not even once.

Virginia choked in disbelief. She was his personal property? "I thought I was your guest!" she cried.

The captain ignored her, as did Mac and Gus. "Mac, you captain this ship," the golden-haired pirate said. "Sail her to Portsmouth. We'll take our bounty from the prize agent there. Drogo, Gardener and Smith will stay on board to crew for you. Handpick ten others. I will be following," he said.

Mac blinked. "Yer comin' with us to Portsmouth?"

He clapped a hand on Mac's broad shoulder. "Our plans have changed," he said flatly. "You will rejoin the *Defiance* in Portsmouth."

"Yessir."

Virginia, listening intently and watching closely, felt her heart sink. Why were his plans changing? She prayed that it had nothing to do with her.

And what did he intend to do with her? It crossed her mind then that she was well enough dressed for him to be thinking of ransoming her. On the other hand, Mrs. Davis was the one with the pearl necklace, the diamond rings and the expensive clothing.

The pirate said, "Mr. and Mrs. Davis, I suggest you go down to your berth. We have a fine nor'easter and we're setting sail immediately. You will be allowed to disembark in Portsmouth."

Clearly in terror, the Davis couple rushed past the pirate and disappeared into the hold below.

Now Virginia had a very bad feeling indeed. Why wasn't he robbing Mrs. Davis? Her rings were worth thousands of dollars. A new fear—and a new dread—filled her.

The pirate started away.

"Captain O'Neill, sir?" Gus hurried after him.

O'Neill didn't stop. "You may address Miss Hughes for the sole purpose of finding the location of her bags and escorting her to my cabin, Gus." He did not look back at Virginia, not even once. He leapt onto the higher portion of the deck where clearly many of his cannons had done a great deal of damage to the middle mast and sails. Several pirates seemed to be about to attempt repairs to the rigging there.

"Lash the mainmast," he commanded. "There's good canvas below. Replace the main staysail. The rest can be patched. Put everyone on it. You have one hour and we set sail. I will not lose this wind."

Virginia stared at his tall, arrogant figure, until she realized that someone was speaking to her.

"Miss Hughes, please, this way, Miss, er, Hughes."

Virginia turned and faced the blond man, who seemed younger than herself. His cheeks were flushed and he was not looking at her, clearly taking his captain's orders very seriously, indeed. "Where are we going?"

Still gazing past her shoulder, he said, "To the *Defiance*. Where are your bags?"

"In the cabin below," she said, hardly caring about her baggage.

Gus turned, grabbed another young sailor, and sent him below for her luggage. Virginia found herself at the railing where a dinghy waited for her in the swells below. She hesitated, filled with desperation now.

He had said he would not hurt her. She didn't believe him. She would be a fool to believe him. She dismissed the notion that he intended to ransom her, for he hadn't looked twice at the wealthy Davis couple. What did he want? *What could he possibly want?*

The Atlantic Ocean was silvery gray, far darker than his eyes, and it looked as immensely threatening. One false step and she would be immersed in its frigid watery depths. It crossed her mind that another woman would jump to a watery death, saving herself from any further abuse.

She gripped the rail tightly. She had no death wish, and only a fool would choose suicide over life—any kind of life.

"Do not even think about it," he said, landing catlike by her side.

Virginia flinched and met his brilliant gray eyes.

He stared back and he was very angry, indeed.

Virginia reminded herself to never forget that this man had acute senses—that he did not miss a thing—that he almost had eyes in the back of his head. Perversely, she said, low and almost as angry as he, "If my wish is to jump, the time will come when you will not be able to stop me."

And he smiled. "Is that a challenge or a threat?"

She inhaled, struck hard by his look, his tone, his words. Something odd happened then. He was standing so close, he was so tall, so virile, so in control, and with the comprehension that he would not allow her to die came a breathless sensation and a fiery tingling to her every nerve. She backed away instantly, nervously, suddenly awash in confusion.

"Get her to the *Defiance*. And if she even looks at the water, blindfold her," he snapped to Gus.

Virginia stared. He stared back. In that moment she knew that in any battle that ensued between them, she simply could not win.

Male arms lifted her over a hard shoulder. She cried out, but it was too late, for Gus was climbing down the rope ladder to the dinghy, holding her like a treasured sack of gold. Upside down, she met the pirate's eyes. It was hard to see clearly from this humiliating position, but she could have sworn that he was frowning harshly at her now.

And by the time she was right side up and seated in the bow, he was gone.

CHAPTER FOUR

FROM THE DECKS OF THE *Americana* the seas had looked pleasant enough. The moment the dinghy was set free, the small boat leapt and bucked wildly as two sailors rowed it toward the hulk that was the *Defiance.* Virginia gripped the edge of the boat, sea spray soaking her. A minute ago, the *Defiance* had seemed so close by. Now it looked terribly far away.

A huge wave took the rowboat high up toward the sky. Virginia bit her lip to keep from crying out and then they were cast at breakneck speed toward the pit of the rushing seas.

But they did not go under. Another frothing swell raised them up again. Virginia hadn't eaten since that morning, but she realized she was in danger of retching. She managed to tear her gaze from the violence of the ocean and saw that none of the sailors seemed at all concerned. She tried to breathe more naturally but it was impossible. Then her gaze met Gus's.

Instantly he looked away at the mother ship, his cheeks crimson.

What nonsense, she thought angrily, to order the men to avoid looking at her. "Gus! How will we disembark?" she shouted at him. An attempt to do so now seemed suicidal.

Another huge sea spray thoroughly soaked her; Gus

acted as if he hadn't heard her question. The ocean was very loud, however, so she repeated herself, now hollering. His shoulders squared and he refused to look her way.

Finally they reached the other ship. A sailor tossed down ropes and a plank attached to the ship was lowered, answering Virginia's question. She could not wait to get out of the bucking rowboat.

The sailors above were staring at her. Their rude gazes gave her a savage satisfaction. Gus said tersely, "She's the captain's. No one's to speak to her, no one's to look at her, captain's orders."

Four crude gazes veered away.

As Virginia was helped onto the plank by Gus, who held on to her with a firm grip, she wondered at the control that O'Neill had over his men. How did he instill their instant submission and obedience? Undoubtedly he was a cruel and harsh master.

"This way," Gus said, not looking at her. He'd released her arm now that they were on the vast main deck of the frigate, for she rode the sea more gently than the dinghy and even than the *Americana*.

A sick feeling began. Virginia gazed about her at the huge pirate ship, wishing she knew her fate. She found herself being led across the deck, where word of the captain's orders had obviously spread, as she was studiously avoided. A moment later she was in a small cabin with her single valise, the door closed behind her.

Virginia hugged herself. It had happened. She was the pirate captain's prisoner—she was in the pirate captain's cabin.

She shivered, realized she was trembling from the cold—she was soaked from head to foot—and she blinked and glanced around at her new accommodations. The cabin was about four times the size of the berth she'd shared with the Davises. It was, in fact, luxuriously appointed. Just beyond the doorway there was a low four-poster mahogany bed, bolted to the floor and covered with paisley silk quilts in a bold red, black and gold pattern. Gold-tasseled red velvet pillows were piled high on the bed, looking distinctly Eastern. Two rows of shelves were on the wall above the bed and two dark red Persian carpets covered the floor. A desk covered with books, maps and charts was in a corner of the cabin.

There was also a fine, small dining table in the cabin, gleaming with wax, its pedestal base incredibly carved, clawed and detailed. Four tall, elegantly upholstered striped chairs graced it. A black Chinese screen, inlaid with mother of pearl, was against the fourth wall. A closet seemed to be built into the wall. A porcelain hip bath was there, as well.

Virginia grimaced, terribly uneasy. She hated being in his quarters, surrounded by his personal effects. Worse, it bothered her to no end that the appointments were far more elegant than those of her own home. She walked over to the bed, ignoring it, but helplessly wondering where she was going to sleep. There were some folded garments on one shelf—she saw what she thought were drawers and stockings. There was a mirror, a razor, a thick shaving brush, a toothbrush and a gold-engraved porcelain bowl. There were also several candles in sterling-silver holders.

Dismay somehow joined the unease.

On the higher shelf were dictionaries: French-English, Spanish-English, German-English, Italian-English, Portuguese-English and Russian-English. And then there were two small, tattered books, one on common phrases in the Arabic language, the other Chinese.

Was her captor educated? He'd had a heavy Irish brogue, but he'd also had the airs of an aristocrat. In fact, he hadn't appeared at all the way she would expect a pirate to appear—he hadn't been toothless, smelly and dirty—except for the blood. It crossed her mind that he had been clean-shaven, too.

She couldn't stand it. The cabin, filled with his presence, now threatened to suffocate her. She rushed to the door and tried it, expecting to find it locked. To her shock, it opened instantly.

She wasn't locked in.

The door ajar, she peered out and saw that the preparations on the *Americana* were almost complete. A new mainsail was being unfurled, which meant only one thing—the ship would soon begin to sail. If only she could manage to get back on board, she thought.

She stepped out of the cabin. It was growing later in the afternoon now and a swift breeze had picked up, chilling her more thoroughly. She shivered, shading her eyes with one hand and gazing out at the *Americana.* No dinghy remained tied to its side, so even if she could have thought of a way to get back over to the other ship, it was too late; the ships were casting off.

Cautiously, Virginia glanced around. Men were climbing the masts, unfurling some sails, reefing others, and other men were hoisting a huge anchor. No one seemed to be aware of her presence.

She hesitated, then saw him on the quarterdeck. Virginia stilled. He was obviously giving orders. The strong wind was now blowing strands of his hair wildly about, even though he wore it tied back, and it was also causing his billowing and still-bloody shirt to collapse against his torso, defining ridge after ridge and plane after plane of muscle. His presence was commanding. Far too commanding for him to be some farmer-turned-pirate. The man was an aristocrat, she decided instantly, an aristocrat gone bad.

He saw her and across a vast distance, he stared.

Virginia found it hard to breathe.

A moment later he put his back to her. The *Defiance* suddenly bolted as if it were a horse let out of a starting gate. Virginia was thrown back against the outside wall of the cabin.

Gus appeared. "Captain asks that you stay below, Miss Hughes," he said, refusing to make eye contact with her.

"Then why doesn't he lock the door?" she asked tartly.

"Please go inside, Miss Hughes. Captain's orders," he insisted, crimson-cheeked once again.

"Gus!" she snapped, gripping his wrist. "I don't care what he's ordered, as he is not my captain!"

Gus blinked and, for one moment, regarded her with disbelief.

She felt a tiny surge of triumph. "Please look at me when you address me. I am not a door or a post."

He flushed and looked away. "Captain's orders, miss."

"Damn your murdering captain! Damn him to hell— which is where I have no doubt he will one day end up, far sooner than later!" Virginia cried.

Gus dared to glance at her again. "Wind's changed. Storm's coming. Please go inside or I am ordered to take you in."

Virginia made a distinctly unladylike sound, very much a snort, and she stormed into the cabin, slamming the door shut behind her. She waited to hear a padlock being put in place, but she heard nothing at all. But they were in the middle of the Atlantic Ocean, and there was, quite simply, nowhere for her to go.

She would escape in Portsmouth.

Virginia sat down hard on one of the dining room chairs, filled with sudden excitement. They were but a day away, if she understood correctly. Surely she could keep the lech-

erous captain at bay for an entire day—and surely, in the
next twenty-four hours, she could come up with a plan.

And Portsmouth was in Britain. Somehow she would
find a way to get from Portsmouth to London, where she
was certain her uncle was expecting her.

Hope filled her. So did relief.

Virginia finally faced the fact that she had nothing to do
other than plot and plan. She was freezing, though, and she
eyed her valise. She was afraid to change. She was afraid
of being caught in a state of undress by the captain.
Rubbing her hands together, she decided to focus on
planning her escape.

Within minutes, her mind slowed and dimmed and her
eyes became heavy, refusing to stay open. Finally, her head
fell onto her arms and she was asleep.

"SIR. SHE'S GONE BELOW," Gus said.

Devlin allowed his first mate to handle the ship's helm
but he stood beside him, studying the racing clouds, the
graying light, acutely aware of the sudden drop in temperature. A gale was blowing in and his every instinct, honed
by eleven years at sea, told him it would be a nasty one.

There was still time, however, before he needed to reef
in the topsails. Now he hoped to outrun the storm, although
doing so was pushing them off course.

And the girl was in his cabin. A pair of huge violet eyes,
angry and outraged, assailed his mind's eye. They were set
in a small, finely formed face. Dismissing the unwanted
images, he glanced at Gus, who was blushing. "Give you
a hard time, did she?" He could not help but find Gus's dis-
comfort amusing.

Gus hesitated. "She's very brave for such a small lady,
sir."

He turned away with a grunt. Brave? That was an understatement. Her huge violet eyes had been disturbing him ever since he had had the misfortune to finally meet the Earl of Eastleigh's American niece. He didn't know whether to be truly amused by her antics, or genuinely furious with her lack of respect and subordination. The girl was as small as a child of thirteen, but he was a fine judge of character and she had the courage of ten grown men. Not that he cared. She was a hostage and a means to an end.

He had been expecting a refined lady with equally refined airs, a fully grown and experienced woman like Elizabeth, a woman he might consider bedding just to sweeten the pot. He had not anticipated a pint-size hellion who would try to murder him with a sniper shot and then had dared attack him again, this time with the butt of a pistol.

It was not amusing. Devlin stalked to the side of the quarterdeck, raising spyglasses to his eyes. A heavy feeling simmered in the pit of his loins, dangerous and hot, and it was the seed of a huge, terrible lust.

His mouth twisted mirthlessly as he gazed through the binoculars. Fucking Eastleigh's niece was a terrible temptation. The savage blood lust smoldering in him felt far greater than any lust he'd ever experienced before, perhaps because the girl was just that, more child than woman, making the act even more vicious and brutal. He knew it would add to the triumph of his revenge. But he hadn't lied when he had said he did not rape and neither did his men. It was not allowed. He was a man, not a monster. He had, in fact, been raised by both his mother, his father and his stepfather to be a gentleman. And he supposed that when he infrequently attended a ball or affair of state, it was assumed that he was just that. But he was not. No *gentleman* could ever triumph on the high seas, not in war and not in peace. No *gentleman* could amass a real fortune by seizing prize after prize. His crew would never obey a *gentleman*. Still, ruining an eighteen-year-old virgin was simply not an option, even if he was intrigued enough to be thinking about it.

He set the binoculars down. Her reputation would be tattered enough when he finally delivered her to Eastleigh. He didn't care. Why should he? She meant nothing to him. And if he learned that Eastleigh was fond of her, then he would be even more pleased to present her with a shredded reputation. As for his own reputation, it was very simple— he didn't give a damn and he never had.

He had been talked about behind his back for most of his life. As a small boy, before his father's murder, their neighbors used to whisper with a mixture of pity and respect that he should have been *The O'Neill* one day, like his ancestors before him. Then they would whisper about his family's current state of destitution—or about his father's love affairs. Gerald had been a good husband, but like many men, he had not been entirely faithful. And the whispers had not stopped after Gerald's murder. There were more whispers then, more stares, mostly unkind and accusatory. They whispered about his family's conversion to Protestantism, they whispered about his mother's love for her new husband, and then they dared to whisper about his real paternity. With stiff shoulders, his cheeks aflame, Devlin had ignored them all.

Now the rumors were spread in society by the English lords and ladies there. They bowed to him with the utmost deference, but their whispers were hardly different. They called him a hero to his face, and a rogue, a scoundrel and a pirate behind his back, even as they foisted their pretty, unwed, wealthy daughters upon him at the balls they invited him to.

And he wasn't worried about his naval career, either. It

was a career that had served him well but it was also one that he was ambivalent about. His life was the wind and the sea, his ship and his crew—of that, there was no doubt. Should his naval career end prematurely, he would still sail the high seas, just differently. He felt no loyalty and no love for his British masters, but he was a patriot—he would do anything for his country, Ireland.

Devlin was very aware that he had failed to follow his orders once again. In fact, he had done more than fail to follow them, he had actually flagrantly violated them. But the Admiralty needed him more than they wanted his head; besides, he would see that this new game with Eastleigh was conducted fashionably, discreetly and with the semblance of honor. Eastleigh had no wish for scandal, and Devlin knew he would keep the abduction and ransom of his niece a very private affair. He intended to conclude it as swiftly as possible—after he toyed with Eastleigh just a bit.

And Devlin smiled at the darkening sky.

SHE DIDN'T KNOW HOW MUCH time had passed or how long he'd stood there in the growing dusk, staring at her as she slept. But suddenly Virginia was awake, and as she lifted her head, he was the first thing that she saw.

She gasped, sitting upright, riveted by an odd glitter in his eyes. Devlin didn't move. He stood in front of the closed door as if he had just entered the cabin.

Virginia leapt to her feet. Her clothes remained damp and wet and that told her she'd slept for just a short time. "How long were you standing there?" she demanded.

His gaze slipped from her eyes to her breasts. Quickly, they returned to her eyes, and then he moved across the cabin, past her. "Not long." His reply was cool and indifferent.

Virginia hugged herself, flushing. Had that man just ogled her bosom? She *had* no bosom, and the cabin was too small for the two of them. "I thought this was my cabin now."

He was opening the closet door. He turned toward her, his expression mild and inscrutable. "It is."

"Then you should leave."

Now he fully faced her. "Has anyone ever told you that you have the tongue of a shrew?"

"And you are rude. This cabin is too small for the both of us and..." She faltered, finally looking at his wet, bloody shirt. It clung to interesting angles and planes. "You smell."

"For your edification, Miss Hughes, this is my cabin and you are in it as my guest. You did not change your clothes. Why?"

She blinked, his sudden change of topic taking her by surprise. "I don't wish to change my clothes," she said warily.

"You like the appearance of a drowned cat?" His dark brows lifted. "Or is it the cold you enjoy?"

"Thank you for the flattery—and the sarcasm."

He sighed. "Miss Hughes, you will catch pneumonia if you do not get out of those garments. My intention is not for you to die."

She jumped at the cue. "What is your intention?"

His expression changed and it was clear he was now annoyed. He half turned and before she could make a sound, he had pulled his bloody shirt over his head, letting it drop on the floor.

She backed away until she hit the door. "What in God's name are you doing?" she cried, her gaze riveted on broad, naked shoulders and a glimpse of an equally broad, rock-hard chest.

She looked lower. His belly was flat and tight, with

interesting lines, and then it began to ripple. She quickly averted her gaze, but her cheeks had warmed.

"I have the good sense to change my clothes," he returned evenly, forcing her gaze to his.

She met a pair of pale gray eyes and knew she should not have stared. Her spirits sank stunningly, with real dismay. *The face of a god, the body of a warrior.* She had seen a few men without their shirts before at Sweet Briar, but somehow, a glimpse of Frank's naked chest had never distressed her in such a way.

Of course, at Sweet Briar, she wasn't being held a prisoner against her will, in such a small, confined space with her captor. "This cabin is too small for us both," she repeated, aware of her racing heartbeat.

He held a new, clean shirt in his hands, but he didn't move. In fact, had she not seen the rise and fall of his very sculpted chest, she would have thought him to be a lifelike statue. Slowly he said, "You are repeating yourself."

Her shivering abruptly ceased as their gazes locked. The cabin had become hot. It had also become airless.

His face was taut. "You are staring again."

She somehow looked away. "You could have asked me to step outside," she managed, carefully looking at the floor.

"I hadn't realized a man's chest would be so fascinating," he said bluntly.

Her gaze flew up. His back was to her now, encased in fine white lawn, but he was pulling one Hessian boot off, and then another. As he reached into the closet, Virginia glimpsed a sparkle of gold, and then a pair of clean, cream-colored britches were in his hands.

She didn't speak. She whirled, about to dash out the door.

He crossed the space of the cabin in a heartbeat and

placed a hand on the door, preventing her from opening it. "You cannot go out on deck that way."

His arm was over her shoulder and she felt the presence of his large body just behind hers. She couldn't turn around to face him because if she did she would be in his arms. "I am not going to watch you undress," she said, and her tone sounded odd and rough.

"I am not asking you to watch, Miss Hughes. I apologize. I have forgotten how innocent a woman of eighteen is."

Virginia froze. Was he now playing the part of a *gentleman?* Disbelief warred with a vast confusion.

In that endless moment, she became aware of the heat actually emanating from his body, as only inches separated them. Abruptly he dropped his hand from the door and stepped back.

Slowly, Virginia turned around.

He still held the clean britches in his hand. He broke the silence. Tersely, he said, "Look the other way. I will be done in a moment and then you may change your gown."

"I prefer to step outside—" she began.

"Good God, woman! Will you dispute my every word? Your gown is indecent." He raked a gaze over her bosom and stalked away, unfastening his britches as he did so.

It was a moment before she comprehended his words. Virginia looked down and was utterly chagrined. The wet silk of her gown and chemise molded her small breasts, enhanced by her corset, and clearly defined each erect nipple, the entire effect so revealing that no one could be in any doubt as to the size or state of her anatomy. No wonder he had stared. She might as well have been naked. She was mortified.

Cloth rustled.

Virginia looked and glimpsed far more than she should

have—high, hard buttocks, muscled thighs and calves—and she reversed, facing the door, breathing harshly against the wood. Suddenly she wanted to cry.

She had been as brave as she could be for an interminable amount of time, but her courage was failing her now. She had to get to London, she had to beg her uncle for pity and the payment of her debts. Instead, she was on board a pirate ship, in a pirate's cabin, a pirate who at times spoke like an aristocrat, a pirate who exuded such seductive virility that she was, for the first time ever in her life, aware of her own body in an entirely different way than ever before. How had this happened? How?

He was her enemy. He stood between her and Sweet Briar. She hated him passionately—and she must not ever find a single inch of him interesting, intriguing or fascinating.

"I'll wait outside," he said, suddenly behind her again.

Virginia fought the tears back, nodding and stepping aside while refusing to look at him. She was aware of him hesitating and staring at her. She walked over to her bag and made a show of finding new garments, praying he hadn't seen a single tear. Finally, she heard the door close.

She sank onto the floor by her valise and wept.

THE WIND BLEW STRONG and hard behind them. Devlin had taken the helm, as if that would make everything right again. Gripping it with the ease of one who could steer a huge ship in his sleep, he focused on the task at hand—outrunning the storm chasing them.

"Will we make it?" a quiet voice asked from behind just as a pair of moist violet eyes invaded his mind.

Devlin relaxed, relieved by the interruption. He glanced at the ship's surgeon, a small, portly man with thick sideburns and curling gray hair. "It's fifty-fifty," he responded. "I'll know in the next fifteen minutes."

Jack Harvey folded his arms across his chest and gazed up at the inky, starless sky. "What is this hostage-taking business, Devlin?"

Devlin stared into the gray horizon. "My own mad affair, I'm afraid."

"Who is she?"

"Does it matter?"

"I caught a glimpse of her on board the *Americana.* She's a young lady. I smell a ransom. I don't know why. You've never ransomed a woman before."

"There's always a first time," Devlin said, having no intention of telling the good surgeon anything at all. "How are the wounded?"

"Brinkley is dying, but I've given him laudanum and he doesn't know it. Buchler and Swenson will make it. Does she need medical attention?"

Devlin became irritated. "She needs a gag, but no, she does not need medical attention."

Jack Harvey raised both bushy brows in surprise. Then he said, "She's a beautiful wild thing, isn't she? Good God, the men are talking about how she tried to shoot you! She—"

"Reams!" Devlin snapped. "Take the helm. Stay true to course." He jammed a finger at the compass heading and stalked across the quarterdeck. He did not know why he was suddenly very annoyed and angry.

"I take it you are not inviting me to join you for a bite of supper before we face the winds of hell?" Harvey called out to his back.

Devlin didn't bother answering. But it was now or never—if the storm caught them, he needed a full belly and all of his strength.

Had she been *crying* when he left the cabin?

Not that he cared. Women used tears for the sole purpose

of manipulation—he had learned that long ago. As he didn't care about any woman to begin with, tears had no effect on him.

He opened the cabin door and saw Virginia seated at his table, which was set with silver and fine crystal and a covered platter, from which savory aromas were wafting. Her posture was terribly erect, her hands were clasped in her lap and two bright pink spots blotched her cheeks. Her gaze, which seemed wild, clashed with his.

He straightened, closing the door, sensing a battle's first blow.

She smiled and it was as cold as ice. "I wondered when you would return...*Captain.*"

Delight tingled in his veins. How he loved a good war. He intended to enjoy this one. "I hadn't realized you were pining for my company," he said with a courtly inclination of his head.

"I only pine for your head—on that silver serving platter," she said, as regally as if she were England's queen.

He wanted to smile. He nearly did. Instead, he approached cautiously and saw the fury in her eyes. "I fear to disappoint you. My chef is French. I have far better fare on that platter."

"Then I shall wait patiently for a better day, when the dinner I truly desire is served," she almost spat.

He refused to chuckle. "You do not strike me as a patient woman, Miss Hughes, and as I doubt the day you seek will come for a good many years, what will you do instead of waiting?"

"You're right. I have *no* patience, none at all! Rogue!" she cried.

He almost laughed. "Bastard" was more like it. "Have I somehow offended you, Miss Hughes?"

Her laughter was brittle. "You murder innocent Americans, you abduct me, take me prisoner, strip in front of me, ogle my breasts and ask me if I am offended? Hah," she said.

He reached for the bottle of red wine. "May I?" he asked, about to pour into her glass.

She leapt to her feet. "You're an officer!" she shouted, and he tensed, thinking she intended to strike him. But she only added in another shout, "In the British navy!"

He set the bottle down and swept her a mocking bow. "Sir Captain Devlin O'Neill, at your service, Miss Hughes."

She was trembling with rage, he saw. He decided to give in to lechery and admire her perfect breasts. "Stop leering," she hissed. "You have committed criminal acts. Atrocious criminal acts! Explain yourself, Captain, sir!"

He gave up. This woman dared to order *him*. It was the single truly entertaining moment of his life. She was on *his* ship, in *his* command and she ordered *him* about. He laughed.

Virginia froze, startled by the brief eruption of that rough sound, with its oddly raw tone. Then, still furious at his deception, and worse, at what clearly was not the dire predicament she had thought herself to be in, she snapped, "I am waiting for an explanation, *Captain*."

He shook his head and looked at her. Very softly, he asked, "Are you not afraid of me?"

She hesitated. What kind of question was this?

"Be truthful," he said, as if in earnest.

"You terrify me," she heard herself say, her pulse quickening. Then she amended, "You have terrified me, and all for naught, damn it!"

His brows lifted. "Ladies do not curse."

"I don't care. Besides, I have not been treated like a lady, now have I?"

He gave her a very odd, long look. "Another man would have had you in that bed—where you belong. But you are hardly there, are you?"

She went still. Alarm filled her. Alarm and such a forceful heartbeat she could no longer breathe. "I har—I har—I hardly belong in your bed!" she stammered. Terrible images of her there, with him, in his powerful arms, assailed her.

"A slip of the tongue." His brows, darker than his hair, lifted. "I agree. Skinny women tend to be exceedingly uncomfortable."

She almost gasped again. Then she cried, "I am only fourteen, sir! You would take a child to your bed?"

His gaze slammed to hers.

She wet her lips. She was perspiring and she desperately needed him to believe her now.

His jaw flexed. His gaze narrowed with speculation, causing her heart to lurch with dread. "This is a dangerous game you play, Miss Hughes," he said softly.

"It is no game!"

"Indeed? Then explain to me the fact of your passage, alone and without chaperone, aboard the *Americana?*"

Her mind scrambled and raced. "I had to lie to Captain Horatio to get passage," she said, and she thought her explanation brilliant. "Obviously he would not let a child travel to Britain alone. I told him I was eighteen—"

He cut her off, his eyes cold. "You did not look fourteen in your wet gown, Miss Hughes."

She stiffened.

His smile was a mere twist of lips. "Do sit down. As interesting as this conversation is, I am here for a purpose. A storm threatens to catch us, and if so, a long night ensues." He moved swiftly to the table and held out her chair.

Virginia found it hard to sit down. Oddly, she hated her deception now; she did not want him to really think of her as a child. But did he even believe her? She did not quite think so. And he wasn't a pirate, oh no! Some of her anger at being duped—and pointlessly frightened—returned. "Why didn't you tell me that you are a captain in the royal navy?"

He shrugged. "Do you care?"

"Of course I do!" she cried, facing him earnestly now. "Because I thought I was your prisoner, although I could not fathom why. Now I know differently, although I still do not understand why I am on your ship and not the *Americana.* I know that the British navy thinks nothing of seizing American ships, as you have clearly done, for your country has no respect for our rights! But we are not at war with you, and you are not a pirate! In some ways, we are allies. Clearly you will release me in Portsmouth!" For this was the conclusion she had drawn upon finding his naval uniform in his closet. An officer in the British navy was not about to ransom an American citizen. But what was he about?

"We are not allies," he said harshly.

This was not the reply she had expected and she did not like the look on his face or in his eyes.

"And I am not releasing you in Portsmouth."

"What?" She was shocked. "But—"

"In fact, I am taking you to Askeaton. Have you ever been to Ireland, Miss Hughes?"

CHAPTER FIVE

VIRGINIA WAS DISBELIEVING. "Ireland? You think to take me to *Ireland?*"

"I hardly think it," he murmured, "I plan it. Now, do sit down, as I also intend to eat." He held out her chair.

Confusion overcame her. "I am not sure that I understand."

"Good God!" he shot. "What is there to understand? I am taking you to Ireland, Miss Hughes, as my guest."

She was truly trying to comprehend him. "So I am your *prisoner*," she managed to say hoarsely.

"I prefer to think of you as a guest." He became serious. "I will not harm you—not even if you are eighteen."

"Why?"

"It doesn't matter. Now, sit."

Virginia had believed her terrible predicament over. She shook her head, refusing to take the offered chair. "I have no appetite. Is it a ransom that you seek?"

"How clever." His smile was cold.

"I have no funds. My inheritance is being sold in bits and pieces as soon as possible, and the proceeds go to the repayment of my father's debts."

He shrugged as if he did not care.

Virginia became very alarmed, but managed to breathe slowly, evenly. "You let Mrs. Davis go. She was rather wealthy."

"If you think to starve, so be it." He sat down and began serving himself from the platter, where a hearty mutton stew was revealed.

Unfortunately, the sight and smell of the stew caused her stomach to growl loudly, but he did not seem to hear. He began to eat, and quickly, as if eating were a mission and he were in a rush to accomplish it.

Finally he took a sip of wine and saluted her with his glass. "Fine contraband, indeed."

Virginia did not reply. A terrible inkling was dawning upon her. He intended to ransom her and he couldn't care less about her inheritance.

He had known her name from the moment they had met.

He must know of her uncle, the earl.

She sat down hard on the chair he had left pulled out from the table. That action caused him to glance up, although he never ceased eating.

But now she was safe enough, was she not? The man was in the navy, even if about to be discharged, or worse— and she hoped he hanged from the nearest gallows. He was no common outlaw. He wanted a ransom, one that would surely be paid, and considering all circumstances, she doubted he would return her to her uncle blemished in any way.

Virginia wondered what the ransom would be and if her uncle was wealthy enough to pay her ransom and her father's debts. Her dismay was infinite.

"You seem distraught," he remarked, leaning back in his chair, apparently having finished his meal.

"You have no morals, sir," she said tightly. "That much is clear."

"I have never said I did." He eyed her. "Morals are for fools, Miss Hughes."

She stared. Impulsively, she leaned forward. "How can

I make you change your mind?" She could hardly believe herself now. "There cannot be a ransom from my uncle, Captain O'Neill. I am eighteen, not fourteen." His face never changed expression. "I will do whatever I must to be freed."

He stared for an interminable moment. "Is that the offer that I think it is?"

She felt ill...breathless...ashamed...resigned. "Yes, it is," she croaked.

He stood. "The storm is upon us. I am afraid I must go. Do not leave this cabin. A chit such as yourself would be blown overboard instantly." He tossed his napkin aside and strode across the now-rolling floor of the cabin as if it were still and flat.

That was his reply? She was incredulous.

At the door, he paused. "And my answer is no." He walked out.

She collapsed on the table in tears, all of which now flowed purely from desperation. She already knew her uncle didn't give a damn about her. He would never pay both a ransom and her father's debts.

Because of the damned Irishman, she would lose Sweet Briar.

Anger exploded and she leapt up, racing across the cabin. As soon as she had swung the door open, a huge gale wind sent her forward helplessly across the entire deck. She had never felt such a force in her life; Virginia saw the raging, frothing sea beyond the railing and it seemed to be racing toward her. She couldn't even cry out and then she was slammed hard, midsection first, into wood and rope.

Pain blinded her. The sea sprayed her, while the wind wanted to push her overboard. Panic consumed her—she did not want to die!

"You damnable stubborn woman," O'Neill hissed, his

strong arms wrapping around her. And she was cocooned against his entire hard, powerful body, the sea and the wind now relentlessly battering them both.

She inhaled, unable to look up, her face pressed against his chest. His grip tightened, and then he was dragging her with him as he confronted the wind, walking fiercely, determinedly into it, a single man against the elements.

He shoved her into the cabin, and for one moment stood braced in the doorway, pounded by the wind. "Stay inside!" he shouted to make himself heard.

"You have to let me go!" she shouted back. Oddly, she wanted to thank him for saving her life.

He shook his head, lashed her with a furious look and began running across the deck, finally leaping up to the quarterdeck. It had begun to rain, pounding and fierce.

Virginia stayed safely within the cabin, out of the reach of the storm, but she made no move to close the door, which had become nailed open by the wind. Now she realized how serious the storm was. The ship was riding huge tidal waves the way the tiny dinghy had earlier, cresting to each huge tip, only to plummet sickeningly down again. She glanced around and saw sailors everywhere, straining against ropes, crawling in the masts. They were hanging there, too.

Then she looked back up and cried out in horror, because a man was hanging from a middle yardarm, and she knew he had fallen and was about to career to his death.

She had to do something, yet there seemed to be nothing that she could do.

She glanced toward the quarterdeck. She was too small to even cross the space between O'Neill's cabin and where he stood, to tell him what was happening. She looked back up—and the hanging man was gone.

Vanished...drowned.

Her insides lurched terribly. He was gone, and she hadn't even been able to hear him scream.

As the ship bucked violently, Virginia saw that all of the sails were tied down save one. She quickly realized that the sailor who had fallen had been sent up the first mast to reef a single sail that remained taut and unfurled.

And the huge ship instantly began to turn over on its side.

Virginia was thrown against the floor and carried all the way across it, downward, until she slammed into the opposite wall, her shoulder taking the blow, and then her head. For a moment, as the ship lay on its side—or nearly so—she remained there, incapable of moving, stunned.

She then realized that the ship was going to capsize if it didn't become righted again. She looked at the doorway, which remained wide open, and now was oddly above her, like the ridge of a hill, the angle severe, perhaps forty-five degrees or more. The black sky shimmered in the open hatch.

They were all going to die, she thought wildly.

Virginia began to climb the floor, using the bolted table legs to help her, then the leg of the bed. Once there, she managed to stretch flat and reach high up to grab the ridge of the floor where it adjoined the door. Her arms screamed in protest, her shoulder joints felt racked. Virginia slowly pulled herself to the doorway, and once there, her back pressed into one wall, her feet into another, gazed wildly around.

The sailors on deck were also fighting the terrible angle of the ship, and its lowered side, while still not submerged, was being pounded with whitecaps. Virginia looked up at the masts and froze.

There was no mistaking Devlin O'Neill, a dagger in his teeth, climbing up the first mast, another man behind him. Above him, the huge foresail billowed, begging the storm to capsize them.

He was going to die, she thought, mesmerized, just the way that other man had. For as he climbed, using sheer strength and will to fight the pitch of the ship, the huge winds and the rain, the frigate rolled precariously even further to its side.

Virginia watched in horror. Even if he didn't die, they were surely doomed, as no man could defeat the wind and the bucking ship in order to cut the sail free.

She watched as O'Neill paused, as if exhausted, the man beneath him also stopping. Virginia could not remove her gaze. She prayed as both men took a brief respite, clinging to the swaying mast.

He started back up. He'd reached the yardarm from which the sailor had fallen and he began to slash at the rigging. The other man joined him. Virginia watched them avidly. A few brief moments passed into an eternity when suddenly the huge canvas broke free of its rigging, sailing wildly away into the night.

The huge ship groaned and sank back evenly into the water.

"Oh, my God," she whispered, watching him begin a precarious but nimble descent. It was obvious he had just saved his ship and crew, and it was also obvious he had dared to do what few others would even contemplate.

She began to shake. The man knew no fear.

She realized she had never been more afraid in her life.

She wasn't sure how long she sat there when a sailor shoved his face at her. "Get inside, Captain says so."

Virginia had no time to react. She was shoved back into the cabin, while the sailor used all of his strength to pry the door free from the outside wall, fighting the gale and eventually slamming it in her face.

This time, she heard the click of a lock.

Virginia stumbled over to his bed, where she collapsed and lapsed into unconsciousness.

SUNLIGHT WAS STREAMING brightly through the portholes of the cabin when she awoke. Every part of her body ached and her head pounded, while her eyes felt too heavy to even open. She had never been so tired in her life, and she had no wish to awake. She snuggled more deeply beneath the covers, cocooned in warmth. Then a mild irritation began—only the back side of her body seemed to be covered.

She groped for the blanket…and realized there were no covers and she was not alone.

She stiffened.

The length of a hard body lay against her, warming her from her shoulders to her toes. She felt a soft breath feathering her jaw, and an arm was draped over her waist.

Oh God, she thought, blinking into bright midday sunlight. And trembling, a new tension filling her, she looked at the hand on her waist.

She already knew who lay in bed beside her and she stared at O'Neill's large, strong, bronzed hand, which lay carefully upon her. She swallowed, an odd heavy warmth unfurling in the depth of her being.

How had this happened? she thought with panic. Of course the explanation was simple enough and she guessed it immediately—sometime after the storm died, he had stumbled into bed just as she had, too tired to care that she lay there. That likelihood did not decrease her distress. In fact, her agitation grew.

Then a terrible comprehension seized her.

His hand lay carefully on her waist.

Not limp and relaxed with sleep, but carefully controlled and placed.

Her heart skipped then drummed wildly. *He was not asleep.* She would bet her life on it.

She debated feigning sleep until he left her bed. But her

heart was racing so madly it was an impossibility, especially as she felt his hand tighten on her waist. Virginia turned abruptly and faced a pair of brilliant silver eyes and the face of an archangel. Their gazes locked.

She didn't move, didn't breathe, and could think of nothing intelligent to say.

Then his gaze moved to her temple, which she now realized truly hurt. "Are you all right?" he asked, also still. His gaze slipped slowly to her mouth, where it lingered before moving as slowly back up to her eyes.

His gaze felt like a silken caress.

"I..." She stopped, incapable of speech. And she could not help but stare. His face was terribly close to hers. He had firm, unmoving lips. Her gaze shot back to his. His face was expressionless, carved in stone and impossible to read, but his eyes seemed bright.

She wondered what it would feel like, to have his hard mouth soften and cover hers. "You saved my life," she whispered nervously. "Thank you."

His jaw flexed. He started to shove off of the bed.

She gripped the hand that had been on her waist. "You saved the ship, the crew. I saw what you did. I saw you up there."

"You are in my bed, Virginia, and unless you wish to remain here with me for another hour, at least, leaving the last of your youth behind, I suggest you let me get up."

She remained still. Her mind raced. Her body burned for his touch and she knew it. It was foolish now to deny. Somehow, his heroism of the night before had changed everything. Anyway, he was perfectly capable of getting up, never mind that she had seized his wrist. She found herself looking at his mouth again. She had never been kissed.

Abruptly he lurched off of the bed and before she could even cry out, he was gone.

Virginia slowly sat up, stunned.

There was no relief. There was a morass of confusion, and more bewildering, there was disappointment.

VIRGINIA REMAINED ON THE BED, sitting there, beginning to realize what she had almost done.

She had been a hairbreadth away from kissing her captor—she had *wanted* his kiss.

Disbelief overcame her and she leapt to her feet as a knock sounded on her door. O'Neill never knocked, so she snapped, "Who is it?"

"Gus. Captain asked that I bring you bathing water."

"Come in," she choked, turning away. *O'Neill was the enemy.* He had taken her against her will from the *Americana,* an act of pure avarice and greed. He was holding her against her will now. He stood between her and Sweet Briar. How could she have entertained, even for an instant, a desire for his touch, his kiss?

Gus entered, followed by two seamen carrying pails of hot water. He set a pitcher of fresh water on the dining table, not looking at her. Both sailors also treated her as if she were invisible, filling the hip bath.

How kind, she thought, suddenly furious with him—and furious with herself. She had never even thought of kissing *anyone* until a moment ago. This had to be his fault entirely—she was overwrought from the crisis of the abduction, of the storm, the crisis that was him! He was somehow taking advantage of her state of confusion, her nerves. In any case, the entire interlude was unacceptable. He was the enemy and would remain so until she was released. One did not kiss one's enemy, oh no.

Besides, kissing would surely lead to one certain fate—becoming his whore!

"Is there anything else that you need, Miss Hughes?" Gus was asking, cutting into her raging thoughts.

"No, thank you," she said far too tersely. Her cheeks were on fire. *She* was on fire. And she was afraid.

Gus turned, the other sailors already leaving.

Virginia fought the fear, the despair. She reminded herself that she had to escape. She had to convince her uncle to save Sweet Briar. Soon, this nightmare that was O'Neill would be only that, a passing bad dream, a memory becoming distant. "Gus! Where are we? Are we close to shore?"

He hesitated, but did not turn to face her. "We were blown off course. We're well north of England, Miss Hughes."

She gaped as he left, before she was able to demand just how far north they had been blown off course. Her geography was rusty, but she knew rather vaguely that Ireland was north of England. Being taken to Portsmouth was far better than being taken to Ireland, and ironically, now she was afraid he'd change his damnable plans and not take the *Defiance* to Portsmouth first.

She ran to his desk and glanced at the map there. It took her a moment to confirm her worst fears. Ireland was north and west of England, and if they had been blown far north enough, Ireland would be smack in their way. But could a mere storm have blown them that far off course? To her uneducated eye, two hundred miles or more were required for them to be on a direct line with the other country.

She glanced at the map of England. Portsmouth did not look to be far from London. She tried to estimate the distance and decided it was a day's carriage ride. At least that one point was in her favor, she thought grimly.

Now what? Virginia's gaze fell on the steaming bath. Instantly she decided not to waste the hot water. She bathed quickly, afraid of an interruption, scrubbing his touch from her body. Leaping out, she barely toweled dry, afraid he would walk in and catch her unclothed. She braided her hair while wet, in record time donning the same clothes. A glance in his mirror showed her that she was frightfully pale, which only made her eyes appear larger. She looked terribly unkempt—her gown was beyond wrinkled and torn at the hem, with a bloodstain on one shoulder. But even worse was the abrasion on her temple. It looked like a terrible gash, and when she touched it she found the wound sensitive.

She looked like a washerwoman in a fine lady's clothes, one who'd been in a fistfight or other battle.

But then, she had been in a battle, she had been in a constant battle since the moment O'Neill had attacked the *Americana*.

Virginia walked over to a porthole, which she levered open. It was a beautiful spring day, the sky blue and cloudless, the ocean almost flat, and she was amazed at how serene the sea was after the horror of the night before. She strained for a glimpse of land or even a seagull, but saw neither. Virginia left the porthole open and stepped out onto the deck.

She espied him instantly. O'Neill had his back to her, standing with an officer who was steering the ship, his legs braced wide apart, his arms apparently folded in front of his chest. She felt an odd breathless sensation as she stared at him, one she did not care for. He turned slightly— the man had the senses of a jungle tiger—and their gazes locked.

He nodded.

She ignored his gesture and walked over to the railing, only too late realizing that this was very close to the spot where she would have been washed overboard if he hadn't rescued her.

She clung to the rail, closing her eyes and lifting her face to the warm May sun. But inside, she was shaken to the core. Last night, she had almost died. It was an experience she hoped never to repeat.

A distinct recollection of the feel of his strong arms wrapping around her, and then the sensation of being pressed deeply against his body, overcame her. Virginia stood very still, allowing her eyes to open, reminding herself that he was the enemy and that would never change—not until he let her go free.

"A fine spring day," an unfamiliar voice said cheerfully behind her.

Virginia started, turning.

A plump man with curly gray hair and dancing brown eyes smiled at her. He wore a brown wool jacket, britches and stockings—he could have been strolling the streets of Richmond, except for the lack of a hat, cane and gloves. "I'm Jack Harvey, ship's surgeon," he said, giving her a courtly bow.

She smiled uncertainly, sensing that he was a good man—unlike his superior. "Virginia Hughes," she said.

"I know." His smile was wide. "Everyone knows who you are, Miss Hughes. There are no secrets on board a ship."

Virginia absorbed that and helplessly darted a glance at O'Neill. He seemed oblivious to her presence on his deck now, his back remaining to her and Harvey.

"How are you holding up?" Harvey asked. "And should I take a look at that temple of yours?"

"It's sore," she admitted, meeting his gaze. "I am holding up as well as can be expected, I think. I have never been abducted before."

Harvey met her gaze, grimacing. "Well, you may know that as far as Devlin is concerned, this is a first for him, as well. He's taken hostages before, but never women or children. He always frees the women and the children."

"How wonderful to be an exception," she said with bitterness.

"Has he hurt you?" Harvey asked abruptly.

She started and stared. An image of his silver gaze as she turned in bed to face him filled her mind. She hesitated.

"You are very beautiful," Harvey said in the lapse that had fallen. "I have never seen such extraordinary eyes. I do not approve of Devlin sharing that cabin with you."

Did she have an ally in the ship's surgeon? She inhaled sharply, her mind racing. Then, carefully, she summoned tears—a feat she had never before performed. "I begged for mercy," she whispered. "I told him I was a young, innocent and defenseless woman." She stopped as if she could not continue.

Harvey's eyes widened in shock. "I don't believe it! The bastard...*seduced* you?"

He would be an ally, she could feel it. "Seduced? I don't think that is the right word."

He was pale beneath his coppery tan. "I will make sure he finds accommodations elsewhere," he said tersely. He glanced over his shoulder at O'Neill, who remained with his back to them, facing the prow of the ship. "Not that that will change what he has done," he said, clearly distressed. "Miss Hughes, I am so sorry. Clearly you are a lady, and frankly, this is entirely out of character for Devlin."

She was certain she had won him over. She pretended to wipe her eyes, making certain that her hands trembled. "I am sorry, too. You see, I have terribly urgent affairs in London, my entire life is at stake, and now...now I doubt I will be able to solve the crisis I am in. Are you his friend?" she asked without a pause and without premeditation.

He started and then became thoughtful. "Devlin is a strange man. He keeps his distance from everyone. You never really know what he is thinking, what he is intending. I've been aboard his ships for three years now and that should make us friends. But the truth is, I know very little about him—no more than the rest of the world. We all know of his exploits, his reputation. I do consider myself a friend—he saved my life in Cadiz—but frankly, if we are friends, I have never had a friendship like this before."

It was almost sad, but Virginia was not about to be swayed by any compassion. Curiosity consumed her. "What exploits? What reputation?"

"They call him 'His Majesty's Pirate,' Miss Hughes," Harvey said, smiling as if on safer ground now. "He puts the prize first always, and I suspect he has become a very rich man. His methods of battle are unorthodox, as are his strategies—and his politics. Most of the Admiralty despise him, for he rarely follows orders and thinks very little of those old men in blue and doesn't care if they know it. The papers fill pages with accounts of his actions at sea. Hell— er, excuse me—they write about his actions on land, too. The social pages always mention him when he is at home, attending this ball, that club. He was only eighteen at Trafalgar. He took over the command of his ship and destroyed two much larger vessels. He was instantly given his own command, and that was only the beginning. He will not accept a ship-of-the-line, however. Oh, no, not Devlin." Finally Harvey paused for breath.

"Why not? What's a ship-of-the-line?" Virginia asked, glancing toward her captor again. Daylight glinted boldly on his sun-streaked hair. The man attended balls and clubs. She could not imagine it. Or could she?

She had a flashing image of him in a black tailcoat, a flute of champagne in his large, graceful hand, and she had no doubt the ladies present would all be vying desperately to gain his attention.

Oddly, she didn't care for the image at all.

"A battleship—they travel and fight in a traditional formation. Devlin is too independent for that. His way is to sail alone, to swoop in on the unsuspecting—or deceive the suspecting. He never loses, Miss Hughes, because he rarely maneuvers the same way twice. The men trust him with their lives. I've seen him give commands that appeared suicidal. But they weren't. They were victorious instead. Most commanders flee—or try to—when they realize the *Defiance* is on the horizon. He is the greatest captain sailing the high seas today, mark my words." Harvey was smiling. "And I am not alone in that opinion."

"You like him!" Virginia accused, amazed. But in spite of the animosity she refused to release, she was also impressed—with his exploits, not the man himself.

Harvey raised both brows. "I admire him. I admire him greatly. It is impossible not to, not if one is in his command."

"He saved the ship last night," she remarked. "Why didn't he send someone else up that mast?"

Harvey shook his head. "Because he knew he could accomplish the mission. That is why we admire him, Miss Hughes, because he leads—he really leads—and then, how can we not follow?"

She hesitated, her heart racing. "Is he...married?"

Harvey was surprised, and then he laughed. "No! I mean, do not get me wrong, he likes his women, and there are many London ladies who wish to entice him to the altar—he was just knighted, you know—but I cannot imagine Devlin with a wife. She would have to be a very strong woman, to put up with a man like that." He became thoughtful. "I don't think Devlin has even thought of marrying, if you must know. But he is young. He is only twenty-four. His life is the sea, I think. I suppose that could one day change." He sounded doubtful.

O'Neill appeared as harsh and hard as he had been heroic—and he also seemed very alone. Virginia realized she was staring at him again. Standing there as he did, controlling the huge frigate, a commanding figure with an inescapable presence, the aura of power almost visible, she instantly amended her thoughts. The man gave no sign that he was lonely. In fact, he seemed an island unto himself, and only a very foolish woman would dare to think him lonely or needy in any way.

"He is not a bad man," Harvey said softly. "Which is why I do not understand what he has done and what he is doing. He certainly doesn't need this ransom."

Virginia started. "Are you certain?"

"As captain, he gets three-eighths of every prize we take. I know what we've been about these past three years. The man is wealthy."

Virginia shivered, staring with dismay and dread. *If this was not about her ransom, then what, dear God, was it about?*

And she decided the time was now. She touched the surgeon's hand. "Mr. Harvey, I need your help," she said plaintively.

HE HAD HAD ENOUGH. His damned ears were burning as if he were some child in the schoolroom—he knew they were talking about him. "Martin, take command of the ship," he said. As the officer came forward, Devlin wheeled and leapt off of the quarterdeck.

His eyes widened as he saw his little hostage with her hand on Harvey's, her eyes huge and pleading, her rosebud mouth trembling. Suspicion reared itself. The chit was acting like some foolish, simpering coquette—and there was nothing foolish, simpering or coy about Miss Virginia Hughes. What was afoot?

His irritation had decreased, amusement taking its place. The one thing Virginia Hughes was, was entertaining.

He almost smiled, until he thought of how she had felt, asleep and spooned into his stiff, aroused body last night. He grimaced instead. He hadn't even known she was in his bed when he had dropped there in absolute exhaustion after the storm had abandoned the ship. But he had certainly become aware of her while asleep, because when he had awoken, his body had been urging him to take instant advantage of her. Fortunately, he prided himself on his self-control—he had been exercising self-will and self-discipline since he was a boy of ten. Ignoring his physical needs was not the easiest task, but there was simply no question that it was a task he would complete.

Surprisingly, she had not felt at all like a bag of bones in his arms.

She had felt soft and warm, tiny but not fragile.

"Good day." He nodded sharply at them both, dismissing his thoughts.

Virginia dropped her tiny hand from Harvey's, her cheeks flaming, as if caught at the midnight hour with her hand in someone else's safe. She looked as guilty as could be.

By God, they were plotting against him, he thought, amazed. The little vixen had enticed Harvey to her side, into insubordination. It wasn't a guess. He smelled the conspiracy in the air the way he had first smelled the approaching storm last night.

"Devlin, good morning. I hope you don't mind my taking some air with our guest?" Harvey smiled cheerfully at him.

"Fortunately my orders did not include you," Devlin said calmly.

"Of course they didn't. I'm the ship's surgeon," Harvey said with humor.

Virginia's eyes widened as she understood. "I hope those ridiculous orders no longer stand!"

He faced her. She was so petite that she made him feel as tall as a mythological giant. "My orders do stand, Miss Hughes." He didn't like the look of the gash on her temple. "Harvey, I want you to tend to that immediately."

"I'll get my bag," Harvey said, striding off.

And they were alone. Devlin stared at her. She, however, refused to meet his gaze. What was this? An effect of guilt? This morning she had been in his bed, on the verge of begging him for his kisses. Devlin was no fool. Desire had clearly shimmered in her hungry violet eyes. "Feeling guilty?" he purred, deciding to enjoy the debate that would surely ensue.

She jumped. "What do I have to feel guilty about? You are the one who should be prone with guilt, but then, you would have to have a heart in order to feel anything."

"I confess," he said, smiling, "to being absolutely heartless."

"How far off course are we?" she asked, and it was more of a demand than a question.

"About a hundred and fifty miles," he said, and he saw her pale. "That distresses you?"

She stared and finally nodded. "Where do we sail now?" she asked grimly.

She was very clever. He admired her wit and decided never to underestimate it again. "There's no point in tacking south to Portsmouth. Besides—" his heart tightened, proving that he was capable of feeling after all. "—I have grave doubts about the *Americana* making port there."

Her eyes widened. "You don't think..."

"I doubt she survived the storm. We barely outran her— the *Americana* could not outrun her. Mac is a fine sailor, but he was sailing with a skeleton crew." A soft sorrow crept over him. He didn't try to shove it away. This was the way of the sea and he knew it very well; it took more lives than it ever let go. Over the years he had learned that it was better to mourn the loss of his men and be done with it. He had also learned not to expect longevity from those who chose to sail with him. It was far easier dealing with death when one accepted its inevitability.

"You don't care," she gasped. "You do have a heart of stone—if you even have a heart at all," she accused. "Those men—that ship—they lie at the bottom of the ocean because of you!"

Now he was angry. He gripped her wrist so quickly that she cried out and he did not let it go. "They lie in a watery tomb because of the gale, Miss Hughes, and as I am not Poseidon, I had little to do with the making of that storm last night."

She dared to shake her head at him. "No! Had you not battled that ship, wounding it terribly—in order to abduct me—they would be alive!"

This woman seemed to have the capacity to ignite his fury as no one else could. He flung her wrist away and was ashamed to find it red. "Had I not battled that ship, wounding it and abducting you, you would be on the ocean's floor with them." He was about to stalk away. It crossed his mind that if he bedded her, he might teach her the respect she so clearly lacked. That, and far more.

But he was struck with his earlier assessment, and he whirled to face her again. "Do not plot against me with Harvey," he warned.

She cried out, appearing frightened. "I...I'm not!"

"Liar," he whispered, bending so close that their faces almost touched. "I know a conspiracy when it forms beneath my nose. Do you know what the fate of a mutineer is, Miss Hughes?"

"There is no mutiny," she began.

He smiled at her coldly. "Should you entice Harvey to your schemes, that is mutiny, my dear. We hang mutineers," he added with relish, and it was not entirely a lie. He wouldn't hang Harvey, but he'd lose a damned fine ship's surgeon, and they were as hard to come by as an Indian ruby, if not even more so.

She shrank away from him, against the wall. "I have something to say to you," she said fiercely.

He had been about to go. He didn't like her tone and he turned, awaiting her blow.

"I despise you," she said thickly.

Oddly, he flinched, not outwardly, but somewhere deep inside his body. Outwardly, he felt his lips twist into a mirthless smile. "That is the best that you can do?"

She looked as if she might strike him.

"Do not," he warned softly.

She clenched her fists. "I am sorry I missed," she said suddenly. "I'm a fine shot, and if only I had waited, you would now be dead."

"But I'm not dead, alas," he mocked. Her words had an edge he refused to feel, cutting deep. "Patience, Miss Hughes, is a virtue. And you, my harridan, lack it entirely." He strode away.

"Why are you doing this? O'Neill!" she cried after him. "Harvey says you are rich!"

He pretended not to hear.

"Bastard," she said.

CHAPTER SIX

JACK HARVEY CLIMBED THE three steps to the quarterdeck. Although his semblance remained cheerful, as was characteristic for him, he was still stunned that Devlin had abused his hostage—stunned and disturbed. But he'd given up trying to understand his captain. He'd served under O'Neill long enough to know that he would never understand him.

Devlin was at the helm and he turned at the familiar sound of the surgeon's short, surprisingly light footsteps. "How is she?" he asked.

"The gash could have used a stitch or two last night, but it's healing nicely now. She hasn't had a headache since she received the blow, which, according to Miss Hughes, was during the storm last night."

Devlin nodded at his first mate. "Take the helm," he said. He stepped away and he and Harvey moved to the deck's larboard side. "You are eyeing me oddly," he remarked coolly.

Harvey no longer smiled. "Damn it, Devlin, I hope she got that blow as she claimed, by falling, and not from some other means."

He stared, instantly comprehending Harvey's meaning. "By God, you think I hit her?" He was genuinely surprised. He had never hit a woman in his life.

"I don't know what to think," Harvey grimaced. "Not now."

Oh, ho, he had a very dark inkling, indeed. "Really?" He gripped Harvey's arm and they stepped down to the main deck, away from prying eyes and listening ears. "You are a fool, Jack, to allow a clever vixen like Miss Hughes to so sweetly tie you up and wrap you with a pretty bow."

Harvey appeared flustered. "What does that mean?"

"That means," Devlin said tightly, "that she has enticed you into disobeying me, has she not?"

Harvey blinked, paling. "Devlin..." he faltered.

"What do the two of you intend? And tell me, how can you justify thwarting me, defying me, when I am your captain?"

Harvey stiffened. "Damn it, you seduced her."

For one moment, he felt as if Harvey had spoken a foreign language, one he had never before heard. "I *what?*"

Harvey blinked another time, now looking worried and uncomfortable. "You seduced her," he said less certainly.

He stared as red-hot fury swept over him. Damn that woman with her clever machinations, her foul lies! "So that is what she told you?" he asked, as if completely calm.

"Er." Harvey hesitated. "Yes."

"You know, it is good luck for you that we are, for the most part, on good terms. Otherwise you would not be wearing such a straight nose. I don't seduce virgins. Innocence does not tempt me." And as he spoke, he was aware of that having changed.

Harvey paled. "Oh, dear," he said.

"You have always been taken in by a pretty face," Devlin said.

Harvey grimaced. "Devlin, I beg your pardon, I am so sorry!"

Devlin didn't know whom he felt the most umbrage at—Jack Harvey or Virginia Hughes. He certainly felt like throttling the latter. "What did the two of you plan?"

Harvey remained white. He shook his head. "I was to bring her a sailor's clothes from one of the boys below decks. Then, when we made port, I was to distract and pre-occupy you and she would simply walk off the boat with the others."

"Very clever," Devlin said, and he meant it. The plan would have undoubtedly worked if he had not sensed the conspiracy between his ship's surgeon and his little captive.

"Devlin, I am sorry, terribly sorry. I knew it was not in character for you! But then, this entire affair makes no sense—you've never ransomed a woman before. Please forgive me. She was so convincing! She wept, for God's sake," Harvey cried, his gaze filled with anxiety.

There would be no forgiveness for anyone. Devlin said, "When we reach Limerick, you will have to find another ship. As of this moment, you are relieved of your duties."

Harvey's mouth opened, as if to protest.

Devlin stared, silently daring him to utter a single sound.

Harvey decided the better of it—then amended that decision. "I am sorry," he said.

Devlin walked away. He no longer cared what Harvey said, thought or did, because their relationship was over.

VIRGINIA SMILED AS SHE STROLLED the deck, uncaring that she had no parasol. In fact, she relished the strong, bright sun. It felt wonderful on her face—it felt wonderful to be alive—and in that moment, she had a sense of why the siren call of the sea was so enchanting. The ship tacked lazily across the wind, the seas were as unhurried, but the breeze was fresh and clean, the skies scintillating, infinity some-where beyond. She smiled happily, reaching the railing and gripping it. Late tomorrow they would make port in Limerick—and Jack Harvey was going to help her escape.

She laughed out loud, throwing her head back, thinking

of how she wished she could see the expression on Devlin O'Neill's face when he found her gone. She had been wrong to think that she would never be able to win any battle between them. Oh, no. There would be a battle tomorrow and her plan was foolproof. Tomorrow she would be the victor, oh yes.

She knew she was gloating—savoring a triumph she didn't quite have—and she could almost hear the headmistress at the Marmott School admonishing her. "Ladies do not gloat. In fact, Miss Hughes, ladies do not have battles with avaricious, unscrupulous sea captains, either—a lady does not battle anyone, ever, at all."

Virginia had to chuckle again. "Well, this lady does do battle, Mrs. Towne," she said aloud, to the wind and the sea. "In fact, she is rather enjoying herself!"

She realized she had meant her every word and she became reflective. How had she come to this place and time, where she so wanted to outwit Devlin O'Neill? Where the idea of doing so brought her such a thrill? Was it because she still recalled that terrible aching moment when she had desperately wanted his mouth to cover hers? She refused to feel any more desire—and she did not—but she could not escape the singular memory. It had somehow become engraved upon her mind.

Virginia turned to lean her back against the railing, thoughtful still. She glanced toward the quarterdeck and was surprised not to see him there. Why hadn't he kissed her?

She started, wishing she had never asked herself the question. But she knew why! She was a skinny little thing, with tiny, shapeless breasts, a sharp, angular face and hair that resembled a rat's nest. Suddenly Virginia felt despair.

It dawned upon her that she wanted her handsome captor to find her beautiful. How foolish could she be?

She drew herself up straighter as the ship rocked over a swell, reminding herself that soon she would be free again, and eventually she would be back at Sweet Briar. Then she would no longer even recall Devlin O'Neill, not by face and not by name. He would not be even the most distant memory.

Somehow she was not reassured.

She suddenly saw Jack Harvey crossing the deck. Virginia's heart leapt and she waved at him.

He started and changed direction, not waving back or acknowledging her in any way.

Virginia froze. *What was that?*

Filled with unease, she did not hesitate to rush after him. "Mr. Harvey!" she cried. "Mr. Harvey, do wait!" Surely he had not seen her; surely he had not snubbed her!

Harvey's steps slowed and Virginia caught up to him. "Hello," she said brightly, but he did not return her smile. "What a glorious day. Didn't you see me wave?"

He halted, facing her. "Indeed I did, Miss Hughes."

Something was amiss, terribly so. "But you did not wave back...or even nod," she said slowly, with dread.

"I am extremely upset," he said bluntly. "You see, I have been relieved of my duties, and when we arrive at Limerick, I am to be cast off this ship."

"Oh," she managed to say, her heart pounding.

"You lied to me, Miss Hughes. You accused Devlin of a terrible crime."

She held her head high. "He *has* committed a terrible crime—I am innocent of any wrongdoing, and he has taken me prisoner against my will."

"You claimed he seduced you!" Harvey exclaimed. "So that I would defy him and aid you in your escape!"

She had lost after all, she thought miserably. How she wanted to weep. But she did not. Keeping her chin high, she said, "He has abused me, Mr. Harvey."

Harvey cried, "But not in the manner you claimed. You have never—and I beg your pardon—been in his bed!"

"I never said any such thing. It was a conclusion you drew yourself—those were not my words."

He blinked. "Does it matter? You understood the conclusion I came to—you encouraged it!"

"The man is a criminal," she said.

"He is—was—my captain. Now, because of you, I shall have to find a different ship. Miss Hughes, I wish you well. Good day." He turned and strode away.

Virginia then trembled. Perhaps it had been wrong to let Jack Harvey think the worst, but she was desperate. She had to escape, she had to reach her uncle, she had to save Sweet Briar. Now she succumbed to guilt, but only because Harvey was a very decent sort and he seemed upset at losing his duties upon the *Defiance*.

It wasn't right. If anyone were to blame, it was he.

Virginia glanced at the quarterdeck once more, but O'Neill was not standing there, commanding the sun, the sky, the sea. She raced back to his cabin.

As she barged inside, she saw him seated alone at the dining table, slathering butter on a biscuit, a plate containing more biscuits and cheese in front of him. He did not glance up as she stared accusingly at him.

She fought for her breath and her composure, then closed the door and approached.

He finally looked up but did not stand. "Would you care to join me for some dinner?" he asked.

She shook her head.

He ate, sipped from a mug, then said, "You are getting sunburned, Miss Hughes."

She felt her temper igniting. "It was my fault. The entire plan. If you wish to punish anyone, it should be me, not Jack Harvey."

Devlin pushed back his chair and rose to his full height, towering over her. His stance made her feel small and vulnerable. She felt certain he knew that his height affected her thusly, and that he did it deliberately. "I would love nothing more than to punish you," he murmured. "Did you have something in mind?"

Her heart skipped wildly. He stood too close for comfort—he was too tall, too strong, his britches too tight, his shirt far too loosely drawn at the throat. Virginia couldn't speak.

"You will remain confined in this cabin until we disembark," he said calmly. "Those are my orders, Miss Hughes."

"Do not dismiss Mr. Harvey! He is your friend!"

He had been about to walk away; he turned back to her. "My friend? I think not," he said too softly.

"No, you are wrong, Mr. Harvey cares about you. He admires you greatly—he told me so. He was—and is— your friend," Virginia cried. "And you must not treat him so callously because of what I have done!"

"I have no friends—not on board this ship, or any other." He strode to the door.

"Then I feel sorry for you!"

He whirled. "You think to pity me!"

Virginia realized she had hit a nerve—she hadn't realized he had possessed one. "Is there anyone in this entire world whom you would call a friend, Captain?" she dared, and it was a challenge.

His eyes glittered, turning dark, like a stormy sky. "Do you dare intrude into my private life?" he asked very softly.

"I didn't know you had one," she said as angrily.

He stalked back to her. "Perhaps you will think twice about involving others in your schemes and lies, Miss Hughes. Perhaps next time you will think about the ramifications of your actions."

"Perhaps I will," Virginia said, "but this isn't about me, not anymore. I cannot let you dismiss a man who considers you the greatest captain upon the high seas because of my stupidity, my perfidy. He is your friend, Captain O'Neill, he is your loyal friend!"

"He was my ship's surgeon and he betrayed me. That is neither friendship nor loyalty. He is lucky I did not shackle him and throw him in the brig." He strode back to the door, but there he paused. "Why? Why attempt an escape? You would be lost in Ireland. Did you even think your scheme through? I haven't hurt you. I haven't even touched you. In a short period of time you will be reunited with your beloved uncle. Why dare to escape? Why dare to defy me?"

Virginia stared helplessly at him. "Because," she managed, "my entire life is at stake."

He started.

She stared for a moment longer, then turned and sat down at the table. She felt despondency settle over her like a huge and weighty cloak, and she listened to him walk back to the table, where he also sat. "Explain that statement."

She shook her head.

He gripped her face, turning it upward so their gazes collided. "I mean it."

His hand was large, engulfing her chin and jaw. She trembled. "What do you care?" she said awkwardly.

He released her jaw. "I don't care. But you are in my custody and everything about you is my affair."

She couldn't fathom why he should be so interested in her personal matters, and while she did not think sharing her burdens would soften him toward her purpose, she could not think of a reason to remain secretive. She sighed heavily, thought of her parents, and felt a familiar wave of ancient grief. "I was born at Sweet Briar," she said, her voice low, not looking up at him. "It is heaven on earth, a plantation near Norfolk, Virginia." She smiled a little, for in spite of the ship's odors and the scent of the sea, she could smell honeysuckle and lilac and freshly harvested tobacco. "My father built our home with his own two hands, planted the first crops alone." Finally she looked up, smiling sadly at him. "I loved my father and my mother. Last fall they both died on a stormy night in a foolish carriage collision."

He said nothing. If he was at all moved by her plight, she could not see it in his expression, as not a muscle in his face changed.

"I am the only child. Sweet Briar is mine. But my guardian, the earl, is selling it in order to pay off my father's debts." She laid her hands flat on the table, gripping the smooth wood until her knuckles turned white. "I won't allow it."

He stared and it was a moment before he spoke. "I see," he said flatly. "You will beat the earl about the head until he agrees to pay off your father's debts and hand you the keys to the plantation."

This was her last remaining chance. Virginia seized both of his hands and was stunned at the feel of them in her small palms and against her fingers, stunned enough by the contact not to see the surprise leap in his silver eyes. She looked up and spoke swiftly, hoarsely. "If my uncle has to ransom me, he will never be moved to pay my father's debts. As he decided to sell the plantation without even consulting me, it will be hard enough to persuade him to change his mind without your ransom! Captain, don't you see? I cannot survive without Sweet Briar. I have to go to the earl. There can be no ransom! Please, Mr. Harvey told me you are a wealthy man and that you hardly need this ransom. Please, let me go—take me to London where I hope I am expected. Please. I beg you."

Devlin removed his hands from hers and stood. "I'm sorry," he said flatly, "that you will lose your inheritance, but my plans are not flexible."

She leapt up with a cry. "I am an orphan now! Sweet Briar is all I have!" she cried.

He walked to the door.

"God, you just don't care! You don't care about anything or anyone!"

He opened the door.

"I am losing Sweet Briar because of you and your damned plan to ransom me," she shouted.

He didn't turn. As he left, he said, "No, Miss Hughes, you are losing Sweet Briar because, apparently, your father was a very poor businessman."

Virginia choked on the insult, but before she could fling some equally wounding barb back at him, he was gone, the hatch closing on the graying twilight sky.

SHE HAD DECIDED THERE WOULD be one final attempt to thwart him.

Virginia stood by a porthole, which remained open in spite of the blustery day, and watched the Irish cliffs passing. High rock cliffs towered above a strip of sandy beach beginning to give way to more gently rolling country. She had decided not to antagonize O'Neill further and had remained in his cabin since the day before. But hours ago, when the first gulls had appeared overhead, she had cracked the cabin door to overhear that they were already sailing up the river toward Limerick within mere hours.

Well, several hours had since passed. The frigate was moving swiftly up the River Shannon. Here and there she could make out a manor or a cluster of huts. The Irish countryside was now lush and green, at times sheep dotting the hills.

How long would it take to go up the river and reach the port at Limerick? She had no idea. A glance at his maps told her nothing. But she was afraid to delay any longer, because if she waited too long to commence her new plan, it would fail.

Virginia went to the cabin door. There was no sign of the young blond man, Gus. But she did see Jack Harvey, looking sad and severe, standing below the quarterdeck. "Mr. Harvey! Please, sir, I would speak with you!"

Harvey glanced her way, incredulous.

Above him, a tall, leonine figure at the helm, Devlin half turned and nodded, saying something to Harvey that Virginia could not hear. Harvey approached so slowly she began chewing on her lower lip. Then she smiled brightly at him. "I must beg a favor of you," she said.

"I am not participating in any of your schemes," he began.

"Would you please find Gus and send him to me? I need to bathe before I step off of this ship. I only wish to ask him for some wash water."

Harvey looked relieved that she had not asked for something else. He nodded and went off.

Virginia closed her eyes after shutting the cabin door, wishing there could be another way—but Gus was scrawny, and while he was a few pounds heavier than herself and a few inches taller, too, he would have to do. She took one of O'Neill's silver candlesticks in hand, and positioned herself so that when he came in, she would be behind the door.

She now prayed he would come in alone.

Upon the sound of his knock, she told him to enter, and

quickly saw that another sailor was with him. She moved away from the wall, holding the candlestick behind her back, smiling, while they filled the tub with steamy water. As they began to leave, Virginia called out, "Gus? Please wait. I have never been to Ireland before and I must ask you some questions. It's terribly important."

As usual, he avoided looking at her, while telling the seaman to go. The other sailor left. Virginia, her heart pounding, walked to his side. "I heard most of the country is Catholic. How will I find a Baptist minister?"

Gus seemed confused by her question. He hesitated. Virginia walked behind him. He said, "I'm sure the captain—"

Wincing, her desire to escape overcoming her reluctance to hurt him, she hit him with the candlestick on the back of the head. Instantly, he crumbled to the floor.

She froze, terrified she had hit him too hard, terrified he was dead. She dropped to her knees and saw that he was breathing, but blood was staining the back of his blond head. "I am so sorry," she whispered, reaching for his belt buckle. She undid it and tugged his rather dirty pants down. The sight of his skinny legs and calves did not affect her at all. In fact, he wore no drawers, but she didn't even bother to glance that way. She did decide to take his dagger—it might prove useful, indeed. She proceeded, with more difficulty, to get his shirt off. Then she dove under the bed where she had stashed a good length of rope. She tied his ankles, then used the same length to tie his wrists. She gagged him with a stocking.

"Please don't hate me," she said, rolling him under the bed. As she glimpsed his pale face, she wondered if escape was worth it. This man had been nothing but respectful toward her.

Of course, he dared not be otherwise, given his captain's penchant for dismissing unruly crew.

Virginia stripped off her corset, gown and pelisse, leaving on only her chemise and pantalettes. Her shoes followed, all shoved under the bed. She hopped into his pants, knotting the belt instead of buckling it. His shirt followed, and finally, she tucked up her braid under his wool cap. Then she looked down at herself, scowling because her bare feet looked feminine. Then she saw a lacy edge of her pantalettes peeping out from under the loose pants.

"Damn it," she cursed, rolling the underwear up. She raced to the porthole and gasped. A good-sized town was in view, a collection of huts on the outskirts, followed by stone houses, a few manors and churches, and finally, the town itself. A dozen ships of varying sizes seemed to be at dock. None were even half the size of the frigate; all seemed to be merchant ships or fishing vessels.

Then she saw a crowd beginning to form.

Children were running from the town along the river, screaming wildly, heading toward the approaching ship. Their shouts became more distinct, forming into whoops and hollers. As the ship drew abreast of the motley, tattered group, she saw boys begin to wave, grinning wildly. The ship was now sailing past the children and Virginia gazed back to see them following.

Then she looked ahead.

A number of people were rushing down to the docks. She grew disturbed. Some appeared to be farmers in their shabby tunics, others merchants, finely dressed in wool coats and britches. Women were in the gathering, too. The younger ones were waving and smiling. No—everyone was smiling.

She was uneasy now.

Virginia heard O'Neill shouting orders as the ship slowed. She saw a titian-haired woman in the simple garb of a peasant step out from the crowd. She was carrying a basket of flowers.

Someone cheered. The cheer sounded suspiciously like, "O'Neill!"

She hugged herself. The cheering began in earnest, then the titian-haired beauty began tossing flowers at the ship. The flowers were caught up in the wind and landed in the harbor's waters. There was no doubt as to what the crowd was cheering. "The O'Neill! The O'Neill!" they hollered and cried. In fact, Virginia felt certain that there were tears—*tears*—on quite a few cheeks.

She did not understand.

Men clad as seamen—not O'Neill's crew—dashed forward to catch the *Defiance*'s ropes. The ship moved laterally now, and Virginia heard a huge anchor being thrown into the river. Why were these people overjoyed by O'Neill's appearance?

She told herself it did not matter. She must be ready to escape and the time was now.

But as she cracked open the cabin door, she knew it did matter—it mattered very much. She simply did not know why.

O'Neill was standing on the quarterdeck, viewing the town and the congregation that had come to greet him as imperiously as if he were a king. He wasn't smiling. But he was, Virginia thought, completely preoccupied. His expression was strange, both intense and strained. She could not help but wonder at his feelings.

Then the titian-haired beauty was crossing the deck and climbing up to where he stood. Virginia watched her reach out, a bouquet of roses in her hand. O'Neill suddenly seemed to realize she was present—he started and turned. The beauty tossed the bouquet aside and leapt forward, her hands finding his shoulders, her mouth finding his.

Virginia blinked in shock.

O'Neill quickly embraced her, clearly accepting and then deepening and finally dominating the kiss.

The assembled townspeople went wild, screaming his name, over and over again.

Virginia could not look away, as if she were hypnotized.

Then her common sense rescued her. She knew the perfect opportunity when it presented itself and she hurried from the cabin, across the deck and joined several seamen rushing down the gangplank as the townspeople rushed up it to board the ship.

On the dock, she look back. O'Neill was setting aside the woman, but someone, an official of the town, perhaps, was offering his hand. O'Neill accepted it, his attention never wavering.

Virginia moved up the dock, hit the cobbled street, passing several drays and wagons, and turned into a tiny cramped street filled with shops below and homes above. Then she ran.

DEVLIN WALKED SLOWLY TO the captain's cabin, the decks finally cleared of townsmen, all of his sailors gone on liberty. He was subdued. It seemed a different lifetime completely when he had walked those streets as a boy with his father, their wagon filled with supplies, everyone bowing in deference as Gerald O'Neill passed, his own small shoulders proud and square. It seemed at least a lifetime ago that he had run those streets, half-wild, after Gerald's murder, with the shopkeepers and merchants glancing after him, whispering about "that poor O'Neill boy" and "that affair up on the hill," a reference to his mother's marriage to Adare.

He'd been home once since he'd joined the navy at thirteen, six years ago, a strapping, cold-eyed youth of eighteen who had just received his first command after Trafalgar. There had been no roses strewn at his feet when he'd sailed his schooner in that day, no cheering throng at the docks. But everyone had snuck out of shop and home to steal a glance at him as he passed their way on his ride to Askeaton. There'd been whispers, but he had refused to listen. He hadn't known what they said.

Devlin realized he was not alone. Jack Harvey stood near the cabin, smoking a pipe. "And the prodigal son returns," he said.

Devlin halted, no longer angry at Harvey—in fact, he had accepted his treachery the way he would have accepted his death, the time for mourning over. He had no remaining feelings at all except for indifference. "I am hardly anyone's prodigal son."

"You are this town's prodigal son."

"They are filled with delusion and desperate for a hero—any hero—as long as he is Irish and Catholic, no matter if he is a figment of someone's too-vivid imagination."

"It's funny how everyone in the fleet considers you obnoxious, rude and overbearing, not to mention excessively arrogant. I, however, know the truth. You are one of the most modest men I've ever had the good fortune to meet."

"Is there a point to your being here, Jack? I haven't been home in six years and I intend to make Askeaton before dark."

"Then I suppose you shall have to hurry," Harvey said.

Devlin knew Harvey wished to linger but he did not; he walked into the cabin. There he started, realizing instantly that Virginia was not present. He was disbelieving—and then, when he realized that she had somehow escaped, he couldn't help feeling a twinge of admiration for her. She was more resolved than even he.

"Clever little witch," he growled.

An odd strangled noise came from below his bed.

Devlin strode over and hauled the naked, hog-tied and gagged Gus Pierson out. He slit the ties and pulled out the gag. Gus was frighteningly white. "Sir, it was my fault. I take full blame for the prisoner's escape, sir!" he cried, standing.

Devlin felt like striking him, but he did not. From the doorway, he heard Harvey murmur, "Well, well, she did it, anyway. Will you dismiss Gus, too, or simply keelhaul him?"

Keelhauling usually meant death and no one used such a method of punishment anymore. "Tell me exactly what happened," Devlin said, ignoring the taunt and tossing Gus a pair of his britches and a shirt.

Gus donned the garments, turning red as he spoke. When he had finished, Devlin said, "You will help me find Miss Hughes, Gus, and when she is back in my charge, you will relieve the watch of this ship. Your privilege of liberty is suspended for the duration of our stay, until I deem otherwise."

"Yes, sir," Gus mumbled, but he looked relieved, as if he had expected far worse.

But Gus was a fine sailor and a very brave lad, and Devlin was well aware that his orders not to even look at the prisoner had aided her in her successful escape. His punishment of Gus was perfunctory at best—he needed the rest of the crew to witness it in order to maintain his discipline of the ship. But he did not blame Gus for her escape. There had been no treachery. Virginia Hughes was simply far more clever than the young Dane.

"And how will you find her?" Harvey asked. "By now, she is surely halfway to the next village—wherever that may be."

Devlin smiled coldly. "Actually, you are wrong. There is only one sane way for Miss Hughes to get to London, and that is by another ship."

Harvey raised his brows.

"Am I not the prodigal son? Did not the mayor greet me with a medal of honor? Did not Squire O'Brien invite me to supper? Did not the captain of the *Mystère* invite me to dine with him tonight?"

"I begin to see," Harvey murmured.

"Two can play this game," Devlin said, turning to Gus. "Put out word on the docks. My reluctant fiancée is trying to find a passage to London, and her return to me, her heartbroken groom, will be amply rewarded. I will speak with the mayor and town council myself."

Gus rushed off to obey.

Devlin left the cabin. Harvey followed more slowly, and he muttered, "Poor lass. She doesn't stand a chance."

CHAPTER SEVEN

SOMETHING WAS TERRIBLY amiss.

Virginia crouched on her knees in the hayloft of a dark, sweet-smelling barn, peering through the window onto the narrow, twisting street. Night had fallen and the street was now entirely deserted. Virginia had been hiding in the barn, which was somewhere in the center of town behind a carpenter's shop, for several hours. In all that time, she had seen only the occasional pedestrian, a few pairs of sailors and a cart or two. Why hadn't there been a huge search party?

Surely her clever captor had discovered her disappearance shortly after she had escaped. Surely he had organized his men into various groups in order to thoroughly search the town. But she hadn't heard a search party, and from her hiding place she could hear the laughter and music coming from the wharf-front inns and bars. From time to time she could even hear drunken conversation on the streets just beyond the one where the barn was situated.

What could it mean?

Virginia stood, her knees aching, and stretched. As worried and suspicious as she was, she knew she must move on. She had to find a ship leaving for London, or if that failed, for any port in Great Britain. That seemed to be the only intelligent way to get to London—traversing Ireland, on foot and penniless, would be absurd.

Virginia climbed down the ladder and left the barn. She hurried toward the wharf, certain that, at any moment, her captor would appear from around a street corner, legs braced apart, a wicked and cool smile on his disturbing features, determined to capture her all over again. But neither O'Neill nor a search party materialized around any bend.

This was very odd, indeed.

Virginia's unease and alarm grew as she faced the docks. Limerick had a few oil lamps on the main public streets, but the wharf was left mostly in shadow, except for the occasional glow of torchlight. It did not matter. Instantly she saw the dark outline of the *Defiance* rocking gently at its moorings, shadowy and huge, proud and beautiful even in the cloak of night. The reefed sails stood out starkly against the inky black sky. No lights burned from the captain's cabin, although one torch signaled the presence of the watch. She half expected Devlin to suddenly appear on the quarterdeck, a ghostly figure in his white shirt and pale britches, but he did not.

Her heart beat far too hard. Why wasn't he searching for her? Had her plea been effective, then?

Virginia suddenly flinched as voices sounded behind her. She ducked her head, pressing against a shop door as she tried to look at the pair of men.

They were obviously sailors. As obviously, they were drunk and boisterously discussing the merits of a wench at the Boar's Head Inn. She did not recognize either of them. But then, she could not possibly recognize all of O'Neill's crew.

Virginia ran up to them, lowering her voice as she spoke. "Hey, mates. I'm lookin' fer a ship to get home to London." She hoped to mime a cockney accent. "D'ye know who's bound that away?"

The men paused, one of them drinking from a mug. The stout one spoke. "*Mystère* sets sail on the first tide, boy. I heard the cap's short his crew, too, an' he's takin' anyone who can walk."

Virginia could not believe her good luck. She beamed. "Why, thank you!"

The man suddenly shoved his face closer, peering at her. "Hey, you look familiar, boy. You been on the *Defiance,* sailin' with us?"

Virginia turned and ran without answering, aware of how fortunate she was that the two sailors were so drunk. The *Mystère* was a sloop, half the size of the *Defiance* and berthed close by. Virginia hurried up the gangplank. Instantly the watch called out to her.

"Name's Robbie," she growled. "I'm looking to set sail tomorrow with ye boys if the cap'n will allow it."

A lanky sailor came forward, shoving a torch toward her. "Cap is dinin'," he said. "But we're real short of men. C'mon, Rob. I'm sure he'll speak with you."

Virginia followed the other youth, her heart continuing to race, relieved he carried the torch while walking ahead of her.

"How old ye be?" the watchman asked.

She hesitated. "Fifteen."

"Ye look twelve, maybe," the lad laughed. "Don't worry, Captain Rodrigo won't care if yer eight. We got a few boys just out of nappies on board."

Virginia grunted as they paused before the small cabin that was just beneath the quarterdeck. The watch knocked, was told to enter, and Virginia followed him in.

"Got a boy here, Cap, lookin' to sail with us."

A barrel-chested man with a gray beard and dark piercing eyes sat at a small table, apparently finishing a supper of bread, cheese, mutton and ale. He eyed Virginia, who stood as close to the door as possible. "Step forward, boy," he said roughly. "Ye ever sailed a ship before?"

Virginia came forward, avoiding looking him in the eye. She needed to get to London, and decided there was no choice but to lie. "Aye, sir. Been at sea since I was, er, eight."

"Really?" The ship's captain wiped his hands on his thighs, then belched. "Which ships?"

Virginia felt herself pale. Then a brilliant idea came to her and she said, "The *Americana,* Cap."

"Never heard of it."

"We were seized by the *Defiance,* sir. Just a few days ago. The *Americana* is probably at the bottom of the sea right now—she'd never have had the sail to outrun the gale that hit us. I was lucky enough to be taken aboard the *Defiance,*" she said, and she smiled at him.

"An' why jump ship?" Rodrigo stared far too closely at her. "Most of my men would give an arm to sail with O'Neill."

Virginia hesitated. "Not me, sir. He likes boys, if you know what I mean, Cap."

The captain's broad face never changed expression. "O'Neill's reputation for fine women is well-known. Seize her, Carlos."

Seize her, Carlos.

Seize her.

Virginia whirled as the lanky youth, Carlos, reached for her. She ducked under his arm easily enough and bolted out the door.

"Get the girl," Rodrigo shouted. "She's O'Neill's fiancée, goddamn it, and there's a pretty reward for her return!"

It all clicked then, as she raced across the deck. O'Neill had not bothered to search for her, knowing she would try to find a ship to London. She hated him then as she ran toward the gangplank.

How could she fail now? When freedom was so close?

A group of men were stepping onto the gangplank from the docks below. Behind her, Carlos cried, "Seize that woman! That's not a boy, it's a woman! *O'Neill's woman!*"

Virginia faltered as the men below hesitated, and then the four of them bolted up the plank toward her.

She looked back.

Carlos stood a few feet behind her, grinning at her, his arms dangling at his side, fingers twitching as if eager to grab her.

Virginia looked to her right as the four sailors ran toward her.

The water was black and iridescent in the starlight.

It looked so calm. She was a strong swimmer, too.

Virginia darted toward the rail. And then she leapt up onto it.

Carlos shouted, "Grab her before she jumps!"

Virginia paused on the top rail, took her dagger from her belt, and held both arms high up overhead. Then she dove.

DEVLIN STRODE TOWARD THE docks, leaving the waterfront bars and inns behind. His mood was dire, indeed. Somehow his dead father had haunted him all day, as if he did not have enough on his mind with Virginia's witty escape. Everywhere he had turned since setting foot on Irish soil, he had almost expected to see Gerald O'Neill standing there, having something to say. But that was only his imagination, of course. Gerald was dead and unlike most people, Devlin did not believe in ghosts.

Besides, what could his father wish to say to him, anyway? Eastleigh was nearly ruined. Long ago, Devlin had decided a miserable impoverished existence would be far better punishment than death, and wasn't that revenge good enough?

Sightless eyes stared up at him from the bloody stump of his father's severed head.

The memory made him angry. He hadn't been tormented with it since he had set sail from London—no, since he had seized the *Americana,* and the absence had been a huge and welcome relief. But hadn't he known that returning home would undo him? *The boy had returned, frightened and uneasy, weak and without confidence.*

Devlin hated the boy—he always had—and he softly cursed.

He needed no haunting, no memories of his past, not when his prisoner was missing. And he could not rest easy until he had his captive back. He reminded himself that if she managed to escape, it really did not matter; she was only salt that he would mercilessly rub in Eastleigh's gaping wounds. But that rationalization did not quell his annoyance. Virginia Hughes was far more than a brat, daring to defy him. This was a challenge, one he could not let pass.

Huge violet eyes gazed pleadingly at him. *I cannot survive without Sweet Briar. Please let me go! Please. I beg you....*

He refused to feel sorry for her, not even in the most dispassionate and clinical way. He did not wish Virginia ill, certainly, but her last name was Hughes, and she would serve him and his purpose well. But oddly, he could not help but recognize that she was a terribly innocent victim of his plans.

Devlin's steps slowed as he realized he did pity her after all. He had no feelings for Elizabeth, but he pitied his captive, perhaps because of her youth and innocence, or maybe because she did not know that Eastleigh hadn't the funds to save her beloved plantation.

Her violet eyes seared him again, this time soft with love. *I was born at Sweet Briar. It is near Norfolk, Virginia, and it is heaven on earth....*

The anger erupted, stunning him with its force. Pity was a weakness. And if she continued to defy his authority, he could easily enough turn her eyes soft and smoky with the plunging hardness of his own body. In fact, he was beyond tempted now. Should he discipline her in his bed, there'd be no more defiance, no more escape attempts. Then, escape would *not* be on her mind.

Cries echoed on the docks ahead.

Devlin started, all thoughts of sex vanishing, and saw a commotion aboard the *Mystère*. A group of men were boarding her. Someone on the deck held a torch, shouting, and Devlin thought he heard his name. Then his gaze slammed to the railing in utter disbelief and instant recognition. Virginia stood atop the rail, arms outstretched, poised to dive into the icy river.

What in hell was she doing?

Devlin's heart slammed to a hard stop.

And as she sailed off of the rail, he ran for the dock. He saw her break the water, and just before he dove in after her, his heart racing with alarm, he wondered if she could even swim.

As he knifed into the frigid water, he felt a surge of fear. Surely she knew how to swim! After all, the woman could shoot, curse like a sailor, strip a man naked and steal his clothes. She was probably an excellent swimmer—but he was not relieved.

The water was pitch-black. As he dove, he flailed for her, but felt nothing. He continued to dive until weeds grasped greedily at his hands, arms and legs. If Virginia became enmeshed in the vegetation at the river's bottom, she might never be able to get free. He continued to search for her by feel, but there was only the occasional piece of wood and rock.

His lungs finally bursting, a seizure of panic beginning, he had no choice but to swim back up to the surface. As his head popped free, he breathed in harshly, the air cold and sweet.

And their gazes locked.

She was treading water and gulping air just a few meters from him. More torches had been carried to the rail of the *Mystère,* lighting up the water around them. She seemed as surprised to see him as he was to see her.

"Are you all right?" he demanded, moving closer to her and reaching for her.

Her answer was a vicious one. As he gripped her wrist, the sharp blade of a knife cut through his own arm.

He was stunned that she had a weapon, much less that she was attacking him with it. For one instant, he could only recoil as their gazes clashed again, her eyes filled with fierce determination. Then he sensed another strike.

Still treading water, she slashed at him again, this time at his face. He caught her wrist, thwarting the ugly blow. "Drop it," he warned, very angry now.

Her eyes widened with alarm. "No."

He was disbelieving again, but would not dwell on her folly. Ruthless fury filled him and he increased his grip without mercy. She whimpered and released the knife. He pulled her against his side.

"I almost won," she whispered, and he realized tears were shimmering in her eyes.

The stab of pity came again. He shoved it far away. "You never came close to a victory, Miss Hughes. And you never will. Not if you think to battle me."

A fat tear rolled down her wet cheek. "One day I am going to dance with *glee* upon your grave, you *bastard.*"

"I have no doubt," he said, suddenly aware of her slim legs entwining with one of his. And the anger vanished. In its stead was lust.

"O'Neill! Take the rope!"

Devlin realized that the men on the *Mystère* were throwing a lifeline to him. He turned, a soft, surprising breast pressing into his rib cage, stunned by the surge of sudden desire. Keeping one arm around her, he caught the end of the rope. As they were reeled in, he thought Virginia began to cry, but he wasn't sure. Her odd, raspy breaths might have been from the cold.

SHE WASN'T CRYING WHEN they reached his cabin. She was shivering violently as she preceded him in. Devlin faced Gus. "Heat up some water for her, before she dies of an ague."

"Aye, sir," Gus said, casting a worried look at Virginia. She was ashamed enough of what she had done to avoid all eye contact with him. Instead, she kept her back to both men, hugging herself and trembling wildly, her teeth chattering loudly.

Devlin closed the door behind Gus, lighting several candles. "You had better get out of those clothes," he said, moving past her to the closet. He took out a nightshirt he'd never worn, as he slept in the buff.

"Go to hell," she chattered.

He looked at her and froze. Gus's soaking clothes clung to her like a second skin, and he could see every possible line of her body—from the tips of her hard nipples to the handspan that was her waist and, goddamn it, the cleaved arc that delineated her sex.

For one moment he did stare, imaging a wealth of dark curls and a handful of moist flesh.

The cabin became torridly hot, humid, airless.

Red tinged his vision; his manhood hardened impossibly, the pain acute.

"O'Neill?" she whispered roughly.

He jerked, still in the throes of the most incredible lust he had ever experienced, and then he found a semblance of sanity and he tossed the nightshirt at her. He walked away, keeping a deliberate distance from her, his heart pounding as if he had just run from Limerick to Askeaton and back again.

Why protect her virginity?

She was the enemy, never mind that she was eighteen. He could take her now, so quickly satisfying himself. Did it really matter? Would anyone really care? She was an orphan, an American, and Eastleigh had no wish to be burdened with her. No one would care if he returned her without her maidenhead.

He would care.

He would care because he was the son of Gerald and Mary O'Neill, and he had been raised to respect women, to know the difference between right and wrong—and to hate the English. God, his captive wasn't even English, he thought grimly.

He poured himself a Scotch whiskey and realized his hands were shaking. Not only that, the blood continued to press and pummel in his loins, the pressure there escalating, not decreasing. He downed one glass, then another. No warmth, no softening, was to be found.

He realized that the cabin was terribly silent. Devlin turned.

She stood where he'd left her, but she was staring at him, her gaze wide and fixed, no longer shivering at all. She hadn't put on the nightshirt—of course she wouldn't obey him—and the moment he faced her, he realized she was as aware of the charged atmosphere in the cabin as he was.

She understood his desire, no matter her naiveté and innocence.

She slowly glanced at the long, hard ridge quivering visibly against the tight fabric of his britches. Then she looked up at his face again. She didn't speak, but her cheeks were brilliantly pink.

"I'm a man," he murmured. "And you are a woman. It's quite simple, really." How smoothly he lied.

She wet her lips. It was a long moment before she spoke. "Are you..." She faltered. "What are you going to do?"

"What do you want me to do?" he heard himself reply.

Her eyes widened with surprise. She whispered, "I don't know."

He heard himself laugh with disbelief. Virginia's nipples remained tight and taut. He only had to glance down to know that she was swelling for him—and he hadn't even touched her. "I think you lie, Miss Hughes. I think you burn for my touch today the way you burned for it yesterday."

She stiffened. "I do not."

"It doesn't matter what you want." He poured another Scotch, and now, beginning to enjoy himself despite the erotic pressure, he walked to her and handed her the glass. "You lost all your rights when you dared to defy me this one last time."

"I never had any rights."

"You had many rights, but you have been relinquishing them one by one. Drink. It will help warm you while we wait for your bathwater."

"I'm not cold anymore."

He almost inhaled harshly, because her words, spoken so innocently, further inflamed him. He tilted up her chin with his fingertips. "Drink," he said softly, and then he decided to touch her.

He slowly explored her lower lip with the pad of his thumb.

She inhaled, and then began to breathe too quickly.

Impossibly, the heat and humidity thickened in the room.

Her lower lip was full, firm, damp. Her mouth had parted for him.

Red hazed his vision again. One kiss, he thought, one long, slow, deliberate kiss. How terrible would that be?

Instead, he closed his hand over hers, lifting it and the glass she held, until the rim reached her mouth. "Trust me on this one small point," he murmured, aware that his voice had become as thick as the tension in the cabin.

She sipped, not once but several times.

"You are no stranger to Scotch," he said, surprised.

She held the glass tightly against her chest between her small breasts, clearly unaware of what she was doing and how interesting it appeared. "My father was very fond of Scotch whiskey and he frequently let me take a sip or two, as long as Mother wasn't watching."

Something twisted inside of him like a knife. *Gerald had shown him how to load a musket at the tender age of six, grinning and whispering, "Mama will murder me if she knows, so don't breathe a word of this, you hear?"*

"You loved your parents very much," he heard himself remark, shoving the pain of the beast away.

"Yes," she whispered, and she looked down at her drink. Her eyes widened and her cheeks flushed as she realized her appearance. "Oh." She looked up wildly, wide-eyed.

"I am enjoying myself immensely," he remarked.

She gulped the Scotch, then shoved the half-empty glass at him, turning away.

"You know," he remarked as casually, "you do not strike me as being the modest type, Virginia."

She didn't answer. But she slowly bent to retrieve his nightshirt.

He could feel her mind racing. What was she up to now? he wondered, and as he sipped her Scotch, he finally felt himself begin to relax. He looked forward to whatever it was that she intended and decided not to even try to guess.

She suddenly looked at him, the gaze sidelong and lingering.

His heart slammed, because it was the gaze of a courtesan, not an eighteen-year-old orphan.

Then she pulled Gus's shirt off.

She wore her chemise beneath it, but she might as well have worn nothing, and she was half-turned toward him, so he had everything to view that he wished to. Then his heart stopped as she removed the sodden chemise as well.

He was still.

Facing him was a perfect profile with a tiny nose and full lips, small, upthrust breasts, a slim rib cage and soft, flat tummy.

Fully aware that he was staring, she slowly lifted the nightshirt over her head. For one moment her slender bare arms were upstretched, her small breasts thrust tautly forward, her back arched, her naval visible as Gus's pants rode lower. His resolve vanished. His clean, soft cotton gown slithered over her head and down her bosom. Then she reached under it and slid off Gus's pants and her pantalettes, all in one motion.

Blood pounded in his groin, in his brain.

She faced him, smiling softly. "Thank you for the clean gown, Captain." And she was walking toward him.

He was in a stupor, one of sheer lust. But even so, he wondered if he were in the midst of a dream, as this had become far too surreal. She was a seductress now, smiling softly, pausing to stand before him, naked beneath his shirt, and in spite of the terrible urgency consuming him, he knew she was up to no good.

"Did you like kissing her?" she asked. "The woman on the docks?"

"What?" he asked, giving in. He closed his hands on her waist, pulling her up against his arousal, precisely where she belonged.

She gasped, eyes flying wide.

He smiled then, savagely, and slid his hands down to her buttocks. He gripped her there, hard and possessive, pulling her snugly over him, so she rode him.

She held on to his shoulders, eyes closing, moaning deeply.

He looked at her. She had the face of an angel and he could no more deny it than he could that he was close to a terrible climax. She was the most beautiful woman he had ever beheld, and he had thought so from the moment he had seen her standing on the deck of the *Americana*, pointing a silly and useless pistol at him. Her hair had been loose, flying in the wind, and she had been both avenger and angel. Now she was nothing but soft, succulent woman, warm and wet and ripe, waiting for him to master her.

He dug his hand into her nape, wishing her hair was free, and he did what he wanted to do more than anything, other than to thrust inside her. He took her mouth with his.

She moaned again as he covered her, as he opened her, not waiting, all patience disintegrating, as he thrust huge and deep. She moaned as he rocked her back, until she was on the bed and he was on top of her, still deeply inside her mouth, trying to touch and taste every possible place. Her hands fisted in his wet hair, her thighs wrapped around his legs. He began to rub the long edge of his arousal over her sex.

She tried to tear her lips away from his mouth desperately.

Amazed, he realized she was on the verge of her climax. He released her lips and looked down at her. She gazed up at him with wild, unfocused eyes. "Oh, please," she gasped, squirming against his shaft.

"With pleasure," he said, and he held himself up and moved more precisely against her, once, twice, stroking her swollen flesh three times, while she clawed and scratched his back and shoulders. He stared, incapable of doing anything other than watch her every expression now, and when he saw her eyes fly open, when he saw the heat erupt in the violet depths, when she arched up, crying helplessly, the pressure became impossible to resist. The dam broke. She clung to him, sobbing unabashedly, as he spasmed as uncontrollably, as suddenly.

Her cries eased.

He lay on top of her, breathing hard, absolutely shocked. He had just committed a terrible faux pas, like the greenest of schoolboys, and his little captive had climaxed—loudly, vocally—with hardly any effort on his part.

Still stunned, but now acutely aware of the soft, limp woman beneath him, he rolled off of her, abruptly sitting up. He did not dare look at her now.

And he did not dare think.

Action. He needed action. He leapt to his feet, grabbed clean, dry clothes from the closet, and quickly stripped. His mind wanted to function, urging him desperately to do so, but with iron resolve, he refused.

Ruthlessly he blocked out every single possible thought.

Instead, he carefully focused on the task at hand. He fastened his trousers, but damn it, he could feel her gaze on him. He became even more grim, almost furious, knowing he must not look at her. But one thought finally crept in. *If only he had resisted, if only he hadn't kissed her—and helped her achieve what was probably her very first climax.*

He whirled, shirtless, and their gazes collided. "Was that your first time?"

She was sitting up against the pillows, tendrils of dark hair curling about her fragile face, her eyes huge and riveted upon him. In his large nightshirt, she looked impossibly innocent. She looked like a goddamned virgin. "Wh-what?" Her cheeks were turning pink.

"Was that your first time coming?"

"C-coming?" She seemed dazed.

"Climaxing," he demanded, furious now, at her, at himself, at Eastleigh, at the world. He strode over. "Climaxing—*le petit mort,* the French call it. It means having an orgasm, if one wishes to be clinical."

"You mean...what happened at the end?" Her gaze never left his.

He nodded. The urge was sudden and huge, to strike her not just physically, but to strike her out of his life. "When you began screaming like a whore," he said coldly, hating himself for being so cruel and helplessly wishing to be even crueler.

She swallowed. "Yes."

Relief overwhelmed him—and only increased the fury. "Remind me to never offer you a Scotch again," he said.

She winced. "It had nothing to do with the Scotch," she said unsteadily, but her head was high. "It had everything to do with you."

He walked away. He did not intend to hear another word, oh no.

"I have never been kissed before, Devlin," she said.

CHAPTER EIGHT

VIRGINIA DECIDED THAT SHE hated her dark blue silk dress and the black pelisse that went with it almost as much as she hated *him*. She stared at her pale reflection in *his* mirror, her eyes impossibly huge, the pupils dilated, her mouth appearing oddly swollen, or at least, it seemed far larger, lusher and riper than before. It was the morning after. She trembled and wished him *dead*.

But what, exactly, would that solve? She would be free, oh yes, to go her unhappy way, but she would not be free of the memory of him.

She flushed.

Something was terribly wrong with her. That fact, at least, was clear. Because while no woman could be immune to a man like Devlin O'Neill, the combination of power, danger and impossibly virile good looks inescapable, only a fool would be held against her will and then think to entice him to kiss her. Therefore, she was a very foolish woman, because last night, alone with him in his cabin, her escape thoroughly thwarted, she had begun to think about his touch and his kisses, when she should have been scheming up another escape instead.

"Are you ready?" he demanded from outside the cabin door. Last night he had disappeared, sleeping God only knew where. And he had locked the cabin door behind him when he had left—Virginia had tested it to be certain.

The worst part was, Virginia decided, still staring at her reflection and wondering who the wanton woman staring back at her really was, she more than ached for his touch. She wanted to know if she had somehow imagined what had happened. Surely she had. Surely the excitement and thrill of being in his arms, his mouth and body on hers, had not been as huge and vast as she recalled. Surely, if he held and kissed her again, she would not be affected. This had to be a terrible mistake!

He walked in, clad in a pale gray coat that matched his eyes, riding britches and worn Hessian boots. His expression was filled with impatience. Instantly their gazes met in the looking glass.

Virginia simply could not breathe.

His gaze raked her. "We'll have your clothes pressed at Askeaton. Come. The coach is waiting."

Virginia bit her lip and turned, moving past him with the utmost caution, as if afraid he might reach out for her—or she would reach out for him. His gaze narrowed as he watched her, and finally exasperation sounded in his tone. "Forget about last night," he snapped. "It was a mistake and it won't happen again."

She whirled. "Why not?"

"So now you are eager to warm my bed? One brief encounter—although a mutually satisfying one, I assure you—and you have changed your tune?"

"I wouldn't mind if you shared my bed." And that was the terrible truth.

His gaze widened.

Virginia wished she were a different woman, one not so amoral and not so outspoken. But the fool remained, oh yes.

"Have you no wish to be innocent and chaste on your wedding night?" he finally asked seriously.

"I hadn't ever thought about it," she said truthfully.

He started. "It's what all women think about—dream of—live for."

She became annoyed instantly. "Not this one! I have no intention of ever marrying, not unless I find the love my parents had."

He stared at her as if she had grown two heads. Then he dared to laugh. The sound was rough and condescending. "No one marries for love," he said flatly. "If the emotion even exists."

She felt like kicking his shin. "My parents loved each other and married for love. I am sorry your parents did not love each other," she said angrily. "Clearly that has scarred you deeply. Perhaps that explains your cruelty and your lack of compassion."

In an instant, he was in front of her, towering over her. "Never bring up the subject of my parents again, as they are none of your affair. Do you comprehend me, Miss Hughes?"

She recoiled. How had this maddened him so? "You could not be more forthcoming."

"And dare I remind you that not once since I have taken you aboard my ship, has anyone, myself included, been in the least bit cruel toward you? Unless you consider the sweet death you experienced last night cruelty—"

"Leaving me to wonder how a woman feels when the act is truly accomplished, and if the sweet death you referred to changes in any manner, that is certainly cruel," Virginia heard herself say.

He looked stunned.

Virginia knew she flushed. "I can't help wondering what it must be like—"

He seized her arm and propelled her out of the cabin. "I am sorry that I cannot control your thoughts," he said tersely.

"You cannot be angry now that I am curious, when it is all your fault!" she cried, looking at his hard, perfect profile.

"My fault?" He propelled her down the gangplank. "I do believe you were the seductress, Miss Hughes."

"I am eighteen. I had never kissed anyone before last night. How could I possibly seduce you?" Ahead of them, she saw a carriage and a liveried driver. A big gray stallion was tied to the back. The mount was saddled. She realized the coach was for her and the horse for him.

How glorious it would be to be astride again, she thought. But she instantly knew she should not let him know the superb rider that she was, just in case another instance presented itself for escape.

Devlin handed her into the coach. She dared to look into his cold gray eyes. He remained angry with her. It was simply ludicrous. "Wait," she cried softly, before he could leave.

Impatiently he did so, his jaw hard with tension.

"What is so terrible about what happened last night? Didn't you enjoy yourself? You seemed to. But again, I have had no experience so I would hardly—"

He slammed the door closed in her face. "Good day, Miss Hughes."

VIRGINIA GAZED OUT OF THE carriage window, eager in spite of herself. Although the day was gray and threatened rain, the countryside was a rich, fertile sweep of verdant green hills, mostly pasture and crop and the occasional stand of woods. The narrow road they were on wound atop a ridge. They were passing a number of small farms, where every cottage looked the same—a garden out back, a field of corn and wandering, grazing cows and sheep. Ahead she glimpsed a stone church and beyond that, some other imposing buildings she could not quite make out.

Suddenly Devlin rode up to her window, which was open in spite of the chill day. "This is Askeaton," he said, his gaze fierce with pride. "As far as the eye can see, the land belongs to me."

"It's beautiful." She smiled at him. "It reminds me of Sweet Briar, Devlin."

He stared at her, then abruptly galloped ahead of the coach.

He angered even more easily than he had when they had first met, she thought, poking her head out of the window and gazing after him. He was letting the gray run, and man and beast were far ahead. But now Virginia could see that the buildings ahead belonged to a manor. She saw several barns, more cottages and a gracious manor house surrounded by flowering gardens, as well as what looked like an old tower or castle in the distance. Excitement caused her heart to pound. She was very curious to see his home and to meet his family—if he had any family, that is.

The carriage paused in front of the manor house. Virginia didn't wait for the driver, leaping out instead. Devlin stood with his fists on his hips, staring at the house, the lawns surrounding it, the buildings they had just passed, and then back at the house again. Virginia could not imagine what he was thinking, although perhaps he was taking an inventory of his holdings. The manor, which was three stories, looked very new, except for the two chimneys and an outer wall. Vines crept up the walls and a gazebo was to one side. She smiled. He had such an enchanting home for such an ill-tempered man.

The front door opened and a man stepped out, tall, lean and dark. "Dev!"

Her captor whirled. Virginia caught his expression and she inhaled, hard, for it was one of bright, pure joy. She stood very still as the younger man rushed down the stone walk. "Sean!" Devlin said hoarsely.

He strode forward. The two men embraced, tightly clinging. Virginia inched forward. This had to be a brother, as they were close in age and Sean was very handsome, too, with the same unmistakable silvery-gray eyes, although his hair was nearly black.

The two men pulled apart. "It's about goddamned time," Sean exclaimed, but he was smiling.

"Yes, it is," Devlin said, his tone rough. "The house looks good, Sean. Clearly it has been well-built, and I like the new door."

"Wait till you see the hall. I think you'll be pleased." Suddenly he stopped, eyes widening as his gaze landed on Virginia. "We have a guest?"

Devlin turned and Virginia received the warmth of his genuine smile. It made her heart speed and spin and then a terrible yearning began. "Yes, we have a guest," he said, extending his hand.

Virginia didn't move. That smile wasn't meant for her, it was meant for his brother. But it was a smile that could melt most of the North Pole. Why didn't he use it more often?

"Virginia, come. I'd like you to meet my brother, Sean," he said, the glorious smile fading. But his tone held a lightness she hadn't heard before.

Virginia summoned up her own smile and came forward. "Hello," she said.

"I wish I'd known we were having company," Sean said with worry. His gaze was wide and went back and forth between Virginia and Devlin. "But Fiona can have the yellow room ready soon enough, I think."

"This is Miss Hughes, Sean. Miss Virginia Hughes of Sweet Briar, Virginia."

Virginia started, stunned he would introduce her so, and then she noticed that Sean seemed even more shocked.

"Miss Hughes?" he echoed.

Why was Sean so surprised by her name? Virginia wondered in sudden confusion.

"Let's have a drink. We have a lot to catch up on," Devlin said, clapping his back.

But now Sean stared at Virginia—and he didn't look pleased, either.

A feminine squeal sounded.

Virginia started and saw a dark-haired woman rushing from the house. For one instant, Virginia saw only thick, straight black hair, a voluptuous figure and a huge smile, while more happy cries sounded. She stiffened as the woman halted right in front of Devlin, her heaving bosom mostly revealed by her low-cut blouse. She was dark and sultry enough to be a Spaniard or a Gypsy. "My lord! Welcome home! Oh, Captain O'Neill! Welcome!" she cried, looking an instant away from jumping into his arms—and his bed.

Virginia folded her arms across her own nondescript chest and scowled.

A look of recognition crossed Devlin's face. "Fiona?"

"Yes, it's me, my lord!" she cried, clapping her hands together. "My lord, it has been so long, and I am so happy you are home—we all are, my lord Captain! The hero of Askeaton has returned! We are so proud of you!"

Devlin said, "Thank you." His tone was polite.

"Fiona," Sean interjected. "It's Captain or Sir Captain or Sir Devlin now."

Fiona nodded, grinning. "What can I do for you, my lord?" she asked, and there was no mistaking her meaning. In fact, Virginia felt certain the other woman had already enjoyed Devlin's lovemaking in the past and intended to do so again, very shortly.

"Please show Miss Hughes to a guest room," Devlin

said, "and bring her a tray of refreshments once she is settled in." His gaze wandered past the house and settled on the ruins of the castle.

Fiona blinked, glancing at Virginia for the first time, clearly not having even noticed her until then. Her gaze met Virginia's, slid down her figure and back up and instantly became dismissive. She turned back to Devlin, beaming. "Yes, of course, my lord. I am *so* happy to see you again." She curtsied and Virginia expected her breasts to fall free of her blouse, but they did not. The woman clearly wore no underclothes, not even a corset.

"I am very happy to be home," Devlin said. He was gazing at the house now, as if inspecting every inch, and not at the maid. His expression was just a bit softer than usual and it made him far less intimidating—it made him seem human.

Virginia almost relaxed. He hadn't seemed to notice that Fiona was pretty and very voluptuous and wishful of being in his bed. And why should she worry? Last night, she was the one who had enthralled him. Virginia didn't have to have any experience with men to know that Devlin O'Neill had been swept up in the same rapture as she.

"Connor, Miss Hughes's bags," Sean instructed another servant, this one an older man. "Fiona, please show Miss Hughes to the yellow room. Bring flowers," he added.

Fiona nodded, never even looking at him. She only had eyes for Devlin.

Suddenly Devlin turned and strode to Virginia. She didn't move. "There is nowhere to go. You know that."

She didn't—just as she wasn't certain she wished to go anywhere, not just yet—but she nodded, anyway.

"As far as the eye can see, the land belongs to me or my stepfather, the Earl of Adare. Do you comprehend me, Virginia?" he asked softly, with real warning.

She thought about how easily he had thwarted her escape in Limerick. She had no doubt that escaping him in the heart of his holdings would be as futile. She smiled at him. "I won't try to escape again," she said as softly. She was far too curious to think of attempting another escape now.

He started. "What I wish to say was that here you will be treated with the utmost respect, your every need will be met, and I will try to see to it that your stay is brief."

She heard him but added, "You have my word."

He stared at her for a very long moment. "Whatever you intend, I suggest you rethink it," he said tersely.

"How do you know that I intend anything?" she asked sweetly. But she *did* intend something. Before she left Askeaton and Ireland, she wished to experience all that she had thus far discovered in her captor's powerful arms—and even more. The urgency he had awakened was simply too great to ignore or even resist.

"Because you are too clever and too stubborn to simply roll over upon my command," he said slowly.

She hesitated. "Perhaps that was then—and this is now. Perhaps I await your command, Sir Devlin," she murmured.

He leaned close. "Do not even think to tempt me again!"

"Why not?" she whispered back.

He seemed utterly taken aback. "Because I am far stronger than you, Virginia, and I suggest you never forget that." He gave her a hard look and started toward his brother, who was listening raptly to them.

But Virginia was beginning to understand her captor. She smiled as sweetly as she had before at him. "I never said you weren't," she murmured.

He flinched but did not halt. Sean appeared very distressed now, and he finally followed his brother inside.

Virginia began to grin. Oddly, she felt as if the tide were turning in her favor—somehow, it felt as if she had won that last encounter. And then she looked up into Fiona's hostile black eyes.

CLEARLY THE "YELLOW ROOM" hadn't been used in years. As Virginia stood in the doorway of a large bedroom where the walls were painted a soft, muted shade of gold, she watched Fiona angrily plump the pillows, dust billowing from them.

Virginia glanced around. This room was far more luxuriously appointed than her own bedroom at Sweet Briar or the two guest rooms there. The canopied bed in its center had gold velvet coverings and matching drapes were held back with gold tasseled cords, while a brown-and-gold Aubusson rug covered much of the scarred but polished oak floors. The ebony wood mantel over the fireplace was intricately carved, a lush chaise and ottoman adjacent to that, and several old portraits and landscapes adorned the walls. Virginia walked over to one window and actually cried out with delight. The view was stunning. Her eyes swept across the rolling fields of corn to an endless series of green pastures and hills and finally to the bare edge of the river itself. The ruins of an old and crumbling stone keep were just to her left.

Virginia gripped the sill. Ireland somehow called out to her the way that her home had, although the country was so very different. She wondered how she would feel if she were at Askeaton under other circumstances. She might never want to leave.

Fiona had stopped fussing with the bed. Virginia turned away from the window and found the other woman staring at her with open hostility. She was, Virginia thought, about twenty-five. "I should like some sandwiches and tea," Virginia said as if she were Sarah Lewis and back at the Marmott School for Genteel Young Ladies.

Fiona stiffened. "Be right up." But she didn't move.

"And I'd like some roses from the gardens," Virginia added, increasing her intonation, so she sounded more like a queen than a genteel young lady. "Oh! This gown. Do help me remove it. It needs pressing immediately. I'd like it back for supper, please."

Fiona looked ready to scratch her eyes out. "Are you to be his *wife?*" she asked with scalding anger.

Virginia started, then, indifferently, she shrugged. *His wife.* One day, Devlin O'Neill would settle down, take a wife, have children. Why did this notion mesmerize her? When that day dawned, she would be home at Sweet Briar, in fact, she might even be old and gray.

The confusion that had so recently begun and that seemed to crop up now whenever she thought about her captor swept over her with full force. She finally looked up. "Perhaps," she managed to say lightly.

Fiona started, scowling.

"And you? Were you his mistress? I thought so at first— but he didn't recognize you, so I am no longer sure."

Fiona stalked forward.

Virginia held her ground, even though the other woman had a stone or more on her.

"He hasn't been home in six years," she hissed. "I was a child back then, I was only fifteen but I loved him and I gave him my maidenhead. I'm a woman now, and I know a trick or two I am certain he will enjoy! In fact, I cannot wait until tonight, my lady, I cannot wait to pleasure him in every way I can think of! By tomorrow he will not even know your name."

Virginia stiffened, afraid the other woman might be right. But now she had to wonder what kind of man stayed away from his home for six long years?

And Virginia began to worry on another score. Devlin

had been eighteen, she thought, when he and Fiona had carried on, and she hated the fact that he had been her first lover. Nostalgia might be attached to their affair.

"How old are you?" Fiona asked with scorn.

"I'm twenty," Virginia lied.

Fiona rolled her eyes. "I'd wager you're sixteen. Let me tell you something, my lady. He won't ever look at you the way he looks at me. You're too skinny! A man likes meat on the bones, a man likes this." She cupped her heavy breasts and then she smiled, sighing and clearly thinking of Devlin fondling them instead.

Virginia turned her back on the housemaid. Her confidence, never high, vanished completely. Who was she fooling? If Devlin had a choice, he would seek out the older woman. She had no doubt.

She should be thrilled. She wasn't. She was upset, distressed, bewildered and even hurt by the prospect.

Fiona laughed at her distress. "So set them eyes somewhere else, my fancy lady," she hissed. "Here at Askeaton we got no use for the English and them royal airs. Here at Askeaton we got no use for you and your kind. Go back to where you came from!" Fiona left the room triumphantly.

Virginia ran after her. "I'm American, you fool. I'm American, not English!"

But if Fiona cared, she gave no sign. She never faltered as she hurried down the hall.

Virginia stepped back into her room, closing the door. Too late, she realized Fiona hadn't helped her undress, she hadn't taken her awfully soiled gown and she hadn't intended to bring water, refreshments, flowers or anything else.

Virginia took a small chair and pulled it up to the window. There she sat in dismal silence, staring out at the countryside, thinking about her captor.

DEVLIN POURED TWO WHISKEYS. Sean faced him with dark, angry eyes. Devlin handed him a glass, ignoring his brother now, his gaze moving around the library, then to the French doors and the terrace beyond. He relished the view, the moment. God, it was good to be home.

Gerald smiled conspiratorially at him. "Don't breathe a word of this to your mother, you hear?"

Devlin walked toward the French doors, no longer smiling, drinking instead.

His father's eyes, wide and angry, staring up at him from the bloody stump that was his head.

"Are you going to explain? Is she Eastleigh's daughter? It isn't enough that you bed his wife?" Sean demanded furiously.

He saluted Sean, forcing the brutal memories aside. "She's his niece. His orphaned American niece." He had expected Sean to be outraged, but that did not mean he liked it.

"So that explains everything. What the hell are you doing!" Sean cried. "And how old is she? Have you seduced a child?" He was disbelieving.

He studied the contents of his glass as if indifferent. "She's eighteen, and no, I haven't seduced her," he said, wondering how his righteous and oh, so moral brother would react if he told him that she might well decide to seduce *him.* "I'm ransoming her, Sean." He smiled, real mirth returning. "Eastleigh is on the verge of debtor's prison. He can ill afford a ransom, much less the one I will demand." He actually chuckled. "I shall, of course, toy with him a bit first. However, to free his niece he may very well have to sell off Eastleigh itself. This may be the moment we have been waiting for."

"And vengeance is mine, said the lord," Sean said harshly. "Vengeance belongs to God, not you, and this moment you have been waiting for—not I!" He slammed his drink down, untouched.

"You may not share my enthusiasm, but I am doing this for you as much as for myself," Devlin said. He pushed open the door and inhaled the clean, floral and grass-scented Irish spring. He did not want to debate Sean on the merits of his revenge against the Earl of Eastleigh. The subject was an old and tired one. It came up every time he saw his brother, once or twice a year, depending on how often they met in London or Dublin.

"You do this only for yourself. God, when will you let our father rest in peace?" Sean cried. Then he added, "Thank God Mother and Adare are in London!"

Devlin turned, his temper igniting. "Gerald will never rest in peace and you know it. As for our mother, she doesn't need to know about this."

Sean stared. "If his spirit wanders, it is because you will not allow him peace! Dear God, you have destroyed the man financially, when will you stop? When will you let go of this obsession and find some peace of your own?"

"Perhaps, if your memory served you as well as mine did me, you would be as bent upon revenge as I am," he said coldly.

Sean's own silver gaze chilled. "Do you think I don't wish that I could remember that day? You speak as if you think I willed my memory loss! I do not know why my mind has failed me so, but do not accuse me of complaisance when it comes to the fact that I cannot remember anything of that terrible day our father was murdered!"

"I'm sorry," Devlin said, but sometimes he resented the fact that he alone was the one haunted by Gerald, for neither his brother nor his mother seemed to suffer as he did.

"And what of the navy? Is the Admiralty going to let

you get away with this, the abduction of an American woman, an attack upon the English aristocracy?" Sean demanded.

"Eastleigh will never allow word of this abduction to come out. He already plays the fool and his pride will ultimately make him pay for Virginia's freedom. I feel certain no one will ever know about this little game, other than ourselves."

"Little game? You abuse an innocent young woman and it is a little game? Father must be turning over in his grave right now. You have gone too far!" Sean cried. "And what about Miss Hughes herself? If she goes to the authorities, you could lose your head! And I do not speak figuratively now."

Devlin laid his hand on Sean's rigid shoulder. "I have no intention of losing my head, Sean," he said softly.

"You think you are invincible. You are not."

"Trust my instincts. Eastleigh will conclude this affair swiftly. His pride is all he has left."

Sean stared, his expression harsh and agonized. "I don't approve, Devlin. I simply cannot. God, I don't even know who you are," Sean suddenly despaired, "and frankly, I never have."

"I'm your brother."

"Yes, my brother. A stranger whom I never see, as you clearly abhor the soil and the earth—as you cannot spend a fortnight on land, it seems. You are a stranger with a passion for vengeance and little else. I pity you, Devlin."

Devlin made a mocking sound, although his brother's words made him very uncomfortable. "You should save your pity for one who needs it—perhaps the beautiful Miss Hughes?"

Sean did not flinch. "I won't deny I find her attractive beyond comparison. I only hope she does not need my pity, ever, Dev."

"When you become more acquainted with Miss Hughes, you will discover that she is not the kind of woman to be pitied." He almost smiled, thinking of her courage and her absurdly independent nature.

A silence fell.

Devlin turned and found Sean staring, his gaze wide and searching. He said, "You almost sound fond of her."

He actually hesitated. "I am hardly fond of her, Sean. But frankly, her courage is amazing—reckless though it may be."

"So you admire her, then," Sean said quietly.

Devlin became impatient. "Enough of Miss Hughes! The subject grows tiresome. When Eastleigh pays her ransom, she goes back. Until then, she is *our* guest." He stressed the plural pronoun deliberately and stared. He softly added, "Your loyalty to me does precede your noble sense of honor and your disapproval, does it not?"

Sean folded his arms across his chest, staring grimly in displeasure.

"Sean?"

He spoke roughly. "You know I would never betray you, in spite of my outrage over what you think to do."

Satisfied, Devlin stalked back to the silver tray of decanters and glasses on the sideboard, pouring himself another, far stiffer drink. The silence lengthened. He finally sighed and glanced up. "All right. What is it? What is it that you wish to say?"

"If Eastleigh is so impoverished, what makes you think he will even wish to pay a ransom for his distant American niece, someone he has probably never seen and does not care for?"

Devlin stared. "He'll pay."

"And if he doesn't?" Sean prodded.

Devlin felt his entire being tense. "Then I will have to

provoke him publicly until he has no choice but to rescue our little guest, until it becomes a matter of honor."

"To destroy Eastleigh, you will have to destroy her, will you not? How can you live with yourself?" Sean cried.

"Rather easily," Devlin said, but even he knew there was nothing simple about his life and that his answer was a lie.

"You bastard," Sean said.

CHAPTER NINE

THE MANOR SEEMED terribly quiet and felt almost empty, Virginia thought, pausing in the grandiose hall. She had spent the afternoon exploring the grounds and visiting the stables, where Devlin had some very fine horses, especially a sweet bay mare. Now dusk was quickly approaching. Virginia had bathed in scented water—Connor had filled her tub—and changed into one of her mother's fine evening gowns, one altered hastily by Tillie before she had left Sweet Briar. The gown was a bright rose silk, with small puffed sleeves and a low-cut bodice. Virginia had gone to great lengths to pin up the heavy masses of her hair. If she were fortunate, the pins would stay in place until she retired for the night.

She wondered where her captor was.

Virginia walked through the hall, admiring several very old tapestries hanging on the walls and the huge crystal chandelier. She paused before two open doors that led to another salon, this one smaller and more intimate, with moss-green walls and green, pink and lavender molding on the ceiling. A man rose from the dark brocade sofa—it was Sean.

"Oh, I didn't realize anyone was in the room," Virginia said quickly. "I hope I am not intruding."

He came forward in a formal blue evening coat, pale britches and stockings. His gaze was openly appreciative as he smiled at her. "You are not intruding, Miss Hughes, not at all. After all, supper is almost upon us. Would you like a sherry or some champagne?"

She had to admire him as well. With his midnight hair and pale gray eyes, he was every bit as handsome as his older brother. Like Devlin, he was tall, broad of shoulder, long of leg and lean of hip. His body looked every bit as muscled and toned. "I would love a glass of champagne," she said.

He quickly poured two flutes from the chilled bottle on the sideboard, handing her one. "You are fetching, Miss Hughes, in that lovely dress," he said.

She wondered if he was blushing, as she remarked two slight spots of color high upon his cheekbones. "You must call me Virginia, Mr. O'Neill, and thank you very much." She hesitated. "This dress belonged to my mother."

"I am sorry about your parents," he said instantly. "And please, it's Sean."

She started, meeting kind and concerned gray eyes. "You know about my parents?" she asked.

"Dev mentioned that you are an orphan."

She nodded. "It was a carriage accident last fall."

"Sometimes there is no comprehending God's will."

"I'm not sure I believe in God," she said.

His eyes widened. "Then that is a shame. But there have been moments, I confess, when I have had my doubts, too."

She smiled at him. "Then we must both be intelligent and human."

He laughed.

She stopped smiling, enjoying his laughter, which was warm and rich and so different from the odd, croaking sound Devlin had made on the few occasions when he seemed to try to laugh. "You and he are nothing alike, are you?"

"No." Sean studied her.

"How is that possible? Aren't you both close in age?"

"I'm two years younger," Sean said. "Devlin assumed responsibility for me when our father died. That is one reason for the difference between us."

"And the other?" she asked, determined now to learn everything she could about her captor.

He smiled wryly and shrugged.

"I do not understand him," she said. "He is very brave, that much is clear, almost fearless, I think—" she recalled how he had defied gale winds to rescue his ship "—and that's not very human, is it?"

"He is fearless," Sean agreed. "I think he doesn't care if he lives or dies."

Virginia stared, Sean's theory stunning. "But no one wishes to die!"

"I didn't say he wished to die, merely that the thought doesn't frighten him as it does us other mere mortals."

Virginia considered that and immediately she felt certain that Sean was right. "But why? What kind of man would be indifferent toward his own life?"

Sean was silent.

Virginia suddenly comprehended the only possible answer—only a man deeply wounded or deeply embittered would be so indifferent. She was shaken. She quickly sipped her champagne, which, she saw, was also contraband, as it was French. How complex Devlin O'Neill was. "His men respect and admire him," she mused aloud, almost to herself, "and the town seems to think of him as a hero. I have seen myself how effective he is on the high seas, so I understand why his men admire him. But the town?"

"You are very curious when it comes to my brother," Sean remarked.

"Yes, I am. After all, he seized my ship, then seized me. I simply do not understand why he wishes to ransom me when he so clearly does not need the money."

"Perhaps you should ask him," Sean said.

"Perhaps I will," Virginia returned thoughtfully, "although I am sure he will only become angry—he is a very angry man. Why is that? You are not angry. I can see kindness in your eyes. You seem as compassionate as he is ruthless."

"I am not a ship's officer upon the high seas, where discipline is crucial to maintain, and once lost, impossible to regain." Sean sighed then. "There is one fundamental difference between us. When we were small children, we saw our father brutally murdered by an English soldier. Devlin has never forgotten that day—I cannot recall a single second of it."

She stared, her mind spinning, trying to understand. "How old was he?"

"He was ten, I was eight. From that moment, Devlin has been a father as well as a brother to me, and acutely aware of his responsibilities as head of the O'Neill clan here in southern Ireland."

"How terrible," Virginia said softly, "and how fortunate you cannot remember. I cannot imagine how I should feel or what I would think if I saw my father murdered. I suppose I should intend to kill the murderer." And now the mind of her captor was beginning to make sense. Of course he was a hard, cold man. He had learned a brutal lesson as a small child, one that clearly had affected his character, his nature. Perhaps that was why he had chosen the rough and merciless life of a career spent at sea.

"Then perhaps you and I have more in common than we think," Devlin murmured.

Virginia whirled and saw Devlin standing in the

doorway rather nonchalantly, as splendidly dressed as his brother, although he wore his naval uniform. In his navy-blue jacket with its gold epaulets and buttons, his stark white britches and stockings, he made a terribly dashing figure, enough so that her heart seemed to stop. There was simply no comparing the brothers, not now, not anymore. Sean might have an innate decency and kindness that she doubted Devlin would ever have, but Devlin fascinated her impossibly, as if she were a moth, he the fatal flame.

She shivered, hoping the image was not in any way a premonition.

"I am sorry about your father's murder," she heard herself say.

He shrugged, coming forward, giving her a cool and indifferent glance. "Life is filled with surprises, is it not?" His gaze moved slowly over her face, her hair, her bare shoulders and finally across her décolletage.

And his look warmed her the way his lovemaking had the previous night. She opened her mouth to speak, but no sound came out, as her thoughts were preoccupied with how she hoped the night would end in his bed, in his arms.

"Sean, escort Virginia in," Devlin said.

Virginia started, surprised and disappointed, and when she turned, Sean was holding out his arm, looking resigned and grim. She quickly smiled at him, but her gaze followed Devlin, who had moved away from them, his back turned as he poured himself champagne.

"You don't have to pretend to be pleased," Sean said. "Your feelings are clear, Virginia."

She quickly focused on him. "I am hardly displeased, and I do not know what you mean!"

"Virginia? I hope the time comes when I may speak with you frankly, because there is something I fear I must say."

She did not like his tone or his expression, and she murmured some vague affirmative, not wanting to continue the subject.

"SOME GROWERS PROTECT THE seedlings with a fine net of cotton," Virginia said happily, her small face animated and her violet eyes sparkling. "But that is far too expensive and not really necessary where we are, as it doesn't get that cold. We found that mulch works just as well. We use a thin layer of straw and chopped grass. The real issue is transplanting the seedlings, which is done in about eight or nine weeks. The soil has to be pulverized, level, disease-free—which is why we burn the fields every spring—and fairly wet. We plant just under an ounce of seed for every two hundred square yards. It is crucial that the seeds are distributed uniformly, which is why we do so by hand."

Sean shook his head with admiration. "Is there anything you don't know about planting tobacco, Virginia?" His eyes were dancing.

"I'm sure there's something." Virginia smiled at him.

Sean smiled back.

Devlin lolled in his chair between them at the head of the long trestle table, absolutely silent—the way he'd been all through supper. And while his expression and posture remained indifferent, he was irritated with the two of them. His gaze moved slowly over Virginia, who seemed to have forgotten his presence at supper. But then, his brother was openly admiring, gentlemanly and attentive, and probably the most rapt audience she had ever had. She was as greedy for the attention as a gambler for a single win, he thought sourly.

His gaze took in her tiny upturned nose, her full mouth, the low-cut bodice of her dress and the small breasts thrusting up against the corset she wore. He stretched out his long legs beneath the table, trying to ignore the simmering pressure in his groin. Only he knew how passionate she was, how fiery and hot, how easily ignited.

I have never been kissed before, Devlin.

The pressure felt explosive, just like that. He shifted in his seat as Sean said something and she laughed. Her bedroom was at the other end of the manor, which he considered fortunate. Because in spite of his determination not to repeat last night, he was very tempted. One touch and she would not be thinking about his brother.

He grimaced. They'd been regaling each other with stories of Sweet Briar and Askeaton all night. However, he did admit that her stories were somehow interesting and even refreshing. Knowing her now, even the little that he did, not a single story of her life in Virginia surprised him. But what father raised a woman to shoot, ride and swim, allowed her to roam a hundred acres freely, allowed her to wear britches, work beside the slaves, forgo teas and dances—in total, what father raised such a little hellion?

Randall Hughes had probably been an interesting man. He had surely been unconventional.

"I still can't believe your father taught you to shoot a musket when you were seven," Sean remarked.

Virginia laughed for the hundredth time that night, the sound as bright as bells. "Mama was furious when she found out. Papa had to bring her trinkets and gifts for a month afterward, to return to her good graces."

Sean laughed as well.

Virginia sobered. "I do miss them," she said.

Devlin started as Sean reached across the table to cover her hand. He stiffened as Sean said, "This is a terrible cliché, but it will get easier with time."

She smiled slightly now. "It has gotten easier, but I think

I will miss them until I die. Sweet Briar will never be the same, not without them."

Sean withdrew his hand. "Do you miss the plantation very badly?"

She nodded. "Sometimes—usually in the middle of the night. But—" she brightened "—I do like Ireland! There's something about it that reminds me of home, even though the climate is so different. Maybe it's the green. Everything is so rich with life here—it's that way at home, too."

"I should like to visit Sweet Briar someday," Sean said suddenly.

"I should love for you to come," Virginia cried, clearly delighted.

That was it—he'd had enough. And did his little hostage find his brother attractive? Only last night she had been in *his* bed, in *his* arms. Was a new romance unfolding before his very eyes? He stood abruptly, shoving back his chair. "I am going to smoke," he announced, trying not to glare at either of them.

"I do hope your tobacco is Virginian," Virginia said sweetly.

He stiffened. And from the corner of his eyes he saw Sean sputter with laughter and the two of them share a glance. He turned. "It's not. It's Cuban. Good night." He was pleased to see her face fall as he uttered his last words, then, having no intention of leaving them alone, he looked darkly at his brother. "Join me," he said, and it was a command.

As he strode out, he heard Sean say, "And his lordship doth speak."

Virginia giggled. "He is so dour tonight."

"He is always dour," Sean remarked.

He debated walking back to them and defending himself, but decided to pretend he hadn't heard their insipid insults. Besides, they'd both drank enough champagne to sink a ship. Still, Sean was far too interested and it was simply not acceptable.

In the study, rebuilt to exactly replicate the study his father had used up until his death, he found a cigar and poured a brandy, then lit up. Exhaling deeply did not ease the tension. And if he brooded further, analyzing the evening in order to decide if the camaraderie he had just witnessed was romantic or not, the pressure would increase. He knew it, as surely as he knew the sky would be clear that morning.

"Captain, sir," a woman breathed.

His annoyance faded as he turned and faced Fiona.

She smiled at him, clad in a tight white blouse and dark skirts, the blouse showing off the full shape of her bosom and hinting at the large areolas beneath. He carefully looked her over now, for the first time since he had returned home. She was actually pretty, and she had the kind of body most men would die to bed. He vaguely recalled a few torrid nights spent in bed with her, many years ago. And while he didn't lust after her, she certainly presented a solution to the problem of avoiding Virginia in the long, dark shadowy hours of the night.

"Kitchen's done and your room's ready," she said softly, her gaze on his. "Is there anything else I can do for you, sir, before I go to my bed?"

He made the decision instantly. "Yes. You can go to my room. I'll be up shortly."

There was no look of surprise, she only smiled and purred, "Of course, Captain, sir." She gave him a promising look and strolled out, her wide hips swinging.

He wanted to compare their width to one particular waif's far too slim ones, but refused to do so. He would satisfy his lust tonight in the way lords of the manor had for centuries—with a willing, comely, insignificant maid.

Sean made a derisive sound, apparently having been standing in the doorway for some time. Devlin ignored it, handing him a cigar and lighting it for him. As Sean puffed, he poured his brother a brandy. He said, "You seem smitten with our little guest."

Sean exhaled and said, "I am nearly so."

"Don't become too attached. She is going to lose her beloved Sweet Briar and blame me for it, I have no doubt."

"That's right. She will blame you, and rightly so, I think. But she certainly won't blame me."

Devlin sat down on the edge of the desk. Oddly, his father chose that moment to cast a presence in the room. "I am going to find you an heiress," he warned.

"I don't need an heiress. You would never stay home to run Askeaton. One day I need a wife who will partner me in all that I do here."

"You mean, a wife who understands crops, markets and shipping, inside and out?" He became angry.

"Maybe." Sean came closer. "Look, Dev, I find her intriguing, and unlike you, I am not using her for some terrible end—for some personal retribution. In fact, after getting to know her somewhat tonight, I think you should end your miserable scheme and help her get to Eastleigh. Who knows? She's charming beyond words. Maybe he'll be smitten, too, and he'll save her home."

Devlin was furious now, furious because if he read Sean right, his younger brother was falling in love with his captive. "No. Nothing changes, and you keep your heart and guard it well. She is not for you—I will not allow it. She is a tool, a tool I am using even as we speak, she is only a tool. Do you understand me?"

Sean was furious, too. "I told you this afternoon—I don't even know you, so how can I understand you? But I grow tired of your orders! I am not a sailor on your ship!

If I choose to admire Miss Hughes, that is my concern, not yours."

"You go very far." Devlin stood, and the two men stood eye to eye and nose to nose, the exact same height. "Since when do I order you? I haven't been at home in six years— I see you perhaps once a year in London! There have been no orders, little brother, until yesterday, and may I remind you that this manor is mine? The land is mine? It is all mine until I die, heirless. Only then does it become yours."

"Do you threaten to give me the boot?" Sean was incredulous. "You may have bought Askeaton from Adare with your damned prize money, but Askeaton would be nothing but bogs and woods without me! I took this land and made it fertile, I took this land with my own bare hands and made it rich! You'd have nothing here without me, and you damn well know it!"

Devlin inhaled hard, stunned at the intensity of Sean's anger and his own answering rage. How had they come to this terrible argument? Virginia's image seared his mind. "Sean." He clasped his arm and Sean flinched but did not pull away. "I know all that you have done. I agree with you. Without you, this house would be a burned-out hull, the fields would be barren and lifeless, bogs would abound. I know that. I appreciate every day you have spent here in my place, planting our crops and harvesting them, collecting our rents, breeding our livestock. I more than appreciate all you have done. You're my brother. We should not fight, not like this, not ever."

Sean nodded, pale now. "And I know how hard you have worked to be able to buy Askeaton, and the house in Greenwich, and all the treasures we now have both here and there. I know you are the lord of this manor, Dev. I don't want to be lord here. God, I want you to take a wonderful wife and have fine sons to inherit all that you have earned—and all that is your rightful due as Father's eldest son."

"I know that, too," Devlin said, relaxing only slightly. And he looked closely at his brother now.

Sean stared back. Very carefully, he said, "We will fight again, however, because I cannot ever approve of what you are doing and the way you are ruthlessly using Virginia."

"Don't fall in love with her," Devlin heard himself say.

Sean hesitated. "Perhaps it is too late."

Devlin reeled, as if physically struck with shot.

"I am going to bed," Sean said, putting out his cigar. He smiled a little, but it was forced, and walked out of the room.

A yawning silence came over the study. Devlin stared at his own cigar, burning in the porcelain ashtray. He was grim. Virginia had been nothing but a pawn in his game with Eastleigh until that night. Now he felt as if she had become a terrible viper in their midst.

But he could not change his course.

He covered his eyes briefly, pain stabbing in his forehead, then paced wildly, allowing the anger in, welcoming it. She had come perilously close to flirting with Sean tonight. She had encouraged his emotions. Her attentive behavior, her pretty laughter, her eager conversation had ensnared his brother thoroughly. She had become a problem, one he must quickly solve.

The sooner he was rid of her, the better. The better for everyone.

Suddenly Virginia materialized in the doorway. He stiffened. She didn't smile, but said, low, "It's a beautiful night. Would you walk with me, Devlin?"

"No."

She jumped at the harsh sound of his voice.

"Come in," he ground out, fully aware of what he must do to end any further dalliance between her and his brother. As she did, her eyes wide and wary, he walked swiftly past her and closed the door.

"What's wrong?" she asked cautiously.

"You are to stay away from Sean."

"What?" she gasped.

He found himself gripping her shoulders. Now his anger had become infused into something entirely different and it was rearing up insistently, the blood there hot and red, pounding. "Let me repeat myself. *Stay away from Sean.*"

"Whatever you are thinking—you are wrong!" she cried, eyes wide.

"Am I? The last thing I need is my brother falling in love with you, Miss Hughes. Do I make myself clear?" He found his grip tightening. She whimpered, but it was too late, somehow his hands had a will of their own, pulling her up against his hard, aroused body.

"Devlin," she whispered, the sound throaty with need.

Triumph surged within him. *She would not think about his brother now.* "Do you wish to know something, an interesting fact?" he asked harshly, palming her backside and holding her up against his arousal, where she began to squirm. "I don't think it will be very difficult to make you forget all about Sean...darling."

Her eyes were glazing over. She gripped his shoulders, her chest heaving, her cheeks flushed. "I don't want Sean," she said hoarsely. "I want you."

Inside his brain, coherence exploded. Devlin crushed her to his chest, taking her mouth, forcing it open. As his tongue swept deep, hers came forth to meet him. More explosions went off inside of his head. Then he felt her small hands sliding over his waist.

Desire thoroughly blinded him. "No, here," he said,

taking one of her hands and pushing it over the hard ridge that was his arousal. She gasped and he almost laughed, but the pain and the pressure was far too intense and he could not get a sound out. Choking, he forced her hand to slide down the length there, and when suddenly she closed her fingers around most of him, he pulled her down to the floor, moving on top of her, claiming her mouth yet again. And briefly, there was no more thought.

She clawed his shoulders and moaned; he kissed his way down her throat, pulled her bodice down, exposing both perfect breasts. And as he stared at one erect nipple, two images came to mind—Eastleigh, fat and gray, and Sean, dark and angry.

What was he doing?

He was so angry he couldn't even think clearly, and this was so fast and furious it wasn't even seduction—it wasn't rape, but because of her and Sean, he was poised to take her, violently and brutally. He had sworn to return her to Eastleigh unharmed—but instead, he had lost all control.

She reached for his face, thrashing beneath him. "Hurry," she begged.

He looked again at her erect nipple, at her small, plump breast, and desperately fought the increasing pressure in his loins, the red haze growing in his head, the frantic urgency. He was out of control. Stunned, he pulled her dress up, covering her breasts, and somehow stood.

What in hell had just happened?

This woman had brought him to a point he had never before reached.

He was a master of self-control—but she had shattered it.

Not looking at her, not daring to, he started swiftly from the room.

He heard her sitting up on the floor. "Devlin," she gasped. "Come back. Please."

He ground his jaw down and did not falter.

"You can't leave me like this!" she cried.

He bounded up the stairs, taking them two at a time. Then he strode down the hall. By the time he reached his bedroom door, he felt as if he had regained some semblance of control—but not all of it.

He was very disturbed.

Because Virginia had just had power over him—and he could not, would not, ever let anyone have any power over him, not in any way, and not his very own prisoner.

He entered his room, quickly shutting the door, shrugging off his navy coat. His erection still raged and he tugged uselessly at his britches but found no relief.

"Oh, do let me help with that." Fiona stepped forward, resplendently naked.

He stopped short, staring in surprise, for he had completely forgotten about her.

She was smiling as she came forward, her pendulous breasts swaying, and before he could even assimilate that she was present because he had told her to be so, she dropped onto her knees, unfastening his britches deftly.

He inhaled hard as he sprang free, then inhaled again as she took his entire length into her mouth and down her throat.

Huge violet eyes, unfocused and glazed with desire, filled his mind as his own eyes closed. He gripped Fiona's head tightly, and as she sucked his engorged shaft as if she wished to swallow him whole, his treacherous mind envisioned a different woman on her knees performing the very same act, a woman small and dainty, impossibly beautiful, outspoken and defiant. The thick straight hair in his hands became soft, silken curls. The large tongue became small and pointed. Full, tender rosebud lips now stretched taut around him. With his hands, he encouraged Virginia to hurry and finish him off.

The dam broke. He cried out and when he was done, he moved to the bed, where he sat, breathing hard and stunned by the intensity of his release. She moved against him from behind. Suddenly aware of the huge breasts against his back, he stiffened, realizing that Fiona was in his bed, that Fiona had just performed fellatio upon him, not Virginia Hughes.

Very seductively, she began rubbing herself against him. "The night has only begun, my lord," she purred.

He sat there almost laughing at himself. How could he have thought, even for an instant, that Virginia could perform such an act? It wasn't even a matter of her innocence, it was a matter of her—and his—size.

But the incipient amusement vanished. He had never experienced such pleasure before. And recalling it, images of Virginia returned to him full force and instantly his manhood rose to the occasion.

"I knew you would return to me, my lord," Fiona said.

He had a choice—dismiss her or take her. Devlin turned, pushing her onto her back on the bed. And closing his eyes, he mounted her.

HE PACED THE MANOR, disturbed.

The events of the past few hours were haunting him.

And a ghost seemed to follow him, the presence as disquieting as that entire evening had been.

It was as if Gerald had followed him from the docks of Limerick, refusing to release him.

A bottle of fine French brandy in hand, Devlin stared at the gun rack that was mounted on the wall. Once, ages ago, he had found his father's gun rack empty in a terrible time of need. That rack had been destroyed in the fire set by

Eastleigh's troops so long ago. Although there was no need, modern muskets filled the brackets—it would never be left empty again.

When will you let our father rest in peace?

Devlin drank. Half the bottle was gone, and he was going to pay for it on the morrow. He hated thinking about Gerald, he hated each and every memory, the good being far worse than the bad—which was why he never came home.

Sightless eyes filled with fury turned mocking.

"Go away," Devlin murmured. "Your time will come." He paused drunkenly before a huge fire roaring in the massive hearth.

The halls seemed to shimmer in the shadows, but no one answered him. Not that he had expected an answer, and besides, he didn't believe in ghosts.

Still, the room felt heavy and full. He did not feel alone.

Vengeance belongs to God, not you...you do this only for yourself!

"Christ," Devlin gritted. He drank some more, and now his stomach burned from the excessive consumption of liquor. Images of Virginia taunted him, standing on the deck of the *Americana,* the wind whipping her hair, aiming that silly pistol at him. Her face changed, smiling brightly, her eyes sparkling as they had at supper, enchanting his brother with her humor, her wit, her conversation, and then there was Sean, dark and angry, claiming to be falling in love.

You will have to destroy her...how can you live with yourself? How?

Devlin stalked about the great room, wondering if, on this cold and windless night, his conscience had decided, finally, to make an appearance in his life. The hall had been furnished with blood money. Elegantly appointed, it was a testament to the hundreds of ships he had attacked, seized and destroyed at sea, the thousands of crew taken prisoner, the hundreds left behind, dead and buried by the sea. His home was as elegant as any lord admiral's, as fine as Adare's. His next intention was to begin reconstruction of the old keep in ruins behind the manor house. Once, family myth had it, a great pirate ancestor of his had lived there and loved a most extraordinary woman, the daughter of the infamous traitor, Gerald FitzGerald, the one-time Earl of Desmond.

Now he had the funds—his last prize, loaded with bullion, had made him a very rich man.

Enough! Give up.

Devlin stiffened as if shot. He could have sworn he'd just heard his father's stern, angry voice echoing in the room. He slowly looked around the huge hall, almost expecting to see someone materializing in the shadows, but the room was still and silent. Through one tall glass window, he saw stars and the night. He was alone. His imagination was playing tricks upon him—either that, or he did have a damned conscience after all.

But the odd feeling of not being alone at all remained.

Give up.

Devlin flinched. Was he actually hearing a voice, or was it his drunken imagination and nothing more? Still, the advice was good. Prowling his home in the wee hours of the coming dawn was as useless as sailing into the wind. He started for the stairs. The sensation remained however, dark and disturbing—the sensation of being watched.

He refused to look back.

And his last waking thought before drifting to sleep as dawn broke over the Irish countryside was that he would never give up, not ever, not until Eastleigh was dead.

CHAPTER TEN

VIRGINIA REALIZED THAT she was starving. She gave the little, very fancy, bay mare another pat, then stepped out of the stall and left the stables. It was a beautiful morning, the sky a brilliant deep shade of blue, cloudless, the sun bright and burning, threatening to make the day extremely hot. In the end last night, she had been exhausted, and the moment she had crawled into bed, she had fallen deeply asleep. But old habits died hard and she had been up at dawn, walking the grounds and exploring the ruins of the old castle behind the house. Devlin's home was lovely, and the ruins had intrigued her. There was something poignant and romantic about them.

Now she started across the lawns toward the manor, aware of a new tremor within her. She had seen Devlin once, briefly, galloping his gray across a distant hill, apparently out for an early morning ride. Astride a horse, he made the same irresistible figure that he did on the quarterdeck of his ship. He remained an enigma, simply impossible to understand. Had he accused her of somehow being too friendly with Sean? Everything had happened so very quickly in the study when she had dared to ask him to stroll with her in the moonlight. He had been very angry with her, but why? Sean was a nice man and Virginia genuinely liked him. She had enjoyed dining with him. She hoped he would one day visit her at Sweet Briar. But not only hadn't

Devlin joined in their conversation, he had seemed to think that she had a romantic interest in Sean. That was absurd! How could he think that, given the intimacy they had shared?

But he had ordered her to stay away from her brother. There was one other possibility. Perhaps he was afraid that she would entice Sean into helping her escape the way she had Jack Harvey.

Virginia's steps dragged so she might have a bit more time to think. It was impossible not to recall *everything* that had happened last night. Her cheeks began a slow burn. When he had held her in his arms, when he had begun to kiss her, when she had felt his huge arousal, all of her sanity had vanished, exactly as it had the other night on the ship. She hadn't imagined her passionate reaction to being in his arms, oh no. The fever and the frenzy he evoked in her was very real and simply stunning. And in a way, it was frightening, too.

Because when he held her, she was not herself. When he held her, she turned into a creature of desire and little else. In fact, when she was in his arms being kissed and aroused, nothing else mattered.

Fortunately it was midmorning now and Virginia was no longer insane with that terrible lust. Her body was definitely changing in response to thinking about the encounter, but at least she was capable of rational thought. Why did he have such an effect upon her?

He was impossibly mesmerizing, impossibly handsome in a terrible, powerful way, but she was his prisoner, not his guest. Devlin stood between her and Sweet Briar and she was starting to forget that, as if she had all the time in the world to play out this interlude in captivity before rescuing the plantation. She needed to be stronger, firmer, more resolved—time was not on her side.

Still, he wasn't a pirate or a madman. He hadn't hurt her, not a single time, and he was clearly trying to respect her. The world worshipped him for being a heroic naval captain. He *was* heroic—he was the very stuff that heroes were made from. But he had broken the law by abducting her—not to mention that he had so arrogantly stepped all over the *Americana,* which had every right to ply its trade. He had committed at least those two crimes, and her spinning thoughts always returned to this final point. The *Americana* lay wrecked upon the bottom of the sea, she was his prisoner and she had no right to yearn for his embrace.

And she still had no idea why he really wished to ransom her.

It was probably fortunate that he had decided to end their interlude last night as if he had just discovered she was a leper. His hasty exit was almost comical in the light of this morning, and she did smile, recalling it. But it hadn't been amusing last night. Last night she had been desperate and crushed and more confused than ever.

Virginia entered the house, becoming grim. She needed to know why. She needed to know why he risked his career for a ransom he did not need. And in spite of the fact that she was actually enjoying being at Askeaton, that she wasn't in a rush to leave, she had to get to the Earl of Eastleigh. If she wanted a home to return to, she must stay focused and resolved and disregard the passionate attraction they seemed to share.

Virginia walked through the hall, wondering if Devlin had returned from his ride. She had seen Sean riding out some time ago, after Devlin but separately and at a more sedate pace. She felt certain he was beginning his day's work. Virginia glanced into the dining room and found only one place set. She sighed, caught up between disappointment and relief.

Virginia raided the breadbasket, giving in to hunger. With one blueberry scone in hand, she began eating a slice of raisin bread, fresh and warm from the oven, as she started upstairs. She decided to give up thinking about Devlin O'Neill. What she would do instead was change into the riding britches she had brought with her from home and take a long ride across the O'Neill lands.

Virginia finished the bread and was beginning on the scone as she entered her bedroom. Fiona was humming away as she made the bed, having opened all of the windows to let in the warm spring day. Virginia ignored her, going to the closet for her valise. "Good morning," Fiona said with abundant cheer.

Every fiber of her being tensed. Alarm began—what was this? Slowly, britches in hand, her riding boots on the floor, Virginia turned.

Fiona beamed at her. "I brought you roses from the garden," she said, pointing to the pink roses in a vase beside her bed.

The alarm began to change, turning into dread. Virginia inhaled, wondering if Sean or Devlin had set her down for her delinquent manner yesterday. "Thank you," she said carefully. "Would you help me out of my dress?"

"Of course!" Fiona practically ran across the room, and Virginia glimpsed her beatific expression just before she turned. As the other woman undid the buttons and helped her out of the gown, she said, "You are inordinately happy today."

Fiona laughed. "It's a fine day, is it not?"

Virginia had a sick feeling. She stepped into the boys' britches, then pulled on the high, worn riding boots. A simple cotton shirt followed, which she vaguely tucked in. "Have you received some good news?" she asked, lacing up her boots.

Fiona laughed again. "I think I am in love," she confided happily.

Virginia jerked up, staring, appalled. "In...love?"

Fiona nodded eagerly, clasping her hands together. "It was everything I dreamed it would be. He was everything I dreamed he would be, I mean! Oh, God, it was glorious, what a man, so strong, so tireless..." She finally faltered, her cheeks splotched feverishly, a similar glaze in her eyes.

"You...you and Devlin?" Virginia managed, the contents of her stomach seriously roiling now.

"Yes," Fiona cried. "He made love to me all night, that man can hold it like a stud! I have never, ever been with a man like that, and I do not know how I will ever wait until tonight!"

Devlin had taken Fiona to bed.

Virginia sat on the edge of the chair, beyond ill, in stupefaction.

"He's so big," Fiona whispered now. "I can hardly fit him in my hand."

Last night Devlin had kissed her and held her and then he had gone to Fiona.

Virginia was about to vomit. And the shattering began in her heart. Somehow she smiled as she stood. Somehow she held her breakfast down. "I am happy for you, Fiona. The two of you make a fine pair."

"We do, don't we! He's so golden, I'm so dark, he's handsome, I'm beautiful," she cried, clapping her hands together.

Virginia left the room, as fast as her legs could carry her without running. She broke into a run as she reached the stairs, not able to breathe, her heart ripping hideously apart. Instantly her slick booted soles slid on the polished wood and she fell hard, tumbling down half of the steps.

On the bottom she paused on her hands and knees,

panting harshly, beyond shock. Then she somehow got up, ran out the front door, and there she threw up on the closest rose bush.

When she was done, she crawled around the side of the house and sat there, shaking. Images of Devlin straining over Fiona taunted her, mocked her, throwing pound after pound of salt in her wounds. It was some time before she could take control of her raw emotions, and it was only then that the horrific images began to infuriate her.

Oh, how they deserved each other!

She was a whore—he was a whoremonger!

She didn't care—she had her maidenhead intact, thank God—no, thank Fiona!

Virginia hated them both.

How could he go to Fiona after being with her? How?

Virginia somehow stood, her knees oddly weak, brushing dirt off of her beige britches. This was for the best. Soon she would leave Askeaton and Ireland, soon she would return to Sweet Briar and never, ever have to see Devlin O'Neill again.

How, how, how?

"She's beautiful and I'm ugly, that's how!" Virginia raged. She stormed past the house and down to the stables, where the bay mare recognized her and whinnied. Virginia found a saddle that looked a bit smaller than the others, grabbed a bridle and blanket and quickly saddled the little mare up. It began to rain. She held the mare's reins and stroked her neck as her hands became wet. "You're so sweet," she choked. Then she led the mare outside, where the sky was blue, confusing her.

Of course it wasn't raining. It was only her tears—they simply wouldn't stop.

Vaguely she wondered if she had somehow fallen in love with the monster that was Devlin O'Neill.

Virginia mounted the mare and gave her a loose rein. A moment later they were galloping away from Askeaton and across the Irish countryside.

THE BAY MARE PICKED HER way along a meandering deer path through a stand of sun-dappled woods. Virginia was herself again and furiously relieved because of it. She was Virginia Hughes, a planter's daughter and the mistress of Sweet Briar. She was an outspoken, independent woman with no interest in any man, with no interest outside of her home and plantation. With the utmost determination, she had spent the past half hour plotting a new means of escape, this time by horseback. Now she was determined to thwart her damned captor. He no longer expected her to try to flee, and once he found her gone, he would expect her to go back to England by ship. To hell with him! She would first cross Ireland on a horse, and she'd sail out from one of the coastal towns in the east. In fact, as soon as she had the opportunity, she would sneak into the library and find some useful maps. Maybe she would *steal* one.

Suddenly the bay mare nickered.

Virginia started, so lost in thought she hadn't been aware of leaving the woods. She halted the mare instantly, wary and alert. She was on a low, grassy ridge overlooking a small freehold. A stone farmhouse marked its center, along with several barns, a vegetable garden, some cornfields and an open pasture where a dozen cows grazed. Virginia saw his gray stallion instantly.

She stiffened with alarm, renewed anger flooding her. The stallion was tied up in front of the farmhouse with four big-bodied country hacks. Three buggies were parked in front as well. What was going on? She didn't think the farmer was having an afternoon tea.

She reminded herself that she didn't care what Devlin

did and whom he did it with. She started to turn the bay to return to the woods, when she looked at the other mounts tied in front of the house. Wasn't the heavyset chestnut Sean's?

What was going on?

Virginia hesitated. Something odd was happening—her every instinct told her that. She dismounted, tying the mare to a tree and letting her graze. Scrambling down the ridge, she ran hard to cross the clearing until she reached the safety of the farmhouse walls. Virginia crept up to a window, her heart pounding with unbearable force. It had no glass and the shutters were wide open.

Inside, many men were shouting in an uproar.

What could this be? If she were lucky, she was going to catch Devlin O'Neill with his hand in someone else's cookie jar. She fervently hoped so. Virginia straightened until her chin was level with the sill and she could peek inside.

Instantly she saw two dozen men, maybe more, most of them peasants and farmers. The second thing she saw was Sean standing on a dais with a Catholic priest, holding up his hands and asking for order in the room. She quickly spotted Devlin, seated in the front row of the crowd. Bewildered, she could not even begin to imagine what kind of meeting was in progress.

"Please, everyone has a turn," Sean was saying with authority.

The shouting turned into disgruntled murmurs and mutters.

"Tim McCarthy," Sean said. "Would you like a chance to speak your mind?"

A big man with shaggy gray hair stepped forward. "It's just more lies, it's always been lies, it's all the English are good for, that and stealing our land!"

"Here, here!" everyone roared.

Virginia stood up, stunned. Was this a *political* meeting?

"They promised us our rights, the same rights as any Protestant, back in 1800, with the Union. And what have they given us? Does a Catholic sit in Commons? Does a Catholic serve the king? An' I still got to take the ungodly oath if I want to buy my land—land that is really mine!" Tim McCarthy cried.

Everyone began speaking at once, clearly in furious agreement.

Sean held his hands up again. "One at a time."

"I ain't done," McCarthy said.

"Fine, do go on," Sean returned.

"We been meeting for two years now, and for what? We need to get them damned bloody British out of Ireland, yes we do, and the time is now! Because nothing will ever change unless we show 'em the day of steppin' on Catholics is over. We need to bloody a few noses and get all of our rights, just the way the French did!"

A huge cheer sounded.

Virginia bit her lip so as not to cry out. This sounded very dangerous—it sounded like treason. And what in God's name were Devlin and Sean doing there?

Virginia didn't know very much about Ireland, but she did know a lot about the revolution in France, which most Americans had fervently supported, at least until Napoleon had begun his campaign to conquer Europe. She wasn't sure what rights Tim McCarthy referred to, but she knew that Ireland was a part of Great Britain, and an Irishman shouldn't speak about driving the English from their midst. That sounded like an impending revolution to her. It was certainly seditious speech.

Suddenly Devlin stood. Before he could even step forward to join Sean, lusty cheers rang out. "O'Neill!" someone cried.

"The O'Neill," more men answered.

"O'Neill! O'Neill! Hurrah!" everyone boomed.

Virginia slammed back against the wall, shaken and shaking. Was Devlin involved in this unpatriotic, antigovernment conspiracy? But how could he be! He was a captain in the British navy!

Devlin had joined Sean on the dais. "May I?" he asked his brother, confirming Virginia's suspicion that Sean was in command of this group.

"They are waiting for your words of wisdom," Sean said seriously.

The room had become silent. Virginia gripped the sill and stared inside, mesmerized.

"I understand your frustrations," Devlin said slowly, his gaze roaming over the room, making eye contact slowly but surely with everyone there. "But a rebellion will only bring pain and death. My family knows that firsthand."

There were some grunts of agreement—and there were murmurs of anger as well.

"But what can we do?" someone cried. "I can't pay my rents, which are triple what they were last year!"

A chorus of agreement sounded.

Sean held up his hands for silence, and instantly the crowd became still. Devlin began to speak, his focus still moving from man to man—and that was when his gaze finally found Virginia.

His eyes widened.

As did hers.

Then she leapt away from the window and back against the wall. *Damn it!*

And then there was no more time for thought. As she began to sprint away from the house, she heard Sean adjourning the meeting. She ran across the clearing, tripped and fell. As she got up, she looked back.

Devlin was just a few lengths behind her. His expression was one of savage determination. And she realized that a dozen men were streaming out of the house, all angry, and a chorus began—a terribly frightening chorus.

"A spy! It's a spy! *An English spy!*"

Virginia bolted. In terror, she took another step when he leapt upon her from behind. The force of his tackle took them both instantly to the ground.

As she went down he twisted sideways and she landed in his arms instead of on the hard ground, where she would have surely broken a bone. A moment later she was on her back, however, and he was on top of her. "You followed me here?" he demanded, and she saw rage in his eyes.

And for the first time since he had captured the *Americana,* she felt real fear. "No! I was out riding—I saw your horse—I thought there was a party!" she cried.

"You little fool!" he gritted.

Virginia looked past his angry silver eyes. They were surrounded now by the angry mob of men, some of them holding muskets, others with pikes. Each and every man present looked as if he wanted to use his weapon on her. Sean stepped through the circle. "It's all right, boyos," he said lightly, smiling. "This is just a little misunderstanding."

Virginia's fear knew no bounds. She knew what she had witnessed and what she had heard. These men wanted to rise up against the English government and throw it out of Ireland. That was treason. She also knew what she had just seen in their expressions. She had seen far worse than anger—she had seen fear.

They were angry and desperate and they were afraid of what she knew.

"He's a spy!" someone shouted.

A rumble of affirmations sounded.

Virginia looked into Devlin's eyes, trying not to panic. He wouldn't let anything happen to her, would he?

He gave her a very angry look. Then he stood, hauling her to her feet.

"It's a wench," someone cried.

"Damned spy's a woman," someone else agreed.

"Miss Hughes is our guest and she is not a spy," Sean said, moving to stand protectively beside Virginia and Devlin.

Virginia nodded, wetting her lips, which felt parched and cracked. She stared into a sea of hostile, suspicious faces and saw their hatred. "I'm not a spy," she tried. "I saw Devlin's horse and—"

Devlin jerked on her, hurting her, a command that meant, "Be silent," and as he did so, someone said loudly, "She's English! The wench is English!"

Virginia started, although this was not the first time she had come face-to-face with people who had never met an American before and therefore assumed her unfamiliar accent to be British.

"Hang her." Tim McCarthy stepped forward. "She knows too much."

Virginia gasped and looked at Devlin but he ignored her, stepping forward. "There's not going to be a hanging, not of anyone, not today," he said calmly, but with an authority that only he could muster. "Miss Hughes is American, not English, and she's my fiancée."

The crowd was silent, but dozens of eyes had widened in surprise.

Virginia seized at the hope he offered. "Yes," she cried, stepping forward, "Devlin is my betrothed and I only came to—"

He took her wrist and almost snapped it off, but before she could cry out, he had jerked her forward and smothered her words with a kiss.

Virginia gasped. His mouth was hard and angry and hurtful. His arms felt like the iron bars of a prison cage, steel bands tight around her. She vaguely heard some mutters behind her, mutters about O'Neill having taken a bride. She tried to press him away, but his grip only tightened, his lips turning more ruthless, and that was when she felt his arousal.

It was red hot, leaving no doubt whatsoever as to his state of mind and body, and she instantly forgot about the terrible meeting she had just witnessed. Instead, as his mouth started to soften, causing her own lips to instinctively yield and part, she thought about Fiona. His tongue swept inside. *Fiona.*

Last night he had been in bed with Fiona.

Virginia bit down on it.

He jerked away from her, but he did not yelp or release her. Virginia stared furiously up at him—he stared as furiously back.

"Let me go," she murmured, low and threatening.

"Like hell, my sweet little bride." And he smiled and swooped down on her again. But this time, before he kissed her, he hissed, "Pretend you love me, *chérie,* as your life might well depend on it."

Virginia felt real despair, as his lips brushed her mouth, and worse, his hands slid so intimately over her back and lower still. But he was right. She was trapped. He pulled her closer still, perhaps thinking to punish her, for the surge of sensation engendered by contact with him was just that, unfair, unjust punishment. "Kiss me back," he ordered so only she could hear.

All the hurt she had thought safely tucked away in some far and distant place where it could never come back crashed over her now. She knew she should kiss him so that the onlookers would think their engagement real. She simply couldn't. It was impossible to kiss a man while crying.

And he knew. His body stiffened far differently, the tightening in his shoulders and spine; his roving hands went still, and his mouth, while covering hers, no longer sought to invade. Virginia finally managed a weak and pitiful closemouthed kiss.

He pulled away and looked closely at her.

She wanted to curse him to hell but did not dare, as the crowd had fallen silent. She felt a dozen pairs of suspicious eyes and she summoned up a smile that had to be as pathetic as it felt frail.

His stare intensified.

Someone cheered, "Captain O'Neill and his bride!"

The cry was taken up.

Devlin smiled coldly. He put his arm around her in such a way that she could not move an inch if he did not let her do so. He faced the crowd, which no longer seemed suspicious. "My little fiancée could not wait for me to return home," he said mockingly.

Rough male laughter sounded.

But McCarthy said, "Will she be sworn to secrecy, Captain?"

Devlin smiled coolly at him, with real warning. "She would never betray me, Tim."

He nodded slowly, not even looking at Virginia, his gaze hopeful and eager and riveted on their leader.

"Let's go," Sean said, appearing with his horse and Devlin's. He was smiling pleasantly, but Virginia saw the wariness in his gray eyes. For one moment, as his glance moved over her, she saw so much of Devlin in him. His gaze was as cold, his expression as controlled. She sensed a new wariness and some hostility. Was he suspicious of her? she wondered, surprised. Or was it the men in the meeting he did not trust?

Devlin's hands closed around her waist and before she

could protest she was seated on his stallion. He swung up behind her and the saddle was far too small for them both. She held her breath, for otherwise she would turn and quell him with a look. He didn't seem to notice as he spurred the gray forward.

"How did you get here?" he asked tightly, his breath feathering her ear.

So he was angry, she thought, thinking of Fiona again. Good, because she hated him and she always would. "I rode."

"Really? And who gave you permission to do so?"

"No one," she said snidely.

He was silent. As the bay mare had become visible, grazing farther up the hill, she knew he had seen her horse. He changed his horse's direction, causing them to canter toward the bay. "What is on your mind, Virginia?" he asked.

"Nothing," she snapped.

"Good, as I have no patience for you today." He halted abruptly beside the bay.

Virginia started to get down, but he wouldn't let her. "You are riding with me," he said, dismounting and untying the mare.

"Like hell I am!" she cried.

He stared at her. Slowly, he said, "I am the one who is angry, Virginia, as you were spying on me. How much did you hear?"

She lifted her chin. "Everything."

He smiled then, so ruthlessly that she shivered. "Then you may never leave Askeaton, my dear."

She gasped, "You don't mean it!"

"Oh, but I do."

"But, my ransom?"

"Your ransom pales in significance right now," he said. "And it is my duty to protect Sean and the others."

Her mind raced. "I didn't hear anything!"

He swung up behind her. "That's not what you just said."

"I lied. I really didn't hear anything!"

"Liar. Pretty little liar." He had yet to ask his mount to move. "Why didn't you kiss me when I told you to? Your life hung in the balance and that was an order, not a request."

"I don't take orders from you," she managed.

He finally looked very irritated, indeed. Then he asked, "And why did you cry?"

"I had dirt in my eyes," she flung.

He stared searchingly. "You are a terrible liar. I would not recommend dishonesty, Virginia, as you are as easy to read as a children's book."

"Then why am I angry?" she asked with false sweetness.

His prying gaze never wavered. "I don't know. But I will find out." Abruptly he spurred the gray forward.

Virginia would have fallen off except for his strong grasp, which tightened as the horse surged forward. She bit off her cry, as she refused now to give him any satisfaction at all. They rode the rest of the way back in a charged and uncomfortable silence.

SEAN WAS WAITING FOR HIM when he came into the library. He had his hip balanced against the edge of the desk, his arms folded across his chest. He was almost scowling. "What did you do with her?"

"She's in her room. Connor has orders to watch her every move."

"Maybe she should be kept under lock and key," Sean said tersely.

Devlin was almost amused. He poured himself a brandy, offering his brother one, who declined. "I thought you were her champion."

"How much did she hear?" Sean asked tersely, not amused.

"I don't know precisely, but I intend to find out—one way or another."

"Damn it!" Sean suddenly exploded, coming off the desk and pacing. "What the hell was she doing at Canaby's farm?"

"Probably following us," Devlin said.

"Now what are you going to do? For God's sake, you can't return her to Eastleigh now!"

Devlin sat down in a huge leather chair, stretching his legs out in front of him, glass in hand. "I'll have to return her sooner or later."

Sean stared, his gaze wide. "That meeting was treasonous and you know it, even if nothing has been planned. We could lose everything—and you, an officer in the navy, could wind up swinging from the nearest yardarm for this, never mind the damnable ransom you intend!"

"It's more likely they would chop off *your* head and stick it on a pike. You're their leader."

"Is that funny?" Sean was disbelieving. "They are looking for hope, Devlin, and I am trying to give it to them."

He sipped. "No, but it's odd, isn't it? Like father, like son."

"And now you choose to be morbid? I will not allow a rebellion. But Devlin, you are holding Virginia against her will. She has terrible information that she could use to bring us both down."

"What do you suggest? Should I send her to the bottom of the sea?" But Sean was right. Virginia needed to keep her mouth closed and her lips sealed, even though what she had seen looked far worse than what it was. He knew from Sean's letters how angry and desperate their people were and that once or twice a year they held local meetings. His arrival home had precipitated this one. Even if he hadn't been invited to attend, he would have done so. But the men were not planning an uprising. They were farmers and cotters, more interested in feeding their families than losing their lives. And while free speech was sedition in wartime Great Britain, everyone was encouraged to speak freely at these meetings. Tim McCarthy and the others had called a meeting mostly because they desperately wanted to hear what Devlin had to say. As Sean had said, they desperately needed hope.

Sean was pacing. Devlin wanted to calm his brother down. "Sean, you need not worry. I will not allow Virginia to bring the British down upon you and the others. If I have to, I will tell Virginia the truth. Our people are frustrated, angry and hungry, but we will not allow a futile armed struggle."

Sean did not appear reassured. "I do not think Virginia is in the mood to listen to anything that you might say."

"She'll listen," he said, instantly grim. What had been wrong with her that afternoon? Why had she been crying?

Sean hesitated. "Devlin, I have a solution, I think, as far as Virginia is concerned."

"Pray tell."

"One of us should marry her."

Devlin spilled his drink.

"I'm deadly serious."

He quickly placed the snifter on a small end table, wiping his hand on his britches. "And who is to have the honor of making Virginia a happy, loving, loyal wife? Oh, let me guess! That honor would be yours?"

"I would marry her if she were willing. But it's not me that she wants."

"I am not marrying that penniless American orphan, Sean," he warned. His heart was racing with alarming speed, as if he were about to sail his ship into a hurricane.

"Why not? After all, you are the one victimizing her, and only you can make this just."

"Are you serious?" Devlin could not get over his brother's suggestion. It was beyond absurd. Virginia was going to Eastleigh directly upon his receiving his ransom, and if her plantation home was sold, she would undoubtedly reside in England with her family.

"I said I am. I do not wish to lose Askeaton, and you certainly do not need to lose your head." Sean gave him a grim look, then continued the pacing he had left off.

"The one thing I am not about to lose is my head," Devlin said wryly. "Cease worrying. There will be no accusations from Miss Hughes."

Sean stared.

Devlin didn't like the unwavering look. "What is it?"

"If you will not marry her, then I want permission to court her."

Devlin started.

Sean began to flush. "I know you've had her in bed. I could lie and say I don't care, but I do. However, if it stops right here, I can live with that. Give me permission to court her, to win her over, to marry her."

"No."

Sean flinched.

Devlin hadn't even thought about it before refusing, and now, as angry as he was, his mind began to tell him that if the little American wanted to cause problems, Sean's idea wasn't a bad one. First he could ransom her and break Eastleigh, then Sean could marry her, undoubtedly winning her loyalty and love. The two of them could live happily ever after at Askeaton while he was gone.

But Sean could do better, and Devlin intended for that to be so.

"So even though I wish to marry her, your desire to have her as a plaything usurps my wishes?" Sean asked coolly.

Devlin did not hesitate. "My desire is for you to marry

a wealthy heiress so you may raise yourself up in this world."

Sean strode to him. "Is it? Is it really? Because I don't think so. I think you are speaking with your prick. Think about it. Really think about it and then give me your answer." He stalked out.

Devlin stared thoughtfully after him, the rush of anger receding. Sean was wrong—he did not intend for Virginia to be his plaything—and damn it, Sean's idea was actually clever. And the man who had made a fortune from the bloody ashes of nothing knew it was worth consideration. He lifted his snifter and stared at the contents, trying not to think about Virginia thrashing wildly in his bed, trying not to recall the feel of her slim little body, her soft, wet lips. *Why not let Sean at her?* At least his intentions were noble ones. And Virginia truly deserved a fine man like his brother. She certainly did not deserve what he was doing to her.

He was so tense he felt like he might snap, so he stood, but there was no relief.

A marriage between Virginia and Sean would solve so many problems. In fact, it would even cover up the crimes he had committed and his life could continue this way indefinitely.

And his life seemed to stretch ahead infinitely, like the bleak gray line of one of the old Roman roads, a strip of nothingness, never used, impossibly dismal, impossibly insignificant, joyless, flat, with no possible end in sight.

Devlin walked to the window overlooking the back lawns, suddenly shaken. He would rather die tomorrow, a murderer and a cutthroat, than live out the interminable travesty that was his life.

CHAPTER ELEVEN

AS PUNISHMENT FOR HER CRIMES, she hadn't been allowed out of her room the entire day or even downstairs for supper. Virginia had been sent her repast on a silver tray. She had simmered in rage all afternoon at the absolute injustice of her sentence. She had only gone for a morning ride. How was she to know that she would be uncovering some kind of secret, political, anti-British society? Had she known what was going on in that farmhouse, she would have stayed away! It was all O'Neill's fault, for bedding that fat Fiona, anyway. Had he not been such a cad, she would not have gone riding so far and for so long. Consumed by such thoughts, she was simply unable to enjoy the cook's fine stuffed pheasant and roasted salmon, which she barely touched.

Had he meant his terrible and disturbing threat, that he would not let her leave Askeaton if she had seen all that she had? Virginia shivered. He had gone to great lengths to abduct her so he could ransom her, and she seriously doubted he would give all of that up.

He had said he had to protect Sean and the others. Protect them from what? Being convicted as traitors to their country?

Virginia stood at an open window in her cotton night-gown, not having bothered to braid her hair, her supper tray removed a long time ago. The night was filled with a thousand shining stars. She knew she gazed toward the river, even though she could not see it, and beyond that lay the Atlantic Ocean and home.

A terrible heaviness engulfed her. She wanted to go home. The feeling of being homesick took her by surprise; it was as vast and consuming as it had been when she had been locked away at the Marmott School in Richmond.

Virginia tucked her chin on her hand. Now she was locked away at Askeaton. Of course she would be homesick, because until this past year, she had never been anything but free to go and do as she wished. Growing up the way that she had, she hadn't realized how lucky she was. She realized it now. If only she had said thank you to her parents for all their love, for their confidence in her, for allowing her to wear britches, ride astride and help Father run the plantation.

A knock sounded on her door.

Virginia thought it was Connor, who remained ridiculously outside of her door, guarding her as if she were a dangerous felon. Perhaps he was leaving to go to his bed for the night. If so, she might be tempted to climb out the window, steal the bay mare and simply run as far away as she could.

Virginia wasn't given a chance to answer. Devlin walked into her bedroom.

For one moment she was shocked. "Get out!" Virginia cried, her rage erupting.

He stared at her, so inscrutable that it was impossible to guess what was on his mind. "We have matters to discuss," he said carefully.

She strode back to the bed and reached for the closest object on the bed stand, finding a water pitcher there. Hefting it, she turned to throw it at him. She hoped to hit him in the head and, if she were lucky, murder him on the spot.

He leapt forward before she could hurl the object, gripping her wrist and causing her to cry out. "Put it down," he warned.

"I'll put it down." She bared her teeth at him. "I'll put it down on your head." She tried to jerk free. Suddenly nothing was as important as breaking his grasp and slamming the pitcher on his head. Images of him and Fiona, starkly naked, passionately entwined, fueled her as nothing else could.

"Stop it, Virginia," he said quietly, tightening his grip on her wrist.

Virginia glared at him, afraid she was going to start to cry, and said, "Fine." She dropped the pitcher, hoping it would land on his foot, and if not, that it would break.

It didn't land on his foot, but it was heavy Waterford crystal, and the handle chipped, the water sloshing over her bare feet and his boots.

"I take it you are still angry?" he asked, easing his hold but not releasing her.

She snorted derisively. "How clever you are, Captain. Now, let me go, you are hurting me."

"You also sound bitter," he remarked, and she saw his glance go once, quickly and in such a manner that it was barely perceptible, past the ruffled edge of her bodice. She knew what he was about—he was looking at her breasts.

Virginia yanked her arm hard to pull away, but failed. "Why should I be bitter? I was on my way to London to take care of the most urgent and personal affairs, when I was abducted off of my ship. I have since been locked in your cabin, at your mercy, and now I am locked in this bedroom. Bitter? Oh, no."

"I want to speak with you. If you think to attack me again, you will be locked in this bedroom for an entire week."

She met his cold gaze. "You are every bit the bastard that everyone says you are."

He shrugged, releasing her.

She jumped away and felt her buttocks hit the edge of the bed. She did not like being trapped between him and the bed, not at all.

"You are angrier with me now than you were when I first seized the *Americana*. You were crying this afternoon and now again. Why? And do not tell me there is dirt in your eyes."

"This time it's the *dust*," she said with false sweetness. "Now, get out of my bedroom, O'Neill!"

"I think not." He studied her, unsmiling and far too carefully.

"But Fiona is waiting." The moment the caustic words slipped out, she regretted them and winced.

He went still. But she saw the spark of surprise in his eyes.

She flushed and she slipped aside, away from the bed and away from him. She walked across the room to the fireplace, where she pretended to be fascinated with the flames. Oh, why had she just said that? Now he would think her upset, jealous even, when she was not. She was glad, fiercely so, that he had reunited with his love.

"What did you just say?" he asked.

She folded her arms tightly beneath her breasts and stared at the flames. Tears hazed her vision. *Why? Just tell me why? Don't you owe me that?*

She never heard him come up behind her and she jumped when his hand enclosed her elbow from behind. "What did you say?" he asked again.

"Nothing." She firmly pressed her lips together, but her heart slammed wildly and she hated being so aware of him, standing behind her.

"No, you said that Fiona is waiting. Waiting where? For whom?" His tone was without inflection.

She whirled to face him. A tiny voice inside of her head warned her not to say what she wished to, but she ignored it. "I don't care if she is in your bed, Devlin. In fact, I am relieved! 'Oh, how big it is, I can hardly fit it in my hand!'" she mimicked.

His eyes flew wide, and she saw him truly surprised, perhaps for the very first time.

"'Oh, he is so tireless, like a stud!'" she spat, aware that her cheeks were flaming. "'Ohhh! I am sooo in love!'" She glared.

He was silent.

She had a terrible suspicion and she looked more closely at him and saw that he was amused, goddamn him, for she saw the light of mirth in his eyes. "So you are angry with me because I took some maid to my bed?" he asked quietly. "You are jealous of Fiona?"

She cut him off. "I am not jealous! I am *relieved.* And I think you are in the *wrong* bedroom now." She smiled widely—falsely—at him.

He regarded her for a long moment.

"Say something!" she shouted.

"I abducted you off of the American ship. I have tried to treat you as I would any guest, but we both know you're being held here against your will. You should be relieved that I eased myself with some inconsequential housemaid, Virginia."

He was choosing his words with so much care and it was obvious. Virginia knew she should be as careful, but she couldn't. "I am relieved, I told you already, and I think you should go back to her this very moment!" she cried, and horrified, she felt tears welling.

He didn't speak.

"Why are you staring at me as if I am a madwoman?" she asked, her mortification growing because her tone was a choke-filled sob.

"I don't understand you," he said softly. "You're my prisoner. How can you be jealous? That would imply that you have feelings for me, your captor."

"I'm not jealous." She turned away, perilously close to allowing those forming tears to fall.

He seized her arm, reeling her back around. "How could I have hurt you?"

"You haven't!" she lied, furiously batting back the tears.

"You're crying—again."

"I'm not. I don't care about you and I don't care that you prefer Fiona," she said. "Please don't touch me."

But as he released her, he also cupped her chin. "Only a foolish man would prefer the maid to you."

She was sure she hadn't heard him correctly. "What?"

"I don't prefer her. In fact, I had forgotten all about her." He hesitated. "I am sorry she spoke so freely to you, Virginia. I had also forgotten that I gave you your very first kiss."

They had never spoken so sincerely before. Virginia bit her lip, then had to say, "But I didn't forget."

His jaw flexed. "I wanted to discuss some important matters with you, but this is clearly not the time."

She shook her head, touching his sleeve. "I thought you liked me," she heard herself say, and it was as if she were a little girl begging to understand.

He was so motionless it was as if he did not even breathe. Very quietly, after a long pause, he said, "Men use women all the time. It means nothing. It is a means to an end. Fiona was eager to service me. I didn't go to her. I didn't seek her out. I can't even recall what she looks like, except that she is fat. But I needed the release physically.

I am sorry if I made you jealous, that was not my intention. To be truthful, I had forgotten entirely about the incident."

She shook her head, incapable of understanding, and now tears wet her cheeks. "I thought you liked me."

And two pale spots of pink seemed to appear briefly on his cheekbones. "You're a beautiful woman. I am hardly immune to that and we both know it."

She stared up at him, suddenly aware of her heart pounding, slow and deep, suddenly aware of how late it was, how dark, how quiet, and suddenly aware that the desire had never died. She was alone with Devlin in her room, which was lit only by a few candles and the fire in the hearth, and he had just admitted that he found her beautiful.

"Do you want me still?" she whispered, but somehow she knew the answer.

His gaze held hers, unflinching. "Yes."

She leaned forward. "Then I still do not understand, Devlin. Why leave me and go to her? I was in your arms—"

"I didn't go to her. She was waiting in my room, Virginia, and I had forgotten she was there."

"Why did you leave me?" she cried, her hands on his chest.

He finally smiled, though it was slight and filled with self-deprecation. "I am the son of Mary and Gerald O'Neill," he said, as if that explained everything. But he didn't move away from her. She felt his chest rising and falling beneath her palms, more quickly than was natural, and she felt his heart there, too, pounding, becoming erratic.

"That explains nothing."

"I had a sister once," he said, his jaw flexing hard. "Had

she survived, she might have been like you—a planter's daughter, a defiant and outspoken woman, someone brave and beautiful."

And Virginia finally understood. "You were trying to respect me and your sister's memory and your parents' teachings."

He didn't speak.

"So you left me in order to save my innocence. Fiona was in your room when you went up—she means nothing," she breathed.

"I see you are becoming a woman of the world," he said. He took her hands and removed them from his person. "Nothing has changed. My resolve remains. I am not going to seduce you and I will not be your first lover. Good night."

He was actually walking away, across the room, toward the door. It flashed through Virginia's mind that the hussy would be in his bed once more, if she wasn't there already. She could not bear that thought—just as she could not bear the thought of his leaving her now.

"I don't want your respect," she heard herself say.

He faltered, but did not turn.

"I want to know what it's like, Devlin," she added softly, her heart racing madly, heat etching its way down her thighs, up her belly, through her breasts.

He made a harsh sound and reached for the door.

She swallowed and said, "Show me. Show me everything that you can, now, tonight—show me, not her."

He whirled, eyes wide, face strained. "Have you no self-control?" he asked harshly.

"Why should I struggle with it?" And she saw what she had been hoping to see. Virginia walked over to him, grasped his shoulders and leaned into his hard, aroused body. "Self-control is for ladies like Sarah Lewis," she whispered.

For one moment she saw the indecision in his eyes; for one moment she saw the battle he waged. She smiled a little and touched his cheek, her heart beating frantically, like the wings of a caged bird. "Devlin."

At once, his arms closed around her and his mouth covered hers. Virginia cried out, and when she felt the rigid line of his erection she began to whimper. His hands moved lower, large and bold. His powerful body was rigid with tension. "Hurry," she managed, as the daze of lust heightened and grew. "Devlin, hurry!"

She was suddenly in his arms and he was laying her down on the bed. "I have never met a woman like you," he said, their gazes locking.

She tried to grin at him and failed. "Good."

He didn't smile, either. His eyes were ablaze. He pushed her open thighs apart with each knee and said, "I wanted this last night."

She remembered instantly and she cried, "Yes."

He released her hands and abruptly ripped her nightgown in two.

Stunned, Virginia stilled, almost afraid, and she saw him look over every inch of her naked body, from the small globes of her breasts with their hard, stiff tips to the delta between her spread thighs, and there, his gaze lingered.

She began to flush, as she had never been exposed like this before. She felt frighteningly vulnerable. She felt powerless—she was at his mercy—and oddly, it made it impossible to breathe. She could only yearn, her desire impossibly heightened.

"You are so beautiful...little one," he murmured thickly, finally lifting his eyes to hers. "I won't hurt you."

Virginia knew she would never forget his eyes. She knew she had been a fool to worry about Fiona. She knew, somehow, instinctively and without a doubt, in that single span of time, that this man wanted her the way he would never want another woman. She knew his desire rivaled hers.

His mouth seemed to twist and Virginia gasped when he cupped her sex. "This belongs to me," he said softly, a warning.

She could only nod, shocked by the barbaric statement. Then his hand eased and she felt his fingers sliding over each full lip and into the crevasse between.

Virginia cried out, eyes closing, arching helplessly up against him. "Devlin,'" she chanted. "Oh, Devlin, do help me!"

His explorations increased, his fingers opened her wide, sliding over slick recess after slick fold, until Virginia was certain she could not stand it. Then she felt his mouth.

At first she thought she was mistaken and she stiffened, paralyzed, eyes flying open—surely he was not kissing her there. She half sat up and saw, shocked, that his head was between her thighs, and there was no mistaking now that it was his lips nibbling hers.

Then she felt his tongue.

A caress beyond any other.

Virginia's vision blackened.

That tongue moved deep and sure, patting the turgid nub of flesh hidden in the broader folds there. Virginia began to faint, the desire so great it was overwhelming her every sense, her ability to breathe, the ability for her blood to go to her brain.

"Come for me, little one," he murmured. His tongue flayed her swollen flesh like a silken whiplash, insistent, brutal, soft, determined.

The blackness lingered and then she was hurled past it, into brilliant light. Virginia held him, sobbing in sheer joy, in stunning pleasure, in ultimate ecstasy. She sobbed and sobbed as he flayed and flayed until finally, she began to float.

She didn't know how long she floated outside of herself in the clouds, but slowly, she became aware of her body again. Every inch of her femininity remained swollen and inflamed, his tongue continued to caress her flesh, his lips moved ceaselessly, in a raw frenzy, as if he were kissing her mouth. Now, with the pleasure, there was pain.

She didn't know if she could stand it again. "Devlin," she breathed.

He didn't stop. His tongue swept up and down, like a starving dog's.

"Devlin," she begged now, the pain vast, and she wanted him to stop, but she also wanted him to continue, harder, because she knew which universe beckoned.

She tried to push him away, but his tongue merely swept deeper; she tried to pull him closer, but he only nipped her, a warning she understood.

"I can't," she gasped, pain and pleasure mingling so tightly now she didn't know if she were living or dying, and she didn't know where the one began and the other ended.

"You can, darling, you can," he choked, and he pinned both heavy folds back with his fingertips and then his tongue encircled the turgid nub, distending it, and she screamed.

He softened and she exploded.

A hundred times, like Independence Day fireworks, her body spinning, tumbling, out of control, flying away, high in the universe. And she was still there when his mouth found hers, his body crushing her into the mattress.

"Virginia," he panted.

Instantly, she felt the huge tip of him against her entrance and she jerked, eyes flying wide, meeting his. She

saw the beast of lust and nothing more in his hot gaze—
she did not see love.

"Virginia." Somehow her name was spoken as a
command and he kissed her deeply and she tasted sex for
the first time. His hard thighs pinned hers down and apart,
and suddenly he was probing against her.

Panic came. *He was too big. She was only eighteen. He
was her captor. She was afraid and she wasn't ready. What
if he didn't love her!*

But his heat was searing into her body and her brain.

"Devlin, don't," she began.

But it was simply too late. Crying out, he thrust into her,
breaking down the barrier of her virginity, causing a brief,
burning pain, and then she felt the huge, hot hardness
inside of her, filling her, hurting her. Stiffening, she closed
her eyes, blinking back tears of sudden despair.

He gasped, not moving, his entire body shaking.
Virginia remained stunned, capable only of feeling him
stretching her apart. Devlin remained still but shaking,
when he suddenly kissed her temple. Her eyes opened,
wide. "Devlin?" she whispered, wondering if she had
imagined his tender kiss.

His only answer was to tighten his hold and she became
aware of being wrapped in his powerful arms, of being
immersed there, and then she felt the insistent throbbing
inside of her own body, huge and hard, but the pain was dis-
sipating. An answering warmth unfurled slowly inside of
her. She felt his mouth move again, this time on her cheek,
and then he moved.

Very slowly, he pulled away, and as slowly, he eased
back inside her. Her body was softening, warming,
tensing—intensely, brilliantly. "Oh," she gasped, surprised,
as he filled her again.

She thought she felt him smile against her face. "Breathe,

little one," he whispered, thrusting again, not quite as slowly.

And as the massive man filled her, so completely, so thoroughly, a tidal wave of intense pleasure swept over her, taking her by surprise. Stunned, the pleasure threatening to turn black, she raised her hands to his shoulders, rippling now, and his back.

He made a sound, choked and hoarse, male.

Virginia's hips found an answering rhythm. She wanted him deeper, faster, harder. She urged him to take more. And he knew, breathing her name, somehow penetrating impossibly, the spasms beginning, for her, for him, and suddenly the man moving within her began to carry her across the bed, across time and space, as the fever of need became a crushing urgency. Virginia cried out, grasping his shoulders, an instant from ecstasy, trying to find his mouth with hers. "Hurry, Devlin, hurry!" she moaned.

He was driving hard and fast now and he turned to take her mouth in another mating as urgent and frenzied as the other one.

Virginia felt her body break apart into a million pieces. Even so, she was aware of the exact moment he gave her his seed—she felt him expand impossibly, then she felt his body convulsing in her arms just as it convulsed inside of her, and she held him tightly, stroking his back, as he simply kept coming.

When he was done, she lay very still, stunned, impossibly aware of the man who lay heavily on top of her, who remained inside of her, half as hard now, half as huge, and she held him in her arms, moved in a way she had never dreamed of.

This was right, she thought, remaining stunned. No wonder she had wanted him so. Nothing was more right than this moment, lying there in his arms, sated and replete, still joined as if one.

She felt the moment he was himself again. His body tensed; he shifted and moved away from her, breaking the union of their bodies.

She lay very still, and unable to help herself, she turned only her head to look at him.

He lay on his back, his eyes closed, still completely clothed, although his britches were open and his shirt askew. His chest rose and fell harshly. She stared at his perfect profile, already strained with emotions she dared not guess at. But she knew he was already thinking.

"Devlin?" she whispered, suddenly worried. She was on the verge of a great happiness, and surely she need not worry now! Not after what they had just done, the beauty of what they had just shared. Surely he was feeling what she was, too.

But he did not answer her and he did not open his eyes.

She knew he was not asleep. Suddenly she wished that he would reach out and stroke her arm, her hair, anything, smile just a little and reassure her that he, too, was feeling simply wonderful.

The bed dipped as he sat up. She also sat, expecting him to turn to her, to say something, and she waited, but he stood, not looking at her—not even once. She glimpsed his expression, and she thought she saw his features rigid and strained with displeasure, and perhaps, with anger.

"Devlin?" she whispered again, and heard how fragile and pleading her tone did sound.

There was the rustle of cloth as he fastened his britches and tucked in his shirt. He finally glanced at her, his face smooth and expressionless. "Go to sleep, Virginia," he said.

She stared, his dispassionate words as painful as the stabbing of a knife.

"It's late," he added, his brief smile forced.

Oh, God, what was he thinking? Why was he behaving as if nothing had happened? Why wasn't he happy?

"Devlin," she began, suddenly panicked.

But he was crossing the room, he was leaving.

"Devlin?" She could not believe he would leave without a meaningful word, kiss, or even a look.

But at the door he paused, not turning to look at her. "I'm sorry I hurt you," he said.

She knew he referred to the physical invasion of his large body into her small, narrow one, and she was finally disbelieving.

He walked out.

HE WAS A MAN ON A MISSION. He traversed the house with hard, purposeful strides, refusing to think. He only knew one thing. *Never again.*

He had failed to keep the vow he had made, to her and himself, and he had failed his parents, both alive and dead—he had failed. In the end he had been caught up in a hunger that was impossible to control or resist. He had never felt such urgency before and he was never going to feel it again.

Never again.

He stood before Sean's closed bedroom door. He did not see the wood there—he saw only violet eyes, wide and glazed, and he heard only her wild cries of pleasure, her begging for more. *What was wrong with him?* A woman was only a vessel. Elizabeth, Fiona, they were objects to be used. Goddamn it. *When he was inside of her, something had begun to break apart inside of him, something had begun to tear apart, almost like a dying man in an endless black tunnel, finally glimpsing the shadow of faraway light and life.*

He didn't like it.

He didn't like it one bit.

Never again.

He realized he was standing in front of his brother's door. He could still hear Virginia's cries, he could still taste her, he could even smell her, all over him. *If he dared, he could walk through the blackness and seize that faraway light.*

The idea shimmered, beckoned. Devlin shoved his terrible thoughts aside and focused on a far more important matter. What if he had gotten her pregnant?

He reminded himself that he wouldn't be around to find out.

His mind was ruthlessly made up. If anything, the thought of her being pregnant confirmed his decision. He banged upon the door twice.

Sean answered it, clad only in his drawers and looking as if he had been soundly asleep. But he took one look at Devlin and his eyes widened.

Devlin meant to smile at him. Nothing was more impossible. "Fine," he said.

"What?" Sean asked, shock in his gaze, for he clearly knew what his brother had just done.

"You have my permission to court Virginia. Court her, woo her, win her love, it's all the same to me—but in the end, you will marry her."

Sean gaped.

Devlin slammed the door in his face.

CHAPTER TWELVE

VIRGINIA ALMOST WEPT.

She no longer felt eighteen, never mind that she was a woman now—the little girl she'd once been had returned, bewildered and hurt. She lay in bed, desperately trying to understand what had just happened. She had just let Devlin O'Neill make love to her. She had let the man who had abducted her and who was holding her prisoner make love to her, and it had been everything she had expected and more. But he had walked out a moment ago as if their lovemaking meant nothing to him.

She refused to cry. Instead she tried to understand him, she tried to make excuses for him. It was late. He was tired. For all she knew, the act exhausted men. Tomorrow he would really smile at her, and he would pull her aside to kiss her and hold her and tell her that he was falling in love.

Virginia moaned. She sat up, absolutely ill with dread. Who was she fooling? She didn't even know the stranger whom she had allowed such complete possession of her body. And what she did know of him did not allow much hope. He was a brave man, but he was also hard and cold. He had just left her bed without a single affectionate gesture or word. And last night he'd been with a different woman. *What had she done?*

Why had she enticed him into her bed? Virginia knew

very well that she had seduced him, never mind how in-experienced she was. Now she simply failed to understand how she could have done such a thing. He was her captor, a man with an iron heart, if any. *But dear God, it had been more than wonderful, it had been right.* Yet she was so shaken now, so confused, at once sick and desperate and even afraid. Never had she felt so lost and alone.

If only he had said something kind to her before he'd so abruptly left.

If only he had kissed or held her, if only there had been one sweet caress.

If only...

And finally, a single tear slipped down her cheek.

Angrily she brushed it away. She was a strong woman and she would not cry over something she had so wanted! Besides, maybe tomorrow he would really smile at her, and that would be enough. One smile to show her that he did care, just a little, after all.

Virginia realized that she was terrified to face him again.

She was terrified that he would not be kind, or worse, that he would be indifferent.

Virginia turned onto her back again. In the morass of her confusion and fear, only one thing was clear. She should go home. If she went home, everything would be all right again. Wouldn't it?

But she didn't even know if she still had a home, and if she somehow did leave Ireland, what about Devlin O'Neill?

She closed her eyes. What if she never saw him again?

Too late, Virginia realized that she could not bear the notion.

VIRGINIA WAS NOT SURPRISED to find her door unlocked, with no one standing in the hall outside. She glanced down the deserted corridor, straining to hear. Yesterday he'd put

Connor on duty outside her door. Clearly her punishment was over, but then, it should be, after what had happened last night.

It was noon. She had not been able to sleep until dawn and had overslept as a result. Carefully dressed in a high-necked gray gown, Virginia went downstairs, filled with tension, so nervous she felt sick. Were they lovers now? *Was she Devlin O'Neill's lover?*

What would he say and do when they first came face-to-face after all that they had done last night, all that they had shared?

Virginia was terrified of their first encounter. She reminded herself to look him in the eye, smile cheerfully and greet him as if nothing had happened—as if she was not scared to death of what he might say and do. She reminded herself that she must carefully feel him out without giving him a clue as to her own feelings. Because if he was not pleasant, she did not want him to know how much she was affected by their lovemaking. She did not want him to guess the extent of her feelings. In fact, she herself was afraid to admit what might be in her heart.

The house was silent, as if nobody was present. Virginia glanced into the dining room and saw that the breakfast buffet had long since been removed. She was very hungry, but she would ignore it.

His study was down the hall. Virginia's steps quickened until she had to remind herself not to run, to slow down, to *breathe*. To her surprise, the study door was wide open and the room was empty.

Dismayed, she stared at the huge desk where she had seen him working. Then she started into the adjacent salon, but that was empty, too. She hurried to the French doors that let onto the brick terrace and stared at the sweeping lawns. She saw a horse and rider approaching.

Virginia left the house quickly, choosing to do so by way of the terrace. Her heart raced with an anticipation she could not hold at bay. Clouds scudded across the sky and she knew it would be a fine day for sailing. She could almost hear him saying so. She smiled, imagining him on the quarterdeck of the *Defiance*.

The rider had yet to come close enough for her to make him out. She paused before the stables, waiting nervously, wringing her hands. Then she caught a glimpse of gray and white from the corner of her eye and she glanced into the barn. To her surprise, she saw his gray stallion was in his stall.

If he hadn't gone riding, where was he? Her heart beat like a jungle drum now. Perhaps he had taken a different horse, she thought, suddenly worried and not quite knowing why. Virginia came out of the barn and she faltered. It was Sean who was dismounting in the courtyard, not Devlin.

She managed to take a steadying breath and plant a smile on her face before approaching. "Good day, Sean," she said brightly.

"Good afternoon," he said, not glancing at her. He handed the chestnut to a young groom. "Walk him until he's cool, Brian, then a nice hot bran will do."

"Yes, sir," the boy said, leading the sweaty horse away.

Virginia continued to smile while her pulse leapt so wildly it made her feel faint. "Did you have a pleasant ride?" she asked.

"Yes," he said, walking abreast of her but staring past her, at the house.

Alarm began. Virginia walked with him, staring at his hard profile, a profile incredibly similar to Devlin's. He seemed sunburned—either that or he was flushed. And it was clear he did not want to look at her.

She swallowed, her first thought being that he somehow knew of the affair last night. But she quickly reassured herself that he could not know. Her bedroom was in one wing, his in the other. But his behavior was so different. He was grim and subdued instead of cheerful and loquacious. "Is everything all right?" she asked cautiously.

"Yes." He finally glanced at her. Then his gaze slammed to her mouth and away.

Virginia's mouth was bruised, her lips were swollen, and she felt certain he not only saw, but understood completely.

She did not want him to know about her fall from grace. "Have you seen Devlin?" she asked, and to her horror, her voice sounded far too high and on the verge of hysteria.

"Yes." Sean seemed angry now. His strides increased, leaving Virginia behind.

She had to run to catch up. "He doesn't seem to be in the house and—"

"He's not here."

She halted. "What?"

Ahead of her, Sean did not pause. "He's gone."

Her mind froze over. She croaked, "Gone?"

Sean suddenly turned, the action violent. "He left. He's not here," he said, his face mottled with a red flush.

She swallowed hard. "What do you mean, Sean?" How hard it was to get the words out. But she somehow knew.

His furious gaze clashed with hers. "He went to London this morning."

Virginia cried out. And for one moment, her world grayed, darkened, became black.

And when her vision cleared, she was in Sean's arms, and he was peering worriedly at her. She started to push him weakly away.

He didn't allow it, holding her upright on her feet, a strong arm braced behind her back. "You were about to faint."

She met his gaze, aware that hers was brimming with tears. *"He went to London?"*

Sean nodded, his expression very grim, his gaze dark with anguish.

And her heart cracked open. Again and again, until it bled, raw. *He had left. He hadn't said goodbye. He hadn't cared enough to say goodbye. He was gone.* "Is he coming back?" she whispered.

"I don't know," Sean said. "He said he will send word."

She stared, her body shaking, her mouth trembling. The eighteen-year-old woman was gone. A tiny child was left in her place, broken and bewildered, abandoned and alone and so very afraid.

"I'm sorry," Sean suddenly cried. "I could kill him with my bare hands, my own brother, a monster I do not understand!"

She cried out, fighting tears now, refusing to weep. *He simply did not care that they had made love. He was gone.*

"I know what he did to you, Virginia. I am so sorry."

She met Sean's gray eyes, eyes that were so like his brother's except that they mirrored compassion and regret and even guilt. He was holding her hands tightly.

"You know?" she whispered, tears seeping.

He nodded. "I saw him last night. It was obvious. But your secret is safe here."

She closed her eyes and shrugged. "I don't care. It's better this way. If Eastleigh thinks to marry me off to some stranger, now I can simply tell the truth about what happened and no one will have me." But she did care. She was in pain, terrible pain, and she had to go away, she had to be alone.

"Don't do this to yourself. This was not your fault. You are young and inexperienced, a perfect target for someone like Devlin. How could a girl like yourself resist my brother's seduction?" His laughter was harsh. "It is times like these that I detest him. He is better off gone and we should hope he never returns."

"You don't mean that," she managed.

"I feel that way now, as I have all night. The truth is, he is my brother, he would give his life for me, and I do love him. But I will never forgive him for this." Sean's eyes were as dark as a stormy sea.

The immense betrayal struck her again. *He was gone.* He had taken her innocence, and now, he had left. *He didn't care.* Not about anyone, not about anything. *He was a monster, not a man.* "I have to sit down," Virginia choked. "My knees are oddly weak and I cannot see."

"You appear as if you will faint again," Sean said grimly, sweeping her into his arms. He carried her to the house.

Virginia had no will to resist. It was too late to do anything about it, but she realized her heart was broken because she had, stupidly, fallen in love with a terrible man.

VIRGINIA LOST TRACK OF THE DAYS. It began to rain, more often than not. Sean gave her free rein and she spent her mornings on horseback while the sky remained clear. Her afternoons were spent wandering the house or reading one of the many books she found in the library. Sean went out of his way to avoid her when once he had been so gallant, amiable and kind. He was courteous when their paths happened to cross, but distant, as if a stranger. Virginia took her supper on a tray in her bedroom.

She thought about escape and made the attempt one single time. She found some coins in Sean's bedroom, where she dared to trespass. Dressed as a boy, she took the bay mare and set out for Wexford, some hundred miles to the east. It was another gray, rainy day. She had expected to be able to find her way quite easily, but at the first cross-roads, she was at a loss, for there was no sign. The choice was north or south, and Wexford lay directly east. She surmised she should go right, which was north. Many hours later she realized she was heading directly north, deep into the heart of Ireland, and that somehow, she was lost. She was also soaking wet and freezing cold, enough so to think about turning around and going back. And the little mare was tired and beginning to falter. But she didn't have to turn back. Late that afternoon Virginia paused at a roadside inn to ask for directions, which only confirmed that she was far off her course. And that was when Sean appeared on a black charger, frantic and furious. But instead of shouting at her, he didn't say a word. He booked two rooms and Virginia was given a hot bath, clean dry clothes and a hearty meal. The next day they returned to Askeaton, riding the entire way in terse silence.

And when the manor lay in sight, Sean pulled his steed to a halt. Virginia halted also and their gazes locked. "I want your word," he said fiercely. "Give me your word you will not attempt another escape. If you do not, I will have to put you under lock and key."

This was their first real conversation since the day Devlin had left. "I don't understand," Virginia said slowly. "You have said repeatedly that you disapprove of what your brother is doing, yet you will not look the other way so I can escape?"

He was grim. "I more than disapprove. But I swore to Devlin I would keep you safe at Askeaton and I will."

"You don't have the backbone to go up against him," she said.

His expression hardened and his eyes flashed. "He wants us to marry."

Virginia choked. Surely she had misheard, hadn't she?

But the walls of her world, already so fragile, crumbled then and there. *"What!"*

"He thinks it would be best, in the end, after the ransom, if we wed," Sean said.

Virginia could not absorb the words, the notion. She spurred the mare into a gallop, racing for the manor and the surrounding barns, reeling from the blow. *She was to be handed off to his brother. He had used her once and now he thought to cast her off to Sean.*

At the house she dismounted, handing the mare over to a groom. Sean galloped up to her and slid off his horse. "I know. It's inexplicable."

"Stay away from me," she warned, striding toward the house. She felt as if she had been punched in the chest. She couldn't breathe and a red haze had formed over her eyes. Pain and anger blurred, impossible to separate.

If she hadn't hated him before, she hated him now.

And images from that night overcame her, heated and lusty, images she wished were a result of her imagination and not the very real past.

She could not wait to be ransomed.

That night, Sean came to her room. Standing in the hallway, he politely asked her if she would come downstairs to dine. Virginia stared at him from the sanctuary of her bedroom, clinging to the open door. He looked grim, an expression now characteristic for him, and he also seemed torn. "Don't do this," she said.

"I'm not doing anything. But after what he did, I treated you intolerably. I want to start over. I am not the enemy, Virginia. The truth is, I am your friend."

She hugged herself. Their gazes locked. "Why did you turn away from me when I was so broken—when I needed a friend?" she whispered.

He hesitated. "Because it hurt me, too."

It was a moment before she thought she understood. Was Sean saying that he had feelings for her, and that Devlin's seduction had made it impossible for him?

He smiled gently. "I think it's time we had a truce. Besides, it's damned lonely in that dining room, night after night. I miss your amusing stories."

She was touched. She plucked his sleeve. "I'm sorry, too. It's not you I hate."

"I know."

Weeks passed into a month, then two. She dined with Sean every evening, and within a few weeks, the tension had disappeared and it was almost as if his brother had never done what he had. Virginia began to look forward to each evening when they would share a fine supper, good wine and never run out of conversation. Sean worked hard managing the estate, and during those evenings, his discourse would include the problems he had encountered and the triumphs, great and small. Virginia quickly learned all about the Corn Laws and how they had saved Ireland; by the month's end she knew as much about that crop as she did about tobacco. Frequently their conversation became political. Liverpool, a man who Sean apparently thought a great deal of, had formed a new cabinet and was now prime minister. In mid-August they both read the *Dublin Times,* learning that the United States had declared war on Great Britain in June, even though the Orders in Council had been repealed. British forces had taken Mackinac, a small settlement in the northwest, and a British squadron had captured the USS *Nautilus.*

Virginia was stunned. "How can your country think to reduce us to colonial status again?" she cried.

"We hardly think to reduce the United States to being our colonies again," Sean had replied. "We did not want this war—our hands are full in Europe. Your war hawks are responsible for this, Virginia."

Virginia knew something about American politics but little about war hawks. "My father was a very intelligent man and he said repeatedly that Britain has no respect for our rights, that she wishes to regain her status as a mother country and she will never allow us free trade! How many American ships were seized like the *Americana* by your navy? How many Americans like myself were abducted off of those ships—and impressed? Do you have any idea how much income your country has cost us due to your restrictive trade policies?" she challenged. And she could recall her father making the very same arguments over supper at Sweet Briar.

"Unfortunately you wish to feed and clothe Napoleon and his armies, Virginia," Sean said calmly. "And that cannot be allowed."

In the end, neither of them won the debate and a truce was called, but now news of the war was avidly followed by them both. An Indian massacre of the American Fort Dearborn followed, as did the British capture of Detroit. This new war, so insignificant to the British and so important to the United States, was not going well for the Americans.

There was no word from Devlin, not a single letter. If a ransom was in progress, he was not keeping them informed.

One evening, Sean suggested that she might enjoy riding out with him to inspect the holdings of some tenants, and she accepted. They toured two tenancies not far from Limerick, took supper there, and the next day, she went with him for the first harvest. She began to join him on a daily basis. Their friendship blossomed.

She almost forgot he had a brother. It seemed to be true after all, that time healed all wounds, and now she managed not to think about Devlin O'Neill. Somehow, she had buried him in some deep dark place and it was almost as if he did not exist—except that, deep in her heart, she knew he was the one man she would never forget.

Toward the middle of September the last days of summer turned hot and humid. Virginia came down for supper one night and heard unfamiliar voices in the front hall. Her steps slowed as she realized that both a man and woman were present, chatting amiably with Sean. From his light tone, she could tell that he was happy. Very curious as to whom their first visitors were, she paused before going in.

Immediately, her eyes were drawn to a tall, dark man with swarthy skin and the bearing of someone with great power. Her gaze veered to a tall woman with sun-gold hair, a lush figure and an elegant bearing. Virginia's heart skipped, for she recognized this woman immediately. Devlin O'Neill looked so much like her in feature and coloring that there was simply no doubt that this was his mother.

Which meant that the tall, dark man with her had to be the Earl of Adare, Edward de Warenne.

Virginia thought about fleeing before anyone saw her, then pleading a headache, as she felt certain they had come to dine, but it was too late.

"Virginia." Sean had seen her and he smiled widely. His gray eyes were sparkling. "Come meet my parents, Lady Mary de Warenne and my stepfather, Lord Adare."

The couple turned simultaneously and Virginia met two piercing stares. For one moment, she felt certain that she was being thoroughly inspected. Slowly, she came forward, filled with unease and dread.

But Mary smiled. "Hello, child. We returned from London yesterday and as soon as we heard the news, we rushed over."

Virginia actually curtsied. "My lady."

"Leave it to Devlin not to say a bloody word," Adare said darkly, staring closely at her.

Virginia looked at Sean in confusion. He seemed bewildered, as well. "How is Devlin?" he asked dryly.

"He was up to his neck in a ruckus of his own causing," Adare said grimly. "He was once again accused of disobeying direct orders—rumor has it he attacked an American ship."

"What happened?" Sean asked grimly.

"There was a hearing arranged by Admiral Farnham with the clever help of Tom Hughes. Devlin, however, claimed to have come to the aid of a foundering American merchantman, insisting he attacked no American ship. Several of his men testified that this was true. The ship, the *Americana,* was apparently lost in a gale and there were no survivors. Farnham was outvoted two to one by St. John and Keeting—the motion for a court-martial dismissed."

Sean was pale. "Christ."

Adare held up his hand. "He is on probation and he was sent to escort a convoy to Spain. My son has nine lives—and he's used up ten."

Virginia was perspiring heavily. There was an explanation now for Devlin's prolonged absence. She would not defend his behavior—for look at how cleverly he had lied to his own admirals!—but somewhere, in a tiny corner of her heart, she was relieved to know that even if he had wanted to return to Askeaton, he could not. She bit her lip hard, then gave up. "Is he returning here at any time soon?" she asked nervously.

"I wouldn't know," the earl said, his tone kind.

Mary beamed at her. "Why, I should hope so! Or does he expect his brother to keep you company while he sails the world?"

Virginia became very uneasy.

"Congratulations, my dear," Mary said, grasping both of her hands. "I am so happy for you both."

"Wh-what?"

Sean echoed her exactly.

Adare smiled. "We are both happy—and relieved, I might add, as this is the last bit of news either of us ever expected."

Virginia had a bad feeling, oh yes. She glanced at Sean, seeking help.

He coughed.

"How on earth did you two meet?" Mary asked, putting her arm around her.

Virginia could not think of an intelligent answer. And she was referring to Devlin—wasn't she?

Adare clapped his hand on Sean's shoulder. "Being as Devlin was not kind enough to inform us of the upcoming nuptials, I will ask you. When is the wedding? Has anything been planned? You know your mother would love to help plan the event."

"The wedding," Sean said cautiously, his cheeks red.

"Yes, Devlin's wedding. The first thing we heard when we got home was the news that Devlin is engaged. The moment we stepped off our ship at Limerick, the mayor was congratulating us—as was every squire and merchant." Adare now stared closely at Sean. "What is amiss, Sean? You seem upset."

Sean and Virginia looked at each other helplessly.

Mary now ceased smiling. "Is something wrong?" She turned to her son. "Sean?"

Virginia spoke, as he seemed incapable of it. Her mouth somehow formed the painful words. "I am sorry. I am not Devlin's fiancée. There has been a terrible misunderstanding."

"I don't understand." Mary was pale.

"Well, this would certainly explain why Devlin did not say a word to us when we saw him in London." Adare was grim and displeased. "I am afraid to ask, then, what this is about. You are Devlin's guest? " His gaze narrowed. "We have not been properly introduced."

Virginia did not want to upset Mary de Warenne, but there was no choice. "I am not a guest here," she said.

"I don't understand," Mary whispered.

"You are not a guest," Adare said slowly. He turned to Sean. "Is she your wife?"

He flushed crimson. "No. Father, perhaps you should sit down."

"I have a very bad feeling. Out with it!" Adare said, and it was a command.

Sean murmured, "Virginia is the Earl of Eastleigh's niece."

A terrible silence fell.

VIRGINIA STARED OUT THE FRENCH doors, which were open, due to the weather, and watched the earl embracing his wife. Mary was crying. She felt Sean come to stand behind her and a moment later she felt his hand cover her shoulder. She turned to face him.

"Now we know why Devlin has not ransomed you," Sean said softly. "He was too busy defending himself against a court-martial."

"Eastleigh probably thinks I'm dead. He probably thinks I lie on the bottom of the sea with the *Americana*," Virginia said uneasily.

"Probably," Sean agreed.

"Why is your mother so dismayed?" she asked. "No one told her about the ransom."

Sean hesitated. "Some of it has to do with how much Mother yearns for Devlin to find happiness."

Virginia stiffened. "He's not interested in happiness."

"You are right, I think," Sean said. "But she is his mother, and every mother wants her child to be happy."

"They both seemed shocked when they learned I am Eastleigh's niece." Virginia said.

Sean shrugged.

"I have asked you a dozen times. Why? Why is Devlin doing this? He doesn't need the money. And you refuse to answer. So now I ask, why is Lady de Warenne so upset? Why did the name Eastleigh almost cause her to faint? Is this about *Eastleigh?*" she cried.

"Yes."

Virginia started. "I don't understand."

"Eastleigh was not always an earl. Harold Hughes was actually the middle son of the late earl. He was a captain in the army, a common-enough calling for the second son." Sean was terse.

She still had not a clue as to what this meant. "What does any of this have to do with me—and with your brother?"

Sean grimaced. "He served in Ireland, Virginia. He was the man who murdered our father when we were boys."

Virginia cried out, reeling. Sean steadied her. She clung to his arms. "This is about your father's death?"

"This is about my brother's obsession with it, yes."

And it struck her then. "My God, this is not about ransom, this is about revenge!"

He nodded.

And the enormity of it, the absolute irony, became instantly clear. She laughed. She laughed wildly, for Devlin was a fool, oh yes!

"Virginia, you are becoming hysterical," Sean said cautiously, trying to lead her to the sofa.

"I think not!" she cried, allowing herself to be led. "Your

brother is a fool, because Eastleigh doesn't give a damn about me and he could not care less that I am someone's hostage!"

Sean pushed her to sit, then walked away.

Virginia continued to chuckle, for now she was the one with the last laugh. Devlin's absurd scheme had certainly backfired. Sean returned, looking very worried, handing her a snifter. Virginia shoved it away. "Don't you see? There is no revenge. If Devlin wants to hurt Eastleigh, he can not do so with me."

Sean sat down beside her, taking both of her small hands in his own large, strong ones.

Virginia thought of Devlin's hands—both men were so alike physically—and she tensed. Slowly she met his gaze.

"No. Devlin has been methodically destroying East-leigh for years. The man has been reduced to a single estate with very little income. He can't afford this ransom, and when he pays it, he will have to sell off all that he has left. He will be finished, Virginia, and my brother will have won."

She stared, stunned, dismayed, and then, aware of him holding her hands, she pulled them away. "And he will have to pay?"

"It will become a matter of honor."

"What kind of man destroys an innocent woman in order to avenge his father?" she asked numbly.

"My brother," Sean said. He took her hand again, but only one, clasping it firmly. "He hasn't destroyed you. You're not with child." He kept his voice low. "He won't touch you that way again, I promise. Very soon, this will be over. One day, it will be a vague memory."

Virginia stared, but she did not see Sean, she saw Devlin instead, and now she began to understand how his eyes could be so cold, how he could lack any kindness, any mercy. He was no ordinary man. He was obsessed with revenge, and apparently, no means was too obnoxious to gain his end. "And what of his career? Surely he will be court-martialed for abducting me."

Sean hesitated. "Eastleigh has already been made a fool by Devlin, many times. He is too proud to go to the authorities, Virginia."

Virginia became still. It struck her then that she had the power to be the means of Devlin O'Neill's downfall. And Sean stared back—clearly, he knew it also.

Suddenly Mary and the earl had stepped into the room, Mary no longer crying. Both were terribly grave. As they looked at her, she slid her hand from Sean's and slowly stood.

Mary managed a smile. "Please, child, come outside and sit with me. It's such a pleasant evening."

Virginia wished she could be saved, as she had little doubt that Mary wished to speak far too intimately with her. She glanced at Sean pleadingly but he shrugged. Having no choice, she walked out to the terrace with Mary. The other woman paused beside the balustrade and faced her.

Virginia gazed up at the stars instead of at the other woman. But it was impossible not to be aware of her kindness and compassion; it flowed from her the way it might from an unearthly angel, in holy, tangible waves.

"Child," she said softly, tilting Virginia's face. "How can I apologize for what my son has done?"

Virginia had to meet her gaze. The woman's sympathy threatened her composure. "It's not your fault."

For one moment, Mary could not speak. "I love both of my sons with all of my heart. I want them to have lives of peace and joy. It is very hard, here in Ireland, to attain such a life. Sean, I think, has come close. But Devlin? He went to sea when he was a boy. I have rarely seen him since. He has chosen a life without joy, a life on the high seas, a life of war and destruction and death. He lives with his pain, closed off to the world, to people, as if he were his own island, as if he did not need any human companionship, any love, any joy." Mary closed her eyes and tears slipped down her cheeks. "I have prayed so much for him."

Virginia had the odd urge to cry, too. "Maybe he doesn't need companionship or love." She was terse.

"He may be cold," Mary said, meeting her gaze, "but he is a man. A heart beats in his chest, filled with red, human blood. Of course he needs companionship and love. We all do."

Virginia wasn't sure that Mary de Warenne was right.

"I wake up in the middle of the night, worrying about him. I have cried myself back to sleep a hundred times. My husband reminds me that he is a grown man and that in many ways, we should be proud of him. He grew up with nothing. We were very poor, once. Now he owns this fine manor, land that has belonged to O'Neills and FitzGeralds for generations, and he has many fine ships, his own fleet, really, not to mention a wonderful home in Greenwich. He was recently knighted, you know." She smiled through more tears. "It is Sir Devlin now."

"He is a very powerful man," Virginia said hoarsely.

"Yes, he is." Mary seized her hands. "But he isn't cruel. Is he?" she begged.

Virginia stared, for a long moment incapable of a response. Finally she whispered, "Not in the way that you mean."

"Oh, dear Jesus, what has he done?" Mary cried.

"I'm fine," Virginia lied, agonized.

Mary studied her closely, searchingly, as agonized and desperate as only a mother can be. "I raised my sons to respect women," she said hoarsely. *"Has he respected you?"*

Virginia did not know how to answer. Had Mary asked her this question even the day before Devlin's departure, she would have said yes without hesitation. But now the hurt came rushing back, a roaring in her ears, deafening her, a haze in front of her eyes, briefly blinding her. *He had left without even the most careless goodbye.* It still hurt, dear God, and if that wasn't cruel, what was?

Mary knew. She covered her bosom with her hand, shaking, and she turned away. "If I didn't love him so, I would disown him—my own flesh and blood." She turned back. "Are you with child?"

There was no more denying anything. Virginia shook her head.

Mary came closer and cupped her cheek. "You are such a beautiful young woman," she whispered. "Do you love him?"

Virginia started. Then she said, "Please. I just can't answer any more questions!" She pulled away, began to run, then turned back. "Lady de Warenne, he didn't really hurt me. I think he tried to be the man you wish him to be. No! I know he tried. But...it just happened!" She knew she was defending him now. She shook her head wildly, panicking, for her defense remained inexplicable. "I don't know anything anymore! I only know that I must go home." She turned and ran inside, past Sean and the earl, stammering out some inane regrets. Then she fled to the safety of her bedroom.

IN THEIR COACH, EDWARD SLIPPED his arm around his wife and held her close. She turned to him, laying her cheek on his broad chest, closing her eyes. He could feel her anguish, and while he loved Devlin as if he were his own biological son, he hated the pain he caused his wife and wished he had the power to prevent it.

It was the ultimate irony that many powerful men dealt with—they might rule a kingdom filled with subjects, but they could not rule an errant son.

Edward stroked her hair. "Don't worry anymore tonight," he breathed. "Tomorrow we will discuss this and decide what to do."

Mary did not answer. He felt her trembling and knew she was crying again. He bent and kissed her temple. She found his hand and clung to it.

"What would I do without you? I love you, Edward, I love you so much."

An ancient thrill swept him. He had fallen in love with Mary the first moment he had ever seen her, when Gerald, his tenant, had brought home his new seventeen-year-old bride. He himself was engaged at the time, the nuptials imminent. He had spent eleven years admiring her from a distance, never once making an inappropriate remark or gesture, while she bore her husband three children and his own wife bore him three fine sons and a daughter. In those years, he had developed respect and admiration for his tenant, as well as a wary caution. He heard rumors about the Defenders having come to Wexford, that their enthusiasm and power was growing. Edward had always favored full Catholic emancipation, as he felt it would enable Ireland to become stronger economically and politically and thus help her to become an equal to the mother country. Others disagreed. Others feared the loss of power and land should newly entitled Catholics seek to restore their ancient claims.

From time to time he dined with Gerald, Mary politely excusing herself so the two men could discuss the land, trade, the economy and, eventually, politics. Two Irishmen could not sit down together without discussion of Ireland's inferior position economically, constitutionally, socially, not even a Protestant and a Catholic. There was always heated debate.

Gerald had never suspected that he was in love with his wife.

Mary had known. She had sensed it from the first, and from that time, she had kept her eyes cast aside whenever he was present, as if afraid that one single shared glance might lead to something terribly wrong.

Sometime before the Wexford uprising he had learned of Gerald's involvement in the secret criminal society. They had fought terribly, almost coming to blows, with Edward demanding he stay out of the conflict. Days before the rebels took the town of Wexford, Gerald had ridden into Adare at a gallop, his appearance one of a madman.

Adare had met him in the courtyard, terrified that something dire had happened to Mary or her children. Gerald had leapt from his horse and seized the earl by the lapels of his hunt coat. "I need you to swear to me that you will look after my wife and children, Edward."

"What?" Edward had been stunned.

"Just in case..." Gerald stared savagely. "They'll only have you to turn to. Promise me, make it an oath. You'll see to their welfare, you won't let them starve. And..." He hesitated. "And you'll find her another husband, a good, decent man."

By then, his own wife had died several months before in childbirth, his second daughter not surviving, either. He was still grieving, and he hadn't even dreamed of what the future held. "Stay out of the rebellion," he ordered. "You have a fine family, a fine wife, and they need you alive."

"My country needs me," Gerald retorted. "Promise me, Edward!"

He had promised, but it wasn't necessary, because he would have moved heaven and earth, anyway, to protect Mary and the children.

It had been an incredible stroke of a terrible fate—his own wife dying and then Gerald murdered by the British. But now, almost fifteen years later, having attained a personal happiness and a joy he had never dreamed possible, he could not imagine his life without Mary as his wife. He stroked her hair again and murmured, "We will send her back to Eastleigh. I'll arrange it on the morrow."

"No!" Abruptly Mary sat up, her eyes wide.

"No? Darling, Devlin has kept her against her will," he said gently, refusing to actually call Virginia Hughes either a prisoner or a hostage. He and Sean had chosen their words around her very carefully.

"Devlin abducted her and holds her hostage," Mary said flatly. "You need not think to mince words around me now!"

He smiled grimly and squeezed her hand. "I only wish to spare you any further hurt," he said.

"I know," she cried. "But what about Virginia? Should she not be spared any further hurt? Should she not have *justice?*"

He searched her blue eyes. "What do you have in mind?"

"Devlin will do what is right," she said flatly. "He is going to fix this in the only possible way."

CHAPTER THIRTEEN

HE SQUINTED INTO THE GRAY day.

Ahead of him the country road from Limerick wound away, disappearing into the now-harvested fields and rolling hills, crisscrossed with stone walls. For one moment he stared, and as he sat his mount, he was very, very careful not to allow any feeling to creep over him. He succeeded. This time, there was no warmth within him in coming home. It was merely another mission he must accomplish.

Devlin spurred the liveried gelding into a canter, well aware that around the next bend he would be able to see his fields, his pastures, his land. But it didn't matter. He had an iron grasp on himself—he had never been more in control.

He rounded the bend and finally took some small, idle pleasure in the sight of the harvested fields that lay bare and brown ahead of him. As he passed the first farmhouse, he noted, almost indifferently, that McCarthy must have had done well that year—his flock of sheep seemed twice the size and his house had been recently whitewashed.

A stone wall cut across the field. Devlin rode his mount at it, and when the animal wavered, he spurred him on, clamping hard with both legs. The gelding took the wall, landing roughly. When he'd recovered his stride, Devlin gave the animal a pat for his courage. The skies finally parted and a light drizzle began.

A field lay ahead, the earth being turned over by a laborer. Devlin saw two horses grazing by its border and he instantly scanned the area for the riders. When saw two figures standing by the edge of a stream, apparently in conversation, he halted his horse abruptly. His heart quickened but he ignored it. One of the figures was small enough to be a child—or a very petite woman—and he knew beyond any doubt who she was.

He was grim. His legs tightened so hard around the horse that the animal shot forward. Instantly he jerked to a halt, causing the gelding to rear. He could not look away from his brother and Virginia.

He reminded himself that he controlled his men, his ship, the enemy. That he had done so for a good ten years, and never more effectively than this past summer and autumn, while patrolling the coast of Spain, while guarding the Straits. His heart mocked him, hammering hard and fast.

He had also controlled his thoughts. He had not thought about anything other than his mission, his ship, his men and the enemy in the course of the past five months. With an iron fist, he'd beaten each and every unwanted thought back into the shadows of the past, where they belonged.

He had come back for one reason and one reason only, and he had come back knowing he was in absolute self-control.

He told himself, very firmly, that he did not care what they were discussing. Let them debate the merits of the Irish soil. He held the impatient gelding at a halt, continuing to stare.

They were too far away for him to make out their features, their expressions or anything other than the fact that Sean's shirt was white, his boots black, and that Virginia also wore pale britches and knee-high riding boots. Her hair seemed to be pulled back—left loose or braided, he could not be sure—but the mass of dark hair fell down her back. He strained, looking for some telltale sign of any pregnancy, but at this distance, it was simply impossible to tell.

His mouth twisted grimly. The insane attraction lay in the past, he felt certain. When they came face-to-face he would feel no differently toward her than he did Elizabeth or Fiona or any other woman. He was through with thinking—he was wasting his time—there was nothing more to think about.

He whirled the bay and galloped to Askeaton.

"IT'S A SECRET RECIPE," Virginia said, smiling, as they walked into the house. "Not my mother's, but Tillie's great-grandmother."

"Tillie, your best friend, the slave?" Sean asked, following. He was carrying a dozen ears of corn.

Virginia nodded, flushed from the mad gallop they'd just had. She wasn't sure who had started to gallop home first, but suddenly they were both flat out and clearly in a race. Sean had won—but only by a length. As a result, they were both covered with red dust.

"I'll supervise the cooking," Virginia said. She was salivating just thinking about the corn pudding they would share that night. "We are lucky we still have any corn," she added.

Sean smiled and said something, but Virginia failed to hear him as she rounded the corner. Standing in the hall was Devlin.

She halted and Sean collided with her back.

Virginia hardly noticed. For her heart had stopped and she failed to breathe. *He was back.*

Devlin stood there nonchalantly, staring calmly at her,

clearly having expected her. His hard thighs were braced as if he rode his ship. His gaze never wavered from her face.

Virginia gulped down air and it burned her lungs and chest. *He had come back after all.* Her heart now slammed, causing more burning, more pain. She began to shake. She turned, realizing Sean had dropped the corn, and managed to glimpse his shocked expression. She bent, inhaling hard, saw how terribly her hands were shaking. As she reached for an ear of the scattered corn, she tried to think, but her thoughts were wild and incoherent.

Oh God, what did she do now?

Images afflicted her, images of Devlin O'Neill getting up from the bed they had shared, not looking at her.

"Devlin," Sean said quietly, but as he spoke he bent and seized Virginia's arm, hauling her to her feet. "We didn't know you had come back." He did not release her, clearly knowing that she might not be able to stand if he did.

There was no response to his remark.

Virginia half turned, fully panicked now, and saw him smiling at them both. Instantly their gazes locked. "The corn," she said, her voice low and husky, incapable of looking away from him.

He hadn't changed. He was seductive and powerful and magnetic; he remained mesmerizing. If only he had changed...

"Leave it," Sean snapped, also staring at Devlin as if hypnotized. "You didn't send word of your arrival."

"I didn't realize you needed to be warned of my return," Devlin said calmly.

Virginia could not look away from him. Almost every moment she had spent alone with him crashed over her then, from their first debate in the confines of his cabin upon the *Defiance* to the last time she had seen him, walking out of her bedroom.

I'm sorry I hurt you, he had said.

"Hello, Virginia," he said now.

She couldn't speak so she tried to nod.

"Sean," he added with an inclination of his head.

Sean finally moved, coming forward slowly. "Father was here the other day. I heard about your tour—and the hearing. I'm glad you're back."

"Are you?" Devlin asked rather coolly.

Sean stiffened. "Yes, I am." He now glanced back and forth between his brother and Virginia. Virginia realized that she was paralyzed and that she continued to openly stare. Although she remained stunned, her mind began to work. She hadn't really ever expected to see him again. And she had been fine with that. He had hurt her beyond words, but she was certain she had recovered, that time did heal all wounds. But now he was back, standing just a few feet from her, and nothing had changed. It was as if the months had never passed. Her wounds, once tightly sewn up, split asunder. *How could he have left her the way that he had? How?*

Suddenly Sean made a sound and walked out of the hall, leaving the two of them standing there, staring.

"You look well," he commented, his tone neither indifferent nor interested. "Other than the dirt."

She inhaled. Did he remember anything, anything at all? But how could he possibly forget!

He strolled forward. "I take it you and Sean are getting on?"

She stiffened. He had once suggested, absurdly, that she would marry his brother. "He has become a good friend."

He didn't seem to care and he shrugged.

She wet her lips. "Did you really tell him...that we should marry?"

"Actually, yes, I did."

"Have you no heart at all?" she whispered.

"I think we both know the answer to that."

"Then can you not show me any sign of compassion?"

"I hardly know what it is that you wish of me, Virginia. I'm sorry you have been so long in my brother's care, but the war delayed my return," he said levelly.

She reeled. He didn't remember, did he? Was it possible that she was so insignificant, so unmemorable?

"What were you and Sean doing?" he asked casually.

"I...what?" She blinked hard. "We were making corn pudding. I mean, we...I was going to show the cook how to make a recipe."

A tawny brow lifted and he said nothing.

Virginia didn't move. Was it possible, she wondered in dismay, to still have some feelings for this man? She hadn't seen him in five months. He had callously left her after the most significant moment of her life. He had given her no sign of warmth, no personal greeting, since he had arrived. But she could feel a desperate tension in herself and she knew, miserably, what it meant.

It meant she wanted him to tell her that he cared, that he remembered every moment of their lovemaking—as she did—and that he wished to beg her for forgiveness.

"Corn pudding," he murmured. "How interesting."

She stiffened defensively and held her head high. But he wasn't going to say anything about their past. She now knew it. "It happens to be delicious. If you're planning on staying for supper, you will certainly enjoy it." How hard it was to keep her voice even, to keep her pride gathered about her.

Now both brows lifted. He seemed amused and mildly incredulous. "This is my home. I had intended to dine before leaving tomorrow."

Her heart slammed to a wild halt. *"You...you're leaving...tomorrow?"*

"We're leaving tomorrow," he said, and finally his gray gaze moved over her, from her eyes to her mouth, lingering briefly, across the white cotton shirt covering her chest, past the thick brown belt, knotted and not buckled, and down the britches encasing her slim thighs. "I'm truly surprised Sean lets you run about like that."

If he felt any attraction, there was simply no sign, not in his tone of voice, not in his expression, and most important, not in his eyes. They were flat and opaque, lifeless.

"We're leaving tomorrow?" she gasped.

"Yes." He finally turned and walked over to the wide, tall windows where he stood, his back to her, gazing out, apparently at the sweep of lawns and the distant hills. "Eastleigh doubts your existence."

She was reeling. "What?"

He didn't turn. He continued to stare out of the window, and no inflection was in his tone as he spoke. "I sent the ransom note from Cadiz. Eastleigh claims you drowned with everyone else aboard the *Americana*. We are going to Southampton to prove once and for all that you are very much alive."

So the time for her ransom had finally come. Virginia was so overwhelmed with hurt and confusion that she could not deal with that matter, even though it meant she would be that much closer to going home. And oddly, in some ways, Askeaton had become her home. She had enjoyed the slow days spent farming and tending to the estate. She had enjoyed the cool days, the mist, the rain. She had enjoyed Sean's company.

But it wasn't her home. Sweet Briar was her home and there was still a chance that it hadn't been sold, which meant that maybe she could find a way to save it. She no longer hoped for her uncle to save the day.

And clearly, Devlin's plans, although delayed by the

war, hadn't changed. She did not know what to say—because the ransom was not what she wished to discuss. "Will Sean come with us?" she finally asked miserably.

"Do you want him to?"

Was there something odd in his tone? "Of course I do," she said, searching his gaze, but he turned away.

"I need him here," Devlin said. "Be ready right after breakfast." He walked out.

In shock, she stared after him. And then the enormity of what had happened hit her. *He had come back and had not said a single word about them.* And with that comprehension came anger.

Virginia strode after him.

She found him pouring a Scotch in the salon. Not looking up, he held up an empty glass. "Would you care for a drink?" he said lightly.

Virginia didn't stop until she was in front of him, forcing him to look at her. "No, I don't want a drink! And I insist that Sean come with us."

He slowly set his glass down and looked up. "You are not in a position to insist upon anything."

"He will be my chaperone," she said tightly. "I refuse to spend one minute alone with you."

He slowly stood, and of course he dwarfed her, making her feel small and vulnerable. "You have nothing to worry about."

"I have everything to worry about," she cried, and she realized she was panting. But the truth was, she doubted she had anything to worry about, as this man didn't seem to recall ever touching her, much less making love to her.

He held her gaze. "Sean stays here."

"Then I'm not going," she cried, as foolishly as a child.

"Don't worry," he muttered, lifting his glass and drinking. "You will be reunited—when I am done."

"You don't remember, do you?" she asked, her teeth starting to chatter. The salon had become frigidly cold. She was cold. Frozen over, in fact.

He sipped his Scotch as if he hadn't even heard her.

She seized his arm, shocking herself and spilling whiskey over them both. "The night we spent in bed together? The night you made love to me?" she demanded wildly.

His jaw tightened and he removed her hand from his arm. "Is there a point?"

"Do you remember or don't you?"

"Barely," he murmured.

She struck him as hard as she could, across the face.

The slap resounded in the hollow silence of the room.

Virginia backed up, shocked at what she had done. But finally a light had appeared in his eyes, even though it was not the light she had wished for. His gaze blazed furiously. At least, Virginia thought, his eyes were no longer opaque and lifeless.

She flinched, panting heavily, expecting to be struck in return.

But he only said, very hard, "Sex is not love."

She gasped, his words far more brutal than any real blow.

"I suppose I owe you an apology," he said tersely.

It was too late. Virginia shook her head, the tears spilling, and she turned to run. But he seized her wrist and somehow she was facing him again. "Let me go," she warned on a sob.

His jaw flexing repeatedly now, he said, "I am sorry. I believe I said so before. I am saying so again."

"How foolish I was, to think 'sex' meant something to you!"

His gaze flickered. "I deserve your reprobation. I had

no right trespassing where no man had gone. Now," he added firmly, "may we allow the past to rest where it belongs—in the past?"

"Yes, please, let's do just that!" she cried, trembling, both hands fisted at her sides, her anger so huge it felt suspiciously like hatred. But the hurt continued to tear her apart inside. She only knew now that she had to get away from him.

Tension rippled across his features and he began to walk out of the room, saying, "Tomorrow after breakfast, Virginia." And it was a warning that she be ready.

She stared, but only for a moment. "And what if I'm pregnant?" She knew full well that she was not, but how she wanted to hurt him, just a little, in return for how he had hurt her.

He froze, and slowly, he turned. "Are you?" he asked, his jaw muscles revealing a slight spasm, his eyes now a stormy and threatening shade of gray—an indication, then, that he had some emotion to share after all.

"No," she gritted. And then, her pride lost, she cried, "You left without even saying goodbye!"

Now his entire body seemed to flex and coil with a very real anger—one he seemed determined to contain. "Why are you doing this?" he demanded. "Have you no pride? I am a bastard, it is quite simple, really. There is a saying, Virginia, one you should heed: let sleeping dogs lie."

"I am not a dog and what we did had nothing to do with sleep!"

"I am taking you to my home outside of Southampton, where Eastleigh is but five miles north. I shall prove your existence, collect your ransom and send you on your way. Is that not enough for you? You shall have your freedom," he ground out.

"It's not enough," she heard herself say. And her pride mocked her now.

He started. "Then I am truly sorry, for that is all I have to offer you." This time, his strides were long and determined, and this time, Virginia sank down on a chaise. She covered her face with her hands and struggled not to cry. He had not wanted to discuss the past and the answers he had given were answers she had not wanted to hear. But it was simply too late. The truth—his truth—was brutal.

DEVLIN ENTERED THE MASTER bedroom and halted hard. He was shaken, enough so that he could not ignore it, but goddamn it, he intended to ignore it. Now was not the time to give in and allow a pair of huge, hurt violet eyes to haunt him...again.

He trembled somewhere deep inside his body and refused to think. Instead, he gripped the post of the bed. *If he had known his control would begin to shatter, he would have never come back. He would have ordered Sean to bring her to Southampton.*

"You should have sent word that you were coming."

Devlin turned, relieved at the interruption, and found his brother on the threshold of the room, looking angry and displeased. "You have nothing to hide. I gave you permission to do as you please. Are you fucking her?" he heard himself say.

And a sordid image assailed him, of Sean straining over her, pumping into her.

Sean attacked.

In a way, Devlin had known he would—and this was exactly what he needed. His brother's tackle sent him back onto the bed, where they grappled as if they were still boys. Devlin had always loved a good fistfight. So did Sean. Using all of his strength, he managed to turn his brother onto his back, but the effort cost them both, sending them to the floor. Sean grunted, as he took most of the fall.

For one moment, Devlin straddled his brother, and he smiled coldly. He said, "A yes or no would do."

"You heartless bastard," Sean cried, and Devlin found himself launched onto his own back, a hard blow landing on his jaw.

Sparks emanated behind his eyes and he welcomed them. But he raised his knee and caught Sean in the gut. Sean gasped, bowled over, and Devlin quickly stood, hauling Sean up and pushing him backward until he hit the wall. There, the two men strained at each other, panting like enraged bulls.

Sean managed to slither free and land another blow to the very same jaw.

Devlin stepped back, pleased as pain exploded in his face. He simply stood there and his brother hit him with all of his strength in his midsection, causing him to gasp and buckle over.

"Fight back, you son of a bitch," Sean shouted.

He no longer wanted to fight. He preferred the beating of a lifetime. He straightened, smiling lopsidedly, realizing his lip was split. "Do you enjoy her cries?" he purred. "And whose name does she keen in ecstasy—yours or mine?"

Sean hit him again. His head snapped back, into the wall, pain exploding in both his eyes. *I'm sorry, Virginia,* he thought suddenly, and anguish pierced his heart. *But I am not the man you want me to be.*

Sean had grabbed him by his shirt. "Do you really think my beating you will make what you did to her right? Damn you, Devlin, damn you!"

He smiled at his brother. "One more blow?"

"Like hell," Sean gritted, releasing him and walking away.

He tested his lip and found it bleeding. Sean was in love with Virginia, how clear it was, far more so than before.

Were they sleeping together?

He walked over to the mirror above the bureau, ignoring for a moment the rag dipped in ice water that Sean was offering. His eye was swelling but might not close. He finally took the rag and held it to his eye.

He reminded himself that he wanted her to fall in love with Sean; he approved of the match. It solved a dozen problems and left him utterly free to do as he pleased for the rest of his life.

Well, not utterly free. There would be one thing he would never be able to do, not again, and that was take Virginia to bed. But that was the entire point, was it not?

"I don't like being manipulated," Sean said.

"Are you sleeping with her? I approve," he added quickly.

Sean grimaced. "No."

A surge of satisfaction filled him—much to his dismay. "Well, you should," he said. Devlin touched his throbbing jaw. "I expected the blow of a boy."

"I am not a boy anymore. Why did you have to surprise us?" Clearly Sean did not want to discuss bedding Virginia Hughes.

"So it is an 'us'?" he asked quickly.

Sean grimaced. "I care deeply for her, Devlin, but no, there is no us. You hurt her terribly when you left. She needed warning, not I."

"Somehow I am not sure I believe that," Devlin said, staring closely at him.

"You can believe whatever it is that you wish to," Sean said roughly. "I am only her friend."

"You don't look at her like a man looks at his friend," Devlin remarked.

"And you may pretend indifference toward her but I can smell the lust," Sean retorted with anger.

"You are so wrong," Devlin said softly, but they both knew it was a huge lie. "And I do not want to argue with you. You're my brother. We are on the same side."

"We are not on the same side anymore, not when you have done this. Free her, Devlin, let this ransom go. Free her and leave Askeaton."

"I can't. I'm taking her to Wideacre tomorrow."

Sean's face tightened. "If you hurt her again, I will kill you."

Devlin stared, trying to decide if Sean meant it, if he could love Virginia so much that he would put her ahead of his family.

Sean flushed.

A terrible silence descended.

"I do hope you did not mean that," Devlin finally said. "After the ransom, she can return here—to you."

"I meant it. I suggest you stick your cock elsewhere."

Devlin smiled, but it felt like a grimace. He wandered the room now, very disturbed. This was what he wanted, he tried to remind himself, a match between Sean and Virginia, but now, his reminder was hollow and so obviously a pretense. He *hated* the idea of them together, no matter how he fought that hate. But then, hatred was what he knew—and did—best.

Finally he sighed and sat down. If Virginia decided to return to Askeaton to be with Sean after her ransom, he would give them his blessing, pretense or not. "You know, I have spent the past three months patrolling the coast of Spain by day and preying upon the few remaining French privateers by night. We seized four ships in that span of time, four ships and eight hundred in crew."

"Are you making a point?"

Devlin glanced at him. "Yes, I am. In all that time, I never spared a single thought for Virginia. Out of sight, out of mind." He did not tell Sean how much discipline that had taken.

"How proud of yourself you must be."

Devlin met his brother's stony gaze. "I am sorry I did what I did. My regret is vast."

"Then maybe you should tell her that!"

Devlin started. "And what would that accomplish?"

Sean snorted in disgust. "What would it accomplish? You broke her heart. Perhaps you can help to mend it!"

"Sean, I beg to differ. I could not possibly break her heart. She is my prisoner—not my lover."

"Now I beg to differ. She is in love with you," Sean said.

Devlin stared, so stunned he could not think coherently, not for a long moment.

"You are such a fool," Sean said, quietly now.

"No," Devlin said, shaken. "You are wrong. Virginia is curious, independent and passionate. That is all. If she thinks she loves me, she is wrong—it is lust, nothing more, and any fondness on her part comes from the fact that I was her first."

"You know," Sean said slowly, "it is possible that a woman might want more from you than your body."

"Yes, a woman might want the wealth, power, position and security I could give her." He was annoyed now. He leapt to his feet, flinging the bloody rag away. "I never expected this, and not from you!"

"Then what did you expect? To do the deed and simply walk away? To have her now choose me? Or hand her off to me, with no regard for her feelings? She is not Elizabeth! She is nothing like Elizabeth! Virginia could not pretend to be anything that she was not, not even for a moment. Virginia wears her affections openly—she wears her heart upon her sleeve! *What did you expect?*"

"Unfortunately, I wasn't thinking at all, much less expecting anything," Devlin said, abruptly sitting down. His heart dared to race and mock his cool demeanor now. His body trembled. Did he dare to confess the real truth, not to his brother, but to himself? "I lost all control," he said slowly. "I swore I would not do it. I swore I would not touch her that way. That night I lost all control. *I have never lost control before.* Damn it, I ruined an innocent young woman!" And he felt the anguish then as it was simply impossible to ignore. Briefly he covered his face with his hands.

He had abused an innocent young woman—he had ruined Virginia Hughes. Gerald must be rolling in his grave, and dear God, his mother's heart would break if she ever learned the truth.

"Then you are human after all. Tell her what you told me—that you are sorry, that you have regret, and that you found her so beautiful you could not stop yourself."

He cursed. "I am not a poet, Sean."

"Then say something kind in your own words!"

"I already have." His intention would not waver now. He was not going near Virginia again and certainly not to bring up the ugly subject of the past.

"Tell her again."

"Absolutely not."

Sean sighed, as if admitting defeat. Then, slowly, he said, "Perhaps you should think about what such lack of self-control signifies?"

Devlin stood. "It means she provokes me in an unnatural way."

"How convenient your theory is," Sean murmured.

But Devlin was pacing now, back and forth, as if on his deck, and he really did not hear. "I have spent these past months exorcising every thought of her from any and all existence," he said, almost to himself. "If I can defeat any French commander, I can defeat myself."

Sean smiled a little. "Maybe it is a slip of a woman whom you cannot defeat."

"Like hell." And he was, finally, furious.

VIRGINIA DEBATED NOT GOING down to supper but decided that would make her appear childish and as if she were sulking. And she was not sulking—she was hurt and angry and determined not to allow him to know just how hurt she was. She looked through her four gowns, already knowing there was no choice, and she took out the rose silk with the low-cut bodice and black lace trim. In this dress, she looked her best, in this dress, she knew she was beautiful, and she hoped he would look at her and regret *everything*. Then she held the dress tightly, turning to face the mirror. What was she doing?

If only he hadn't come back!

Things had been fine recently, for she had been content and almost happy, having managed to forget and bury the past. Now she was ill, her stomach so tight and knotted she could barely breathe, and once again, he consumed her every thought and moment, against her very will. At least, she thought rigidly, her reflection unearthly and pale in the mirror, he had admitted that he had deserved her slap. At least he was moral enough to know that what he had done was wrong. But she would never accept his apology, sincere or not.

She should not be wearing her only seductive gown.

But she wasn't trying to seduce him—Virginia had no intention of ever going there again. He might remain the most interesting and disturbing man she had ever met, not to mention the most magnetic, but she would never make the mistake that she had. *Sex is not love.* She had been a fool once, but never again. How those words hurt.

She had wanted an admission that he had been stunned

by their passion, too, that he had cared, that he still did. But none of those sentiments would be forthcoming, not ever, and she remained a fool, to think he might admire her at all in her dress, when it was clear that he didn't find her attractive anymore.

Virginia rang the bell pull, wanting a bath. An icy fear seemed to grip her now. And she dared face her darkest thoughts: he hadn't admitted anything that she had secretly hoped for because he was a man of the world, and she was only one more woman out of the hundreds he had already used.

Virginia knew she was growing up because she did not shed a single tear.

IF DEVLIN WAS SURPRISED to see her, he gave no sign. He nodded politely, sitting on the emerald-brocade sofa, legs crossed in soft beige britches that delineated his every muscle, not having bothered to change his Hessians for stockings and shoes. He wore a navy-blue velvet coat, a sapphire blue and silver-brocade waistcoat beneath, his ivory shirt exquisitely ruffled at the cuffs and throat, the jabot carelessly tied.

He did not even glance at her; instead, he sipped his red wine as if deep in thought.

But Virginia stared. He had been in a fight. His left eye was swollen and bruised, as was the same side of his jaw. What in God's name had happened?

She was diverted when Sean leapt to his feet and rushed to the threshold to escort her inside. He smiled but glanced searchingly at her.

"I'm fine," she said to his unspoken question. She stole one more glance at Devlin, then told herself, quite firmly, that she did not care if he had been fighting the devil himself.

Sean smiled again and squeezed her hand. "He's taking you to his country home tomorrow. It's close to Eastleigh. He plans for you to meet him. Are you all right with this, Virginia? Will you be able to manage?"

She nodded, glancing over at her captor, who now, finally, eyed them. No expression could be seen on his implacable face. It crossed her mind that she could thwart him easily by denying that she had ever heard of Virginia Hughes and claiming to be someone else. And if she really wanted to hurt him, to thwart him, she could go to the authorities once she was freed. Devlin would wind up in prison for years, unless he had a plan for that contingency, too.

Neither alternative gave her any pleasure. She only wanted to go home—if her home still existed. Unlike Devlin, she had a heart and it was human and kind. She would never deliberately hurt him, and not out of revenge.

"You are lovely tonight," Sean added. Then he added, "You are always lovely, Virginia."

Something in his tone caused her to start and she met his gaze. "If you are overly kind, I might lose what is left of my composure," she said softly.

Sean smiled a little. "Don't do that!" Then he said, "Virginia, would you step outside with me? We have to speak."

"Now?" She knew it was seven and they always dined precisely on the hour.

"Please."

Something was afoot. She nodded, searching his expression for a clue as to the matter at hand and they crossed the room. She had no idea what was on his mind. Devlin murmured, "Do not mind me."

Virginia decided to hell with it and she glared at him.

He saluted her with his glass and then picked up a Dublin newspaper.

Outside, the night was pleasant, a few stars beginning to emerge in the inky blue vastness overhead. To Virginia's surprise, Sean gripped both her arms. "I am going to miss you," he said roughly.

Her eyes widened. "I will miss you, too," she said.

His gaze searched hers. "I don't want you to worry about Devlin. I have become your protector, Virginia. You do not have to fear another episode like the last one. I won't allow it and..." He hesitated.

She was becoming moved beyond words. "And?"

"And he is resolved to treat you with all of the respect that you deserve."

Oddly, the twinge of dismay was at once rude, surprising and strong. "I doubt he said that."

"He didn't have to. He is very sorry, Virginia—"

"Don't! If that man cares about what he did, how he did it and how he left, he can tell me himself."

"He may never have the courage," Sean said softly.

Virginia started. As Devlin was the bravest man she knew, what in God's name was Sean talking about?

Sean touched her cheek. "Virginia, I must ask you something."

She was suddenly wary, though Sean had become her best friend.

"Do you still love him?" Sean asked.

Virginia gasped. She was so flustered and so stunned she could not respond for a moment. "Sean!" She gripped his hand, causing it to drop from her face. "I do *not* love that man," she said fiercely. "Maybe, once, for a brief moment, I was deluded into thinking that I did. I do not even know him! He has treated me abominably. There is nothing, absolutely nothing, there!" she cried.

But so many images of Devlin O'Neill assailed her now. She saw him standing strong and proud on the quarterdeck of the *Defiance,* the scourge of the seas; she recalled Devlin staring at her fierce with pride, telling her that all the land, as far as the eye could see, was Askeaton, that all the land belonged to him.

And finally there was Devlin, his body hard and aroused, covering her, his eyes brilliant and unfocused with the maddened haze of his lust.

Virginia tried to breathe and calm herself. He hadn't always treated her abominably. He had treated her well until those last few hours—and if she dared to remember, she had sought to seduce him then, never dreaming what her success would mean.

"I'm afraid I don't believe you," Sean murmured, his hands sliding around her now.

She stiffened, stunned. "What are you doing?"

"I have tried very hard to think of you only as a friend," he said slowly, his gaze holding hers.

And in the fading light of dusk, Virginia saw every emotion that he was feeling in the pale gray disks that were his eyes. Unlike Devlin's, they shimmered with sorrow, with sincerity and with something far greater than friendship. *He was in love with her.*

His hands tightened. "I will always be your friend," he said grimly. "But what I want to know is if there is any chance that you could forget him and what you have shared with him. If there is any chance, no matter how small, that you might ever think of me as something more than a friend."

Virginia reeled. She did not know what to say. And she was so touched that she cupped his face in her hands, a strong, handsome face, his features as hard, defined and angled as his brother's, a face so terribly similar except for his dark brown hair and brows. But she had never confused the brothers, because his eyes were windows to his soul, as Devlin's were not. "I don't know," she began hoarsely. "I am so surprised...."

His hands moved into the heavy weight of her hair, which she had pinned back but left down. "I lied to my brother," he said as hoarsely. "I am in love with you, Virginia."

His words were a terrible trigger. She loved him, too, but not that way—and what a fool she was not to love him as a man. Because she knew him completely. He was a man incapable of treachery while capable of loving a woman deeply, forever. "Sean, I can't." She dared not admit why, not even to herself.

He nodded, not speaking now. But he held her for one moment longer before dropping his hands. Instantly she seized them and clung. "Don't leave me now! I need you now more than I ever have!"

"I know." He smiled sadly, then the smile turned grim. "I will always be here for you, Virginia, but I am not going with you and Devlin to Wideacre. It is a terrible idea. I prefer not to be with the both of you."

"But—"

"No. Let me speak. I have wanted to speak frankly for some time."

She tensed but she nodded, for she owed him this. Still, what more could he possibly say after such an admission?

"Devlin is not a bad man. But the day he saw our father murdered, he changed. That was the day he stopped smiling, the day the laughter disappeared. That was the day he became obsessed with revenge."

She swallowed and nodded. It was impossible not to feel sorry for him, but she steeled herself not to now.

"Virginia, I am telling you this because I love him. Like my mother and stepfather, I worry about him and what he has spent his life doing. His naval career? He couldn't give a damn about the navy, Virginia. And he cares very little for Great Britain."

She thought about the secret meeting she had witnessed. "But why?"

"A man like Devlin can become rich and powerful in the navy, and as you have seen, that is exactly what Devlin has done. He used the navy to acquire enough wealth and power so he could destroy Lord Eastleigh."

She shivered.

"He went to sea at thirteen. His system of revenge began that day, Virginia."

"Oh, God." She began to realize the enormity of his obsession.

"He would die for me, our mother, our stepfather or our stepbrothers and stepsister. Gladly. He would die to save his men, his ship. He would die for Ireland. But I suppose his fearless courage is not at issue here."

"No, it's not," she whispered, mesmerized in spite of knowing how dangerous it was to allow such an intense fascination to overcome her now. And where was Sean leading?

"He is powerful, wealthy and fearless, he is widely admired as a great sea captain, and he is both respected and feared. But he is not kind. His ability to be kind died the day our father died."

"I am sorry," she heard herself say.

"Don't be. He is not a ruthless monster, either, though, and I know you saw that. Virginia, I love my brother enough to tell you now that I think, possibly, there is hope."

"Hope?" she echoed.

He gripped her shoulders. "The Devlin I know would never succumb to his desire for a young, innocent woman. God, we were raised with a stepsister whom we were sworn to protect! And even more important, the day our father died, our baby sister was left by the British to burn in the fire they had set. I can't remember, not any of it. But Devlin remembers it all. He would never use an innocent woman. To be very crude, if he needed a woman it would be a harlot like Fiona."

"What are you trying to tell me?" she whispered, trembling, afraid, and oddly, so filled with hope.

"I think you have reached a part of him he lost a long time ago, and I think—no, I hope and pray—you can reach that part again and pull him back into the light of a new day."

"What?"

"He is sorry," Sean said. "He told me, and I know him well—it is the truth. But it is not over."

She could only stare.

"He is not indifferent—it is a sham, a pretense, a huge theatrical act. If you do not hate him, if you can ever forgive him, maybe you are the one who can help him find his soul."

"Are...are you mad?"

He smiled and released her. "I am sad."

She quickly moved to embrace him. She hugged him hard.

In her arms, Sean whispered, "My brother needs the love of a good woman, and if you cannot love me, then maybe you can give him another chance."

Virginia began to shake. "What are you asking me?" she whispered.

"I am asking you to save my brother."

CHAPTER FOURTEEN

VIRGINIA STARED OUT OF THE window of the coach as it left Askeaton. Sean stood in the courtyard waving, and as the coach traveled down the road, he and the manor became smaller and smaller until finally Sean became indistinct. There was a terrible lump in her throat, and the fact that a part of her, a large part, did not want to leave became glaring. Was it Sean she already missed, or was it the safety she had found at Askeaton, the safety and comfort, the friendship?

Or was she afraid of what the future held?

I am asking you to save my brother.

Virginia inhaled harshly and the cold, wet air somehow burned her lungs and chest. She could see nothing now but the harvested fields and the woods that the road wound through. Panic came, hard and fast. *I don't want to save anyone—much less him!* she thought wildly.

Virginia stole a quick glance at her captor. He sat beside her in the back seat, dwarfing her as well as the interior of the coach. The cab was too small for them both, never mind that a few very solid inches remained between them.

I think you have reached a part of him that he lost a long time ago.

Virginia winced, wanting to plug up her ears the way a small child might, only that would not stop Sean's voice, so loudly speaking in her head.

He is not indifferent. It is a sham, a pretense, a huge theatrical act.

Inwardly, Virginia moaned. Why had Sean urged her to befriend his brother, to awaken him, to heal him? Why? Why not throw such a monumental task on someone else, someone stronger, more experienced, more womanly? She did not want to be his savior. Sean had been mad last night, to think she was the one to help this man recover his humanity.

My brother needs the love of a good woman....

Now she moaned out loud, caught herself, and bit off the sound somewhat belatedly.

She felt his stare.

It felt cool, calm and terribly indifferent.

She dared another sidelong glance at him, her hands clasped in her lap.

"Are you ill?" he asked.

"I...I have a terrible headache."

Their gazes had met, but only for a moment, because he accepted her excuse and looked indifferently out the window at the passing countryside. It began to rain heavily.

She looked at the edge of his hard jaw, the angle of his straight nose, the slash of a cheekbone. Her heart tightened, and an oh-so-familiar tension, already within her, grew. She remained terribly attracted to this man, against all reason and all common sense. It was as if he were a powerful magnet, she a tiny clip. She could feel the pull that arose from him. Like the very ocean itself, waves emanated from his body, crashing over her and trying to pull her far out to sea.

It was such a waste, she thought. But Sean was wrong in many ways. Devlin was indifferent and he did not care—this could not be an act. And she was not the one capable of guiding him back to his lost soul.

*But everyone deserves a second chance. What is there
to lose, my darling?*

Virginia shot up, for it was as if her mother, smiling and
benign, had spoken.

"We do not have a ship's surgeon, but if you are in
extreme pain, I do know where the laudanum is kept."

She turned to stare at him, aware of how wide-eyed she
must be, and his gaze narrowed in return. He was wearing
his naval uniform, making his presence even more
powerful, more formidable and even more seductive. "I
won't need any laudanum," she breathed.

Her mother had been the kindest person Virginia had
ever met. No one in need was ever left without, not if
Elissa Craycroft Hughes could help it. Children were her
greatest cause, and one Sunday a month they had made the
long trip to Richmond so Father could make repairs to the
orphanage there while Virginia and her mother handed out
baked cookies and homemade toys. Every other Sunday
they went to church in Norfolk. After the sermon they
would mingle, with Elissa always asking the poorest folk
how they were and what they might happen to need. The
townspeople were proud and it was a rare day that anyone
would admit to any lack, other than to being sick.
Somehow, Elissa always knew what was needed, whether
it was a poultice of her own making or a freshly washed
and repaired hand-me-down shirt. And finally, they'd stop
by the black folks' church, Virginia always hoping to catch
the last of the singing of the hymns and the dancing. Elissa
was welcomed there as warmly as if she were a slave
herself. She was never empty-handed; her grapevine
always told her if Grandma JoJo needed a new pair of
shoes or if Big Ben's boy had the fever again. And no
needy stranger passing by Sweet Briar had ever been
turned away, either.

"What is it, Virginia?" he finally asked. "Are you anxious about finally meeting your uncle?"

She started. "No. I was thinking about my mother," she said slowly, still consumed with the memories, and she smiled at him.

Instantly he glanced away.

Her mother, Virginia thought ruefully, would agree with Sean. Especially as her daughter was not immune to the man to begin with. She sighed and finally regarded her captor openly. Her heart skipped a little. "We missed you at supper last night," she murmured, as he had remained in his study, apparently immersed in estate ledgers.

He shifted and turned his head, settling a cool glance on her. "I doubt that."

In the past, such a cold remark would have hurt her. But she understood him a little now. As a child he had lost far more than his youth the day his father had been murdered, and what she had witnessed from the moment of meeting him was the result of that. This man was heavily scarred. And Sean was right. He wasn't a bad man. She had never seen cruelty, sadism or evil. What she had seen was a ruthless discipline, forced upon others and forced upon himself. And what she hadn't seen was any sign of happiness, not once in all the time she had spent with him.

She was torn and confused, not certain of what tack to take, and as uncertain whether she wanted to feel any compassion for him, but whether she wanted to or not, the fact now was that she did.

"You know, Virginia, I am feeling like an insect in a laboratory glass."

"I'm sorry." She smiled a little at him. "Were you ill?"

He sighed with annoyance, said tersely, "I had a migraine," and stared out of his window again.

She started to laugh.

He glared at her.

She bit it off and widened her eyes innocently and said, "Men don't have migraines, Captain."

He simply stared at her, very coldly.

He was in a worse mood than usual this morning. She decided to ignore it. "And even if they did," she continued, "you are not a man who would ever have such a headache."

"Pray tell," he said grimly, "why we are having this conversation?"

She faced him more fully, her heart racing now in her breast. She felt as if she shared the coach with a dangerous lion, one who might choose to bite off her head at any moment with the least provocation. "Well, it is a good hour to Limerick and we are enclosed together in a very small coach and I am being polite."

"There is no need."

"And you did not join your brother and myself for supper last night," she added.

"I wanted to allow the two of you one last meal alone," he said mockingly.

She blinked. "Are you being serious?"

"My brother is in love with you, Virginia," he exclaimed. "By now, surely, after that sweet scene last night, even you must be aware of it?"

She inhaled sharply. *"What?"*

He smiled at her, but it was mirthless and she realized he was angry.

Was he referring to the conversation she had had with Sean on the terrace before dinner? Had he been eavesdropping? "What scene?"

He erupted with rough laughter. "Oh, please, the scene where you held my brother in your arms—or was he holding you?"

"You were spying on us?" she cried, sitting up, aghast and then feeling her cheeks flush.

"I wasn't spying on anyone, Virginia," he said sharply. "I wanted some air, but the two of you were so engrossed I decided not to step outside. It was a perfect night for a pretty pair of lovers."

She gaped. Her mind raced. "How much did you hear?"

"I heard nothing," he said sharply. "Did you enjoy his kisses, Virginia?" he demanded suddenly.

She gasped. And her racing mind realized how it might have looked to Devlin—as if they were lovers, in a prolonged embrace. "What happened last night was between me and Sean," she managed, still stunned, "and it is none of your affair."

"But I approve of the match," he said. "I always have and heartily so."

She stiffened, his words hurtful. Then she recalled that he had said that Sean was in love with her—and he was right. She stared at him. Surely he was not jealous? The instant she thought it, she almost laughed. Jealousy was a result of affection or love, and this man did not care for her in any way—although Sean would disagree. Carefully, she said, "Sean is only a friend—a dear friend, my dearest friend."

He made a derisive sound. His face was so taut the flesh looked like it might snap free from the tendon and bone that lay beneath.

"But you are right. Unfortunately, he has come to have very strong feelings for me, feelings that I do not return."

"Why not?"

"Why not?" she gasped, and then she was so angry her fists balled up. His gaze moved to them, then back to her own eyes. "I am not a whore. Or have you really forgotten that you took my virginity, Devlin?"

He flinched and their gazes held, and unfortunately, Virginia thought him to be far more in control of any emotion than she was.

"How can I forget," he asked, "when you are forever reminding me?"

She ached to slap him. She did not. "I think that night precluded any possibility of my ever falling in love with Sean."

"Why?"

"Why?" She was in disbelief.

"Yes, I asked why. The past needs to remain dead and buried, Virginia, and very shortly you will be free to go where you please. You were very sad to leave Askeaton—and Sean."

Virginia hesitated, still incredulous, hurt and angry. *He is not indifferent to you. It is a sham, a pretense.*

She couldn't believe Sean, but dear God, she wanted to. But if he cared at all, why would he be doing this? Why would he be pushing her toward his brother? Softly staring at him, she said, "There is magic at Askeaton, Devlin. In the five months I have been there, it has come to feel like my home."

His gray eyes were impossible to read. Then his mouth twisted into a parody of a smile. "Well, that is good. Because when the ransom has been delivered, you may return there happily, if that is what you wish."

"Is it guilt?" she asked. "Is it guilt that drives you now? Do you think to have your brother clean up the mess of your making?"

"That's enough," he said harshly.

"That's it, isn't it?" she cried, stunned. "It's guilt! You have some heart after all! You said you were sorry—Sean says you are sorry—you even said you deserved that slap. So you know you have behaved monstrously. But you would never offer marriage—not that I wish you to!" she added hastily. "But if Sean did, why, how convenient for you! You could forget there was a day when you became the kind of man your mother would not recognize, that your mother would—"

He seized her by both shoulders. "Enough."

She tensed, the grasp of his large hands causing her heart to slam, and for one moment, her body shifted toward him, expecting him to pull her close and kiss her. Instantly, her mind told her otherwise and she pulled back. As instantly, his gaze plunging to her mouth, he let her go.

"Never bring up the subject of Lady de Warenne again," he warned.

She hesitated. "I met her."

He paled.

Oh-ho, this was interesting indeed! "She is a very kind woman. I liked her very much." Virginia became sly.

"I am going to kill Sean," he said.

She grabbed his arm, but he was too close, too male, and it was not a good idea, so she dropped her hand quickly. "It was not Sean's fault! They came calling as they had heard of our engagement."

"Our engagement?" he gasped.

Virginia stared and then she had to try very hard not to smile. She had thrown him off balance, and God, it felt so damn good. So she did not reply; far more slyly, she waited.

"We are not engaged," he choked out.

She was enjoying this moment. She wished to engrave it in stone. She smiled and shrugged, refusing to clear up the misunderstanding.

"Jesus, the people," he said. "It must be all over the village, the town, that you are my fiancée."

"I suppose," she murmured.

"Why are you grinning like the Cheshire cat?" he

snapped. "We both know I fabricated that story to save your pretty little neck."

He liked her neck? "You find my neck pretty?"

"Is that what they still think? My mother and Adare?"

She sighed. "No, Devlin, that is not what they think."

The coach became very silent, very tense. She looked at him. His silver eyes were hard and unwavering. She shivered. "Sean chose his words with care." Then she gave up. "Well, what do you expect! To take your blood enemy's niece hostage and fool your family, who live but a dozen miles away?"

He cursed.

"This is all of your own making," she reminded him sweetly.

He gave her a dark glance. "The sooner I break East-leigh, the better. The sooner you are gone, the better," he added as darkly.

His words did hurt, when she knew better, and they also somehow dismayed her. Carefully, she said, "You are right. And when I am ransomed, I am going home to Sweet Briar—I can hardly wait." But the odd truth was that she hadn't thought very much about her home in these past few months. Memories that had once been a lifeline had become vague and distant, replaced by the day-to-day existence she had shared at Askeaton with Devlin and then Sean. "If it still exists," she added grimly.

ONCE AT SEA, ITS MAIN SAILS unfurled, the *Defiance* took off, fighting the rain and the sea, tacking across the wind to the south. Virginia did not like being back in his cabin. His presence was everywhere, powerful, heavy and over-whelming. She sat down at the dining table, finally overcome with confusion and the gravest of doubt. A part of her so wished to tame the beast and eventually heal it, but she had no confidence, and Devlin's continued insistence that she should marry his brother did not help. She suspected he felt guilty, but he was so arrogant, so impossible to read, that he left her feeling terribly uncertain and terribly naive. She wished the conversation with Sean had never taken place.

By dusk, the rain had ceased and the skies had cleared, the seas growing calm and sweet. Virginia dined alone, not surprised that her captor was avoiding her—she knew that much, at least—and then, donning a pelisse, she slipped from the cabin.

Devlin was at the helm, although he did not steer the ship. He stood beside a sailor she recognized, his strong legs braced, facing the prow and the stars shining ahead. Virginia hesitated, her heart quickening, and then she walked over to the quarterdeck. As she climbed up, he turned.

She took the last step, expecting him to order her away, but he met her gaze, his eyes a flash of silver in the twilight, with a mere inclination of his head. Virginia walked over to him. "It's a fine night for sailing," she breathed, meaning it. Behind them, the moon was rising in the east, a spectacular sight.

Devlin seemed to flinch, though she could not be sure. But he glanced at the rising moon and nodded. "Yes, it is. We'll have a moderate breeze for an hour or two and we must make use of it. It's a good fourteen knots."

She studied him as he stared ahead. He had removed his naval uniform some time ago and wore only a loose shirt with his britches and boots. *How she would love to be in his strong arms again.*

Virginia started with guilt, dismayed by her wayward, uncalled-for thoughts. That was the last place she ever intended to be! She had learned her lesson and learned it well. "You didn't come down to dine," she said softly.

"I ate on deck." He didn't look at her as he spoke.

She decided to enjoy the night, the stars, the wind, the sea and even his impersonal company. It wasn't a bad life, she thought, sailing the world by day and night. "It's so free," she whispered.

He didn't respond, his arms now folded across his chest.

Suddenly she was struck by a comprehension and she faced him. "Do you think to outsail your childhood memories?" Was that what he was doing? Running away from his past under the guise of being a naval captain in a time of war? "How convenient," she gasped.

He seemed to choke.

"I mean, this is a life without family, without responsibility. If you wanted, you could sail the world forever."

Not looking at her, he said to the first mate, "Red, I'll take the helm."

Red said, "Aye, aye, Cap," and he stepped aside.

Virginia watched Devlin's large hands close on the helm, firm and assured, neither hard nor gentle, and she was breathless. Blood pumped in places it should avoid. She looked away, taking a huge breath, suddenly faint with the most urgent desire. *His hands had been on her like that, almost exactly so.*

"I think you should go below," he said tersely, still refusing to look at her—and it was as if he knew.

"Is that an order?" she asked. But she knew her dazzling insight was right.

He finally turned his head and their gazes locked. He seemed to hesitate. "No."

"No?"

His jaw was most definitely flexing. "The nights are long."

She began to smile. "You don't mind my company."

"As long as you are quiet."

Her smile widened—how quickly he could make her heart sing and dance! "You want my company," she teased.

She thought she saw him hold back a smile. "I hardly said that. But I do not mind it, if you are *quiet.*" He stressed the last word.

"I promise." She grinned, and she leaned on the siding, gazing up at the stars. Tendrils of stray hair whipped her face; she loosened her pelisse. "If I were a boy, I could have been a sailor," she mused.

"No, you couldn't."

She turned, leaning her back on the ship, facing him. "You dispute me?" she bantered, praying their conversation would remain light and thrilled with it this far.

"You love the land." He added thoughtfully, "One might think you are like the sea, a flighty mistress, ebbing one way, then another, forever free, but you are really like the dark, deep earth, solid and immovable."

She stared. "How wrong you are, Devlin. You are like the earth, not I."

He started.

"Did you always want to be a sailor?" she asked, aware of the depth of the tension between them. The light conversation, as brief as it was, had not done anything to dispel it.

"No."

She tilted her head. "No? Do you care to elaborate?"

He seemed to caress the helm, steering the ship.

"Devlin? Has it ever occurred to you that it is easier to converse than to be in a speechless war?"

He sighed. "Askeaton has been in my family for centuries. I thought to do what Sean is doing."

She became still. Suddenly she realized that she was touching his wrist. Desire crashed over her but she ignored it. "And then your father died and it all changed."

"My brother has a big mouth. What else did he say?"

"He said you used the navy to become rich, so you could destroy your father's murderer—my uncle."

He looked directly at her. "And he is right."

She stared boldly back. "If you expect me to swoon with hysteria and fear, then you do not know me at all."

He seemed to smile in the darkness. "I would never expect you to swoon, Virginia," he murmured.

She went still. She had not misheard the sexually seductive tone of his voice, oh no. And she trembled, reminding herself that she must never allow herself to wind up in bed with him again. He truly thought to hand her off to his brother and a few moments of pleasure would not change anything.

He cleared his throat. "And what will you do after the ransom, Virginia?" he asked, surprising her with the question.

But she knew what he was doing—he was changing the subject to distract her from the attraction she could not ignore. She met his careful regard, wetting her lips. "I will go home, of course."

He turned and stared at her. She stared back. It lay there unspoken between them—his desire to wed her to Sean. She said, low and careful, "I will not return to Askeaton, no matter how I have come to love it, and even view it as my home."

He looked ahead, into the slightly frothing waves beyond the frigate's prow. "And if Sweet Briar has been sold?" he asked after a long moment.

They were actually having a serious and sincere conversation. She hesitated. "It can't be sold. It simply can't, Devlin. It has been my entire life—it belonged to my parents—it belongs to me. It is my birthright," she added firmly.

"You must face the fact if it has been sold," he said, glancing at her. "I made some inquiries in London. As of last month, it was still available for purchase."

She smiled, thrilled. "Thank God!"

"If you have no home to return to, you may have to stay in England with your uncle."

"No!" She stared at his hard profile. "Never," she added fiercely. She hesitated and said, "I would return home, anyway."

"To what possible life?"

She tensed. "I really don't know." She looked up and found him watching her now, closely. "It's been five months, Devlin, since I first came to Ireland. A child set sail on the *Americana,* a cosseted, stubborn child, filled with naive hope, and a woman will return, a grown woman who has experienced something of the world. If Sweet Briar has been sold, I will go home anyway and find some kind of livelihood."

It was a moment before he spoke, and when he did, his voice was calm. "You are still a child, Virginia, and hardly experienced. You are not suitable to take employment as a schoolteacher or a governess," he said, "and I cannot see you as a seamstress, either. Your best recourse would be marriage."

She inhaled harshly. "To Sean?"

He seemed rigid. But his gaze locked with hers. "To Sean—or to some fellow American."

"If I ever marry, it will be for love."

He made a harsh sound. "As I said, you are still a child, and a naive one at that."

She tensed, anger flaring. "Of course I appear a child in your worldly, jaded eyes. But then, you did not think me much of a child when you had me in your bed."

His hands tightened on the helm, his knuckles turning white.

She hesitated, torn, the anger instantly vanishing. The evening had turned into a pleasant one. Her only complaint was that she still felt a raw and terrible attraction for this man. She did not want to argue, to fight. She wanted to continue a light but sincere and pleasant conversation. She wanted to be friends.

His face seemed flushed. For one moment—until he spoke—she did not know if it was with anger or embarrassment. "Will we forever dredge up the past?"

She knew she had made a terrible mistake. But she could no more stop herself from speaking what was in her heart than she could from seizing his arm. "Please tell me one thing, Devlin," she heard herself say quietly, with dignity and pride. "It is very important to me. *How could you leave me like that afterward?*"

There was no mistaking the flash of silver in his eyes. "I had business in London," he said smoothly, and they both knew it was an utter lie.

"Coward," she cried.

He straightened as if shot. Slowly he turned wide, incredulous eyes on her. "What did you just call me?"

Her heart raced with some real alarm. "You heard me," she managed.

"A man would die for such an utterance," he said very softly, as if he hadn't heard her plea.

"I suppose I am lucky I am not a man," she said as lightly as possible.

He did not smile at her lame jest. "I have faced entire fleets alone, Virginia, choosing to engage, not run. I may be a ruthless bastard, but I am not a coward."

She wet her lips. Her heart pounded with destructive force. Her ears rang. "You are a coward when it comes to personal matters," she said firmly. "And you sail this sea merely to run."

His eyes widened with more disbelief.

She decided she had gone too far. She backed up. "But you are only heartless because of the terrible circumstance of your father's murder, which you unfortunately witnessed. That would scar anyone, Devlin," she cried in a rush. "But I understand you now, I do!"

His gray eyes huge and disbelieving, he leaned over her. "If you are such an expert on my character, Virginia, then you will know that you expect more from me than I can ever give. I sincerely hope that you will return to Askeaton after your ransom, that you will marry Sean—who loves you—and that the past will be forever buried, where it belongs." He straightened. "Red!" he barked. "Escort Miss Hughes below."

The first mate materialized from the deck below.

"No!" She stood her ground, refusing to move, although a terrible dismay and hurt claimed her and she doubted herself, in spite of the conviction with which she spoke. Because she wished to save this man, but feared it was impossible. "I understand now! I understand your anger toward my uncle, your obsession with revenge! No matter what you say and do, I am not the enemy, I am your friend!"

Very grimly, Devlin said, "Take her below."

"Aye aye, sir. Miss Hughes? Captain says—"

"I am not afraid of you, Devlin O'Neill," she flung, cutting the sailor off. "But apparently, you are very afraid of me."

He had placed his broad back squarely to her; now he whirled. "Why do you think to provoke me?" He leaned close, actually leaving the helm, which Red seized with a gasp of horror. "I suggest you rethink your position, Virginia, because you had damned well better be afraid of me."

"I'm not," she lied, because now her heart was slamming in fear. "I'm just sorry, I am so sorry about your father, and that's all I wanted to say!"

Devlin took her arm and handed her over to Red. "Get her off of my quarterdeck," he said.

October 29, 1812
Eastleigh Hall, the south of Hampshire

WILLIAM HUGHES, LORD STUCKEY, heir to the earldom of Eastleigh, strode into his father's suite of rooms without knocking. He was a man in his mid-thirties, already a bit thick in the middle, dressed in a fine scarlet coat, britches and stockings. He wore a number of rings, his hair was thick and black and his attractive face was flushed. "Father!" he demanded, his pale blue eyes flashing. He had a wife whom he did not care much for and two children whom he adored.

The Earl of Eastleigh, Harold Hughes, had once looked exactly like his son. Now he was a very heavy man, hugely overweight, and because of it—and his penchant for tobacco—his complexion was distinctly pasty. He wore his gray hair pulled tightly back, his sideburns thick and long. At first glance, he seemed a well-dressed and wealthy man. Only a second glance revealed that his once-fine gold velvet frock coat was tired and worn. Only a second glance showed that his britches boasted several stains that the laundress could not remove, that his stockings were carefully turned so as to not reveal the beginning of a fine run or two. His patent shoes gleamed but were heavily scratched, the soles so thin a hole might soon be in the making.

Eastleigh sat at the desk in the sitting room that adjoined the master bedroom and William could not imagine what he was penning that was so important. William ran the estate—or what was left of it—along with the steward, Harris. Any regrets to be proffered due to the social engagements his father refused to attend fell to his wife. His father looked up, setting his quill aside.

"Father!" William paused beside the desk and with some disgust, he saw that his father was composing a letter to a male friend, and the subject was horse racing.

Eastleigh clasped his hands calmly in front of his face. "You seem upset, William. Do you bring me poor tidings?"

William was furious. They hovered on the brink of real destitution because of a single man—and he did not know why Sir Captain Devlin O'Neill had decided to bring the Hughes family down. But last month they had received an absurd letter from the man. He claimed to have William's American cousin at his home in Ireland, as his *guest*. Apparently he had taken her off the *Americana* as it foundered, saving her life. "As graceful as my hospitality shall be, the time soon comes when Miss Hughes shall wish to go forth to meet her British family," he had written. "I am certain that such a reunion can be arranged to all parties' satisfaction."

William had no clue as to what that odd statement meant. His father had read the note, torn it up and put the pieces calmly in the fire. He had been utterly dismissive and refused to discuss the subject at all. In fact, he never discussed anything having to do with O'Neill, not since he had been forced to sell the man their Greenwich home.

"The *Defiance* has just sailed into Southampton port, Father, with that lunatic O'Neill. I can only assume he has come to visit his new country home! What if he thinks to stay in residence for a while, with Wideacre but miles from Eastleigh?"

Eastleigh stood and laid his hand on his son's shoulder. "He has every right to reside at Wideacre, if that is what he wishes to do."

Impatiently, William tore free and paced. "Goddamn it! I knew it was only a matter of time before that scum of the earth would appear here, to taunt us beneath our very nose! He must intend to take up residence at Wideacre. Damn those stupid fools at the Admiralty! Damn them for letting him off the hook again! I do not understand how this hearing failed—Tom swore it would not!"

Eastleigh folded his hands in front of him. "I don't understand why you are so upset. It is not our affair if he resides so close to us."

William whirled in disbelief. "The man stole our home in Greenwich! He lives there like a goddamned king! He stole Tom's mistress and flung it in his face! I happen to know that the countess—" He stopped.

"The countess what?" Eastleigh asked mildly, his brows lifted.

William stared, trembling with his rage. Then he drew himself up stiffly, his mouth pursed. He had discovered a year ago that his stepmother was having an affair with the man he so hated. It was beyond belief and he had been outraged, enough so to confront her about it. She had denied the entire affair, but he had managed to hire a spy to confirm what he had already guessed. He didn't know why that, at every turn, the goddamned pirate—and that was what he was, a pirate, not a naval captain—was always there, a huge thorn in his side. It was as if O'Neill were an avowed enemy of the Hughes family, but that, of course, made no sense.

And what did that insane letter mean?

William grimaced. "Nothing," he said. "Have you forgotten that absurd letter?" he said more calmly.

"Of course not. Perhaps he thinks to bring my brother's daughter to our doorstep? If she is alive, if she truly lives and did not drown, we are indebted to him for saving her, are we not?"

"Virginia Hughes was on the *Americana* and it sank, Father, it foundered in a huge storm, and there were no survivors." William confronted his father angrily. "Devlin

O'Neill has dared claim she lives, as his guest, in his home, and I begin to suspect a fraudulent plan! She must think to pose as my cousin in order to secure some kind of allowance from us! Of course, we have nothing to spare," he added in warning.

"We have nothing to spare, but if she is alive, perhaps he deserves a reward," Eastleigh said idly, toying with the letter opener on his desk. It was a small, pearl-handled dagger.

William felt like pulling his hair out. "Father! O'Neill has been trying to wound this family for years. He has stolen everything we most love, but we do not know why! And now you think to give him a reward? This is some scheme, Father. Virginia Hughes is dead, there were no survivors, so some actress comes forth at O'Neill's prodding to leech us of more blood."

"You have a fanciful imagination, my boy," Eastleigh said, walking over to the window, the small dagger in his hand. He stared outside at lawns that had once been manicured but were now overgrown, as they could not afford more than one gardener, and the gardens, once a riot of color and bloom, were now decayed and devoid of life. He touched the dagger to his finger and was rewarded with the gleam of his blood. He smiled.

"I shall send for Thomas," William decided, "because I have no doubt that O'Neill will invite us to Wideacre in a neighborly gesture to meet the impostor. But our cousin is dead. And we do not have the means to support her, anyway, am I not correct, Father?" And William cared not one whit if the girl were his cousin or not. As far as he was concerned, his cousin was dead—a very fortunate circumstance, given their financial state and her being a sudden orphan and not yet of an age to wed. As far as he was concerned, O'Neill was up to no good and the woman was an impostor.

But why?

Why did O'Neill, as controversial as he was, choose to toy with the Hughes family?

Eastleigh turned. "Fine. Summon Tom. The two of you can put your heads together and bemoan our loss of fortune." He smiled, and it did not reach his eyes.

Making a sound of disgust, William turned and rushed from the room.

Fury exploded then. Eastleigh jammed the dagger into his wall, a wall that badly needed painting. And he stared at the quivering weapon.

"So you think to stab me again, you bastard?" he said. "If my niece lives, I hardly care, and I will not pay the ransom you so politely request."

He tore the dagger free of the plaster. "My sons are fools. I am not. This war is not over yet."

And he imagined beheading Devlin O'Neill as he had his father, so many years ago. It would please him to no end.

CHAPTER FIFTEEN

"I DON'T SEE WHY WE COULD not have stopped at your estate before calling on my uncle," Virginia said, her tone purposefully low. It had taken two and a half days to reach Southampton and it was late in the evening. Since she had dared to bait Devlin upon his quarterdeck two nights ago, she had not been given the chance to do more than greet him before he would walk away. Unlike her first voyage on the *Defiance,* he had not dined in his cabin, slept there or used it for any purpose whatsoever. Every time Virginia had gone out on deck, hoping to attempt another civil conversation, he had been at the helm of the ship. Apparently he had given orders that she was not allowed on the quarterdeck anymore, as her way had been quickly barred.

He was, she thought, either very afraid of her or absolutely disinterested in her company.

Now Devlin didn't answer her. They stood in the front hall of the Eastleigh mansion, Virginia aware of how miserably unkempt she was and how desperately she needed any help that her uncle could offer. She could not help but wring her hands, and she so wanted to make a good impression.

What if the entire matter of her ransom was instantly resolved? She dared to look at Devlin, oddly disturbed. If that were the case, she would be spending the night at Eastleigh and she doubted she would ever see Devlin O'Neill again.

Her heart lurched, leaving her in no doubt as to the state of her true feelings.

I am asking you to save my brother.

Virginia felt like telling Sean that she could not save his brother if he would not even have a decent conversation with her. "Devlin? I really need to freshen up," she said.

"Virginia, your appearance is fine," Devlin said, his attention clearly elsewhere. He had not glanced at her even once, he was so hugely preoccupied.

She trembled. "I so want to make a good impression," she whispered. "Not that you care."

He finally faced her and his eyes held hers. "Why? Eastleigh is nothing but a murderer and you know it for a fact."

She swallowed, queasy now with the impending affair, and said, "I need his help, which you know, or Sweet Briar will be lost. And Devlin, I don't know all the details of your father's death, but I doubt it was deliberate. I'm sure it was an accident, one that, with the passage of so many years, you have re-created to be a deliberate act."

Devlin's eyes blazed. "When a man uses his sword to decapitate his victim, that is deliberate, Virginia," he said coldly.

She was so stunned that she was paralyzed. Images of a grotesque beheading assailed her. "Your father—he was *beheaded?*"

His face was flushed. But his tone continued to drip venom. "Yes, that is correct. I did not re-create the act with my imagination. I witnessed it firsthand, as did my poor mother."

"Oh, God," she gasped, reaching for his hand and squeezing it tightly.

For one moment he gazed at her palm as it covered his, and then he shook it off. "This is neither the time nor the place to discuss my father's death. Am I clear? You may greet your uncle and cousin as you will, but I will do most of the speaking."

She remained shocked. Her compassion for both Devlin and his mother knew no bounds. And her uncle had done this? But how could this be?

And now she really began to understand the depth of Devlin's scars. And Sean thought there was hope?

Suddenly a handsome man with regal bearing in a burgundy coat entered the room. His pale blue eyes were cool as he strode toward them, his air one of authority. Virginia flinched but knew he could not be her uncle; after all, he was only thirty or so, if that. "Captain O'Neill," he said, smiling, and it was more a baring of his teeth. "Welcome to Eastleigh." He bowed.

Devlin inclined his head. "Good afternoon, my lord," he said politely. "We have just arrived in Hampshire as we are on route to my estate, Wideacre." His mouth twisted into what might have been a smile, except Virginia knew it was a mere contortion of his lips. "However, your cousin expressed such an eagerness to be reunited with her family that I simply could not refuse her. Come, meet Miss Virginia Hughes."

William glanced at her, his expression mildly astonished, both dark brows lifted. "But I had heard, dear God, I had heard that she drowned aboard the *Americana!*" he cried. "I heard that there were no survivors!"

"You are mistaken. As you can see, Miss Hughes is very much alive." Devlin's eyes seemed to dance with glee.

"It is I, your cousin," Virginia managed, wishing she was not there. "I have hardly drowned, as you can see."

William looked at her, his expression comically arranged—his eyes were hard but his face was not, it was arranged into the angles of surprise. "But how can this be?" Clearly mockery was in his tone. "The navy has said the

Americana foundered in a gale. The statement was an official one. There were no survivors."

Now Devlin appeared incredulous. "You accuse Miss Hughes of treachery, of fraud?"

Virginia felt her cheeks heating.

"I have accused no one of anything," William said, his smile wide and fixed. "And I do apologize, Miss, er, Hughes, if I have given that impression."

"There was one survivor," Devlin returned smoothly, before Virginia could speak. "I know it for a fact, as I am the one who conducted her from the *Americana* to my ship."

"Well." William smiled again. "How odd this is! Two contradictory claims, it seems!"

"I suggest you summon the earl," Devlin said. But it was not a suggestion; clearly it was a command.

"I think I will do just that," William said, and relieved, he hurried from the hall.

Devlin glanced at Virginia, his gaze narrow with speculation and satisfaction. But Virginia was mortified. "He thinks I am an impostor," she whispered.

Devlin smiled. "He knows you are his cousin. He will insist until kingdom comes that you have drowned, however, in order to avoid any ransom and any future financial support which you are rightfully due."

"Can't this wait?" she pleaded.

His gaze hardened. "It cannot wait. It has waited too long. Surely you wish to meet the earl? Surely you wish to embrace your freedom?"

She inhaled harshly. "Not this way. Look at how impoverished they are!" she cried, gesturing at the hall. Some of the marble in the floor was cracked and chipped, the walls badly needed repainting, and a glance into an adjacent salon showed her a room filled with family treasures and heirlooms, but nothing was new, everything was tired and worn. How could her uncle possibly pay off Sweet Briar's debts, much less ransom her? Virginia was devastated. There did not seem to be any possible way now to save her home.

Footsteps sounded on the broad staircase to their right. Virginia turned and saw a tall, heavyset man with a gray complexion descending the stairs, William following. His gaze was on Devlin, and Devlin had turned and stared back. For one moment, she felt a seething tension in the room, a hostility that sizzled between them. And then her uncle smiled, his expression benign. "Captain O'Neill," he said, coming forward. "How good of you to call."

"My lord," Devlin said calmly, bowing slightly.

He turned to Virginia, who hastily curtsied. "And this is...my niece?"

Virginia leapt forward. "My lord! Yes, it is I, Virginia Hughes, your brother's daughter and only child!"

His gaze was piercing. Instantly Virginia stiffened, instinctively alarmed. But he continued to smile. "I was told that there were no survivors," he said softly.

She inhaled but could not dwell on her odd reaction to this man, her uncle. "Captain O'Neill saved my life, my lord, not once, but twice. He...he took me aboard his own ship when it became clear that a storm was at hand and that I would be safer upon it." She would never tell anyone that he had attacked the *Americana.* "Had he not done so, I would now be dead! And the storm was so violent I was almost blown overboard—but he rescued me then, too. I am incredibly indebted to him," Virginia said in a rush, aware of Devlin staring at her in surprise.

She refused to look at him, but now he knew she would never tell the world what he had really done.

Eastleigh looked her over. "And all this time, you have

been the guest of my friend, the captain. How wonderful, truly."

She hesitated. "I am hardly a guest," she whispered, but Eastleigh did not seem to hear. She glanced at Devlin. His arms were folded across his chest and his eyes gleamed with a predatory light.

"Sir...my lord...uncle!" She could not help herself and she grasped his plump, damp hands. "Please tell me that Sweet Briar hasn't been sold! Please tell me my home is intact!"

Eastleigh removed his hands, glancing at his son. "Have we sold the plantation yet?"

"Unfortunately, no."

Virginia almost cried out, and she covered her racing heart with her hand.

All three men looked at her. Then Devlin said, "I wish a word with you in private...my lord."

Eastleigh continued to smile. "I am afraid we are late for a supper engagement. I suggest you call later in the week."

Devlin now smiled and it was chilling. "I insist upon a moment of your time."

Eastleigh seemed to be a statue until he spoke, so quickly that Virginia had to strain to hear. "I grow tired of your games," he said softly. "I grow very tired, indeed."

"Unless you wish for the entire world to know of the countess's indiscretions, I suggest you give me the moment I am asking for."

Virginia had no idea what Devlin spoke of, but William gasped, and she glanced at him and found him pale. Then she saw that Eastleigh was turning red, dangerously so, in an apoplexy of rage.

William came forward. "I will call the constable," he cried. "This man cannot come into our home, flaunting an impostor and making accusations against the countess."

"I have hardly made any accusations yet," Devlin said. "I merely threatened to do so."

"There will be no constable," Eastleigh choked. "State your business, O'Neill, and leave—before I have you thrown out."

And Devlin was clearly amused. "And just how would you do that?" He started to laugh.

Virginia saw the absurdity. As if this old man and his pampered son could defy a man like Devlin, a man who did not think twice of attacking and destroying innocent ships. She hurried to him. "We should go."

But he didn't hear her—no one did. He said, "Virginia wishes to be reunited with her family—with you. Your reputation for generosity precedes you, my lord, and I wish to discuss the nature of the reward you will want to bestow upon me." He seemed to be laughing now.

Eastleigh just stood there, looking as if he wished to strangle Devlin but did not dare. He was crimson now.

"Reward?" William gasped. "Good God, the man thinks to ask a ransom! He wants a ransom!" he cried. Then, "Oh, ho, your head will roll for this! Even you cannot abduct a woman like my cousin and get away with ransoming her!" He had become gleeful.

Eastleigh and Devlin stared at each other, neither of them smiling, and if their eyes were daggers, they would both be dead.

"There will be no constable," Eastleigh said finally. "And you will not, William, mention this to anyone! Not even your brother, do you hear me?"

"But..." William sputtered.

"I do not seek a ransom," Devlin said far too softly. "I seek merely to have my expenses reimbursed, and we shall call it a reward. Fifteen thousand pounds should do." He turned. "Let us go, Virginia, our business here is done—for now."

He had taken her arm. She glanced back and saw East-leigh in his impotent rage, and William, more stunned than anything else. *Fifteen thousand pounds*. It was a vast sum of money, a sum Eastleigh clearly did not have.

They were at the door when Eastleigh called out to them. "We are not paying it," he said. "You have lost this time, O'Neill, for you see, I do not want the girl and I am not paying any ransom at all. You may keep her." And he laughed.

VIRGINIA HUDDLED IN THE COACH. This time Devlin had the coachman tie his horse to the back of the carriage and he climbed in beside her. Closing the door, he settled back against the leather seat, knocking on the partition. The carriage took off, rumbling down the paved drive.

Virginia looked at him with wide eyes. His face was hard. So were his eyes. He seemed deeply thoughtful, but if he was dismayed about the interview—or Eastleigh's refusal to pay her ransom—she could not tell. She shud-dered. What would happen now? She had little doubt that Eastleigh had meant his every word. He did not care if she lived or died, was captive or freed. She had never seen such cold eyes—except for Devlin's.

She shivered again. Somehow, Eastleigh's eyes were worse. Two things now were clear. Devlin's hatred knew no bounds—but Eastleigh hated him as ferociously. And both men were at an impasse, were they not? As Devlin was demanding a ransom that Eastleigh refused to pay.

If only she could make Devlin change his course. Would anything stop him from exacting his revenge on his enemy? She did not think so and she despaired. "Devlin...this has to stop."

He looked at her. "This stops when I say so and not a moment before."

She stiffened, as his gaze was chilling. "And are you pleased with yourself? Do you get pleasure from what you have done, and what you are doing? My uncle is destitute! You have clearly ruined him. Why continue? Who would choose to live this way—to live a life of hatred and revenge!" she cried.

Something in his gaze flickered. His mouth tightened. "I heard you once say that if someone had murdered your father, you would kill him yourself."

She stared, for she had said that to Sean. "I'm not sure that I meant it."

"You meant it. You see, in this one instance, we are not that different, Virginia."

"We are very different! I have every reason to hate you and to exact my own vengeance. But I don't hate you—and I never will. And I will never tell the truth to anyone about what you have done. You see, I refuse to walk the path of revenge, Devlin, I simply *refuse*."

His face grew hard as he stared at her. "I owe this much to my father."

"Your father is dead! He has been dead for years!" She could not yet give up. "Devlin, they do not have the ransom, and even if they did, they would not think to pay it. Surely you, a fine judge of character, saw that."

He did not glance at her now, clearly having no intention of answering her.

Virginia turned away in despair. She had a bad feeling. She knew he was planning something, and whatever it was, she dreaded it. But there was nothing more that she could say. She was clearly not capable of persuading him to give up his course, to change his life—Sean was so wrong! Perhaps he was a madman—for was not *obsession* a clinical term for a psychiatric disorder? And what would happen to him in the end? If only she did not care! Would

Eastleigh's son call the constabulary? Wasn't Devlin afraid of being caged behind prison bars? She knew how he loved the wind and the sea and she thought that imprisonment might kill him.

But then, this man did not fear death, so maybe he did not fear incarceration, either. He certainly did not seem at all worried about his future. She was the one, dear God, worrying about *his* future, when she had her own future to worry about, a future that seemed very bleak.

They had left Eastleigh's tattered estate behind. Lush green hills were crisscrossed with old stone walls and wildflowers bloomed along the roadside. They drove through a quaint village filled with small whitewashed stone houses, the shops below and the apartments above, before passing the local church, built in Norman times and never renewed. A few minutes later they turned off the main road, between a pair of rusting iron gates. Virginia saw a pleasant sweep of lawn and a modest stone cottage, two stories high and perhaps two rooms wide. A stone carriage house was behind it, as rundown and ramshackle. Virginia blinked, surprised at how small and shabby this country home was. This could not possibly be Devlin's home—it had to be the wrong address.

But Devlin helped her down, annoyance in his expression. He took a long, hard look at the house, giving Virginia the impression that he had never seen it before, and she knew they were in the right place after all. Then, his hand on her arm, he guided her up the stone walk. At least the roses blooming against the side of the house were pretty, Virginia thought.

The front door opened before they even reached it and a man and woman came out. "Sir Captain O'Neill?" the tall, dark-haired woman asked. She was middle-aged, quite lean, and her features were hawkish. She wore the severe black dress of a servant.

He nodded. "Mrs. Hill, the housekeeper, I presume?"

She smiled tightly at him. "Yes. We have been expecting you. I hope the house and grounds meet with your satisfaction, Sir Captain."

"I will let you know," he responded noncommittally.

"Sir? I am your butler, Tompkins," the smaller, dapper man by the housekeeper's side said. He wore a dark wool coat and trousers. "We are so pleased that you have finally come home, Sir Captain."

Devlin grunted. "Take all the bags and install them in my suite," he said.

Virginia was startled—what about her bags?

"And may I introduce Miss Hughes?"

Mrs. Hill smiled at her, as did the butler. The housekeeper seemed tense, her smile rather thin, but the butler seemed quite the opposite, rather jovial, in fact.

"Miss Hughes is to lack nothing," Devlin announced. "She is my very special guest, and anything that she wishes is to be met."

Virginia stared at him, a very bad feeling coming over her now. What was he up to?

"And where shall we take her bags, sir?" Tompkins asked.

Devlin's dark brows lifted in surprise. "Why, to my rooms, of course," he said.

A moment of surprised silence fell.

Virginia opened her mouth to protest, but he suddenly had her by the hand and he was lifting it to his mouth. Virginia wondered if she was dreaming. He smiled and kissed her hand, his lips firm and warm on her skin.

Her body responded instantly, shockingly, and she could only think, what was he doing? And dear God, why?

"Your suite, er, sir?" Tompkins managed, flushing.

"Miss Hughes is sharing my rooms," Devlin said, smiling warmly at her.

And Virginia, her heart racing with exertion, suddenly sensed what was coming. "Devlin," she managed, a feeble protest.

"Hush, darling," he said. And he smiled at the servants. "Mrs. Hill, Mr. Tompkins, meet Miss Virginia Hughes, my mistress."

Part Two

The Bargain

CHAPTER SIXTEEN

VIRGINIA KNEW HER SURPRISE was evident. She felt her jaw drop, and it certainly seemed as if her eyes popped. She was only given an instant in which to react, however, an instant in which Mrs. Hill turned grim and severe, a knowing glint in her eye, while Mr. Tompkins flushed. "Come, darling," Devlin murmured, tugging on her hand.

What game was this?

Anger rushed over her in one hot wave. She refused to move, turning what she hoped was a murderous glare upon her captor. Still, her disbelief knew no bounds. *What could he possibly be doing?*

Devlin swept her up into his arms and carried her into the house. "Do not argue with me," he murmured. "And do not kick."

"I'll do better than that! Put me down and I am not—"

He covered her mouth with his.

Virginia could not have been more surprised. She stiffened, but his mouth was far more than terribly familiar. When she did not kick or beat at him with her fists, his lips softened. She felt him push open the door as her heart lurched wildly and then picked up an insistent, faster beat. His mouth covered hers, demanding that she open and admit him. How she wanted to yield... Her anger vanished, as did all thought. Her lips parted; her hands curled around his shoulders. His tongue swept deep inside her.

And the answering desire was a piercing bolt, directly to her heart.

He raised his head as he trotted up the stairs and their gazes met. His gray eyes smoked, but otherwise, Virginia could not fathom what he was thinking—much less what he was doing. And what was she doing—kissing him back, her entire body burning with a desperate need? On the landing he paused, finally breaking their stare, glancing around.

"Put me down, Devlin," she said more calmly than she felt. Her sex was full, a terrible testimony to how easily this man aroused her, but she was not about to share his bed, no matter how he might attempt to seduce her, no matter what he had said.

His answer was to push open the first door with his shoulder, glance within and back out. "Be quiet," he said tersely. "And stop squirming." He strode to the next door.

"I am not squirming," she said rather breathlessly. "And I—"

He entered the next room, sliding her to her feet. Virginia made contact with the singular most fascinating piece of his anatomy, and she went still. He was also aroused. He still wanted her. How was she going to manage this?

He turned and closed the door, faced her, and said low, "This is only a pretense. I will sleep on the..." He looked around, and resigned, said, "Floor."

"What?" she gasped, realizing that the master bedroom, if it was that, had a fine four-poster bed and one chaise, two end tables, a bureau, a hearth and that was all.

He walked over to her.

Virginia tensed, still breathless and still wishing desperately that she did not burn to be in his arms. "What are you doing, Devlin?" she asked quietly.

"Unfortunately, I will have to provoke your uncle into paying a ransom," he said flatly. "You will live in my rooms as if you are my mistress, and in public, we shall act like a very shameless pair of lovers. I expect your cooperation, Virginia," he warned, "and I remind you that your interest remains in being freed quickly. The sooner Eastleigh cannot stand my parading you so openly about, the sooner you will be on your merry way home—or wherever it is that you choose to go."

She simply gaped.

"I once thought to enjoy toying with him over this." He was so grim. "But actually, I am sorry he will not pay me directly so that we might be done."

It took her a moment to truly understand his plan and her comprehension of it made it impossible for her to hear his last words. "We will *pretend* to be lovers? We will *share* this room? You will ruin me in the eyes of the *world*—but you are not going to share my *bed?*" She heard disbelief and the tremor of hurt in her own tone. What he suggested was more than incredible, more than shocking. He would ruin her good name—flaunt her in society. She was stunned.

"That is the gist of it, yes," he answered, his hands on his hips and his strong thighs braced. In fact, he looked braced for a very real storm.

"A gentleman does not live openly with a woman other than his wife—a gentleman does not escort his mistress about his neighbor's halls."

"There is no other way."

"How can you do this to me?" She found it hard to breathe now. For here was the ultimate proof that Sean was wrong and Devlin did not care—he would callously use her and ruin her name, all for the sake of the ransom.

Maybe you are the one who can help him find his soul.

Absolutely not, Virginia thought in response to Sean's terrible words. Devlin could not care about her, not at all, if he thought to destroy her reputation this way. To use her so deliberately, he could not have any soul left to save. She was now horrified.

"You know what motivates me," he said rather harshly. "Again, I have no wish to abuse you, but there is no choice. I did not come this far to have Eastleigh simply laugh in my face and refuse to pay your ransom." And he turned away, as if he could not face her now.

But she was imagining that. "They are impoverished! They cannot pay it and it is obvious!" She had to sit down as her legs had become useless. "Even if they could...how could you do this...to me?"

"They can sell off the estate, Virginia, or borrow more funds; they might even succeed in selling Sweet Briar. I hardly care what they do." He stalked toward the door, his strides stiff. Then he turned. "We both know you don't care what anyone thinks—you just spent five months un-chaperoned at Askeaton—and that does make this easier. I know that if I actually made you my mistress, you would be pleased. So cease this sham of hurt and outrage!" Inexplicably, he was trembling.

She did not know why he was so distressed and she could not care. What if her uncle sold her home in order to pay her ransom? "No one knew I was at Askeaton, and the villagers thought I was your fiancée. I am hurt, Devlin," she said with what dignity she could muster. "I am hurt that you care so little for my reputation that you would flaunt me as your lover just to gain your ends. You justify ruining me for the sake of your revenge."

And he was furious—so much so, that for a moment, he could only stare. And what he saw was the most hurt, vulnerable expression he had ever beheld. Tears filled the violet pools of her eyes. In fact, Virginia was looking at him as if he had betrayed *her.* In that moment, he hated himself for what he was doing—but there was no choice. Was there?

And for one moment he hesitated, aware of the oddest urge to back down—to let her go and be done with it all.

Then Eastleigh's cold laughter came to mind, followed by the terrible memory of his father's sightless eyes staring up at him from the ground. *Eastleigh could not win. Justice had to be served.* "You are making far too much of this. I am sparing you actual degradation. I am not making you my mistress in fact. And when this is over I will tell the world, if you wish me to, that it was all a lie to humiliate your uncle. But as you intend to return to Virginia, what happens here is of no consequence—there, no one will know what has happened here." And he knew his attempt at rationalization was a pathetic one.

She raised her chin but her tone was so soft, it was barely audible. "If we were *really* lovers, you would *guard* my reputation fiercely and no one would ever know of the affair."

She was right. He felt as if he had been struck a severe and physical blow. "I fail to see the difference," he lied. "There is no other choice."

"There is always another choice, Devlin. Even if you use me so callously, what makes you think they will pay, even if they can sell my home or borrow the funds?" she cried.

He gripped the doorknob but did not face her, as he could not. "It will be a matter of honor," he said. "They will pay—I will make certain of it." And he walked out as quickly as he could, as if in doing so he might forget the atrocious plan he had set in motion, a plan that would, in fact, destroy Miss Virginia Hughes once and for all.

VIRGINIA WAS AFRAID.

It was crystal clear now that Devlin was so obsessed

with his revenge that nothing and no one would stand in his way. It was equally clear that Sean was so very wrong—she could not show him the light of a different way, because if he were not completely lost, he would have some guilt over what he was doing to her. But she hadn't seen an inkling of guilt—she had only seen utter determination. Of course, Devlin O'Neill was a master at controlling his emotions.

I am asking you to save my brother.

"Sean, do go away!" Virginia cried, splashing the water in her bath and just realizing how cool it had become. "He is beyond saving!"

She became still, an odd despair coiled around her. Was he beyond any and all help? Was anyone, as long as he still lived and breathed? Virginia closed her eyes tightly. His every other action somehow hurt her, yet even now, she could not hate him, as foolish as that was.

She was at a loss. She had become a child again, bewildered and hurt. She did not know what to do. Somehow she remained consumed with her captor, defending his actions to herself, and still secretly hoping to save him from himself. But was there anything that she could do? From the moment he had attacked and seized the *Americana,* she had been but a pawn, tossed this way and that, at his very whim. And now there was this new terrible twist in his game, a twist that proved his indifference toward her.

Virginia sighed, beginning to shiver. She should hate him for holding her a prisoner yet again. She should hate him for planning to flaunt her as his mistress. She should hate him for a lot of things, but she didn't hate him at all. She felt sorry for him, deeply so. She felt sorry for the small boy who had seen his father murdered, and she felt sorry for the man that boy had become.

She got out of the bath, wrapping herself in a towel, and went to stand before the fire in the bedroom.

Virginia stared at the dancing flames but only saw Devlin. Now, as before, she had no choice but to play his game his way and see where it led. She was strong enough to do so. Devlin had been partly right. She did not care what society thought of her—or not very much. Then she stiffened.

But why not be more clever than he?

Why not play his game to *win?*

Stunned with her thoughts, Virginia began to dress, thinking very carefully. She wanted her freedom and she wanted Sweet Briar, but that was not what she wanted most. Did she dare admit to herself what she really wanted?

Unfortunately, what she desired most was her captor.

Her heart lurched as she realized exactly what it was that she wanted from him, and she felt faint, her knees buckling.

Dressed only in her chemise and pantalettes, Virginia gripped the mirror and stared at her reflection there. Her violet eyes were huge and bright hot spots of soft pink marred her complexion. She wanted Devlin to think her beautiful, to be overwhelmed by his passion, and most of all, she wanted him to love her.

She wanted his love.

Terrified, Virginia managed to find the chaise, where she sat, shaking. Most people who knew him would claim he was incapable of love. How could she be such a fool?

Did she dare even hope for the impossible?

And more important, did she dare try to make him love her?

Virginia bit her lips, tears forming in her eyes. She wasn't even beautiful, although he clearly found her attractive. She wasn't a lady, either, which he already knew. How could she think to entice such a man?

But what was the alternative? To be ransomed and set free, so she could go home or stay and marry his brother?

Virginia trembled and it had nothing to do with being wet and cold. Somehow, sometime, somewhere between the *Americana* and Wideacre, she had fallen in love with Devlin O'Neill, and nothing was ever going to be the same. There was no choice. She was going to have to do whatever she had to do in order to save his soul—and make him love her, too.

As VIRGINIA WENT DOWNSTAIRS, she was very preoccupied and very somber. Her terrible new comprehension—and her new plan—consumed her thoughts, and her steps were faltering and filled with trepidation.

"Is there anything that you need, Miss Hughes?"

At the sound of Mrs. Hill's firm voice, at once conde-scending and obsequious, she started, turning. "My blue day gown and the matching pelisse need laundering, if that is at all possible," Virginia said with a pleasant smile.

"Of course. I'll send the maid up." She smiled tightly at Virginia. How strained her expression seemed.

And her dark eyes were twin mirrors of disapproval. Virginia smiled back, said thank you, and added, "Where is the captain?"

"In the library," she said.

Virginia met her regard and thought that it was far too knowing, as if she suspected that Virginia wished to find her captor for a very illicit and carnal reason. As Virginia walked away, she was disturbed. She was surprised to realize that she did not like being judged and disliked—but she reminded herself that she did not care what people thought of her and the housekeeper's opinions meant nothing. After all, everyone had looked down on her as a country bumpkin at the Marmott School, and she had not given a damn.

But it was terribly familiar, the condescension. Her entire childhood she had been accused of being more like a boy than a girl, of being a wild child in her britches and on horseback. Those asides and snide glances had bewildered her then, although there was nothing bewildering about the rigid housekeeper's thoughts now.

Virginia quickly dismissed the unpleasant memories. Her childhood was far behind her and only a very uncertain future remained. Not to mention an even more tenuous present, she thought somewhat grimly.

She passed the open doors to a shabby salon with a faded gold velvet sofa, the draperies a sober mustard color, the chairs a grim brown paisley. The next door opened to a study where a medium-size desk was in one corner, a dark green sofa facing the fireplace. All of the walls were lined with bookcases crammed with books, and with the dancing fire and the sun setting outside behind the overgrown lawns, the room became a pleasant one.

Except for Devlin, sitting on the sofa, a glass of Scotch in his hand. He had been staring as if entranced into the hearth; now he turned and their gazes locked.

Her heart careened and crashed. Oh, ho, his mood was dire, indeed, and what did it mean? She went on alert. Worse, he continued to stare, his expression quite harsh and very forbidding, and then his gaze dipped and slipped over her, causing an instant tightening within her, and a heightening of her already profound tension. "You are in a fine kettle," she murmured, standing in the doorway, not brave enough to enter.

Did she really think to play his game and win? Did she really think to make him fall in love with her?

But he stood and inclined his head. "Care for a Scotch? I'd offer you wine but the stuff in the cabinet has turned."

She thought about the sip or two of Scotch she'd shared

with him in his cabin on the *Defiance.* "No, thank you." She smiled cautiously at him.

His eyes widened and she knew he sensed some purpose on her part; then he eyed her with far too much speculation, like a big, slothful lion sunning himself—not quite sated and not quite starving, but very capable of pouncing for his evening meal. "Are you no longer inclined toward good Scotch whiskey, or are you suddenly afraid of me, Virginia?"

She stepped into the room, never one to refuse a challenge. "I am sure your Scotch is fine." She smiled again. "I remain taken aback," she said, and it was true. "Not only can I not fathom you, your impossibly dark humor has somehow become even darker."

He merely gazed at her, as watchful as before. He had shed his uniform and wore only a silk shirt of the finest quality and his britches and boots. As usual, the britches fit far too suggestively and he had left the shirt carelessly unbuttoned at the throat. "The Earl of Eastleigh hardly brings out my best mood."

"You are not enjoying the hunt? You are not enjoying stalking a poor, fat old man?"

He eyed her as he moved to the sideboard, a huge and heavy piece of furniture that was simply ugly. "I am enjoying the hunt. Of course I am enjoying it. But if you dare to pity that murderer, I suggest you keep your feelings to yourself." He handed her a glass of Scotch.

"I don't pity him," she said softly. "It is you I feel sorry for."

For one moment he stared and she expected his temper to flare. It did not. Instead he shrugged and said, "You have said so before. If you think to arouse me, you will not. Feel what you will and do sit down. I won't bite. Besides, the servants are expecting you to enjoy my company." He drained his glass and poured another one.

"I am only joining you because there is nowhere else to go and nothing else to do," she said quietly, sitting on the far side of the sofa, although that was as far from the truth as could be.

He finally smiled at her and sat as well, his big body dominating the sofa, the room, herself. "Really? Frankly, I believe you enjoy my company," he said. His gaze became hooded. "Although I cannot think why," he added in a silken murmur.

Virginia started and became even more rigid and more breathless. "Are you in your cups, Devlin?"

He saluted her. "Only a little."

"Only a foolish woman would want and enjoy your company," she said, flushing, aware of how many women must leap at his beck and call.

"Then many women are foolish, I suppose," he returned evenly. Another half a glass of Scotch had vanished.

Was he trying to become inebriated? And if so, why? But more importantly, how many women did he mean? "How many?"

"How many what?"

"How many women have enjoyed your company?" she dared—for she simply had to know.

"I beg your pardon?" His eyes widened and he looked torn between disbelief and laughter. "Are you asking me how many women I have had in bed?" He now choked.

"Yes, I think I am," she said, clasping her hands tightly in her lap and blinking furiously. She felt her cheeks begin to burn.

He began to laugh. His laughter had that rough, raw, unused quality, but it was not unpleasant. "I think what I like most about you is your rampant curiosity," he said, "as it is so unique." His laughter died. But he smiled now with real mirth and her heart lurched wildly. She had never seen such a handsome man.

"No, strike that, I like your outspoken manner. Has it ever occurred to you not to reveal your every thought, wish and desire?"

She blinked, trembling. Not only had she made him laugh, really laugh, he was flattering her—he liked her curiosity, her manner! Did he know what he was doing? Was this another game, or was she finally glimpsing him relaxed, his guard down, the truth allowed out due to the Scotch he had imbibed? *Did he like her just a little bit?* "How much have you drank, Devlin?"

"A Scotch or two," he said softly. "Very well, this is the third. No, the fourth. I am not drunk, Virginia. I do not get drunk."

"I think you are," she said, and somehow their gazes met and held. His eyes had become soft, with no hint of ice, as if he was feeling warmly toward her now. She was so elated she could not breathe properly. "No one likes my outspoken manner. Even my parents despaired."

He smiled again. "You are unpredictable—I never know what you shall say or do. It is interesting."

Her heart raced. "So you like me, a little, after all?" Dear God, had that been a hopeful tone in her voice? She prayed not.

He tore his gaze from hers and slowly got to his feet, the slumbering lion preparing to feed. He gave her a seductive glance, sidelong and direct, and slowly began to pace. "So many questions," he murmured. Then he added, "I sent Tompkins to the *Defiance* for some wine. The cook has prepared venison and I think a hearty cabernet will do. But I know you prefer white, and I asked him to bring some, too." He paused, facing her, leaning one slim hip against the sideboard. The posture was at once indolent and suggestive.

She leapt to her feet. "Don't change the subject."

His lashes lowered. "There have been many women, Virginia, and I do not count," he murmured.

How clever he now was, avoiding the subject she so wished to discuss. "It is hardly the end of the world if the great and oh-so-cold Captain O'Neill actually likes another human being," she said.

His lashes lifted, revealing the gleam of silvery eyes, and then he looked away. "You are like a dog with a bone. What is it that you want me to say? That I find you beautiful? That I yearn for your kiss? That I cannot live without you? I'm afraid that while I do find you unpredictable and interesting, I am not the kind of man to grovel over a woman, to yearn for true love or any other such nonsense. Leave it alone."

She stared, swallowing, for he was too astute, and it was almost as if he knew her thoughts and feelings. "You started this," she began. "And we both know I am not beautiful, so I am not asking you to find me so. We also both know it takes little to arouse you, so clearly you yearn for my kiss—or something along those lines. And as for living together? Are you madder than I previously thought? Of course you can live without me—without Sean—without anyone! You are an island, Devlin, an island unto yourself and the whole world knows it." She was very pleased with her brisk tone and how firmly she had rebutted him.

For a long moment he stared, so intensely that she backed away. "No, I'm afraid that you started this, Virginia, by wanting something from me that I cannot give." His tone was soft but firm and very sincere.

Virginia almost hugged herself, staring back at him. Was he telling her that he would never love her? Could he be that perceptive? Had the liquor allowed him to speak so honestly with her now?

"I do not know what you mean," she whispered, perspiring.

He shrugged with a small smile, the gesture meant to convey that he did not believe her, not for a single moment.

An idea struck her then, a wonderful idea that might help her attain her end. "But there is something that I want, Devlin," she said.

He studied her, half a smile on his face, waiting.

"There is something that I want from you and I *know* you can give it," she said firmly. How tense her expression felt.

"Oh, ho! I sense a new battle. Darling, you cannot win, so do not even think to take to the field." He smiled, but she saw the wariness in his eyes. She realized then that, drunk or not, he would always be a dangerous adversary.

"I am not your darling," she breathed.

"But you are—in the eyes of the world." His soft tone was a deadly caress.

She wet her lips, praying hard, wondering if he might actually be trying to seduce her, in spite of what he had said earlier. "I want your friendship, Devlin. Nothing more, just your friendship."

His eyes widened, then quickly narrowed. "A new twist," he murmured, inclining his head with real respect. "As I said, forever unpredictable. I think not."

"No! You must hear me out!" She finally walked over to him and took his hand.

He stared first at her face and then at her pale hand, and he made an incredulous sound. "Virginia," he warned, and it was clear that the seductive dance between them was now over.

Bravely she stood her ground. "I want your friendship, freely given, until the ransom is paid and I am free to go."

He stared at her. "I have no friends."

"That's ridiculous!" His brows lifted. "Sean is your friend."

He pulled slowly away from her and folded his arms across his broad chest. "Forever interesting," he mused softly. And his tone hardened. "I sense a negotiation. Negotiate."

She wet her lips. His gaze lingered on her mouth. She noticed, but only vaguely, as her heart slammed with undue force. "In return, I will play the part of your mistress so well that even you will believe me your shameless lover," she said.

He looked at her in absolute surprise.

She smiled, savoring a moment of triumph. "Well? This game will end much sooner if I cooperate. I am offering you more than cooperation—I am offering you full participation."

He slowly smiled at her, but it did not reach his eyes, which remained dark and thoughtful. "I know how clever you are," he said. "And I know you have some scheme upon which this bargain rests. Whatever it is, whatever you think to truly accomplish, you will fail—if it is not what I want."

She shrugged, weak with the desire to win. "Just make the bargain."

"Patience, *darling,* is what you must learn if you are to be a real player in the game of life."

She sighed with real exasperation, while inside she was very close to elation. "Do we have a bargain or not?" she cried.

"We have a bargain," he agreed softly, with a slight smile. "Let me guess. We seal it with a handshake?" His tone remained soft, but it was mocking.

"I don't think so," Virginia said boldly, barely able to believe her courage, and she moved into his arms. "We seal it with a kiss."

His smile told her he had thought so. And he waited.

Her heart raced with such strength that she felt faint.

Virginia stood on tiptoes, clutching his shoulders, too ex-
hilarated to be annoyed that he made no effort to bend
down to her. She turned up her face and closed her eyes,
the last thing she saw being his silver gaze, suddenly hot,
suddenly bright. He wanted this, too. And then she moved
her mouth firmly over his.

He remained utterly still.

She pushed at the seam made by his lips, using her
tongue, and when he gave, she felt real triumph and she
invaded, her small tongue against his much larger one.

His hand closed on her nape, hard, and instantly he bent
her over backward and his tongue swept deep into her
mouth. In that one instant he took over the kiss, branding
her and letting her know it. Virginia didn't care. She held
on tightly, pressing against him, allowing him every
possible liberty, should he wish to take any. And when the
hot, hard kiss was over, he lifted his head and stared.

"Whatever your game, darling, it's a dangerous one."

She smiled, but fiercely, while trembling in his arms. "I
merely want your friendship, Devlin," she lied.

He made a mocking sound.

THE MOMENT THE DOOR OPENED, Virginia pretended to be
asleep.

She lay absolutely still, on her back, listening intently.
As no footsteps sounded, she thought he stood in the
doorway, staring at her.

He sighed and walked in, closing the door. "I know you
are awake, Virginia, your cheeks are turning pink," he said,
holding a candle aloft.

She sat up. It was midnight. She had tried to go to sleep
two hours ago, but her mind had refused to cooperate. No
longer confused, she remained scared, the feeling distinct,
as if she were standing on a cliff high above a lake, pre-

paring to dive into icy, unknown depths far below. All she could think of was what she was doing. Did she really think to beat him at his game? Did she really think to win his friendship? Did she have a chance of making him fall in love with her? And how in God's name were they going to share a room? She could think of little else than a far better way of spending the night in the same bedroom together—even though her resolve not to leap into his bed remained.

"I see you made my bed for me," he said, glancing at the pile of sheets and pillows on the floor. "How thoughtful."

She hugged her knees to her chest, watching him yank a sheet free and then lay it flat. When his makeshift bed was made, he sat down in the room's single chair and tugged off his boots. When the second one hit the floor with a thump, he looked up, his eyes hard and narrowed. "Do not make this difficult, Virginia."

"Why not?" she flung. "You have certainly made my life difficult."

"We are not sharing that bed." He stood, unbuttoning his shirt.

She had to watch, mesmerized by the swath of golden skin slowly but surely revealed. "That's right, we're not. This is pretense and I know it better than you."

"Really?" He clearly did not believe her.

"Now you plan to undress?" she asked breathlessly as he tossed the shirt aside. She made sure not to inhale, but he was an Adonis, impossibly beautiful, his body hard and muscular, every sinew and tendon sculpted and defined.

Not looking at her, he blew out the candles. "I am sleeping in my britches, if that is any comfort to you."

"It's such a relief!" she mocked. Her eyes adjusted to the darkness, and with the moonlight streaming through the window, she saw him lying quietly on the white sheets, one arm flung above his head. A moment passed and she wondered if he were already asleep, as he did not move at all. "Devlin?"

Remaining motionless, he said, "Yes, Virginia?"

"Are you thinking about what I am thinking about...at all?"

"No," he said calmly.

She stared at him suspiciously. "Yes, you are! How else would you know what I am thinking?"

"You are thinking about going home," he returned smoothly. "Good night." It was a warning.

She hugged her knees harder, her pulse racing, and finally, softly, she said, "I am not thinking about going home. I am thinking about that kiss in the library."

"Good night," he said very firmly.

She sighed with exasperation and frustration and flopped onto her back. Instantly images of his eyes, blazing with lust, filled her mind, followed by another image of how he had just looked, shirtless, and her body responded completely. She bit her lip hard. How would she ever fall asleep when he was right there on the floor, a temptation like no other? And why did she have to be so tempted? She had a plan now, one that frightened her, but one she intended to follow. Would it really matter if she was his mistress in fact as well as in fiction?

It would matter to her, she thought. It would matter a great deal, unless he gave her his love as well as his body. She sighed. She might as well resign herself to a very long and uphill battle, including the one against herself.

"Virginia," he warned. "You are acting like a child."

She sat up and moved to the end of the bed, where she could see him quite clearly. "How am I acting like a child? I simply cannot sleep with you there on the floor!"

He remained on his back, but he was looking at her. "You don't want to sleep," he muttered. "You want to argue...among other things."

"What other things could I possibly want, Devlin?" she asked innocently, although she was smiling.

"Count sheep," he said firmly. "Or leaves of tobacco. Good night."

"I think I am a bit mad," she said reflectively. "That must be it. I mean, six months ago I was on the *Americana* and we had never met. No, actually, I was still at that awful and horrid ladies' school in Richmond. Since then you have abducted me, taken me to Askeaton, had your way with me, left me, handed me off to your brother, and here we are, man and mistress—almost."

"Good God," Devlin said. "Are you going to be this garrulous every night?"

"And after all of that, I still enjoyed that kiss. Of course, I refuse to ever entertain you in bed again."

He sat up. The sheet dropped to his lap, revealing the hard slabs of his chest and his lean, flat abdomen. "You have an eerie mind, Virginia, and it seems to be on a single path. And, darling, I entertained you, not vice versa."

That was it. She thought about his mouth and tongue against her sex and she could not breathe, not one drop of air.

He suddenly leapt to his feet. "I am going downstairs to read for a while."

This was never going to work, she thought, staring at him. He was aroused, the rigid line impossible to miss in his snug, pale britches. "Too bad Fiona isn't here," she heard herself remark.

"Yes, it is," he said, crossing the room and not looking at her.

"Devlin, this will not work. Our sharing a room, it's

simply impossible. You have to sleep somewhere else. To hell with the servants!"

He leaned against the closed door, facing her. "Servants gossip madly, and I would bet my fortune that Mrs. Hill's telling everyone she can think of how shameless a barbarian her new Irish master is. So this will have to work, and it will, but only if you make an attempt, Virginia, an attempt not to think about your passionate nature."

"Like you are doing?" she challenged softly.

"Like I am doing," he said with a smile that was a simple baring of his teeth. "It is called self-will, Virginia, and while I realize you have never thought to exercise it, now is a good time to start."

"This is not my fault," she reminded him.

"Lie down, close your eyes and count sheep, Virginia, sheep—or bales of tobacco, if you will—or battleships. Then I am certain you will be able to rest." He walked out.

"We do not bale tobacco," she muttered crossly.

Virginia flopped back down, arms crossed, oddly pleased. He wasn't that hard to provoke, she decided, and she did enjoy stirring him up. And he did find her attractive, of that there was no doubt.

Virginia closed her eyes and began to count tobacco leaves. But the tobacco faded, replaced with a striking image of Devlin O'Neill. Virginia suddenly smiled. Maybe her plan would work after all.

CHAPTER SEVENTEEN

"MISS HUGHES? YOU HAVE callers in the parlor," Tompkins said.

Virginia had awoken that morning quite late, as it had taken her hours to still her mind and fall asleep, and the bedroom had been empty. It was now noon and she had been strolling the back lawns, finally pausing on the small terrace behind the house. She smiled at Tompkins. "Callers?"

"Yes," he beamed back at her.

He was not at all like the horrid Mrs. Hill, whom Virginia had seen in passing that morning. The housekeeper had made a remark that breakfast was taken between eight and nine, an explanation for the empty sideboard in the small dining room. She had refused to look at Virginia, as if doing so might make her a mistress, too. Virginia had ignored her growling belly, politely asking for some coffee, toast and chocolate. A maid had brought her the requested refreshments, as it was clearly beneath Mrs. Hill to wait upon her master's lover.

As they turned to the French doors, Virginia asked, "How long have you been at Wideacre, Tompkins?"

"Ten years, if I do say so myself," he responded cheerfully.

"And you love it here?"

"Yes, I do. The missus died some time ago, my two

daughters are married with children, one in Manchester, the other in a small village to the south, and Wideacre has become my home." He shrugged a bit, his cheeks pink.

"You do a wonderful job," Virginia assured him. They stepped into the parlor.

Devlin stood speaking to a country gentleman and his plump, pretty wife. Virginia halted the instant she laid eyes on him and for one moment, she admired him in his fine brown frock coat and tan britches. She had never seen him in a casual coat before. It hardly made a difference; he remained such a stunning man.

He saw her and their gazes locked. She wondered if he had ever come up to their room last night; when she had finally fallen asleep, he had yet to return. *Their room.* It was still almost impossible to believe, as was the state of her heart, now that she had admitted her worst fears and greatest dreams.

"Do come in, Virginia," Devlin said, smiling. "Squire Pauley and his wife have been so kind as to call."

Virginia hesitated, aware of the game they would now play. It had already begun, in fact, with his calling her by her given name so intimately. Both the bewhiskered squire and his blond wife were regarding her curiously, smiling. Virginia knew they did not yet know that she was a fallen woman.

She would change that. She smiled and swept forward, going right to Devlin, where she stood on tiptoe and kissed his cheek. His skin was warm and smooth—he had clearly shaved recently. Her heart leapt as she withdrew her mouth and she said, "Good morning, darling," her voice husky without any effort on her part.

He started, but then, ever the better gamesman, he took her hand and lifted it to his mouth, pressing his lips firmly there. "You are ravishing, Virginia," he murmured. "I see you slept late. No doubt you have deserved it."

Their gazes held. "I was so tired I simply could not get up," she breathed, and deciding to outdo him, she stroked his cheek, just once.

He started yet again. That gave her no satisfaction, however, as her heart was racing from the feigned intimacy. It was as if they were really lovers, and in that brief moment of pretense, it had felt as if they were alone.

"May I present Miss Virginia Hughes of Sweet Briar, Virginia," Devlin said, looping her arm in his.

The squire and his wife were wide-eyed; now, quickly, they both smiled, at once. "How nice to make your acquaintance, Miss Hughes," the squire said, his gaze shooting back and forth between them. Virginia knew he was trying to fathom their relationship.

"It is my pleasure," Virginia said, as if she had been the most stellar student at the Marmott School. She extended her hand and he brushed the air above it with his lips. She turned to his wife. "Hello, Mrs. Pauley. Do you live far from here?"

"We live just a few miles away," the blonde replied, attempting a smile and not quite succeeding.

"The captain tells us you have just arrived," Squire Pauley said, tugging at his cravat.

"Yes, yesterday. I have spent the past five months at Devlin's home in Ireland," Virginia said, giving him a sidelong glance.

His brows lifted with amusement. He was clearly no longer surprised by her gamesmanship. "While I, alas, was patrolling the coast of Spain." He sighed heavily as if he had yearned for her every day they were apart.

Mrs. Pauley's cheeks were bright red. But she turned her blue eyes on Devlin then. "We have heard so much about you, Captain. You are a hero to us all."

"Yes, sir," her husband added. "We are so pleased that you have a home here now."

"Thank you," Devlin murmured.

"How long will you be in residence?" the squire asked.

"I think a week, certainly no more," Devlin said.

Virginia was surprised. "Only a week, Devlin?" she asked softly.

He pulled her close. "Has my little country home grown on you the way that Askeaton has?"

She smiled up at him, acutely aware of the length of his body against her side. She was practically in his embrace, nestled against him and in the hard curve of one arm. It felt right. "I fear that it might...darling," she said.

The squire coughed. Or perhaps he choked. Virginia glanced at him and saw his face had turned the color of beets.

"Are you...are you betrothed?" his wife managed, her expression mesmerized.

"Betrothed?" Devlin echoed. Virginia heard the disbelief in his tone and she inwardly stiffened, but she smiled and looked up at him. Devlin's brows lifted. "I am afraid I am not a marrying man."

The blonde stared. So did her husband.

Virginia broke the silence. "I am merely his mistress," she announced boldly, and she felt Devlin stiffen with surprise.

"I believe Virginia meant she is a dear old friend," Devlin murmured.

"Er, right," the squire mumbled, now definitely choking on his words.

Virginia looked at him and she looked at his pretty wife. Their shock and distress were evident. She also thought she knew their thoughts, racing through their heads. *She lives with him as his mistress? Good God, does she have no shame?* And as they turned their eyes upon her, she saw the disbelief and dismay turning to condemnation. She smiled bravely back.

For she truly did not care. Did she?

She slipped free of Devlin and walked over to a table to fiddle with some trinkets there. She was *not* embarrassed and she was *not* dismayed, she told herself fiercely. The stakes were too high now. This was only a game, a bargain made betwixt her and Devlin, and if she won, she would have her freedom and his love.

Nothing and no one else mattered.

Tompkins was wheeling in a tea cart piled high with miniature cakes. Virginia had the urge to rush outside for some fresh air. Thankfully, Devlin was breaking the increasingly strained silence. "I have heard there is a wonderful market every Sunday in the local village."

"Oh, there is," Mrs. Pauley cried, smiling widely in relief. "You must go, Captain, really, for there are wonderful homemade pies, a dancing bear, pony rides for the children and one of our cabinetmakers always shows his wares. He makes the most intriguing chests, in all sizes, filled with dozens of hidden drawers! You should bring Miss Hughes—Virginia—I mean, Miss Hughes, as I am sure she would find it most entertaining!" she cried in a rush, her face flushed with her embarrassment.

Virginia wanted to flee. She felt miserable, but what was even worse was using these good and decent people, all to further Devlin's obsessive scheme, and to so humiliate them. But she faced everyone, smiling. "I should love to go, darling."

She realized that Devlin had turned away to examine a porcelain dish.

"You shall most enjoy it," the squire said gamely. "Beth? I do think we must be on our way, as we have taken up enough of the good captain's time."

"Yes, of course," Beth Pauley said, her gaze darting to Virginia with a mixture of fascination and horror.

Devlin came to life. He shook the squire's hand. "Do come again," he said politely, and Virginia had no idea if he meant it or not. "Mrs. Pauley, it was a pleasure," he said, so gallantly that Virginia gaped.

Mrs. Pauley flushed, but with pleasure, and Virginia knew she was smitten. "Do come to the fair, Captain," she said, her eyes soft and glowing.

"We shall make every attempt," he returned. Then he faced the door, where Tompkins somehow magically stood. "Do escort the squire and his wife out. Good day."

Virginia had plastered a smile on her face. She watched the couple hurry out. Devlin strolled to the door and closed it so that they were alone. He faced her, no longer smiling, his expression strained.

He stared speculatively. "You are a good player, Virginia."

"But?"

"But as I said last night, you are forever outspoken."

She did not want to be berated now. "You like my outspoken ways. You said so."

"You are my dear good friend, Virginia, not my mistress. This is polite society, not a gaming hall. You almost gave the squire an apoplexy." He turned abruptly away.

It was almost as if he did not like his own rules. "I'm sorry, I had no idea I was to mince words. Will you excuse me, Devlin? I didn't sleep well last night and I think I am going to lie down." She avoided his eyes.

He didn't answer, as he was avoiding looking at her, too.

That was fine and she went to the door, trying not to hurry, though she was so upset she had to flee so she could rationalize away her distress and boldly continue their game. His words halted her in her tracks. "We leave for my Greenwich home tomorrow," he said.

Now what? she wondered, her heart tight with worry. She shrugged, not looking back.

And as she left, he added, "I am sure there will be more callers, Virginia, so prepare yourself." His tone was oddly grim.

Finally she gave in and fled.

"VIRGINIA, DO COME MEET Lord Aston and Mr. Jayson."

It was about five o'clock in the afternoon. Virginia's smile was plastered with sheer willpower upon her face. There had been four other callers since the Pauleys, three couples and the village parson. There had been five teas, five conversations, five long and interminable acts. Five smiles, five kisses and perhaps fifty "darlings" exchanged between them both. Sometime between noon and now, her heart had frozen over, all emotion simply replaced with one, dread. Virginia stood frozen on the threshold of the parlor, all three men staring at her.

The two gentlemen who had come to call seemed to regard her far too eagerly. Devlin's expression was inscrutable, although she sensed his impatience. How dare he be impatient with her? she thought, the first flurry of anger stirring. She was doing her best to play her part in the damnable bargain she had once thought ingenious. She had not known how much it would hurt.

Devlin was suddenly at her side. "Darling, are you ill?" he asked, his tone filled with concern.

She could not look at him. "I am fine...darling."

He slipped his arm possessively around her. "Lord Aston, Mr. Jayson, may I present my dear friend Miss Virginia Hughes of Sweet Briar, Virginia?" he said politely.

The two men rushed forward, then Lord Aston, a blonde with brown eyes, bowed over her hand. "I am so pleased to make your acquaintance, Miss Hughes."

She felt as if she were in a dream; this was simply too much to bear. Then she realized that Aston still held her hand. Suddenly she felt like a bone being fought over by two dogs—or a whore being passed around. She tried to dislodge her hand and failed.

"My uncle is the Bishop of Oxford," Aston said with a grin, his gaze penetrating. "Have you ever been to Oxford, my dear? I should love to show you the country if you ever happen by that way."

Virginia swallowed and said, "I should so love a tour of Oxford, my lord, if ever the opportunity arises."

He grinned eagerly. "Well, perhaps when Captain O'Neill is called back to duty, you can extend your stay here at Wideacre. Do you ride, Miss Hughes? We have some fine horses."

"I ride," she said mechanically.

"Oh, do let me introduce my good friend, Ralph Jayson," Lord Aston exclaimed.

"I thought you'd never stand back," Jayson grumbled, but he flashed Virginia a roguish grin. He lifted her hand. "I am enthralled to make your acquaintance, Miss Hughes. And while Aston may be a bishop's nephew, I own several factories and mills. I have a wonderful home just south of London, and the next time you are in town, you must call, or come to one of our balls." His dimples deepened.

"I should love to," Virginia somehow managed. She knew what these men wanted. They wanted to use her the way they thought Devlin was using her, they wanted her in their beds.

"My balls are infamous," Jayson added almost conspiratorially. "Prinnie usually attends."

Virginia had no idea whom he was speaking of. "Prinnie?"

Devlin leaned close. "The Prince of Wales, darling, the Prince Regent. Virginia is an American and newly arrived in our country," he explained.

Both young men laughed.

"Actually, Devlin, it has been a long day and I am not feeling well," Virginia suddenly remarked. "It was a pleasure to meet you both. Excuse me." And not waiting for any response from anyone, she hurried out of the room.

TERRIBLY TIRED, VIRGINIA REQUESTED hot water for her bath. When her tub was full, the maid gone, she sank into the steaming water and leaned back, trying very hard not to think or feel, closing her eyes. It was impossible.

She had known it would hurt to be paraded as his mistress, but she had never guessed at the depths of degradation and humiliation, or the extent of the anguish. And now she no longer felt like a mistress, she truly felt like a whore.

She reminded herself that she had wanted this bargain, because she had so foolishly fallen in love with him. But they were an entire day into their agreement, and though he had what he wanted—the entire shire seemed to know who she was—she had nothing, for they had not become any closer to being friends. And after this last visit, after being so forcibly presented to the lascivious Aston and Jayson, she no longer knew if she wanted to be his friend. And on that thought, she began to cry.

And then she was furious. She was furious with herself for being so weak. She wiped her eyes, refusing to shed another tear while reminding herself that Devlin O'Neill seemed able to hurt her at every turn the way no one else could. She had known that before and she knew it better now. So what was she going to do about it?

She could surrender—or she could fight.

He walked in without knocking.

Virginia gasped and looked wildly about for her towel as Devlin stopped short. The towel lay on a chair, too far for her to reach it. She looked up. Devlin stood not far from the threshold of their bedroom, staring into the smaller adjoining chamber where she bathed. She sank deeper, not quite certain if the rim of the claw-footed tub would shield her body from his eyes, expecting him to walk out.

Instead, he slowly walked over to the open doorway of the chamber, his gaze unwavering and bright.

Virginia tried to be nonchalant. "I beg your pardon, Devlin, I am in the bath."

He leaned his shoulder against the doorjamb and looked right into the tub. He seemed to almost smile. "I can see that."

She felt her cheeks heat. She looked down and saw that the soapy water hid nothing, her entire body was clearly visible, and her breasts almost appeared to be floating. "I'd like some privacy," she managed.

He folded his arms across his chest and studied her, his gaze nowhere near her face. After a tense, interminable moment, he looked up. "Are you crying?"

"I got soap in my eyes," she said swiftly. "And would you care?"

"No." His jaw flexed. He made no effort to leave and he looked her over even more carefully than before. "But if you were crying, I wish to know."

Her nipples were taut and so was her sex. She wanted to cover herself. "I was not crying. Please hand me my towel," she said calmly.

His lashes lowered, shielding the gleam in his eyes. He walked over to the chair where she had left her towel, that action bringing him dangerously close to the tub. He lifted it and held it wide open for her.

She inhaled harshly, having no intention of getting out of the tub and letting him wrap her in the cloth. "Just hand it to me," she said.

"Of course," he murmured, stepping over to the edge of the tub.

Virginia stood, reaching for the towel, ripping it from his hands. She quickly wrapped it around her naked body, still knee-deep in the bathwater.

He reached for her.

"Don't," she said hoarsely.

He froze, his arm extended but not touching her. Then he gripped her arm. "I am only helping you out so you do not fall and break your neck."

"How kind," she said tightly.

"I have never pretended to be kind."

"We are friends now."

"A mere bargain does not make a friendship."

"So now you are a philosopher?" she cried furiously. She tried to fling him off.

"Step out of the tub, Virginia," he said, his expression strained.

She stepped out, and the moment she had both feet on the wood floor, he released her. "I didn't know it would be this hard!" she cried.

He stared, silent.

"Those men made me feel like a whore."

He hesitated. "I'm sorry."

"Are you?" she cried wildly.

"Actually, yes, I am."

"How relieved I am, you have some capacity for compassion in you," she said, marching past him and into the bedroom.

He followed. "I have changed my mind. We won't stay here long. London will be easier."

"Why?" She faced him. "Because there are many mistresses there—and many whores?"

"You are not a whore, Virginia."

"Tell Lord Aston and his friend." Then, because he continued to stare, she flung, "And tell yourself, as you have certainly looked at me as if I am!"

His expression hardened. "I have never looked at you as if you are a whore. No one knows better than I that you are practically a virgin. No one!"

She could only stare, as he was almost shouting. What did this loss of control signify?

He calmed. "And I was not looking at you as if you were a whore."

"Oh, you did not stare at my breasts and..." She could not continue and she felt her face flame.

"I was merely admiring a beautiful woman." He stalked out.

His words sank in. She ran to the door and stared after him in real surprise.

WHEN HIS BROTHER WALKED into the library, having just arrived from London, William threw his quill aside and did not stand up. He stared at him, a slender, handsome man with the pale blue eyes the Hughes men were renowned for, and he scowled. Thomas Hughes, Lord Captain R.N., was in his naval uniform, and he slapped a pair of gloves down on the desk. "I hope that there is a damned good reason you have called me down to Eastleigh, Will," Tom said bluntly.

"I sent you a letter a week ago!" William exclaimed, leaping to his feet.

"I had matters at the Admiralty I could not leave unattended," Tom said darkly. "We are in a war, Will, or have you forgotten? Actually, we are in two wars, as the damned colonials have gotten their feathers all trussed up after all that squawking no one gave any credence to. Did you hear the latest? We lost the *Macedonian* and the *Frolic*."

Will calmed. "No, I haven't heard—not two of His Majesty's battleships?"

"They were both frigates. Amazingly, those bloody colonials seem to know how to sail and, worse, how to fight." He turned away from his brother and began to pace.

"It was pure luck, I am sure. There is simply no way the American navy, which I read has maybe a dozen old ships, can engage our fleet and survive."

"I agree—and that is the thinking at the Admiralty." Tom turned, legs planted apart. "But they also captured the *Detroit,* the *Guerriere* and the *Caledonia* last month. We are routing them in Canada, however."

"That is also rather amazing," William murmured, as everyone he knew believed the war on land in Canada a certain lost cause, since the British and their Indian allies were terribly outnumbered and the question of supplies was insoluble.

"Liverpool came down yesterday. I was asked to be at the meeting by Admiral St. John. He is forever sticking his nose in our business! He does not want any more lost battles at sea. He is furious over our losses there," Tom said harshly.

William straightened, struck with a notion. "This might be good news, actually."

"How so?" Tom sat in a large and fading red damask bergère chair.

William walked to stand before the empty and cold fireplace. "I asked you to come home because O'Neill has taken up residence in Wideacre, although my sources tell me he plans to leave for London in another day."

Tom made a disparaging sound. Hatred filled his eyes. "Ignore the rotten bastard."

"That's a little hard to do when he is holding our cousin hostage, demanding a ransom and parading her about Hampshire as his mistress," William said with a grim smile.

"What?" Tom shot to his feet.

"I do believe you heard my every word," William said coolly. "The son of a bitch is living openly with her! It is beyond shocking. And he has demanded fifteen thousand pounds. Fifteen thousand!"

Tom had turned starkly white.

"The scoundrel flaunts her in good society, dragging our name through the mud, ruining us all by association! So far I have kept this whole scandalous affair from Father, but he will learn of it sooner or later. I am receiving three or four callers a day, and eventually everyone wants to know about my cousin! It has become awkward and humiliating and we need to stop this lunatic from furthering his damnable game. But of course, we are not paying one pound for her release!"

"Good God, what the hell does O'Neill want? Other than the ransom? Why does he hound us this way? I knew he was the scum of the earth, but to destroy a young woman this way? And he knows we have no funds!"

"I wish to God I knew why he has chosen us to hound," William muttered. "But there is simply no possible explanation."

Tom folded his arms across his chest. "You know the Admiralty almost got him, back in June. He disobeyed orders yet again, failed to complete his tour. He somehow talked his way out of a court-martial. Is the countess still sleeping with him?"

"She returned from town yesterday. I feel certain she is home because he is just down the road," William returned.

"I have had it with O'Neill. First my mistress, next our stepmother, and now our cousin. Who is next? Our stepsister? The man has a reason for what he is doing, and it is, I think, time we found out what that reason is."

"I think I may have a solution, Tom."

"Do tell."

"Send O'Neill over to America. The navy is losing battles at sea over there. Why, who better to engage the Americans? Is not O'Neill the scourge of the seas? Undefeatable?" William smiled. "You do still have Farnham's ear."

"That's a bloody brilliant idea," Tom said. Suddenly a movement caused him to start. He turned and saw his father standing in the doorway. "Father!"

Eastleigh smiled at his younger son, his expression impossible to read, just as deciding how long he had been standing there was also impossible. "Thomas. I did not know you had come down from town. How wonderful this is. When did you arrive?" He sauntered into the room, his gaze hooded, and as always, his tone held a sardonic note.

Tom politely kissed his father's cheek. "Just a moment ago. You look well, Father," he lied, for Eastleigh had to have put on another stone since the summer.

"I am very well." Eastleigh glanced sidelong at William. "And hardly in my grave yet. What are you two discussing? Did I hear you mention our new neighbor, the so very heroic Devlin O'Neill?" Mockery crept into his tone.

William and Tom exchanged glances. The earl's heir apparent spoke. "You do nothing, Father, nothing, while O'Neill pricks us with this dalliance of his. The situation has become a crisis and we are all being played for fools. I can hardly hold my head high while out in public!"

Eastleigh chuckled. "The only fool is O'Neill, as he can strut the tart about the royal court for all I care and it will do him no good."

Tom and William looked at each other again. Tom stepped forward. "He hates us, that much is clear. And now it becomes clear that you hate him as well. Why? Why, Father? Damn it, you owe us an explanation—if one is to be had!"

"He stole my fastest stallion, my best dogs, my favorite house. And now he has my brother's daughter in his bed and you ask me why?" His bushy brows lifted. "I have every reason to despise the man, who claims to be a gentleman but is actually a pirate."

"No." Tom confronted his father, his legs braced wide apart. He was half his size and far shorter. "Why does he seek to punish you? And us? *Why?*"

"Because he is a bloody savage, that's why, exactly like his father," Eastleigh said.

William and Tom exchanged startled glances. "You knew his father?" William asked in real surprise.

"Knew him?" Now Eastleigh smiled widely. "I killed him, my boy, in the coldest blood."

SHE SIMPLY REFUSED TO believe it.

The Countess of Eastleigh sat rigidly in her personal coach, her husband's coat of arms engraved on a gold banner on each side, resplendently dressed in a low-cut ruby-red silk dress and a black pelisse. Her gloved hands were clasped in her lap and she found it hard to breathe. This was impossible, was it not?

She had heard the rumor in London from a lady friend whom Elizabeth suspected guessed of her affair. That friend, Lady Farthingham, had mentioned over tea that Captain Devlin O'Neill was at his country estate in Hampshire, apparently with a new mistress whom he was openly abiding with. Elizabeth had not believed it, although at the time her smile had been plastered in place and her heart had raced. Devlin was many things, but he was a gentleman and gentlemen did not live with any woman out of wedlock. She had finally shrugged at Celia, saying she doubted he would spend any time on his new property, as she knew the place well and it was entirely rundown.

And she did know it well, as it was so close to Eastleigh. In fact, she had been to Wideacre on many occasions before its previous owner had passed away without any heirs. Devlin had also mentioned the manor once or twice in the time she had seen him over the summer in London, difficult times in which he had been immersed in a hearing, fighting for his survival. He had mentioned the old manor with very little interest. She had told him what she knew about it, but he had only shrugged. He had murmured once, "I doubt I will ever actually see it." Elizabeth had known he had meant his words.

Two days ago she had heard the same rumor that he was at his country estate in Hampshire. Elizabeth had been surprised and dismayed. She was in London—and he was within miles of her home at Eastleigh. She'd left the ball early, ordered her maid to pack her things, and they had returned to Eastleigh the following day.

It was all she could do not to rush over to Wideacre the moment she arrived home, but not only did she need to visit her husband and concern herself over his welfare and health, she had two daughters she dearly loved and missed. Instead, she had seen to Eastleigh's health and had spent the day with the girls. It was her stepson, William, who had casually let the cannonball drop.

"I suppose you have heard about our new neighbor, Elizabeth?"

Elizabeth sat outside, watching her younger daughter riding sidesaddle over a series of small jumps. She applauded enthusiastically. Not looking at William, she had said, "I beg your pardon?" She very much disliked her eldest stepson.

"Oh, come!" He sat down next to her in a lawn chair, his long legs sprawling out. "My, Lila is such a fine horsewoman." He faced her, his face too close for comfort. "We both know why you have hurried so quickly home in the midst of the new season!"

"William, I have no idea what you are speaking of," she had returned, standing and fanning herself. "Lila!" she called as her daughter rode her chestnut horse up to the edge of the terrace. "That was wonderful, simply wonderful!"

"Thank you, Mother." Lila beamed, her blue eyes sparkling. She whirled the horse and cantered off, clearly wishing to impress yet again.

William also stood, just behind her, uncomfortably close. When he spoke, it was in a whisper, and his mouth practically touched her ear. "Devlin O'Neill is in residence at Wideacre, and he has openly installed his mistress there."

And Elizabeth's heart had stopped.

Now she saw the brick pillars and the drive just ahead. Her heart felt as if it were lodged rudely in her throat. And there it burned. This was a mistake, she thought, a terrible mistake. Devlin could not possibly have a mistress at Wideacre—she was his mistress!

Of course, she had always known there were other women. But she did not care about Spanish barmaids and Sicilian whores. She did not care what he did when he was gone for months on end on a tour.

She did care, very much, what he was doing now.

VIRGINIA HAD ESCAPED THE house hours ago, taking a very long walk into the village and back. Now, as she entered the drive, she saw the carriage parked in front of the manor and froze. Dread began. She firmly—grimly—shoved it aside. Three days had passed since their first caller and there had been a dozen callers since. Apparently half of Hampshire knew that the infamous Captain O'Neill was living openly with his mistress and everyone had to come see for him or herself. She thought she was playing the game well. She kept her head high, her tone soft, she called him darling, touched and kissed his cheek, and the scandalmongers were satisfied. Devlin was satisfied. Only she knew how hard it had all become.

She hated every moment. It was like being a fish in a fishbowl. Or worse, it was like being a naked woman in a fishbowl, gawked at by lechers with terrible intent. And Devlin did not seem to care. But then, she would never let him know that the game had become such a terrible indignity.

She paused, staring at the front of the stone house, hugging herself. She was simply not up to another performance; she was not up to a severe and judgmental inspection. She debated going back to the road and continuing her walk when she noticed the banner on the carriage.

She knew it well. Her father had had a book of coat of arms and she had been shown the Eastleigh emblems at an early age. Her heart lurched. She did not know whether to be thrilled or dismayed. But Eastleigh must have come to pay her ransom. And maybe it was time to give up, maybe it was time to simply go home.

A part of her shrieked inwardly, refusing to be such a coward. Virginia ignored the silent tantrum, but as she hurried toward the house she wondered how easy—or how hard—it would be to walk away from Devlin O'Neill now.

"They are in the library, Miss Hughes," Tompkins said, his eyes wide. And he was not smiling.

Virginia halted, confused. Devlin always entertained their callers in the parlor. And Tompkins always smiled. "Is something amiss?" she dared to ask.

His smile appeared, terribly strained. "Of course not. They are behind closed doors," he added with significance.

Virginia had been about to walk away. She halted and

looked right at the butler. "It is my uncle, the Earl of Eastleigh?" she asked.

"It is the countess," he said.

Virginia blinked. How odd, she thought, instantly envisioning an old woman as fat and gray as her husband. But maybe the countess had come to ransom her, as the earl seemed so feeble. She started forward, began to open the door, and the moment she did so, she heard the soft, cultured and sensual tone of a woman who was neither old nor feeble. The tone was of a young woman in distress.

Virginia froze.

"I don't understand this, Devlin."

The countess was calling him Devlin? Virginia peeked past the door, which was ajar by mere inches. She gasped.

A very beautiful blond woman, old enough to be William Hughes's wife, not Eastleigh's, stood facing Devlin, clearly aggrieved. She was more than lovely; she had a lush, seductive figure and a face of terrible, haunting beauty. Beyond dismayed, Virginia's gaze shot to Devlin, but his face was a mask, impossible to read.

Her heart began to pound.

"Is it true?" the countess asked softly, touching his chest. *No, God, no,* Virginia thought, *this cannot be.*

"I'm afraid so, Elizabeth," he said, and he walked away.

The woman cried out, a flush covering her cheeks, and she stared after him distraught, trembling, a woman with a breaking heart. "But I am your mistress," she said. "And suddenly you replace me, like this?"

"I am sorry." Devlin returned, handing her a brandy. "I never made you any promises, Elizabeth. I am afraid things have changed."

Virginia clung to the door. *Devlin's mistress had been Eastleigh's wife?* It was too horrid to be believed and while she felt deeply for the countess, she was ill. She could never, ever compete with a woman like this.

Elizabeth held the brandy to her full, very bare bosom, her knuckles white. Her pallor was increasing. "I know you never made a single promise. Oh, God. I still fail to understand. I somehow thought that here in Britain I was all that you wished."

"Perhaps you should sit down?" Devlin asked politely and so impersonally.

"I am in love with you, Devlin," she cried.

"And I told you once, that would not be wise."

"Oh, God." Suddenly she looked ill enough to faint and she sat down with Devlin's help. She clutched the drink but made no effort to sip it. "You don't care. You don't care at all, do you?"

His jaw flexed. "As I said, things have changed."

"No, you were always heartless—I merely prayed that it was not true!" She somehow stood, eyes wide and moist. "Who is she? Is she an actress?" The countess was holding on to her dignity with what was clearly a great effort. She set the untouched brandy down. "I mean, you are living here openly with her. You have jilted me for some harlot?" Tears finally filled her eyes.

"You do not wish to make a scene, Elizabeth," Devlin said calmly.

"But I do!" she cried. "And I wish to meet this woman you have so callously replaced me with!"

"I am afraid that is not possible," Devlin said. "I am sorry if I have hurt you. Perhaps you should leave, before you say something you will regret on the morrow."

"I have been your mistress for six years, and just like this, it is over?"

Virginia gasped and in that moment, she somehow pushed the door wide open and fell into the room. She landed on the floor in a heap, not far from where the lovers stood.

Virginia looked up slowly.

Devlin's brows were lifted while the countess stared, still agonized and shocked. He said, "Spying, Virginia?" And he helped her to her feet.

Virginia wanted to ask him why, why had he done this? Why was he doing this? How many innocent people would he hurt to avenge his father? But she was incapable of speech.

"That's her?" the countess cried. "But she is a child!"

Virginia fought for a degree of composure. "I am eighteen," Virginia said. Then she curtsied. "My lady."

The countess covered her brow with her hand, turning away. Virginia looked at Devlin, wanting to berate him and wishing, desperately, that she had never met this woman, not knowing what she did now.

The Countess of Eastleigh had been his mistress for six years. Virginia remained stunned and heartsick. *Devlin would never fall in love with her, not if he had never fallen in love with the countess.*

A terrible silence had fallen. Devlin broke it, speaking quietly. "Virginia, the countess is leaving. Why don't you go upstairs for a moment or two? I shall be up shortly."

Before Virginia could respond, a refusal on the tip of her tongue, the countess turned. "Virginia? Her name is Virginia?" Her gaze became wildly accusing and it turned to Devlin. "That is not my niece, is it?"

"I am afraid so," Devlin said, and he seemed braced for her reaction. The countess cried out.

Virginia could not stand it anymore. She ran to her and said, "Please, do sit down. You are suffering a terrible shock. And you need not worry, really, he doesn't love me—or even care for me—at all."

The countess blinked at her, tears falling now. She said, "You would be kind to me?"

Virginia nodded. "Because you are right, he is heartless, and no one deserves to be cast off in such a manner." She glared at Devlin. He was actually grim, as if displeased or unhappy with the entire affair.

The countess wiped her eyes and stared. "We thought you drowned."

"No. I was transferred to his ship and—"

Devlin seized her arm. "You need not bore the countess with the details," he said in real warning.

She glared at him and struggled to shake him off. "You are a bastard. Let me go!"

He started and released her.

Virginia sent him another murderous look. Perhaps, finally, she hated him.

He spoke to the countess, but never removed his stare from Virginia. "Elizabeth, I am afraid I must ask you to leave."

"Yes, it is time that I left." But she stared intensely at Virginia now, so much so that Virginia forgot how furious she was with Devlin and apprehension began. And finally the countess glanced at Devlin. "Have you hurt her?"

His brows lifted. "Hardly."

The countess turned to Virginia.

Virginia flushed. "I am fine—all circumstances considered."

"I hesitate to wonder what that may mean. Virginia, you are far too young, in spirit if not age, for a man like Devlin. I fear for you, my dear."

Virginia didn't know what to say. "His bark is worse than his bite," she said, hoping her tone was light. Then added, "Usually."

The countess glanced back and forth between them

again. "Don't make the terrible mistake that I made. Do not allow yourself to fall in love with him. He will never love you back." Her smile was twisted and sad and she walked out.

It's too late, Virginia thought. She walked to the door, staring after the countess, admiring her for her dignity and pride. She was unbearably saddened.

CHAPTER EIGHTEEN

DEVLIN PACED THE DINING ROOM, stiff with tension. He glanced at his watch fob—it was well past seven. He glanced at the door, but Virginia did not appear there.

The table was set with crystal, fine china and gilded tableware, all brought from his ship. Covered platters steamed between the candelabra. Virginia was late.

She was avoiding him.

She had been avoiding him for three days, ever since Elizabeth's visit, but that was for the best, as it was becoming harder and harder to trust himself around her. It was becoming harder and harder to use her callously as an instrument of revenge. He knew damned well their bargain and her charade was taking a huge toll upon her. He *was* sorry, when he did not want to be, and it *would* be easier in London.

He had only to recollect her teasing humor, or her sincere desire for friendship, her passion or her outrage, to sorely wish to set her free.

If he set her free, all temptation would be gone.

Those men made me feel like a whore.

Guilt shackled him now. It was an emotion he was rarely visited with. He had wished to throttle Aston and pummel Jayson, instead, he had somehow played the game. Now, Gerald's sightless eyes seemed to be accusing him of perfidy instead of begging him for justice.

His temples throbbed. He paced to the terrace doors, rubbing his neck, as if that might remove the turmoil and tension from his body, his being, his mind. Gerald's accusing gaze turned into Virginia's huge eyes, as accusing, and then they became wide with hurt, an expression he had come to know so well. He truly wished she had not come home to meet Elizabeth. He wished he could have spared her that afternoon.

But she had thought to befriend and comfort Elizabeth. She was the most unpredictable woman he had ever met. She was also the kindest and most sincere.

She lay naked in the bath: small perfect breasts, long, slender legs and in between, an intriguing cleavage covered by dark curls.

He knew that Virginia had no clue of how difficult it was, living with her like this. She did not know that he slept in the library, only coming to his makeshift bed just before dawn. He had let the servants think he suffered from insomnia and worked into the wee hours of the night.

He finally bounded up the stairs. Guilt continued to assail him. His path of revenge, once smooth, had become a twisting rocky road. He was doing what he had to do, what his father would want him to do—he was fulfilling his duty as Gerald O'Neill's son. There was simply no other choice, not for him. His life was meant to be one of hatred and revenge. Sean was the one entitled to family and love.

He stumbled on the steps. What in God's name was he thinking? *Family and love?* Those concepts had naught to do with him and they never would.

He did not feel reassured. Elizabeth's soft, tearful words echoed in his mind, her advice to Virginia. *Don't fall in love with him. He will never love you back.*

He genuinely hoped that Virginia heeded her advice.

He debated knocking, thought about catching her in her bath, and as relish replaced the guilt, he walked in unannounced. But Virginia lay in bed in her childish nightgown and wrapper, reading a book.

She smiled a little at him. It was forlorn. "I'm sorry. I am not joining you for supper. I'm afraid I have no appetite." Apparently she was no longer furious with him.

He paused at the foot of the bed. The gown might be childish, but he knew every inch of the perfect body that lay beneath, a body that belonged to a woman. "Are you ill?"

"No." She carefully closed the book. "You never loved her, did you?"

He hardly wished to discuss Elizabeth with her now. "No."

"Was she also a part of your revenge?"

"Yes." He felt himself grimace.

She inhaled, paling. "That's disgusting, Devlin, horrid and disgusting."

"Is it?" He grew angry then. "She enjoyed every moment in my bed. There was no pretense, no insincerity, no promise on my part! She dared to cross the line—a line I made clear—she dared to fall in love. I am sorry she did, I am sorry if I hurt her, but I do not apologize for what I did. Eastleigh deserves everything I can do and more!"

"Then why don't you simply murder him, as two wrongs make a right, and end this stupidity once and for all!" she cried, sitting up straighter. Her small bosom rose and fell and her cheeks flushed.

"I thought about it," he said, hoping to shock her, and he knew he did. "But a long time ago I decided death was too good for him."

"So you think to make him suffer." She shook her head as if she could not fathom it, him. "Please tell me that you genuinely feel guilty for using Elizabeth the way that you did."

"But I don't. I was not her first lover, Virginia, I was not her first adulterous affair. She wanted my attentions and made that abundantly clear. It was little different from our bargain, Virginia." He knew he glowered at her. It was becoming harder and harder to play poker with her as he did with the rest of the world. Virginia somehow triggered reactions in him—and feelings—that no one else could.

That was distinctly disturbing.

"It was vastly different because you knew she had feelings, and dear God, it's been six years. You made love to that woman for six years!" she cried, two pinks spots coloring her cheeks.

"I never made love to her or anyone," he said, and the moment he spoke, he was ashamed.

She was pale and she lifted her chin and held her head high. "Of course you haven't," she whispered.

He knew he had wounded her and he hated it. He hated that fact and the fact that he had been the one to take her innocence and teach her passion, and he hated that she had to be so vulnerable now. But what he hated most was that she wanted him to make love to her and he knew it beyond any doubt. *But love was not for him.* And what he also hated as passionately was that she had somehow made him even think this last, terrible thought. "Virginia, we have a bargain, my friendship for your charade."

She stared. .

"Do not think of asking for something more, something I cannot—will not—ever give," he warned her now, deliberate and purposeful. He gripped the footboard with one hand. His knuckles turned white.

"I only asked you for your friendship, Devlin. You are deluded if you think I want more than that. I mean, what more could I possibly—sanely—want from a man who has abducted and imprisoned me?"

Her pride had always impressed him. Now it also relieved him. "Tomorrow we are going to London," he began.

"No. I beg to point out a fact. You have been so busy parading me about as your mistress that you have failed utterly to be any kind of friend. Sharing supper does not count as friendship, especially when you brood over your wine and glower at the food."

He started, then controlled the smile that wanted to come to his face. "You are right," he said, relieved now and surprising them both.

"You admit this has been quite a one-sided bargain?"

"I do."

Her eyes widened and her face softened and a sparkle appeared in her eyes. "So what are you going to do about it, Captain?" she teased.

His heart leapt strangely. "When we get to London, I will take you shopping, to a fair, to the theatre, perhaps even to the racetrack, and we will rectify this vast injustice," he said, feeling himself smiling back. And it felt so good to be sharing a moment of humor with her.

She grinned, and it was like the sunshine emerging from the gray Irish sky. "Well, it's about time," she said.

He hesitated. "Are you certain you will not come down and dine with me?" he asked softly, and oddly, her answer mattered very much.

She became still. Then, her mouth pursed, she nodded. "Give me a few minutes to dress."

He left, pleased.

LONDON. VIRGINIA HAD SEEN drawings and sketches and there had been the stories told to her by her father. She had always dreamed of one day visiting that city. They had arrived within hours of leaving Southampton and they had departed at dawn. Now Virginia clutched the windowsill of the carriage, trembling with excitement as their coach took them through the city toward Greenwich, where Devlin kept a home on the river. She could not keep her gaze from every sight and scene. She had never seen so many fine vehicles and conveyances, so many well-dressed gentlemen, so many stunning ladies. The street they traveled on boasted fine shops and gracious hotels, the occasional theatre and park. Virginia craned her head to look twice at a lady in a shocking pink ensemble—pink boa, pink parasol. She turned to face Devlin and asked breathlessly, "Did I just see a harlot?"

"Or someone's very bold mistress," he said with a smile.

His smile was easy and genuine and it made her heart tighten as she automatically smiled back. She reminded herself that he had used the countess shamelessly and callously, while that poor woman was in love with him, but her internal meandering had no effect. She sighed and faced the street again. Now they passed a series of stately and gracious mansions, all with perfectly manicured lawns, rose gardens and stone statues and water fountains. Virginia smiled and shook her head. "One would think the wealth of the entire world resides here," she said.

"A significant portion of it does," Devlin returned. "But there is also terrible squalor. I would never drive you through the human misery that exists side by side with the opulence you are now witnessing."

She faced him seriously. "Why not? We have horrible poverty at home, too. We simply do not have so many displays of such lavish wealth."

"Virginia, you are a lady, and one does shield the fair sex from such sights."

Exasperated, she rolled her eyes at him. "Oh, please." Then she narrowed her gaze at him, aware that he was smiling at her, as if she were amusing. Her heart sang a little, just a little bit. "At home we gave everything that we could to the poor. Mama demanded it, and of course, Papa was happy to oblige. Do you give to charity, Devlin?" She realized the question was terribly important to her.

"Yes, I do. But I give to the Irish poor, Virginia. The British can take care of their own."

"Hunger and sickness know no national boundaries," she remarked. She half turned and saw that they were turning to race up a road that ran parallel to the Thames. Even larger, statelier homes lined its banks. "Are we there yet?"

"Soon," he said, a smile in his oddly soothing tone.

She glanced at him. "Do not patronize me as if I am a child."

"You are as excited as a child today."

"I hated Wideacre!" The moment the words had erupted from her mouth, she regretted them immensely. "I mean..." She faced him again, flushing. She did not want him to ever guess how horrid it had been, being paraded about Hampshire like that: "I mean that I much prefer to be in London, as I have never been here before."

But he had turned away, gazing out of his own window.

Virginia had the chance to stare at his gorgeous profile and her body tightened, leaving her breathless and confused. She would never forget the countess—how abused she had been, how hurt and how utterly sensuous—so why did she still wish to be in his arms? And why couldn't her heart move on, to far safer ground? For she would never forget the countess's belated warning, either.

"You need a new wardrobe," Devlin said suddenly. "I will see if Madame Didier can accommodate us tomorrow."

She blinked. "I hardly need new clothes." It was a terrible lie. Now that she no longer lived in her britches and boots, she desperately needed a well-made dress or two.

"There will be teas and that kind of thing, and there will be the occasional ball," he said. "You need some day dresses and a ball gown."

A ball? But she could not dance! "But you make it seem as if we shall be in town for some time."

"We will be in town for as long as it takes," he said firmly.

She was not attending any ball. Or could she somehow learn to dance—merely so she could go to a London ball and one day tell Tillie about it? She began to worry. She did not want to look like a country bumpkin! Now she regretted refusing to pay attention to the dance master at the Richmond school.

"Is something wrong, Virginia?"

She met his searching gray stare. "Of course not!" she exclaimed. "I would love to go to a ball—we had many balls at home and I adore dancing," she cried.

His brows lifted in an expression she had come to know so well, one of mild disbelief and of mild amusement. "We're here," he said.

She whirled and leaned out of her window and gasped.

Silhouetted against the river and the London skyline was a castle. Or at least, Waverly Hall looked like a castle to her, with two towers that graced either side of the giant limestone house. The gardens were magnificent—she had never seen such color in the fall. Then she saw a green court of some sort with a net dividing its center. She turned and pounded on Devlin's arm. "Is that what I think it is?" she demanded. "Is that a tennis court?"

He laughed at her. "Yes, it is."

"I want to play." She had never played the game before but it sounded like so much fun.

"You may play all the tennis that you want, Virginia, as this is presently your home."

Her excitement faded. She had briefly forgotten their bargain because Devlin had been behaving so amiably it was as if he were really her friend. But they did have a bargain and he was buying her a new wardrobe and taking her to balls—he intended to parade her about London now, humiliating her and her uncle until Eastleigh capitulated and paid her ransom.

She moved away from him. "This isn't my home. It's my prison, but I had forgotten it, and that is not a good idea." Suddenly the aching sadness she had been afflicted with yesterday, upon seeing the countess leaving, assailed her again.

"Try to think of it as your home," he said quietly.

She barely managed to smile at him.

AN IMPOSSIBLY STRAIGHT-FACED butler showed them in. Virginia gaped at the immense front hall with its high ceilings, crystal chandelier and works of art. One life-size nude statue was a masterpiece—a Roman soldier mounted on a warhorse.

And the floors beneath her feet were marble. Good God, Devlin was even wealthier than she had thought.

"Good day, sir, we are so pleased to have you back," the butler intoned, taking Virginia's hat and gloves and then Devlin's gloves as well.

"Benson, this is Miss Hughes. Have her bags brought to my rooms, which she will be sharing," Devlin said.

The butler did not bat an eye. "Yes, Sir Captain."

Virginia felt drawn to a huge painting depicting some kind of ancient battle. Mounted soldiers, perhaps Greek or Roman, were invading a citadel filled with frightened women and crying children. The scene was grim, but so powerful and so beautifully done. She stared in awe.

"Ty," Devlin said with surprise.

Virginia turned to see a man standing in the opposite doorway, backlit by the sun.

"Dev." He came forward and she instantly recognized him as the Earl of Adare's son. The resemblance, the sense of power, the dark good looks, were remarkable. She watched with real curiosity as the two men embraced, and decided that they were more than stepbrothers—clearly they were genuine friends. Then the man Devlin had referred to as Ty stepped back and looked curiously at Virginia.

"Virginia," Devlin said, holding out his hand and smiling at her.

She faltered, because once again it was as if Devlin were truly her friend. And suddenly she wished that he was—that he could be a real friend, even if he might never come to love her as a woman. She could settle, she thought, for that crumb.

"Virginia," he said again. But there was no impatience in his tone.

She came forward, the tall, dark man staring far too directly at her, as if he were inspecting her inside and out. She felt herself flush. Was she to play her part now, again? She paused before Devlin, but he did not put his arm around her as he had when they had performed their charade at Wideacre. "Miss Virginia Hughes," he said quietly.

Ty nodded, his jaw flexing, his eyes dark. Virginia realized he was angry as he turned to Devlin, not speaking, as if he dared not utter a word.

"My stepbrother, Tyrell de Warenne," Devlin said to Virginia.

She realized that no charade would be necessary, not with his family.

Tyrell faced her with a bow. "I apologize, Miss Hughes. Your beauty has left me speechless."

She blinked and smiled at him, relived that she did not have to play the trollop now. "I doubt that."

He straightened. "I beg your pardon?"

She bit her lip. "I mean, thank you very much."

Devlin choked.

"Sean speaks very highly of you. He sends his warmest regards," Tyrell added, not glancing another time at Devlin.

Her heart tightened a little. She smiled, instantly somewhat sad. "How is he?"

"Well, if you mean his state of health," Tyrell said, "he is fine."

She met his gaze. Did this man somehow know that Sean was in love with her? Or that he had once been in love with her? And why was he angry with Devlin? "When did you see him? Was it at Askeaton?"

"Yes. A fortnight ago, we actually supped together there." Tyrell reached into his fine, nearly black coat and withdrew a sealed letter. "For you, Miss Hughes."

She took it, seeing her name and recognizing Sean's handwriting instantly. She didn't know whether to be worried or pleased. Then she felt both men staring and she glanced from Tyrell to Devlin. His expression had turned aloof. "Thank you for delivering this," she said to Tyrell. Then to Devlin, she said, "Your home is lovely. I have never seen anything like it. I am going to step outside and explore while you and your brother get reacquainted."

Devlin merely nodded at her.

Clutching the letter tightly, Virginia hurried out.

Tyrell faced Devlin then, finally allowing his anger to show. "She is sharing your rooms? I heard an insane rumor, Dev, about you living openly with some woman in Hampshire, but I did not believe it."

"Tread with care, Ty," Devlin warned, walking into the adjoining salon. He stared across the room. Huge windows let out onto the terrace there and he could see Virginia, opening the letter with her fingernail. Was she in a rush?

Anger enveloped him then.

It was a love letter, he was certain, and she had been moved to receive it and could not wait to read it.

"What the hell are you thinking, Dev?" Tyrell demanded, pausing by his side. He also glanced out of the windows at Virginia, who was now reading the single page she held. Clearly her hand trembled, as the page wavered like a flag.

"I am afraid that whom I wish to bed is not your affair."

"Oh, ho! So you think to play me for a fool!" Tyrell was incredulous. "She is Eastleigh's niece. I know now for certain that you continue on some torturous path of self-destruction."

"The only person on a path of destruction is Eastleigh himself," Devlin said more calmly than he felt. He thought he saw Virginia's shoulders shake. Was she crying?

"Sean is in love with her. You would cuckold your brother?"

Devlin finally tore his gaze from Virginia, an instant from striking Tyrell, his fist raised. Ty was as tall as he, but heavier and more thickly built, and in any actual fight, stronger, although not quicker. The two men had never exchanged blows. "Leave this alone, Ty," he warned, but all he could think about was Virginia outside, crying over Sean's love letter.

"No." Tyrell's jaw was hard and a fierce glint was in his nearly black eyes. "I am your brother and I will not leave this alone. Sean told me your absurd plan to ransom her. You left Askeaton three weeks ago. Where is the ransom, Devlin? Why is she now your mistress when it is your brother she should be with?"

Devlin's fury knew no bounds because Tyrell was right. In a red haze, he saw Virginia and Sean in an unholy embrace. "She remains with me, doing as I choose, until I say so," he ground out.

Tyrell gripped his shoulders. "I have never seen you like this, so thoughtless, so furious. I cannot believe you would destroy her this way—for my brother would never do such a thing! And when this is over? Do you think to escape with your head?" he now cried.

Devlin shrugged him off, Sean's words suddenly echoing disturbingly in his mind. *You will have to destroy her, will you not?* First Sean and now Tyrell. God, what was he doing? He knew damn well that Virginia did not deserve to be a pawn in his schemes. "Virginia will survive," he said grimly. "I will rectify everything after the ransom."

"And how will you do that? Will you marry her to salvage her reputation?"

Devlin started, his heart skipping uncontrollably. "No," he heard himself say. But Tyrell was right. He had not faced the whole truth before—only marriage would save Virginia from the critics and gossips he had set upon her.

Family and love were *not* for him.

His life was one of destruction and death.

Tyrell wrenched him around. "And what of your career? It hangs by a thread now! One more false move and I am certain there will be a court-martial! This abduction is criminal, Devlin, and don't tell me you do not know it. Men hang for less."

Devlin pulled away. "I will not hang." And he started, because beyond Tyrell, through the windows, he saw that Virginia was ashen and as immobile as a statue.

Tyrell followed his stare. Suddenly he said, "Are you in love with this girl?" His tone was incredulous.

Devlin recoiled. *"No!"*

"I see." Tyrell stared thoughtfully. Then he asked, "Will Eastleigh pay?"

"When I am through, he will." He paced, shaken and disturbed.

"How can you do this to her?" Tyrell demanded. "Look." He jerked his head at the window. Outside, Virginia trembled, covering her face with her hands. "She weeps. She is weeping, Devlin. I know it has to bother you, because I know you better than anyone, better even than Sean, and I know you are not ruthless, not completely, at least."

"Fine," he said grimly. "Fine! It bothers me! Are you satisfied now, goddamn it?"

Tyrell jerked with surprise, eyes wide and stunned. Devlin stalked to the sideboard, pouring a large Scotch, his hand shaking. He ignored Tyrell, trying to come to grips with his anger and other, more confusing, insistent feelings he did not wish to own or understand. Virginia wept over Sean. Was it possible that he was jealous?

It was an emotion he was unfamiliar with. He had never been jealous of anyone or anything at any time in his life. But this red-hot anger, coupled with the tremor of fear and doubt, felt suspiciously like jealousy.

"Fuck." He threw his drink as hard as he could at the wall. It shattered loudly, sounding like buckshot.

"I have never seen you lose your temper, not ever," Tyrell said quietly. "From the day Father brought you home when you were ten, Gerald just murdered, you have been the most stoic and dispassionate person I have ever met."

Devlin waved at him in real disgust. He had no response to make, as none could be had.

Virginia ran into the room. "God, what happened? Are you all right?" she cried, her cheeks flushed but not tear streaked.

Devlin couldn't respond to her, either. He could not believe his rage and he could not believe his jealousy—for that was what it was, enraged jealousy—and he stared at her in disbelief.

"I thought someone fired a musket," she said nervously, glancing between him and Tyrell.

Devlin turned away. He still couldn't speak.

"No one fired a gun," Tyrell said quietly. "Could you find Benson and tell him there has been an accident?" He smiled kindly at her.

Virginia nodded, turning to look wide-eyed at Devlin's back, and she hurried out.

Devlin poured another drink, and this time, he drank it.

Tyrell approached. "I see all is not as it appears," he said quietly. He laid a hand on Devlin's shoulder.

Devlin shrugged it off. "All is exactly as it appears," he returned, his iron control returning. "Would you like a drink?" he asked far more calmly than he felt.

Tyrell de Warenne made a derisive sound. "Actually, I would." He paused thoughtfully. "I would also like an invitation to supper," he said.

"Hot loaves! Muffins and crumpets! A penny for a scone!"

Virginia stumbled, reaching for Devlin's hand. They were making their way up Regent Street, which was, he had assured her, the best shopping in London.

"Chairs to mend!" another street vendor cried, stepping in their path to bow before Devlin, who did not wear his uniform but a fine dark blue velvet coat with his britches and stockings. "My lord, sir, I mend any kind of chair," he cried.

"No, thank you," Devlin said politely, and trying not to release Virginia's hand, he pulled her past the chairman.

"Fish! Fine goldfish fer the lady!" an old woman cried, waving a bucket at them. "Pretty goldfish! Fine fer the lady!"

Devlin smiled at Virginia, pulling her out of the fish lady's way as well.

But she pulled back. "Let's look at the fish!"

"Virginia," he began.

"It's my turn," she reminded him, smiling and jerking free. "May I see your fish, ma'am?" she asked.

The old lady grinned, with most if not all of her teeth missing, and she lowered the pail so Virginia could see numerous goldfish swimming about, including several black-and-white striped ones. "How beautiful," she cried.

"A penny fer a dozen," the lady smiled at her.

"Virginia, please do not tell me we are buying you fish," Devlin said, but amusement was in his tone.

"We are not, no, thank you," she apologized to the vendor.

"Hot loaves! Muffins and crumpets! A penny fer a scone!"

Devlin looked at her, smiling.

Refusing to move she said, "Please?"

"Thank God, you are not fat," he said, walking over to the muffin man. "Which is it this time?" She'd had a muffin and a scone already, all digested in the span of an hour.

"I'll try a crumpet," she said, having not a clue as to what that might be.

Devlin made the purchase and Virginia was presented with a warm and crusty golden bun, which she eagerly tried. "Yum," she said, then to her horror, realized her mouth was full.

He shook his head, then laughed. "Come on. It's taken us an entire hour to navigate a single block."

But Virginia cried out, handing him her crumpet, and ran

instead to the huge window display. "Devlin, look," Virginia cried. "Look at the beautiful black lace!"

He came up beside her, still holding the crumpet in its paper napkin. "Do you wish to buy it?" he asked as they stared into the draper's shop.

She did. Oh, how she wished to adorn herself in that black lace, in a red dress trimmed with tons of it, and she looked at Devlin, simply breathless. They would attend a ball together, dance the night away.... Then she thought about the countess. She sobered.

Who was she fooling? She was not the kind of woman to wear red or black lace. "No, I don't think so," she said.

"Change your mind so quickly?" he asked, studying her intently.

"No, I...I don't think it's suitable, really. But it's beautiful," she added wistfully.

"Come. We must make our appointment with Madame Didier," he said, taking her arm and looping it in his.

She glanced at him as they strolled up the block, her heart racing. He kept taking her arm as if they were really lovers—or even a couple. "You do know that one would almost think us real friends," she said hesitantly.

"It is your turn," he reminded her easily. "Are you enjoying yourself?"

She had to beam. "How can I not? Those wonderful muffins—those pretty fish—they sell everything on the street, do they not? I saw a man selling dust! He was selling brick dust," she cried.

"It's used for cleaning knives," Devlin said. Then rather casually, he asked, "So what did Sean have to say?"

Virginia faltered. And she hesitated, uncertain as to how she should respond.

His letter had both warmed and saddened her. He hadn't spoken of his feelings, but it was clear that he still cared deeply for her, and after telling her all that had happened at Askeaton in her absence, he had told her that it simply was not the same without her there. She knew his unspoken thoughts—he missed her. And reading it had made her miss him, too, but the way one would a dear old friend, not a lover. It was wonderful hearing from him, but it was also terribly sad, reminding her of a time and place when she had been so crushed and hurt, though she'd refused to admit it. She had been so lonely those five months she had been left behind at Askeaton.

His letter and her reaction to it had only confirmed her real feelings for him. She had never loved him more as a friend. But she hoped that, one day, he would fall passionately in love with a woman who would love him back the very same way.

She sighed. "I'm afraid that's none of your affair, Devlin," she said.

"Actually it is, as I have been responsible for my brother's welfare and happiness since he was the age of eight. But do not bother to reveal his secrets, as I can already guess what they are."

"So you are now a fortune teller? Or rather, a Gypsy mind reader?" She poked him with her elbow, smiling and hoping to change the subject.

"Hardly," he said, but he smiled in return.

The seamstress's shop was not what Virginia had been expecting. She had anticipated a small shop filled with tables and ladies sewing industriously there. Instead, a stunning young woman with red hair, superbly dressed, unlatched the front door and allowed them into a front hall with polished wood floors and fine Persian rugs. Display cases lined the two walls on either side of the store, boasting hats, gloves, purses and the occasional swatch of fabric or pair of earbobs. Stairs carpeted in red swept up directly ahead.

"Captain O'Neill?" The redhead smiled at Devlin. Her accent was French.

"Madame Didier?" he asked, clearly with some surprise. The woman was no more than twenty-one or two.

"I am Mademoiselle Didier, her niece," the redhead replied softly, her regard not quite seductive. And she faced Virginia. "Mademoiselle Hughes, I presume?"

Virginia nodded, her gaze darting from the elegant and seductive Frenchwoman to the stunning items on display in the hall. It was impossible to decide whether to stare at Madame Didier's niece or at what was for sale in the shop.

"Please, Captain, Mademoiselle, do come upstairs, my aunt is waiting for you."

Devlin touched the small of Virginia's back and she preceded him up the wide staircase, following Mademoiselle Didier.

The salon above had a marble floor and several gracious seating arrangements. An older woman, dark-haired, fine-figured and handsome, came out of another room. "Captain O'Neill, it is such a pleasure to meet you, at last," she cried, rushing to them with a wide smile, her accent stronger than her niece's.

He bowed over her hand. "The pleasure is all mine, Madame, and I am very grateful that you could see us at such short notice."

"For you, *mon capitaine,* I would need no notice at all." She turned to Virginia. "Mademoiselle, ah, what beauty, what petite beauty, ah, this will be so easy and such a pleasure. Look, Sofie, *regardes la petite!*"

A flurry of French followed, the two women beaming.

Virginia flushed, feeling foolish and flustered and wishing she wasn't being called beautiful, as Madame ushered her into the adjacent room. "Does the captain wish to stay and approve our choices or shall you leave the se-

lection of gowns and fabrics up to the ladies?" Madame
Didier asked, her eyes twinkling.

"He is leaving," Virginia said quickly as Devlin sat down
on a delicate green velvet love seat, dwarfing it. She gaped
at him.

He smiled lazily back. "I prefer to approve, Madame.
Virginia needs a number of ensembles for day and some
ball gowns, perhaps two. I prefer her to be in shades that
match her eyes—violet and amethyst would do nicely, I
think."

Virginia knew her jaw hung open, but she could not help
herself. He was staying? She was to be fitted, and that
meant some state of undress.

"And ruby red, *mon capitaine,* and of course, silver."
She snapped her fingers and Sofie held up a swath of iridescent silver fabric that rippled and glowed as the air
simply brushed over it.

Devlin's eyes brightened. "Oh, yes," he said instantly.
"I like it very much."

Virginia went still, closing her mouth and staring at him
as Madame made a happy sound, Sofie now draping the
fabric over Virginia's shoulder and chest. He looked indo-
lently over her at her and smiled, but there was nothing
indolent about his eyes—the gleam there was bright.

Her mouth went dry.

He wanted to clothe her in the silver tissue and he clearly
found the idea arousing. She swallowed hard. "Devlin,
why don't you make your suggestions and then leave us
for a bit?"

"I am staying." He settled more negligently on the small
settee.

Madame chortled happily. "Sofie, where is *le rouge noir?*"

Instantly Sofie found it and, smiling, held up a sinfully
rich dark red satin.

"*Mon capitaine,* look at this!" Madame cried.

Virginia wanted to tell them that she could not wear that, oh no, that was for a woman like Mademoiselle Didier, it was for a woman like the countess.

Devlin nodded, his eyes warmer and brighter than before.

Madame Didier gave an order to Sofie in French and she began to unbutton Virgnia's dark pelisse as Madame sat down and began making notes.

Virginia gasped as it was removed. "I...what are you doing?" she asked warily.

"You must undress. We must take your measurements," Sofie said softly, unbuttoning the back of her dress.

Virginia looked at Devlin for help.

But no help was to be had from that quarter, as he merely crossed his long legs. "Do not mind me," he murmured, apparently relaxing and preparing to enjoy the entertainment.

Virginia felt the dress opening down her back and the delicate touch of Sofie's nimble fingers. She was disbelieving, but not angry. Devlin's eyes continued to gleam and what was actually happening was making her breathless.

Her heart beat far too hard. She swallowed and lifted her arms and allowed the couturier's niece to remove her dress over her head. Madame Didier looked up from her notes and clucked when she saw the pantalettes. By now, Virginia's cheeks were warming, but so was the rest of her body.

She glanced around, to see if there was a window that could be opened, but there was not. "It is still the fashion in America," Virginia lied. She shot Devlin a glance.

He hadn't heard her, as he was quite obviously distracted. His gaze was on her ankles, clad in a wisp of silk stocking, and then it moved to the tips of her breasts, which were, naturally, hard and covered only with the thin wisp of her chemise.

Before Virginia could blink, Sofie removed that garment as well, so she stood clad only in her corset, pantalettes and the drawers beneath. Her breasts were bare, upthrust by the corset, and she was briefly stunned. Her cheeks went on fire and she slowly looked at Devlin.

And he, of course, he was staring very intently now.

The air thickened in the room.

It thickened enough that it was very hard to breathe.

"Capitaine?" Sofie asked, and before Virginia could react she held the red satin over her chest, a stunningly sensuous caress against her breasts, and she said, as softly, "Imagine that, *Capitaine,* imagine that."

Virginia bit her lip to cut off a moan. Every inch of her body was now turgidly raised.

"I more than approve," Devlin said far too quietly, his tone rough.

The red satin was whipped away.

"Mademoiselle needs undergarments." Madame stood. "Two corsets, one black, one white, both trimmed with ribbons, with lace. And for each, a chemise to match. *Oui?"*

Sofie now held up a section of black lace and as Devlin seemed to nod, she whisked it across Virginia's chest. Virginia didn't have to glance at herself to know the lace was transparent.

Devlin's gaze was rapt.

"*Le Capitaine* is happy?" Sofie said softly.

"Very."

The lace disappeared, followed by a sheer ivory linen, and when that was gone, several ribbons in shades of ivory, cream and pink trickled down Virginia's breasts.

"Oui?" Madame asked briskly.

Virginia tried to swallow, but the ribbons were silk and swallowing was now as difficult as breathing.

Devlin nodded, no longer speaking. His gaze moved over the ribbons—over her breasts—and finally lifted to her face.

She could not look away.

"Use them all with the ivory," he said.

"*Superbe, mon capitaine,*" Madame agreed wholeheartedly. "Drawers to match in the latest fashion, *oui?*"

"Yes," Devlin said.

"I wish to show you something. A special silk, for the undergarment, very special, mademoiselle will love it. It is downstairs, *un moment, s'il vous plaît.*" Madame walked out.

Virginia wondered how she was going to survive the fitting.

Sofie now held up a rich, shimmering dark purple silk against Virginia and a hollow feeling overcame her as Devlin slowly nodded. This time Sofie did not toss the silk aside. "How low, *mon capitaine?*" Sofie murmured. She adjusted the fabric so that only the topmost swells of Virginia's chest were revealed. "*Pour la jour?*"

"Lower," he said.

Virginia felt as if she were in a trance, a sexual one, and she blinked, not sure if she was horrified or not. She had never worn such a low neckline in her life, much less even lower.

"Here?" Sofie asked, lowering the garment by an inch.

"Very nice," Devlin said thickly. And suddenly he spoke quickly in fluent French.

"*D'accord,*" Sofie said when he was through. She sent Virginia a glance and hurried out, closing the door behind her.

Virginia met Devlin's gaze as he slowly stood and she

turned, reaching wildly for the closest fabric in order to cover herself. But she knew.

"Don't," he said, a command.

She froze, a wisp of silk in her hand, her nipples hurting, her sex ripe.

He tugged the silk from her hand.

"What are you doing?" she whispered hoarsely, her eyes wide.

"You are so beautiful," he said in return, sliding his hands over her breasts and clasping them firmly.

Virginia wanted to be quiet and she failed—the terrible sensuality that had been building in her erupted and she cried out. Her eyes closed as he rubbed her nipples, making them harder and tauter and tighter than before, until she was trembling helplessly, moaning, her sex engorged and throbbing wildly for relief.

"Look at me," he commanded softly.

Somehow her eyes obeyed, opening, and their gazes met. His were silver flames.

He smiled a little and bent and touched one tip with his tongue.

Virginia cried out, clasping his head, wanting to tell him not to do this—in the back of her mind she knew that Madame or Sofie could walk in on them—but she couldn't, and as he licked her nipple she began to thrash, the explosion imminent.

Then she felt his hands slide down to her waist and begin to tug her pantalettes down.

In a haze of lust, she managed to worry about what he was doing. As if reading her very thoughts, he murmured against her aching, swollen nipple, "Let me please you, darling."

"N-not here," she managed.

But his face was against her navel now and she felt him

smile through the corset she wore. "They won't disturb us."
He tugged on her pantalettes and they disappeared, pooling
at her ankles.

And finally mindless, Virginia grasped his shoulders,
clawing him, pushing him down.

"Patience is a virtue," he reminded her, sliding his face
down until he rubbed his cheek over her mons.

"Oh, Devlin," she wept.

He kissed the delta there, not once but twice and then
three times.

She fell.

He caught her and laid her down on piles of silk and
satin, and as she spread wide for him he separated the
heavy folds of her sex and inserted his tongue there.

Virginia arched, sobbing, exploding, shattering and
flying high. "Devlin!" she wept.

He sucked it deep then teased it softly as she shattered
another time, sobbing and moaning and shaking like a leaf.

When she began to float, her mind came back to life. She
gasped, opening her eyes, still on her back on the floor,
naked except for her stockings and corset. Devlin crouched
between her thighs, which remained spread shamefully for
him. She quickly began to close them but he palmed her
sex. "Don't."

Desire surged. She lay still, panting. "What if—" she
began, barely able to think of an intrusion by the couturier
or her niece.

He began toying with the folds, combing through the
hair. "They won't interrupt us."

Virginia wanted to refute him but forgot the subject,
arching high against his hand. His fingers entered her, and
now there was no barrier. The sensation was so powerful, of
his being inside her, even if it was just his two fingers, that
her stomach seemed to disappear and the room blackened.

"Can you come for me again, little one?" he asked roughly.

She somehow looked at him and was met with a blaze of silver. "Please...put more...there," she whispered.

He shoved harder, fiercely, and she saw sweat rolling down his brow.

But it wasn't enough. And Virginia knew what she wanted. She began to sit, reaching for him, brushing her hand over the stiff, rigid line raised brilliantly against his pale britches—but he pushed her hand away.

Incredulous, she met his gaze.

He moved hard in her.

She gasped, her stomach disappearing again, collapsing back onto a pile of discarded lace and linen. His fingers moved deep and deeper still, large and strong, surge after surge. Virginia was vaguely aware of his gaze upon her, knew she was shameless, and she began to writhe and beg. "Please, Devlin, please, come inside me...*please!*"

He grunted and leaned over her somehow and she felt his mouth on hers, his tongue thrusting deep, even as his hand continued to rock her, and she knew she needed, wanted, had to have *more.*

And suddenly his hand was gone. She was in his arms and his phallus rubbed over her sex and she shouted, gripping his shoulders, exploding into a thousand pieces, not once but many times, while he ground himself over her, again and again, panting and murmuring her name.

This time, she lay for an eternity upon the soft piles of silks and satins on the floor, and he lay on top of her, breathing hard, unmoving, still hard and aroused. She began to blush. She began to think. She began to wonder and to worry.

He sat up.

She met his gaze.

His eyes slid over her entire body. A flush mottled his high cheekbones.

Virginia sat, reaching for a fabric and covering herself. She had not expected this. She was stunned but not ashamed, not at all. And she wanted more, so much more.

"It's a little late for that," he remarked, eyeing the wisp of pink silk she held.

She wet her lips. She still ached to have him deep inside her, and not just with his fingers.

"I have longed to do that again," he said quietly, meeting her gaze. "You are incredibly passionate, Virginia."

His words went straight through her heart. "What about your pleasure?" she asked as quietly, her trepidation growing. But even a real union of their bodies would not be enough. *If only he would reach out now and touch her with real affection.*

But he did not. He shrugged, standing. "I'll survive."

She also stood, refusing to be disappointed, and quickly stepped into her drawers and pantalettes. "You appear ready to mount a cannon," she managed, and then she gave up. She was disappointed.

"What?" he choked.

She did not understand him at all. She did not understand why he couldn't become fond of her, why it had to be simply sex, and she would never understand the line he had drawn and what it really meant. "I mean, I am sorry you won't take your pleasure, too."

"I heard you the first time," he said, and he actually smiled at her. "A man loves to have his size appreciated."

"I am sure you have had more than your share of appreciation." She faced him. "Devlin, I'm confused."

His mask reappeared. "Don't be. It was just...a moment. I should have never stayed here for your fitting."

"And what? I am so *beautiful* that you lost *almost* all control?"

"Frankly, yes."

She stared, about to berate him for his mockery, when she realized he wasn't mocking at all. "Are you being serious?" she gasped.

"Yes." He pursed his lips in indecision, and then said, "Yes, I am being very serious."

Elation crept over her. She smiled. "But—"

He touched her lips. "Why don't you accept the flattery and enjoy it?"

She grinned. Inwardly, a song was bursting from her heart, the last bar of which was a dance. *He thought her beautiful.* All disappointment vanished.

"You know, I think that I will."

CHAPTER NINETEEN

REGENT STREET HAD CALMED by the time they left Madame Didier's shop. It was late in the afternoon and only a few vendors remained; some of the shops had closed, signs in the window pronouncing this fact. A few pedestrians also remained; however, all were gentlemen, when earlier the reverse had been true.

"Is it later than I think?" Virginia asked quietly. Devlin had absented himself for the remainder of the fitting, but only after explaining exactly how he wished Madame to design and trim her gowns.

"It's four. But the ladies of the ton are preparing for their evening affairs at this hour," he said as quietly.

She was trying to avoid eye contact. It was impossible, just as was avoiding her very distinct recollection of his touch and how it had affected her. Virginia was shaken. What should she do now? How could she proceed with their bargain when it meant so much more to her than a mere game?

She should be thrilled that he found her beautiful enough to *almost* lose all of his control, and while that had pleased her, despair now outweighed that.

"You will have some beautiful gowns, Virginia. I know you do not really care about fashion, but you may keep them when you leave."

Instantly the anger came and she could not keep it at bay. "I don't want the gowns."

He hesitated, facing her squarely in the middle of the block, his coach, drawn by four handsome grays, parked a short distance ahead. "But I am offering them to you."

"And does it make you feel less guilty, your grand gesture?" she said with open bitterness.

He stared.

She flushed, wishing desperately that she had not spoken, that she could stop revealing her every thought, wish and desire.

"I should feel guilty?" he finally said, slowly, as if choosing his words with care. "For pleasuring you?"

"For everything," she flung with heat.

"Offering you the gowns has nothing to do with guilt," he said. "You seem downcast. I was hoping to raise your spirits."

"You could always pleasure me again," she said tightly, "that would certainly do the trick."

He started.

She strode away, wishing she had not said that, either; besides, the ecstasy he could bring was only the forerunner of pain. If only she were a woman of the world, a woman who could enjoy his favors indifferently without foolishly yearning for his love. If only he felt guilty for using her at all.

"Lady? Pretty puppies fer sale. Real fancy puppies, my lady, come, see!"

Virginia was blinking back tears. She looked up and into the broad face of a fat black puppy with huge floppy ears, big brown eyes and a pink tongue.

"Real fancy, ain't he?" The toothless man smiled.

But Virginia didn't see. The puppy was wriggling madly, an extension of his wagging tail. She smiled and took the pup into her arms, cuddling it to her chest, her cheek against its fur. He was soft and warm, and she hugged him harder, wishing suddenly that she were back at Sweet Briar, where her life had once been so simple and so happy.

The tears ran then, fast and furious, freely.

"And what kind of breed is that?" Devlin's stern tone sounded.

Virginia blinked back the remaining tears and smiled at the puppy, which licked her cheek enthusiastically.

"A rare breed, sir, a very rare breed. From the north, I believe, is where the dogs come from. They make fine house dogs, sir, for they do not grow much at all. Just to the knee, perfect for a lady."

Devlin snorted.

Virginia hugged the pup harder and it licked her face again. She looked up fiercely. "I am taking this dog, Devlin." And she stared, daring him to refuse her now.

"That dog is a Dane, if I do not miss my guess." His gaze held her eyes. Not looking from Virginia, he sighed and said, "How much?"

"A shilling, sir."

Devlin handed him some coins. "Five pence and consider yourself lucky."

"Yes, sir, my lord!" The man beamed and walked back to the other puppies that slept in a crate.

Virginia turned, softening. "Thank you, I love him. I truly do."

Devlin hesitated, and then he softened, too. "Good. I'm glad," he said, and he felt himself smiling, just a little, but he had lied. The guilt remained, festering now, a wound.

THE NEXT FEW DAYS PASSED slowly. There were no callers, unlike at Wideacre, and the mansion was so large that Virginia had no trouble avoiding Devlin, which she now felt that she must at all costs do. As he did not seek her out—they only shared a terse supper together—she was successful. She began to teach her gangling puppy to sit and lie down. And then they did have a caller—Tyrell de Warenne.

Virginia liked Devlin's handsome stepbrother, whom she had learned was exactly Devlin's age. Upon learning of his visit, she instantly went to greet him. He and Devlin were in a quiet conversation, Devlin clad in his naval uniform. Surprised and dismayed to see Devlin so dressed, she halted in the doorway as both men turned. Tyrell had said something about President Madison, she was certain. "I'm sorry," she said breathlessly, trying not to stare at Devlin in his uniform and wondering if he was about to leave on another tour of duty, "I heard that Lord de Warenne had called. I didn't mean to interrupt."

"That's all right. We were merely discussing your presidential election." Devlin smiled at her, but it did not reach his eyes. His gaze was unwavering and direct, searching hers, as if for some sign of her real feelings.

It was difficult to break the stare. "Hello, my lord," she finally said to Tyrell, managing a smile.

"Miss Hughes." He smiled warmly at her.

"Has President Madison been reelected?" she asked, hoping so.

"Unfortunately," Devlin said wryly. "The news just arrived on one of our battleships."

"He is a very good president," she said firmly. "Capable and clever," she added.

"Your capable and clever president declared war on Great Britain, in spite of the fact that the Privy Council rescinded the Orders in Council, which he and most of your countrymen demanded we do in order to avoid the foolish war we now find ourselves in."

Virginia glared at him. "This war is about far more than

trade and Britain's desire to prevent us from becoming a wealthy and equal sister nation."

"Here, here," Tyrell murmured.

She glared at him, too. "This war is about your country wanting to reduce us in fact, although not de jure, to colonial status again."

"This war is about many things, including your Republican party using it as a means for their own political agenda—to crush the federalists and maintain power," Devlin smoothly returned.

"Do you deny that Britain wishes for us to be impoverished colonies?" she cried.

"No, I do not. But Britain had no desire to go to war with you. Virginia, the British government wishes Ireland to be less than a sister nation, and of course she wishes the same for your country. But no one here is dreaming of reacquiring the American colonies. That is your war hawks' propaganda."

"You are wrong. Your nation is an imperialist one." She was fierce and would not back down, for she knew she was right.

"May I refute?" Tyrell asked smoothly. He was grinning and looking back and forth between the two of them.

"Please do," Devlin said with a sigh.

"The Americans are as imperialistic as the British, Virginia. Everyone knows the agrarian agenda is to conquer Canada and expand in that direction."

"We are suffering terrible defeats in Canada," Virginia said, more quietly. She read Devlin's newspapers every day, and somehow the small British forces in the Canadian territory had managed the impossible, defeating American troops repeatedly. A half-dozen important forts and settlements had been abandoned. "But no one wishes to claim British-held territory there. We wish to trade freely, unimpeded by your navy, and it is our right."

Tyrell glanced at Devlin. "Have you met your match at last, Dev?"

"Perhaps," he said nonchalantly, gazing at some items on his desk. Then he looked up. "Did you wish to see me?"

She faltered. "I merely wished to greet your brother."

"Is that all?" And finally, his careless expression softened.

She blushed. "Yes. Yes, that is really all." Then she looked closely at him. "Why are you in uniform? Are you leaving?"

"No, Virginia, I am not off to sea. I have a meeting in town. Are you disappointed?"

She held her breath. "No," she finally admitted.

His brows lifted, indicating mild surprise. Devlin held her stare.

Her heart raced as she quickly turned away. It was too soon for him to leave again and she was foolishly glad he would stay. She smiled at Tyrell de Warenne. "Would you join us for supper? We should love for you to do so."

"It would be my pleasure, Miss Hughes." He bowed.

She smiled warmly. "Wonderful. Excuse me." She started for the door.

"Virginia?" Devlin called.

She hesitated and turned. "Yes?" And there was no choice but to meet his unwavering stare.

"There is a ball tomorrow evening at Lord Carew's London home. I have accepted the invitation."

Her heart dropped through her entire body, the sensation sickly. "I have nothing to wear!" She wasn't ready for this, not after the other day at Madame Didier's, and not now, after the solitude she had been allowed there at his Greenwich home. She could think of nothing worse than to be flaunted openly as his whore.

"Three of your gowns came today, including the silver ball gown." His jaw flexed with an effort she did not understand.

She tried to smile but nothing happened, nothing at all.

"We'll leave at seven tomorrow evening," he said.

"You ARE LOOKING WELL, Devlin, as always," the Earl of Liverpool said.

Devlin nodded and walked into the prime minister's office, Liverpool informing his clerk that there were to be no interruptions before closing the door behind him. "Tea? Brandy?" he asked.

"No, thank you."

"Have you enjoyed your stay at your Hampshire estate?" Liverpool gestured at a seat.

Devlin sat, as did the earl. "The interlude was a pleasant one," he lied. He hoped to never set foot in Hampshire again—unless it was to receive his ransom money.

"I hear you have taken a most fetching mistress, an American," Liverpool said.

"I have," Devlin returned, hardly perturbed. "So the gossips are hard at their work."

"I believe there is a broken heart or two here in town," Liverpool returned. "Shall we get down to business?"

"Please do."

"Tom Hughes has been pushing for your transfer to the American theater, Devlin. With Napoleon retreating from Russia, his troops decisively routed, the ones that are left decimated and starving, I approve wholeheartedly of the idea—in spite of that fiasco last spring."

"I have no conflict with engaging in action against the Americans," Devlin said, the first wave of excitement washing over him. A good war was just what he needed to get his mind off of Virginia and the odd feelings and notions she aroused. "We've suffered some grave losses at sea. Perhaps I can change that."

"Yes, we have suffered losses that worry me. However,

my concern now is twofold. This American woman—does she present a problem for you?"

"How so?"

"Her allegiance to her country may be strong. Your allegiance to her may also be strong. I hardly wish to send you over to battle her countrymen if you are unwilling in any way to do so."

Devlin's mouth curved. "My lord," he said, "my mistress is a rather unique woman, and she is a patriot, but any regard which I hold for her shall not interfere with my duty."

"I rather expected that would be your answer. Now answer this. I cannot fathom why Hughes is so eager to send you to the north Atlantic. I know the two of you do not get along, but there must be more to this than an ancient dispute over a French actress. Do you have a clue?"

"She was Hungarian," Devlin said smoothly. Liverpool would know the truth about Virginia's identity after the Carew ball, anyway, so he said, "Perhaps it is because my mistress is his cousin."

"I beg your pardon?" Liverpool gasped.

Devlin shrugged. "I have taken up with a very engaging young woman, and I am afraid she is Eastleigh's niece."

Liverpool stared, taken aback. "Devlin, have you no honor? That is despicable."

"I am afraid I have little honor, but I have answered your question."

Liverpool remained shocked. He stood, as did Devlin. "And Eastleigh allows this...trespass?"

"Eastleigh has no choice, really." Devlin shrugged.

"This behavior is simply not acceptable," Liverpool said firmly. "And you may not care, but as an officer of His Majesty's navy, you are expected to be both honorable and a gentleman. Eastleigh will insist you marry her—as will I."

He stiffened, his heart lurching oddly. *Will you marry her to salvage her reputation?* Tyrell had demanded. But her freedom would surely be enough. If he had to, he would make certain she returned to Virginia, where her reputation would not be blemished. "When will my new orders be given?" he asked tersely, his thoughts shifting to Sweet Briar. Had it been sold? If so, Virginia would have no place to go.

"In a week or two."

"She will be free when my tour commences," he said. "But marriage is out of the question."

Liverpool looked at him, clearly stunned and appalled.

"Is there anything else?" He suddenly hated himself. An honorable man would marry Virginia to make amends, but then, an honorable man would have never used her as he had in the first place.

"I have never understood you," Liverpool said heavily. "But you are a great officer, you have done your country one great service after another, and I have nothing but admiration and respect for your stepfather, Adare. Now I am at a complete loss. A senior officer of His Majesty's navy, willfully destroying a woman of family and breeding—it is not to be had."

"I suggest you think to court-martial me when my tour is over. Just now you need me, James, once again." Devlin bowed and walked out.

VIRGINIA STARED AT HER reflection in an oval mirror. She was astonished that the seductive and beautiful creature she gazed upon was herself. It simply did not seem possible.

"Oh, Miss Hughes," the maid, Hannah, breathed. "Captain will never be able to look at another woman again after he sees you!"

And staring at the slender woman in the low-cut tissue

gown with its silver-velvet cap sleeves and sash, Virginia almost believed her. She turned to glance at her profile. Her breasts seemed voluptuous in the dress and she was acutely aware of her new undergarments, all sinfully black, sinfully sensuous, trimmed in ribbon and lace. She should feel like a whore, considering the underwear she wore, but she did not—she was too frightened of the evening to come, and all she could feel was a dreadful anxiety and a genuine faintness.

"You are so elegant, Miss Hughes. How proud the captain will be," Hannah murmured.

At least she did not look like a whore—or like a mistress. She looked very regal and very rich. Virginia touched the beaded silver lace that ornamented her tightly coiled hair and looked far better than any turban or headdress. All that was missing was a necklace and earbobs. She did not dare complain.

But how would she face an evening filled with the ton's most elegant, most aristocratic ladies and gentlemen? How?

"Virginia, we are late," Devlin said.

She glanced into the mirror and saw him pause in the open doorway. His eyes widened as he saw her, moved over the reflection of her face and dropped to her bosom. "Turn around," he said softly.

As ill with dread that she was, she understood the silver gleam in his eyes was one of appreciation. She obeyed, wanting to make light of the moment—and all the moments that would surely come during that evening. She curtsied. "I hope you approve of Madame Didier's work," she said with a forced smile.

"I approve. I more than approve, Virginia, and you will be the most beautiful woman at Carew's tonight."

She made a derisive sound.

His mouth quirked. "You may leave," he said to the

maid. She nodded, eyes downcast, and fled. "Come here," he said softly.

It did not cross her frozen mind to disobey or even question why. She walked over to him. He smiled a little and reached up, and for one instant she thought he was going to take her face in his strong hands. Instead, he clipped an earring to each earlobe, turned her around, and placed a necklace about her neck. Virginia looked down, trying to see, and gasped at the sight of so many diamonds dangling about her throat. "What is this?"

"Do you like it?" he asked, his hands moving to her shoulders.

Virginia found herself facing the mirror, with Devlin standing behind her, his hands clasping her shoulders. Hundreds of diamonds, all cut like stars, dangled from the necklace in random sizes. One large pendant dangled from the center. The earbobs matched.

Virginia swallowed. "Yes," she managed, wondering when he had gotten the necklace and why. Surely it was only for her to use—surely it was not for her to keep. She could never ask.

"Shall we?" he asked, releasing her and lifting her gray satin wrap and settling it about her shoulders.

She nodded, inhaling harshly and beginning to tremble. If only, she managed to think, they were going somewhere else, as something other than man and mistress.

"We will not stay too long," he murmured as he guided her from the room, as if guessing her thoughts.

One minute was too long. She wisely refrained from saying so.

He gave her an odd look. "I promise this will soon be over, Virginia," he said.

THE CAREW MANSION RESEMBLED a palace. Situated on the outskirts of Greenwich, surrounded by hundreds of acres of both park and wood, the house could easily accommodate all three of Devlin's homes. As Devlin's carriage entered the square drive, passing a maze and a sculpture garden, Virginia saw that the line ahead consisted of the most elegant and grand coaches she had ever beheld and the dread congealed. As they waited their turn to alight, she asked, "How many guests will be present?"

"Several hundred, I think," Devlin replied.

He did not speak again, sitting beside her, his long legs crossed, as dashing as ever in his uniform. Virginia was immobilized—it was hard to breathe. Devlin did not seem to notice. He appeared distracted, but what matter could so preoccupy him she did not know. His tension seemed to match her own—and it belied his bland facade.

A half an hour later their carriage door was opened and a footman helped Virginia down, Devlin following. They started up the wide stone staircase that led to the open front door, following a dozen other parties.

"Captain O'Neill, sir, how fine to see you again."

"Lord Arnold, Lady Arnold." Devlin bowed to the smiling couple. "May I present my dear friend, Miss Virginia Hughes?"

Virginia felt her cheeks flame as two pairs of interested eyes came her way. Lord Arnold was a portly man with a kind face, his wife of average looks and figure, her eyes bright and indicating a superior intelligence. Arnold bowed; his wife nodded. "A fine night for a ball, is it not, Miss Hughes?" He smiled.

He had no clue yet as to her terrible status. Virginia nodded. "Very fine," she managed. She glanced at his wife, but Lady Arnold simply regarded her keenly, not saying anything, a polite smile on her lips.

They followed the Arnolds inside, Devlin and Arnold briefly discussing a motion recently passed in the Commons.

Virginia gaped at the ceiling above—it was several stories high—and just beyond the huge front hall, she could see into an even larger, grander ballroom. There, a good two hundred guests were mingling already, and the room was alive with the jewel tones of the ladies' gowns and the thousands of crystals shimmering in the overhead chandeliers.

"So you are an American?" Lady Arnold said as they paused on the receiving line.

Virginia started and swallowed. "Yes." Knowing she flushed, she added, "We do not have balls like these at home."

"And where is your home, my dear?"

"Virginia, my lady." Virginia waited for the next terrible, inevitable question.

"And how did you come to be in England?"

Virginia wet her lips. "My parents died. My uncle is the Earl of Eastleigh and I came to spend some time with him."

"Oh, I am so sorry about your parents," Lady Arnold said. Virginia thought that beneath her very bright eyes, she was kind. "Yes. Thank you."

"And Captain O'Neill? Is he a family friend?"

Virginia hesitated. Should she get this over with? Would it not be better to do so, sooner rather than later?

Lady Arnold said politely, "I do not mean to pry, of course, but I have never seen the captain in the company of a single woman."

She wet her lips. "He has been very kind. I am...staying at Waverly Hall."

Her brows lifted with mild interest. "Oh, yes, the home he purchased from your uncle. Is your family in residence there?"

"I'm afraid not," Virginia said. And she simply could not

go through with it. "Excuse me, my lady, but the captain beckons." And aware of some surprise, she hurried over to Devlin. His regard was searching.

"I am afraid I may not play our charade well tonight," she said tersely.

"You need not play any charade, tonight, Virginia," he said. "You need to merely be with me, at my side, until we leave." His jaw flexed and he looked away, as if he could not meet her eyes. "My lord Carew." He bowed, facing an older, heavyset gentleman. "May I present my dear friend, Miss Virginia Hughes?"

Virginia's headache knew no bounds. She stood apart, watching the many dancers, having no recollection of the steps as the line of men and women formed and broke, partners circling and changing couples before meeting yet again. Devlin spoke with several men but a short distance away, and she knew from their repeated glances in her direction that these men distinctly understood her status in the world.

She was miserable.

"Would you like to dance?"

She whirled and met Tyrell de Warenne's smiling countenance. "My lord! I'm afraid I have forgotten the steps," she confessed. Then she realized she had forgotten to curtsy and she hastily did so.

He touched her, restraining her. "Please, Miss Hughes, I feel we know each other well enough to dispense with formality."

She was relieved. "You British are all so formal!" she explained. "It has been shocking, trying to adjust."

"Yes, I imagine so," Tyrell said gently, with a benign smile. He held out his arm. "Shall we take a turn about the gallery?"

She glanced at Devlin, who had turned to stare at them.

"I doubt he will allow it. I have been insufficiently flaunted."

Tyrell's smile vanished. "Virginia, may I speak freely?"

She tensed. "Please do."

"My entire family is furious with Devlin for his behavior and his bringing you here is the least of it."

She gaped. And she was aware of Devlin leaving his group of gentlemen and striding calmly toward them. She was not deceived. She saw the purpose in his stride and sensed the determination, as well.

"I merely want to advise you that there will be justice, Virginia. You will be shortly compensated for all you have been through, my father will see to it."

She had no idea of what he meant. Compensation? Suddenly she was seized by hope—would they aid her in paying off her father's debts? That would surely be compensation for all she had been through!

Devlin paused, taking Virginia's arm. "Are you trying to lure away Virginia's affections, Ty?"

"As if I would ever trespass upon *your* affections, Devlin," Tyrell said.

Devlin nodded while Virginia ignored the exchange, too busy thinking about the compensation that would soon be hers. Finally it seemed as if her terrible turn of bad luck was about to change.

"Shall we dance?" Devlin asked almost formally.

She started. "I lied. I cannot dance, not a single step."

He finally smiled at her. And the warmth reached his eyes. "I find the whole pastime rather boring myself. Shall I get us some champagne?"

She nodded, wishing he had suggested that they leave. She felt fortunate to have thus far escaped any unpleasant and humiliating encounters.

Devlin nodded and walked away.

Tyrell said, "As you are otherwise engaged, good evening. I hope we shall see each other soon." He bowed.

Virginia smiled, curtsied and watched him leave. And suddenly she was truly alone.

It was an odd feeling, and not a pleasant one, to be surrounded by three hundred and fifty guests yet to be standing conspicuously by oneself. And she *was* conspicuous. With Devlin and Tyrell gone, several groups had turned to gaze at her and she had the distinct feeling that she might be the topic of conversation. One group of ladies stared and spoke rapidly, fans fluttering. Virginia felt certain that they were discussing her.

She turned her back to them and was faced by three handsome gentlemen, and in unison, they all smiled at her. She took a step back.

They approached. The nearest one, a gentleman of thirty or so with shocking red hair and extremely pale blue eyes, bowed. "I do not believe I have had the pleasure of making your acquaintance," he said.

She smiled, summoning up all of her courage now. "No, I do not think so. I am Virginia Hughes."

"John Marshall, at your service," he said, with another, more cursory bow. "You are an American?"

She nodded. "Yes. But I have come to England to visit my uncle, the Earl of Eastleigh." That story had served her well and she decided to continue it.

"So Eastleigh is your uncle?" Marshall seemed delighted. "And you are in Captain O'Neill's party tonight?"

She could not decide if he knew that she had accompanied Devlin alone. "Yes." Her smile was fixed.

"May I present my good friends, Lords Halsey and Ridgewood?"

Virginia smiled and exchanged pleasantries as the men bowed. She felt as if she were surrounded by the enemy—which she most certainly was.

"And how is it you have become acquainted with Great Britain's greatest—and most notorious—war hero?" Ridgewood asked. He was tall and pale.

"Oh, come, George, we all know O'Neill always takes the prettiest for himself." Marshall laughed and the others joined in. But then, his smile not reaching his eyes, Marshall said, "It's no secret O'Neill is quite at odds with your cousin, Tom Hughes. How interesting that you accompany your cousin's bitter foe to this evening's soirée."

Virginia shrugged helplessly.

"Miss Hughes and Captain O'Neill are dear friends—I have heard it said so," Halsey said with a grin. He jabbed Ridgewood with his elbow. "Very dear friends. You are residing at Waverly Hall, are you not?"

"Yes," Virginia managed, hating them all and hating Devlin, too. She could not do this anymore. She hadn't won his friendship; the bargain worked only for him; she had had enough.

"May I call on you, Miss Hughes? Tomorrow, perhaps?" Marshall asked, leaning far too close for comfort or civility.

"Excuse me," she cried, turning and rushing into the crowd.

It was hard to see. The room was a blur of brilliant reds, blinding gold, purple, blue and green, with stark black evening clothes in between. But how could she see? Tears had interfered with her vision and she could not breathe. It was so damn hot and airless in the ballroom...if only she could be transported across the ocean back to her Virginia home.

There will be justice. You will shortly be compensated.

Tyrell de Warenne's singular statement brought some small measure of relief as she stumbled into the gallery outside of the ballroom. There, perhaps a dozen guests strolled. Virginia hurried down the gallery and turned the corner. Another gallery ran down the side of the house, barely lit with the occasional wall sconce. Most of the illumination came from a series of huge windows and the moon and stars outside. Thankful to finally be alone, she went to a window and leaned on the stone sill. Pain had seized her abdomen, cutting through it with the intensity of a butcher's knife. She had to get away. She could not go on like this.

They are dear friends—I have heard it said so.

Virginia kept breathing until she was no longer panting, until some of the pain had lessened. If only she could hate him. She knew she should, but she simply could not.

He is not a ruthless monster...but he is not kind. His ability to be kind died the day our father died.

He is not indifferent. It is a sham, a pretense, a huge theatrical act.

I am asking you to save my brother.

Virginia cried out, because Devlin was beyond salvation and that had become terribly clear. Her stomach so hurt her again that she clutched herself, bending over.

"If it isn't my dear, dear, American cousin."

Virginia straightened, gasping with dread, and slowly, she turned.

A naval officer, lean and handsome, faced her, smiling. He bowed. "Lord Captain Thomas Hughes," he said. His smile remained in place and it did not reach his gleaming eyes. "How thrilled I am to finally make your acquaintance."

Virginia needed air. "My lord," she said cautiously, glancing wildly around. But Devlin was nowhere to be seen.

"You act afraid," Tom Hughes purred. "But surely, my dear cousin, you are not afraid of me?"

She simply could not speak. She sensed a terrible intent on her cousin's part and backed up against the stone windowsill.

"Are you enjoying the ball, Virginia?"

She couldn't even nod. "Ex...excuse me," she whispered, and somehow stumbled past him.

But he seized her arm, whipping her back against the stone ledge. "Are you enjoying the ball as much as you are enjoying Captain O'Neill's bed?"

She cried out, alarmed, and tried to shake him off. "Unhand me. You are hurting me, sir!"

His grip tightened. He leaned close. "I heard he fucks like a bull. Is that what you like? What you want? My little cousin—my little whore?"

The pain shot through her entire arm and she thought she might faint. "Please," she gasped.

"Oh, yes, yes, indeed, the word I have so waited to hear." He jerked her forward and before she even knew it, he had his mouth on hers.

Virginia tried to struggle. But he pressed her brutally into the stone wall with his body, grinding down on her mouth with his teeth as well as his lips, so violently that instantly she sobbed. He thrust his tongue deep and she gagged; as he raped her mouth, she felt his hand delve inside her dress and he seized her breast, crushing it in his hand. More pain exploded in her, and then she felt his arousal against her thigh and blackness began. She fought it as she tried uselessly to fight him. But he kept her pinned against the wall as he mauled her. She had not a doubt that if she fainted she would be raped. Still she began to swim into the beckoning depths.

"I will kill you."

Devlin's strangely fierce words stabbed through the darkness and suddenly Tom Hughes was gone. Virginia collapsed to the floor, still sobbing, her chest and her arm throbbing with pain, and she heard a man scream.

Choking, she looked up.

Hughes lay on the floor, and above him, on the wall, was blood.

Coherence came.

Devlin kicked him. "Get up, coward," he said very softly.

She had to stop him. He had meant his every word. He was going to murder Hughes.

But Virginia could not yet speak.

Hughes got to his hands and his knees. "She's only a whore." He spat blood.

Devlin lifted him to his feet and threw him against the stone wall. Then he caught him as he fell, lifted him again and slammed his gloved fist into his face. Something shattered there.

Virginia ignored all pain and got up. "Devlin, stop! Stop it now!"

But Hughes, his face bloody, withdrew his sword.

Virginia was in disbelief.

Devlin smiled. "A very unwise move," he said. His sword rang as he unsheathed it. And the two men began to dance softly about each other, each with fatal intent.

"Devlin, no," Virginia cried.

He gave no sign that he had heard, feinting once. Hughes misread the feint and thrust to receive a blow; instantly, Devlin thrust and slashed open his uniform. Blood welled. Hughes cried out.

Tyrell. Virginia ran around the corner and into the brightly lit gallery, glancing wildly everywhere, and it wasn't until she was halfway through the hall that she became aware of the people she passed turning to gape and stare. She realized then that her hair was coming down, her gown was torn and that what had happened was terribly clear. But her obvious downfall could not matter now. She paused on one threshold to the ballroom, saw the huge crowd there, and despaired. *Devlin was going to kill Tom Hughes, she simply knew it, and he would hang for the offense.*

Then she saw him, on the dance floor, partnering a stunning blonde.

And eyes were turning her way.

Summoning up all of her courage, she lifted her skirts and ran. "My lord de Warenne!"

Tyrell was stepping back into line, facing his partner, and he stiffened.

She shouted again. "Tyrell! My lord! Help!"

He turned, saw her, and his eyes widened. Then he ran to her, the dancers ceasing at once. "What happened? Are you hurt?"

"Devlin is killing Tom Hughes in the hall behind the gallery," she cried.

He took off like a shot. Virginia ran after him, aware now of a terrible silence overcoming the ballroom, of the furor of gasps and murmurs. It was too late to care. And as she chased Tyrell through the gallery and into the hall, she did not stop to discover how many guests were on her heels.

In the hall she found the two men parrying, with Hughes a tattered, bloody mess. Devlin was pristine in his uniform, pristine and untouched; his adversary could barely keep to his feet. The two men exchanged blows, and Hughes's sword clattered across the floor and out of reach. Devlin's sword thrust against his chest, where it lay, unmoving. And Devlin smiled with ruthless, lethal intent.

"Enough," Tyrell said, moving to stand behind Devlin.

Hughes stood, his back to the wall, swaying as if about

to become unconscious. The crowd behind Virginia gasped and began murmuring in disbelief and amazement.

Devlin's entire face was a taut, tight, controlled mask, one Virginia had never before seen. She knew he wished to kill. His smile was more than chilling; it was terrifying. "I think not. I think it is time for Tom Hughes to die."

"And all for your whore?" Hughes managed.

As Devlin moved to deliver a fatal blow, a thrust meant to pierce Hughes's heart, the crowd cried out and Tyrell gripped his wrist, forestalling him. *"Do not."*

Devlin's smile was savage. *"Get out of my way."*

"You will not kill him," Tyrell returned, and as he held Devlin's wrist, his knuckles were white.

Virginia closed her eyes and prayed.

"He is not worth it. He did not kill Gerald, Devlin. He is not the one you seek," Tyrell said softly.

Virginia opened her eyes and saw Devlin standing there, poised to kill, wanting to kill, a truly savage man.

"Virginia is not hurt," Tyrell added even more softly.

Devlin's entire face tensed. He glanced at her briefly then back at Hughes, and suddenly his posture relaxed and he stepped back.

A number of sighs escaped from the watching guests. Virginia felt her knees buckle in the same terrible relief that one and all were feeling.

And then a dozen officers were rushing to Hughes to administer to him. Devlin suddenly sheathed his sword, turning, and his gaze found hers again. Instantly he strode to her. "Are you all right?" he demanded, staring, not touching her, his eyes moving over her face and hair, finally to linger on her lips, which she thought were bloodied but could not be sure. His glance then took in the torn bodice of her gown. His eyes turned chilling again.

The ability to speak escaped her. She could only nod,

incapable of tearing her gaze from his. In that instant, he was the safest harbor she had ever known.

His jaw tightened, his eyes darkened, and he put his arm around her. "We are going home," he said.

CHAPTER TWENTY

VIRGINIA COULD NOT STOP trembling. She knew it was foolish—she was bruised, but other than that, she was hardly the worse for wear—and she did not want Devlin to see how cowardly she was. Still, the tremors did not cease. She could not forget Thomas Hughes's brutal assault. She could not forget his hand cruelly twisting her breast, or worse, his tongue invading her mouth. Her stomach heaved as Devlin's coach swerved wildly and then bounced over a rut. Virginia closed her eyes and hung on.

"Virginia?" he asked softly.

She did not want to speak to him now. She doubted she could—she remained far too close to hysteria. She hugged herself, huddling in the coach's far corner, other images afflicting her now. *Devlin had wanted to kill Thomas Hughes.* She had seen it in his eyes.

"We will be home shortly," Devlin said, his tone odd, as if uncertain. "Within minutes," he added.

She nodded, refusing to open her eyes because his tone sounded suspiciously concerned and she was afraid she might cry. Of course he had wanted to kill Tom Hughes. He had spent most of his life burning with the need for revenge against Eastleigh and all that was his.

"Virginia, are you in pain?"

She simply could not speak, so she shook her head, and

it was not really a lie. Her wrist and breast throbbed, but it was so much more than that. Devlin seemed to want to know what was wrong. But she could not tell him.

Tom Hughes had treated her like the whore the world thought she was. She could never play this game again, and if it meant losing any chance to win his love, so be it. It had become crystal clear, anyway, that he did not have any soul left with which to love any woman, much less herself.

How easily he had been triggered to murderous intent.

"We're here," Devlin said, sounding grim.

The coach had slowed and was now stopping; Virginia opened her eyes and saw the terribly welcome sight of Waverly Hall. A footman leapt off the back of the coach to open her door. Devlin adjusted her satin wrapper, concealing her torn dress.

Virginia's heart tightened. Why did he bother? She knew she had a split lip, a telltale sign of her disaster. She wanted to thank him, but she still didn't trust herself to speak.

She stood and allowed the footman to help her down to the sidewalk before the mansion's front steps.

Devlin jumped down behind her, as agile as a jungle cat, and she was swept back in time to another place—to the deck of the *Americana,* as she had gripped the railing and gazed at the fierce ocean, wondering what her fate might be at the hands of the pirate captain. *If you think to leap to a watery death, think again. I will not let you die.*

Oddly, his refrain pierced the night as if she were back on the *Americana,* newly seized, as if Devlin stood there behind her, as if he had just uttered those words again.

Devlin carefully took her arm, and Virginia leaned heavily against him. Once in the hall, he circumvented Benson from assisting her with her wrap. "Send Hannah to the master suite instantly with hot water, towels and brandy. Miss Hughes has had a fall."

Benson nodded and hurried away.

He would guard her reputation now? Virginia choked, wanting to weep.

Devlin suddenly lifted her into his arms and began striding through the hall.

"What are you doing?" she managed. "I can walk."

"I am doing what I have wanted to do ever since I allowed Tom Hughes to live," he said grimly.

She finally looked up at him as he bounded up the stairs. His face was taut with anger and regret and, she thought, with anguish. He hit the second level and their eyes met and held. He did not speak and neither did she. Stunned, she realized how distraught he was.

Devlin opened their door with the toe of his shoe, followed by his broad shoulder. He carried her through their sitting room, where a fire blazed in the hearth, and into the master bedroom. There, another fire crackled happily and their bed was turned down. He set her down on it, removing her wrap and breaking eye contact to do so. "I'll help you out of that gown before Hannah arrives," he said. It was not a suggestion.

Virginia realized she was hugging herself, that she still trembled, though she was not cold. Why did he go to such lengths? All of society would know the truth by the next morning.

"Turn around, please," he said softly.

Virginia started. Then she said hoarsely, "I have never heard you say *please* before."

His jaw flexed. "It's a word I rarely feel the need to use. Virginia—" He stopped.

She stared, realizing that he was distressed, perhaps even uncomfortable, and that he wished to say something. Her heart leapt with hope. "What is it, Devlin?"

A silence ensued. Then, "I am so sorry," he said roughly.

Her heart turned over so hard that there could be no doubt that her feelings remained in full force, that nothing had changed, that she still loved this man. She opened her mouth to tell him that this was not his fault—but it was. Everything was his fault.

"Please turn around," he said, his tone as rough as before.

Virginia shifted, and his hands nimbly moved down her back, unbuttoning the gown. When he had removed it she began taking down her hair, acutely aware of him in the room, placing the dress on the back of a chair. A huge silence ensued. Virginia became impossibly aware of her state of undress. She wore her new undergarments—the black lace chemise, black linen corset and black silk drawers, all trimmed in ivory and pink ribbons, all sinfully sensuous. She needed a wrapper, she thought, stabbed with a sudden, new urgency. "Would..." She paused, wet her lips and tried again. "Would you hand me a robe?"

He glanced briefly at her, and if he noticed her undergarments he gave no sign. He opened the armoire as a knock sounded. "Come in," he said very sharply, and perplexed, Virginia thought she heard relief in his tone.

Hannah entered, her eyes wide, carrying a tray with a bowl of water and towels. Devlin slipped a lavender silk robe over Virginia's shoulders, also courtesy of Madame Didier, and she belted it firmly, relieved. "Oh, mum," Hannah whispered. "You had a fall! I'm so sorry," she cried. She set the tray on the bed. "Captain, one minute, sir."

He nodded, standing by Virginia's side, and Hannah went to the door and received another tray from a servant standing outside, this one with a bottle of brandy and two snifters. He took a small towel, dipped it in the water, and then looked at her directly. "You have blood on your lip," he said.

Virginia could only stare, amazed at what was happening, her heart fluttering madly.

He sat down beside her and gently wiped the blood from her mouth.

She could not breathe. What was he doing? And more important, why?

He tilted up her chin, studied her mouth for a moment, and then lifted his eyes to hers. "I'm afraid you will be bruised for a few days."

She didn't know what to say; she said nothing. His touch was beyond gentle. She had never seen this side of him before. Had she not been so upset, she would have been elated.

Hannah had returned, holding two snifters. Devin nodded at the side table, where she set them down. He lifted Virginia's wrist, which still throbbed. And she saw his face tighten, his eyes turn black. He cursed.

"It's not that bad," she lied, her heart pounding now with terrible force.

His gaze lifted. "Like hell. I think he meant to snap your wrist in two. It is lucky for him that he did not."

Virginia could only stare. *He cared.* There was simply no other possible way to read this man's reaction to her condition now.

He handed her a snifter. "This will help. I advise you to drink the entire glass. You will sleep like a baby," he added, trying to smile. But he failed utterly and gave it up.

Virginia sipped, her mind racing, filled with more amazement, more disbelief and, finally, the seed of elation. But how could this be happening? What if she was wrong? He had hurt her so any times—did she dare hope now, that at long last he had come to really care for her? But what else could it be? This man knew no guilt.

Devlin stood. "I will sleep in a guest room so as not to bother you tonight, Virginia."

She blinked hard, in dismay. The last thing she wished was to be alone, even if he slept on the sofa in the next room, as he was wont to do.

"Hannah, please apply an ice compress to her wrist."

"Yes, sir," Hannah whispered.

Virginia wet her lips. "Devlin, no," she said hoarsely.

He stiffened.

"I don't want to be alone—not tonight—please, stay here with me," she cried softly. And tears filled her eyes.

His own widened, his visage far sterner than before. He could not seem to speak.

"I'll get the ice," Hannah whispered and discreetly she fled, closing the door behind her.

Virginia could not move. She could only stare up at him, the tears trickling down her cheeks, wishing she could stop crying, wishing he would not leave, wishing he would take her in his arms and gently hold her.

He remained stiff with a conflict she could not fathom. "Virginia," he said hoarsely, "this is my entire fault. I have used you shamelessly. I am sorry."

She gasped, stunned.

He closed his eyes as if agonized, then sat down beside her hip. He took both of her hands in his. "I will not ask for your forgiveness, little one, because I do not deserve it."

"You are forgiven," she whispered instantly, meaning it.

His nostrils flared, indicating huge emotion, and he stared, never releasing her hands. "How can you be so kind after what I have subjected you to? Tom attacked you because of our charade—the charade I insisted upon. God, I wish I had killed him," he cried.

She had never seen him emotional like this before; he was a man who only expressed anger. "It's all right," she whispered raggedly. Her own fingers tightened on his hands. "He didn't rape me in the end."

His eyes widened. "Is that what he was about? In a public hall?"

Virginia saw the fury in his eyes and she hesitated. "I think so."

He leapt up. "I will kill him after all."

She sat up straighter, confused. "Because of me?"

"What other reason would there be?" he asked in some amazement.

She stared. "Your father."

His jaw flexed. "This is not about my father."

She reeled, his words having the most profound, dizzying effect, and she sank back against the pillows, stunned. *This was not about his revenge.*

"I must go," he said suddenly.

"No!" And her gaze blurred. "Please don't leave me now."

He stared.

She stared back and held out her hand, imploring him to come.

His expression remained impossibly taut and she saw the battle he waged in his eyes.

"Please, Devlin," she whispered. "Please stay—please hold me—just for a moment." Her voice cracked.

He reached her in a stride and sat down, taking her hands again. "You ask too much of me now," he warned.

She shook her head, leaning toward him, and when he did not move, she placed her cheek on his chest.

She felt him stiffen, she heard him inhale, and then his hand clasped her back. Virginia almost smiled, as more tears fell, rapidly now, and the gold buttons and braid of his jacket rubbed unpleasantly against her face. His hand stroked down her back, over the silk of her robe and her underclothes, and she half sighed and half choked.

"Please don't cry," he said harshly, and it was a plea. "It

is over now, you are safe, and we will end this absurd game."

She lifted her face and looked up at him. "I can't play it anymore—it hurts too much."

He nodded, his gaze odd, almost moist, and then he leaned down and brushed her mouth lightly with his. "It's over, Virginia, I swear," he said.

His tone was husky with regret and something far different, desire. Virginia's hands found the epaulets on his shoulders and she held him that way as he brushed his mouth over hers, again, very, very softly.

A huge sigh escaped her, the tears ceasing, her entire body tightening with incredible urgency. His mouth had paused, firm and still, and she opened against him, seeking another kiss.

For one moment he did not move as she brushed her mouth over his, again and again, faster and faster still, every fiber of her body taut with need now, because her entire life had been reduced to this single moment—she had to be one with him. Nothing else mattered, and in that union she knew nothing else would exist. Not his revenge, not the near rape. Not the humiliation of the past month. Nothing else would exist except Devlin and herself and her love.

"Don't," he warned. "This is dangerous, Virginia."

Virginia thrust her tongue into his mouth as he spoke and he tensed—the invasion was so sweet that she moaned, licking his teeth, the inside of his cheeks, his lips.

"I cannot," he gasped, pushing her onto her back. His eyes were wide, brilliant, silver. "I cannot promise you restraint."

She shook her head—she did not want restraint—and she gripped his neck and pulled his face down toward hers.

He groaned and claimed her mouth frantically—but he

was holding himself back, clearly afraid to hurt her, and she felt his entire body shaking with the effort it cost him.

Virginia pushed.at his jacket.

"Am I hurting you?" he cried, flinging the coat off. "I don't want to hurt you!"

"You're not hurting me," she gasped, unbuttoning his pale ivory waistcoat and pulling it off. His eyes widened and when she tugged his shirt out of his britches, he helped her, whipping off the cravat and shrugging off the shirt, tossing both aside.

She cried out at the sight of his naked upper body and found her hands on his chest, exploring the slabs of rock-hard muscle there.

He found her mouth again, and now, as he kissed her deeply, he opened her wrapper, and then pulled away, staring, as he lifted her chemise up. He froze.

Virginia glanced down and saw her bruised breast.

"Oh, God," he whispered.

He was straddling her, clad in his britches, stockings and shoes, clearly aroused and clearly about to abandon her.

Virginia's need was so vast that her entire body was shaking. She knew he had lost almost all of his control, she knew they were instants away from making love, and she took his hand and covered her bruised breast with it.

He cried out.

"You cannot leave me now," she whispered.

His gaze met hers, filled with anguish and heat.

She took his hand and moved it to her other breast, rubbing it over the hard nipple there.

He inhaled harshly. And then he had her in his arms again, their mouths mating, tongues entwining. Virginia knew she had won and she held on to him, hard.

He tore off her wrapper and chemise, kissed her breast, slid his hand down her belly and over her silk drawers.

Virginia gasped, eyes closing, as he delved through the slit drawers, where he found wet, hungry flesh throbbing against his fingertips.

He made a choked sound. She heard his shoes hit the floor, heard him tear off his stockings and britches, and then she felt his strong bare legs against hers and his velvety smooth, rock-hard shaft. Virginia cried out.

He smiled once, hard and tight, and bent and kissed her sex.

Virginia meant to hold him down. He evaded her, slipping her drawers down her legs and tossing them to the floor. She looked at him.

He was completely naked, all power, all muscle, huge and strong. He smiled a little, something primitive and triumphant in his expression, and he moved over her. "I don't want to hurt you, darling," he whispered roughly.

"You won't," she managed.

He smiled a little, as they both knew it must be a lie, with her so tiny and him so huge. "Virginia," he said, kissing her slowly.

She moaned as he probed against her, the sensation too much to bear. Blackness threatened, and with it, an explosion of fiery sparks.

Stroking himself once, twice more against her sex, he murmured, "Are you ready for me, darling?"

She did not answer because she could not, she only cried out.

"I think so," he said roughly, stroking over her again. And his entire body shuddered.

Devlin pushed against her.

For one moment, Virginia tensed, having forgotten just how massive his invasion was.

"Darling," he said roughly against her temple, pressing slowly into her.

Virginia cried out as he filled her, inch by deliberate inch. When it seemed he could go no farther, she clung, panting hard, as tense as a drum.

"Relax, little one, let me bring you pleasure—vast pleasure," he said harshly, and he moved.

He moved deeper yet.

Virginia clawed his back, about to tell him to stop, when her body yielded and a wave of heated pleasure began. She gasped in surprise as Devlin began to ride her, slowly and rhythmically, his body shaking with his restraint as he did so.

The pleasure mounted impossibly. Virginia held him, wrapping her calves around his thighs, causing him to gasp with pleasure and thrust harder, deeper, now. Yes, she managed to think, blinded by the pleasure, the man, and she clawed him, wanting more, demanding it. He responded. As he thrust deep, carrying her across the bed, she held on, crying out, wave after wave of ecstasy washing over her, through her, and still he pounded, gasping out, crying, "Darling, let me give you more," and she wept, shattering, far above the earth.

He continued to plunder, his entire body hard and slick now beneath her hands, shaking wildly as he moved. Virginia floated back down to their bed and finally to a degree of reason, and she was stunned, stunned by the depth of the passion she had just experienced and even more stunned now by the depth of love. It was a huge wave, washing over her and through her the way her orgasm had done.

She looked at him, holding him tightly, amazed by the vast feeling in her heart. "I am hopelessly in love," she thought, and as she thought so, she was acutely aware of him within her, smooth and rock hard, and she looked at him.

His eyes were closed. His face was strained. Sweat beaded on his temples, his brow. He was in the throes of lust—she sensed his climax was near.

Her heart tightened and her belly lurched and the desire, always incipient, throbbed around him.

She murmured, "Ooh," in soft surprise.

"Will you...come for me...again?" he said thickly.

She tried to nod, an impossible task with the man so huge and aroused inside of her.

He bent and kissed her recklessly, tongue to tongue; he feathered her face, licked her nipple, biting it once, all the while embedded deep and hot inside of her. The pressure escalated rapidly and she could not move, as she was so thoroughly impaled.

He knew. He laughed harshly and pulled away; Virginia cried out, furiously protesting, but he bent and licked her sex, prying between the lips there, and when she began to keen he thrust inside, pushing her back up to the headboard of the bed, and she was exploding again when she felt him begin to pulse. A moment later he was crying out and heaving hotly against her.

Virginia seemed to float in a delicious aftermath for a long time. When her mind began to work, she could only feel—his body against hers, their legs entwined, his palm on her belly, perilously near her sex, which was still acutely sensitized, the stiff bones of her corset—and the ballooning feeling of love in her breast. She did not want to feel anything else, but so quickly worry and the beginnings of dread began.

This had happened once before, and she would never forget the heartbreak that had followed.

She was lying on her back and he lay beside her. Her small leg lay over one of his and their hands were side by side, just barely touching. Virginia realized he was awake and as thoughtful as she was. Dread tightened every fiber of her being; she closed her eyes briefly and prayed.

Then she turned her face and looked at him.

He stared up at the ceiling. She had one moment to feel the depth of her love when he turned to look back at her.

Her heart stopped.

He smiled a little.

Relief dared to begin.

Their gazes held. His was, she realized, searching. "Did I hurt you?" he asked quietly.

Perhaps, just perhaps, this was a new beginning. "No," she whispered.

He smiled just a little again, then turned and pulled her across his chest and into his arms. And he kissed her temple.

Virginia almost fainted with disbelief and relief.

"Are you uncomfortable?" he asked after a moment.

Her cheek was on his chest, his arm draped over his abdomen, his other arm around her. Virginia was afraid she might cry with happiness if she spoke. It took her a moment to say, "I am fine."

He hesitated, then his fingers moved up and down her forearm. And he kissed her temple again.

Virginia was afraid to move—afraid to break the moment—afraid that if she did, it would vanish, as if it had never been. So she froze there in his arms.

"Maybe I should sleep in the sitting room," he said.

She jerked, looking up at him and meeting his gaze. It was grave—but it held a gleam she instantly recognized. "Why?"

His mouth twisted in self-deprecation. "I am afraid once was not enough, little one. I want you again, but I refuse to abuse you."

She saw what he meant and her heart tightened. She

smiled at him, uncertain, and very daringly she swept her hand across his taut belly and lower still.

His eyes widened. "Virginia?"

She caressed the velvet length.

He choked.

"You won't abuse me, Devlin. I may be petite but I am not porcelain."

He didn't speak.

She was somewhat fascinated by what she had dared to do, nevertheless, she did look up.

His eyes were squeezed closed. He was beginning to breathe hard. She saw a bead of sweat on his brow. She became very intrigued. "Devlin?" she asked, moving her hand to lightly touch his chest.

He seized it and replaced it. "Don't stop," he said, his voice thick.

And Virginia suddenly had an inkling of the power that might be hers. "What?" She became still, stunned. Was it possible that a mere touch could so immobilize him?

He seemed to fight to speak. "Virginia, do not stop," he said, and his tone was so thick she could not tell if it was an order he gave—or a plea.

Virginia was in disbelief.

"Please," he said thickly.

He was begging *her?*

He stared—she stared back. Then she smiled a little, made absolutely breathless by the fierce blaze in his eyes, and she stroked him again, now carefully, and he gasped and reared up, his chest now heaving.

"Oh, my," Virginia said, elation beginning. She smiled slyly at him.

"Witch," he said harshly.

Virginia grinned and kissed him.

He cried out, grasped her and hauled her up the bed, and

she found herself on her back, her legs spread, with Devlin fiercely intent and as fiercely poised to enter her. "Wicked little woman," he said.

She laughed and pulled him closer, until her laughter died.

IT WAS MIDMORNING. Devlin sat at his desk in the library, an empty Scotch glass in front of him. Virginia had fallen asleep at dawn and he had quietly left her then, knowing he would not be able to sleep.

He was grim, torn, confused. It was hard to breathe. Tension filled his body as if he had not been sexually sated a single time. He did not have to close his eyes to see Virginia lying in his arms, smiling warmly at him, love shining in her eyes.

What was happening to him?

When he had discovered her being mauled by Tom Hughes, he had actually seen red, wanting to kill the man for daring to trespass on what was his, for daring to hurt her. His murderous rage had had nothing to do with his father's murder and everything to do with his feelings for Virginia.

He trembled violently now. He was no fool. Virginia was not his and she never would be his. Yet he had never touched or kissed any woman the way that he had done last night, and insist as he might to himself that it all meant nothing, in his heart he knew differently. Somehow, his admiration for his captive had become something far more—something far worse.

He reached for his Scotch and found the glass empty. Grimly he stared at it. No amount of Scotch would erase what he had done—from the very first, when he had taken Virginia as his hostage, intending to use her so callously as a tool of revenge, to this last devastating plan to flaunt her in society as his lover.

The moment he had first seen Virginia in the hold of the *Americana,* he had known that he should not abduct her—with the finely honed instincts of a true warrior, he had known he should jettison his plan and avoid her at all costs. Instead, he had held true to a fatal course, she the mighty storm and he the tiny sloop. And now their course was run, having come to this final, singular moment in time.

He lurched to his feet with a curse. He could no longer subject her to his whims. He could no longer use her in his terrible scheme. He wished, desperately, that he had not made love to her, not ever. Family and love were *not* for him.

Eastleigh would still have to pay—Devlin's revenge was hardly complete—but Virginia had paid far more than she ever should have, and now he hated himself for all that he had done.

He strode to the hearth, where last night's embers glowed. He had received his new orders and he was leaving shortly for America. Before then, he needed to free her and he would take her home. At Sweet Briar, there would be no malicious slander to haunt her. In fact, she would probably forget all about him in the span of a few months.

Inside his chest, it almost felt as if the devil were ripping his heart in two.

Are you in love with this girl? Tyrell had asked.

He was *not.* He had never experienced the emotion, and he never would. He knew that for a fact.

Devlin returned to his desk, trying not to contemplate the fact that once Virginia had returned to her plantation, their paths would never again cross. Almost ill, he began to pen instructions to his solicitor to purchase Sweet Briar anonymously from Eastleigh on his behalf. He would give her the plantation in a very futile attempt to make amends. He did not seek forgiveness—he did not deserve it.

And then, when Virginia was gone, he would finish Eastleigh, one way or the other.

Because the stakes had forever changed and now there was nothing left to lose.

VIRGINIA HESITATED OUTSIDE of the closed library door where she had been told that Devlin was. It was almost noon and she had recently awoken. She could think of nothing other than her lover. Last night he had made *love* to her. She knew it the way she knew that the air she breathed was filled with oxygen. Everything had changed between them. She hardly knew why—she only knew she had to race back into his welcoming arms, to make sure the night had not been a dream.

But she hesitated because their long history had taught her how ruthless and unpredictable he could be. A part of her recalled every slight and hurt, every single rejection, and that part of her was almost faint with dread. But last night had *not* been a dream.

She smoothed down her lovely gown and knocked on the door. "Devlin?"

There was no answer.

Virginia opened the door and glanced inside. The room was empty. She saw a stack of letters on his desk, one unsealed, and a cup and saucer. She walked in, and at the desk, saw that the teacup was half-full. She touched the cup and found it warm—he had only just stepped out.

And then her gaze fell onto the letter that lay open in the center of the desk. Her gaze widened and she glanced up, but Devlin had not appeared in the doorway. Somewhat guiltily, she lifted the letter and read.

Lord Admiral St. John to Sir Captain Devlin O'Neill
Waverly Hall
Greenwich
November 20, 1812
Sir Captain O'Neill,
Please be advised of the following. Your orders are
to proceed by December the 14 to the coasts of
Maryland and Virginia, where you shall commence
the blockade of the Delaware and Chesapeake Bays
in conjunction with the HMS *Southampton*, the HMS
Java and the HMS *Peacock*. All American vessels are
subject to search and seizure. A determination is to
be made thereof, and any American vessels, including non-naval ships, deemed to be engaged in
military action, are to be seized or destroyed. All
efforts are to be made to avoid harmful intercourse
with American noncombatants; any suspicion of
military involvement on the part of such American
civilians is to be investigated and treated accordingly
with His Majesty's rules of engagement.
The Right Honorable Lord Admiral St. John
The Admiralty
13 Brook Street
West Square

Virginia trembled violently and set the letter containing
Devlin's orders down. Devlin was leaving to go to war and
he was leaving soon—within two weeks. She trembled,
sick with fear for his safety.

She inhaled raggedly, reminding herself that Devlin had
been going to war since he was a boy of thirteen. It did not
help—she feared for his welfare now. She feared for his
life.

And then she thought about the rest of his orders. She

grasped the back of his chair. Dear God, he was going to war against her country. His orders were to seize and destroy any American naval ships and any other vessels suspected of military involvement. He would be fighting her country and her people within miles of her home. And suddenly it was so terribly clear that there was a war raging on the Atlantic Ocean and on American soil, a war between his country and hers.

"Virginia?"

She started and saw him approaching. She swallowed and said, "I did not mean to pry. I was looking for you. I saw your orders."

He paused, glancing at the open letter. "My orders are classified." His gaze was steady upon hers.

"Classified?"

"They are meant only for my eyes and those of the Admiralty and the Department of War."

"I am sorry." She was breathless; she didn't know what to do now. "You're leaving?"

"Yes." He was staring grimly at her. "As soon as possible."

He could have merely acknowledged the fact; his choice of words was a dark blow. She gripped the desk. "As soon as possible?" she echoed.

His gaze did not waver. "Yes."

Surely this did not mean anything, surely this had nothing to do with her or the night they had shared. She wet her lips. Her pulse pounded. "Can you not delay awhile?"

"I don't think so." He faced her soberly. "I will take you home—back to Virginia."

Her heart felt as if it had dropped right out of her body and through the floor. *"What?"*

He was far more grim than before. "I will find another way to ruin Eastleigh. It's time for you to go."

Virginia sank down in his chair. She was in utter disbelief. He would send her away now? After their passion, their love? "But..."

"But what?" he asked too sharply.

"But last night," she implored. "Everything is different now...isn't it?" And she prayed she would not cry.

He did not look at her, pouring a drink. Were his hands shaking? "You need to be freed, that fact has not changed."

She was quickly becoming devastated. "But," she said, frozen on the inside, and on the outside, too, "but we made love last night."

He tossed back a shot. "Don't," he warned.

Virginia managed to stand up, holding on to his desk as she did so. "I know it," she insisted stubbornly.

He finally looked at her, his face taut, his expression so similar to the one he'd worn last night after the ball. "I do not want to hurt you again, Virginia."

"Then do not do so," she cried.

"Why do you still demand the impossible of me?" he cried in return. "Why not leave this alone? I will return you to Sweet Briar. This is what you want!"

She stared, her heart, so badly pierced, beginning to break apart into small pieces. "It's not what I want," she whispered.

He stiffened and he was clearly angry. "Do not ask me to give you something I cannot, and will not, give."

The tears fell. She could not stop them. She stared, and with the hurt, there was almost hatred. "So it meant nothing...last night?"

He drew his shoulders back. "I enjoyed myself very much, Virginia, as I know you did, too. But it meant nothing."

She cried out, and had she been closer, she would have struck his handsome face.

"Clearly, I should not have given in to my passion last night. You are too young and too innocent to understand men, Virginia—and I am only a man, and not a romantic one. I am sorry. I am sorry you think last night meant more than it did. Now, I have a ship to attend to." His shoulders squared, he turned and started for the door.

She somehow stood. Her tone sounded frigid to her own ears. "How odd it is," she said harshly.

He froze but did not turn.

"They say love and hate are the opposite sides of the same coin. I never understood that before."

He stiffened even more—and he looked back at her.

She smiled without any mirth. "Last night I gave myself to you with joy and love."

He stared, no expression on his face or in his eyes, none at all.

"Today there is only hate." And even as she heard herself utter the terrible words, she wished she had not—she hated herself, too, for her cruelty.

His face twisted and he bowed. "It is your right. Good day, Virginia." He walked out.

CHAPTER TWENTY-ONE

DEVLIN TOOK THE WIDE front steps to the Admiralty two at a time, his mouth set in a grim line. He had received notice of this meeting but an hour ago. He had been expecting such notice; after all, all of London would be talking about the affair last night and the befuddled old men in blue were no exception. His conduct had not been that befitting an officer and a gentleman.

Other officers and their aides were coming and going; Devlin did not nod at anyone, as he saw no one. A beautiful pale face with furious violet eyes haunted him instead. *Last night I gave myself to you with joy and love. Today there is only hate.*

His mouth twisted. There was a terrible piercing in his chest as her hurtful declaration echoed, but he was glad, fiercely so, that she had come to her senses. He deserved only hatred, not love, and he was relieved, as fiercely, that finally she would cease imploring him with her every manner to love her in return.

"Captain O'Neill, sir?" A young lieutenant was waiting for him inside at the top of the marble staircase.

Devlin shoved his thoughts of Virginia aside. His feelings were not so easily shunted; both guilt and regret tormented him. He calmly accepted the lieutenant's salute. Inwardly he remained in turmoil.

"Admiral St. John is waiting, sir," the young officer added.

Devlin knew the way—how many times had he been called to Brook Street to be set down? A dozen, perhaps more. He preceded the junior officer down the hall, knocked on St. John's office door and was instructed to enter.

He did so, saluting smartly and giving no indication of any surprise or any other feeling when he noticed Admiral Farnham present. He removed his bicorn, tucking it under his arm, remaining at attention.

"Do sit down, Captain," St. John said, his florid expression grim.

Devlin nodded and took a chair.

St. John took his seat behind his desk, while Farnham sat in an adjacent chair. "I am very sorry to have called you in today," St. John said grimly, "especially after the most unpleasing hearing of last summer."

Devlin said nothing.

"The events of last night have come to my attention, rightly so. Do you care to explain yourself, Devlin?"

"Not really."

St. John sighed. "Tom Hughes has taken a dozen stitches. His head is concussed. He states you attacked him unjustly and unfairly. How do you rebut?"

"He is well enough to make an accusatory statement?" Finally, Devlin smiled. "I should have inflicted far graver wounds, then."

St. John shot to his feet. "This is hardly amusing. This is conduct unbecoming an officer, sir."

Devlin also stood. "And the unprovoked assault on a lady of character is conduct becoming an officer?"

St. John was flushed now. "I beg your pardon, but a woman of no virtue has no character."

Devlin stiffened, real anger rushing through him; he controlled it. "Miss Hughes is the Earl of Eastleigh's niece. She is a gentlewoman of both character and virtue."

"Do you deny that she is your mistress?" Farnham accused, still seated, his black eyes gleaming.

Devlin did not hesitate. "I do. I am afraid there have been malicious gossips at work—Miss Hughes has been my guest and nothing more."

Farnham snorted. "The world knows she is your mistress, Captain. A woman of no virtue, she undoubtedly provoked Tom's attentions."

"She did not," Devlin said flatly, fighting the urge to smash his fist in Farnham's large red nose. "Eastleigh's conduct should be at question here."

"Were you there?" St. John asked.

Devlin turned. "No."

"Hughes said she invited his interest, clearly and openly. She suggested he meet with her at a later date, perhaps on the morrow. She was so seductive he lost his patience, which is when you happened upon the scene."

Devlin's fury knew no bounds. "And it is the word of Thomas Hughes against the word of a whore?"

"Those are your words, not mine," St. John said. "Your attack on Tom was beyond the bounds of gentlemanly conduct. This is my last warning, Devlin. One more incident and you will be court-martialed on the aforementioned grounds. There is no room in His Majesty's navy for a ruffian and a scoundrel."

Devlin knew that once again this was a battle he must lose. Nothing ever changed. The admirals ranted and raved over his insubordination and independence, but in the end, he was always given his liberty again. They dared not lose his competence of command and his superiority in naval battle. This time, though, his heart knew no mocking triumph. This time, he felt ill.

Defend Virginia as he might, it was more than time for her to go. She had no future in Britain, thanks to him.

An honorable man would simply marry her.

He was astonished with his thoughts. He dismissed them instantly. An honorable man would have never used her so abominably in the first place.

"Do you comprehend me, Captain?" St. John asked.

Devlin jerked, his brooding far too intense for comfort, and he bowed. "Completely."

"Good." St. John came forward, smiling. "Will you have a brandy?" he asked, the crisis clearly over.

Devlin nodded; three brandies were poured and passed around.

Sipping appreciatively, St. John then said, "You have received your orders?"

Devlin nodded. "Yes, I have."

"When can you set sail?"

"As you suggested, sir, within two weeks."

St. John nodded. "Try to hasten your departure, Devlin. The news arrived today. The HMS *Swift* was captured by the USS *Constitution*. I do not know how they are doing it, but the Americans are owning the seas and I am counting on you, my boy, to swiftly change that fact." He saluted him with his glass.

Devlin set his snifter down and bowed. "Of course, my lord," he murmured. "I shall make every effort."

St. John beamed, pleased.

"WHAT THE BLOODY HELL HAPPENED?" the Earl of Eastleigh demanded coldly of his younger son.

Tom Hughes lay in bed, his torso and one arm bandaged, as his manservant took his breakfast tray from the room. "My head pounds, Father. Would you please refrain from shouting?" he said.

Eastleigh stared. "I was not shouting."

William stood beside him, pale. "This is simply insufferable."

"Be quiet." Eastleigh looked his youngest son over. "How badly are you hurt?"

"I will live," Tom said. His face tightened. "That bastard only got a set down. He went before St. John and he only got a set down."

"He is probably paying them off," Eastleigh spat. "Either that or the man has had nothing but luck his entire life." And that would change, he silently vowed.

"This is beyond insufferable!" William erupted. "First he parades our cousin about Hampshire, openly flaunting their liaison, destroying her and, by association, our entire family! Lord Livingston did not receive my wife the other day. She is always received there—Lady Livingston loves Cecily! But now the best of friends are the worst of friends—after all, we have a whore in the family! This is beyond insufferable. It has to stop!"

"I admit that I never expected him to go so far as to take her to the Carew ball." Tom was clearly disgusted.

"And you had to pick a fight with him?" Eastleigh asked, his tone icy.

"He attacked *me,*" Tom exclaimed with indignation. "She is our cousin—and she is a fetching little thing. I think I had every right to sample her charms—but the savage attacked *me!*"

"You have only encouraged the gossips." Eastleigh was outwardly calm, but inwardly, he seethed. He agreed with his sons. O'Neill had to be stopped. But the question remained, how? He felt certain that nothing short of killing the man would dissuade him from his revenge.

"I am sure all of London will do nothing but speak of last night's entertainment now. Do you know I dread the dinner party we are attending tomorrow?" William finally sat down. "At least we have an offer for Sweet Briar. Although the buyer wishes to remain anonymous and we are selling the place for half its market value."

"I didn't know!" Tom smiled, pleased. "This shall help ease our depleted coffers for a while. Father, you must be thrilled."

Eastleigh did not really hear him. His sons were both weak; they were both fools. But he was not weak, never mind that he was older, impoverished, obese. He had killed once before with as much chagrin as one felt when swatting a fly. The Irish were mostly savages. He knew that first-hand, having spent his youth as a soldier stationed among them. He had never favored Catholic emancipation and he despised the fools who did. No Catholic should be able to vote or own land—and no Catholic should be as wealthy and powerful as that savage, O'Neill. What would it matter if he killed one more time?

He had so little now to lose.

Eastleigh began to plan.

VIRGINIA STOOD AT HER WINDOW, looking out at the Thames as the twilight grew, where several yachts sailed among the more plebian traffic of dories, dinghies and skips. It was suppertime, but she had no intention of going downstairs to dine. Although she could not remain hateful—she would never hate Devlin O'Neill—her heart had been broken for the very last time. She smiled sadly, bitterly, recalling every moment of her conversation that morning—and every moment spent in his arms last night. But she had had enough. It was over now and she was going home.

Her sadness felt like grief, heavy and depressing, a weight that threatened to sink her down.

Virginia heard voices on the terrace below her window. Her puppy came to stand beside her, whining.

She started, as she had not known they were having company. She heard a man's and a woman's voice, both terribly familiar.

Her cheeks heated. She recognized the woman instantly and she thought, oh no! For it was none other than Mary de Warenne, which meant the man with her was the Earl of Adare.

A knock sounded on her door. Virginia was hardly surprised, and reluctantly she turned. "Come in."

Hannah smiled at her. "Captain asks fer you to come down to dine, Miss Hughes. Her ladyship and his lordship are here, as well."

Virginia smiled grimly. "I have a headache," she said. "Please send my regrets, but I will not be going down to dine tonight."

"Shall I bring you a supper tray?" Hannah asked, instantly concerned.

"I have no appetite," Virginia said.

When the maid was gone, she walked over to the sofa and sat down, pulling the puppy, whom she'd named Arthur, close, staring at the fire in the hearth while stroking him. Then she buried her face in his fur, but she did not cry.

It hurt so much. The heartache this time was worse than it had ever been, because she had truly allowed herself to hope and dream of Devlin's love. But how foolish and naive could she be? Devlin had no heart. He was incapable of loving anyone. He had proved it once and for all. She simply could not wait for the future, for a day when he was not even the vaguest memory.

And that day *would* come, she insisted to herself. It *would*, although perhaps it might take some time. But surely in a year or two, or maybe even three, she would not even recollect his features.

She felt even more anguished and more saddened than before.

"Virginia?"

Virginia gasped, turning.

Mary de Warenne stood in the doorway in a ginger silk evening gown, trimmed with bronze lace. She smiled. "I knocked several times. I'm sorry, but when you did not answer I thought to come in and check on your welfare. Are you all right?"

Virginia stood. "I have a headache, but it will pass," she said tersely.

Mary smiled. "May I?"

Virginia had no choice but to nod. Miserably, she whispered, "Do come in."

Mary did so, closing the door behind her. She paused at Virginia's side, her expression far too inquisitive and far too searching. "How are you, my dear?"

"I suppose I have a bit of an influenza," she managed. She dreaded the interview she sensed would follow.

Mary searched her eyes. "I understand you and my son have been living together openly."

Virginia flushed. "You are very direct."

"I am very ashamed," Mary said, and although she was blunt, her tone was soft. "I raised Devlin to know right from wrong and to treat women with respect."

Virginia backed away.

"He has used you terribly, I fear," Mary said.

Oh, dear, the anguish had returned, vast and full force, threatening to break like a flooding dam. Virginia turned away.

"I am truly furious with him. But what I want to know is if he has hurt you—other than your heart?"

Virginia gasped, whirling. "I cannot answer that!" she cried.

"I believe I have answer enough," Mary said gently, and she came forward. Before Virginia could protest or elude her, she had embraced her. "I like you very much...daughter."

Virginia knew she must not cry. Then she realized what Mary had called her and she flinched. *"What did you say?"*

Mary smiled and brushed some curls away from her eyes. "I called you daughter."

Virginia shook her head, speechless.

"For you shall be my daughter—very soon. Edward and I have discussed it at some length. Some small length, actually, as there was so little to discuss. My son will do what is right."

Virginia shook her head, disbelieving, backing up.

"He will marry you, Virginia, have no fear, and he will treat you with the respect owed a wife. Of that I have no doubt," Mary said firmly. "Edward is speaking with him now." And she smiled, waiting for Virginia to tell her how pleased she was.

But Virginia could not speak, not for a long moment. She was in disbelief. Briefly, she saw herself in her wedding finery, Devlin in his dress uniform, standing before a priest. Then she shook the terribly fanciful image aside. She finally said, hoarsely, "Thank you, my lady."

"Come, let us go downstairs," Mary said, placing her arm around her.

Virginia prayed for help. She said, "My lady? I truly must rest in bed this evening. I am afraid I would be very poor company if I joined you in my present state."

Mary kissed her forehead. "I understand. I will have a light supper sent up. Virginia?"

Virginia turned away to avoid eye contact. "Yes," she whispered.

"Everything will turn out for the best, I feel certain of it," she said.

Virginia could not nod. Mary left, gently closing the door behind her. Virginia sank down in the nearest chair.

Nothing would turn out well. For it was simply too late. She would not marry Devlin, not even if he were the last man on this earth.

DEVLIN OFFERED HIS STEPFATHER a glass of red wine and then sat down in an adjacent chair. Edward sipped and said, "This is damnably good."

"Yes, it is," Devlin returned, glancing at the open door. But his mother and Virginia did not appear. The standing grandfather clock in the corner of the room chimed half past the hour. He hadn't seen her since their terrible conversation that morning and he could not deny that he wished to see her now. He sincerely hoped that she had recovered from the encounter.

"I heard you have received new orders," Edward commented, setting his glass down and comfortably stretching out his long legs.

"Yes. I leave in two weeks. I am to participate in our war with the Americans," Devlin said.

Edward nodded. "It's ironic, is it not? The triumphs in Canada, when we are so outmanned there, and the losses in the Atlantic, when we are the greatest navy on the earth."

"The Americans are a tough and fierce lot," he remarked, a pair of huge violet eyes, flashing with hatred, in his mind. He shifted, aware of a seizure in his chest. But it was her right to hate him and he was glad—he merely had to remind himself of this yet another time.

"And that affair last night?"

"I was wondering if you had heard," Devlin said, bracing himself for the censure he felt certain was to come.

"Devlin, for God's sake, what did you expect, bringing her there, that way?" There was disapproval in Edward's tone.

Abruptly Devlin stood, wine in hand. "I was called in by St. John today. I've truly heard it all. Yes, I made a mistake, and frankly, I am sorry for it. However, Hughes got a beating—which is almost what he deserved."

"And Virginia?" Edward stood. "What did she deserve?" He tensed.

"Or rather, what *does* she deserve?"

"Edward, I am well aware that I have behaved shamefully. She did not deserve to be used in my scheme of revenge. But I have made amends, I hope." He met Adare's unwavering gaze. "I have purchased Sweet Briar, which I intend to give to her, and I will take her home when I set sail," he said tersely.

"The son I raised knows what she presently deserves, and it is not to be tossed away over your father's bloody grave."

"I regret all that I have done," he said sharply. "Isn't it enough that I have bought Sweet Briar for her?"

"You tell me."

Devlin met his dark, blazing eyes. "You know the life I have chosen—you know the man that I am. I am not a family man, Edward," he warned.

"But your father did not raise you to be a rogue. He raised you to be the family man you have just spoken of."

The blow was a fierce one, for Edward was right. "Do not bring my dead father into this," Devlin said sharply.

"Why not? Your father's murder is the crux of this matter—as it is the crux of your life. Good God, he died fifteen years ago! When will you let him rest in peace? When?"

Devlin turned away, trembling. Sean had said the exact same thing, but he could not let go of the past, the effort being beyond his capacity.

"There is only one manner in which you may make

amends to Miss Hughes, and you damn well know it," Edward said softly to his back.

He did know it. He had known it for some time now, though from precisely when, he could not be certain. The only real way to make amends was through marriage. And Virginia's violet eyes flashed. *Today there is only hatred.*

Hatred, so much hatred... It was all Devlin knew and he had taught Virginia the horror of it, too. "I doubt she would have me," he heard himself say.

"Of course she will have you! Will you marry her, then?" he demanded.

He faced his stepfather and the devil had returned, ripping not just his heart but his entire being in two. And he actually wished that he were a different man, one incapable of ruthless vengeance, a man capable of letting go of a ghastly past, a man worthy of Virginia's love. But he was not.

Nothing had been resolved, nothing yet was finished.

"When will you decide that you have had enough of this terrible obsession? When will you decide that there is a chance for happiness? When will you choose joy over pain?" Edward demanded softly. "When will you choose to live?"

"If you had been murdered as Gerald was, Tyrell, Rex and Cliff would do just as I have to avenge you," he said, speaking of the earl's three sons.

"I hope not," Edward said. "You know what you must do. I imagine that somewhere in the back of your mind, you have known all along."

Mary stepped quietly into the room, closing the door behind her. " Devlin? I love you the way only a mother can love her firstborn, but this is about right and wrong. It is about honor and dishonor, and it is about duty. If you are truly my son—the son I have raised—you will do what is honorable and you will stand up with Miss Hughes." Tears filled her eyes. "I know you will honor Virginia with marriage—I know it," she said.

And he was lost. He could not refuse the woman who had borne him into this world, the woman who had raised him, loved him and succored him until his thirteenth year, when he had gone to sea. He could not refuse his mother, who somehow retained a remarkable and unrealistic faith in him, and they were both right, this was the only real means of making amends.

Last night I gave myself to you with joy and love.

He closed his eyes, fiercely resistant, sweating. He did not want this. He did not need joy, he did not need love, but surely he could marry Virginia and maintain a proper distance between them. Surely he could marry her while maintaining his true course—revenge. Nothing had to change, really, except for her title and the fact that her stay with him would now be a permanent one.

"Devlin?" Mary asked.

He turned and met her gaze. With a bow, he said, "I will marry Virginia. Plan the nuptials, I will be there." And there, it was done, the act of honor, what was right, because there was no choice after all.

Mary cried out and rushed to embrace him, tears wetting her cheeks. "Darling, she will make a wonderful wife, I am certain of it."

Devlin nodded but he felt dazed. And oddly, he was also relieved. He had thought to return Virginia to her home, never seeing her again. Instead, they had a lifetime to share.

God, he would have to tread with care or he might truly fall under her spell, he thought with a stab of uncertainty and panic.

"Edward, we have a wedding to plan," Mary was saying

with delight. "And no time in which to do it!" She smiled at Devlin. "I expect you wed within the next two weeks, well before you set sail on the *Defiance*."

DEVLIN FOUND IT IMPOSSIBLE to concentrate on the task at hand. His first officer had presented him with a list of supplies that he needed to authorize, but the words on the vellum blurred. The oddest feeling of relief consumed him, and he could not get over the fact that he was to marry Virginia before the *Defiance* set sail on December 14.

He finally pushed the page away. Where the hell was Virginia, anyway? He understood that last night she had pleaded a headache and had taken a supper tray in her room. Her avoidance of him had been to his advantage, then, too—he had hardly wished to speak with her so shortly after agreeing to their marriage. But it was noon, another day, and he felt quite certain that she had not come downstairs for breakfast, either. Virginia did not loll about her bed. What was more likely was that she had gone out at dawn for a long walk. In any case, she continued to avoid him, and now he felt pressured to meet with her and discuss the fact of their future. Surely they could structure an arrangement that suited them both. He felt it urgent to do so, and he intended to put her on notice that little would change in their relationship except for her official title. And as important, surely she was pleased with the impending nuptials—surely she no longer hated him.

Benson appeared in the doorway. Devlin tensed and sat up more stiffly, expecting Virginia. But it was William Hughes who was ushered in.

He was very surprised. He stood.

Hughes inclined his head in a parody of a bow. Devlin imitated him exactly, becoming wary and cautious. "This is an unexpected surprise," he murmured. What could Will Hughes want?

"Shall we cease with any pleasantries?" William returned, standing stiffly where Benson had left him.

"Oh, I don't know," Devlin replied, moving out from behind his desk. William was very unhappy, very displeased—why? His curiosity knew no bounds. "Brandy? Scotch? Wine?" he offered, his blood heating with the call to arms that this visit signaled.

William made a dismissive gesture.

Devlin smiled at him. "And how is the health of your brother?"

William seemed to choke. "Cease with all pretense!" he cried. "I have had enough! You have sullied the good Hughes name for the very last time. I have come with an offer, O'Neill."

His cold smile fixed, his hands clasped behind his back, Devlin said, "Do tell." Had Eastleigh, the coward, sent William to do his dirty deeds?

His nostrils flared. He held out a banknote. "This is the best I can do. It is not fifteen thousand pounds, an absurd sum. It is three thousand pounds, and it is yours if you release my cousin."

Devlin made no move to take the offered note. He was stunned—and then he almost laughed, as the money being offered him had been his to begin with, undoubtedly garnered from their sale of Sweet Briar to him. "Does your father know what you offer me?"

"Does it matter?" William asked caustically, telling him that he did not.

Devlin shrugged, accepting the note. "Actually, it does not."

William looked at him with real disgust and walked out.

Devlin laughed softly, wondering what he would say and do when he learned of the impending nuptials.

When Hughes was gone, he glanced at the bronze clock on his desk. Now it was almost one. He went to the door. "Benson?" he called.

The butler appeared as if by magic. "Yes, Sir Captain?"

"I wish to speak with Miss Hughes."

Benson nodded, swiftly leaving.

Devlin returned to his chair, eyeing the first list at hand, one of rations for his men. Salt beef, salt pork, peas, oatmeal, butter, cheese...he sighed and gave up. It had become an urgent matter, to discuss the impending wedding with Virginia. Was she actually ill? Or had she decided to walk all the way to London? He looked up as Benson stepped inside, drumming his fingertips on the desk. "Is she coming down?"

"She was not in her rooms, sir. But I did find this upon the bed. Most curiously, it is your seal—yet it is also addressed to you." Benson handed him a sealed letter.

Devlin leapt to his feet, almost snatching the letter, instantly suspecting what was at hand. "That is all," he said tersely.

Benson left, closing the door, and Devlin slit the seal, opening the letter.

The hand was feminine and it was addressed to him.

December 5, 1812
Dear Captain O'Neill,
I cannot marry you. By the time you receive this letter, I shall be gone. It has occurred to me, with no small amount of reflection, my behavior has been foolish in the extreme. It is definitely time for me to go home.

I have many regrets. Our failure to forge a genuine friendship is foremost among them. I also regret the harsh words spoken yesterday. Please know that I hold no grudge, and that in spite of all circumstance, I bear you no ill will. Indeed, the opposite is the case. I do consider you a friend, even if the feeling is not a mutual one. I wish you all the best, always.

Please give my best regards to your family, as they have been nothing but kind.

Sincerely,

Virginia Hughes

CHAPTER TWENTY-TWO

THE COUNTESS OF EASTLEIGH wasn't certain that she had heard the servant correctly. "I beg your pardon?" she asked, her arms filled with the flowers she had picked from the greenhouse. She set them carefully down on the huge center table in the kitchen.

"Miss Virginia Hughes has called, my lady," the liveried manservant replied.

For one moment Elizabeth stared, careful not to allow her face to change expression. But she was more than surprised, in fact, she was stunned. What could Devlin's mistress want? Why had she come calling? Had they returned to Wideacre? And if so, why? Elizabeth knew all about the sordid affair at the Carew ball.

And she still did not know what to make of it. It was astonishing that Devlin had brought his mistress into polite society, but she had come to grips with the fact that she did not know the man who had been her lover for six years. Her neighbors, Lady Philips and Lady Cramer, had been very quick to tell her all about the ball and the duel almost to the death between her stepson and O'Neill. Lady Cramer had been present at the scene (she also knew, Elizabeth was certain, of her own involvement with O'Neill until recently), and she had been very obliging, regaling Elizabeth and Lady Philips with numerous details of the duel. According to her, O'Neill had been intent on murdering his rival and only his stepbrother had prevented him from doing so.

Elizabeth managed a smile and she quickly handed a dozen tulips to a housemaid. "Please set these in a vase and put them in my room," she murmured. Why on earth was Devlin's new mistress here?

She had yet to recover from his rejection, or worse, his using her so baldly to abduct her husband's niece. If she did not hate William so, she would demand to know what it all signified. If she had not been a faithless wife, she would have asked the same of Eastleigh. But she could approach neither man.

Yet Elizabeth was no fool. She had been O'Neill's mistress. Now her husband's niece had that dubious distinction, and Devlin had purchased Waverly Hall from the family some years back. Elizabeth began to sense that some terrible plan was afoot.

"Bring refreshments, Walden," she said, a decision made. Her curiosity won and she removed her apron, washed her hands and left the kitchen.

Virginia stood in the yellow salon, a pretty room quite large in size with a half a dozen seating areas, the furniture obviously tired and worn, and two large chandeliers hanging from the pink, gold and white ceiling. She wore a pale lavender dress with long sleeves and a black pelisse, her dark hair tightly coiled to the back of her head. Her posture was stiff and erect, indicating extreme tension, but Elizabeth had only to look at her strained little face, devoid of all coloring, and then into her large eyes, to realize with shock that she was heartbroken.

Her own heart lurched and the awkward urge to comfort the girl came. "Miss Hughes?" She smiled more naturally now as she stepped into the salon.

Virginia tried to smile back, but it appeared to be more

of a grimace. "I am sorry if I am disturbing you, my lady," she said, her tone low and hoarse.

"You are not disturbing me," Elizabeth said, gesturing at a seat. "Although I will confess, I am quite surprised by your call."

Virginia smiled sadly and sat down, perching on the edge of a faded bronze satin chair.

Elizabeth also sat, and thought, *She really is terribly pretty, and I think I begin to see why Devlin would wish to have her. But she is so young...* Elizabeth refused to recall her own age, but her husband's niece was almost twenty years her junior. "Are you in residence at Wideacre?" she asked politely.

Virginia shook her head. She smoothed down her skirts, gazing at her lap.

A silence fell. Elizabeth felt terribly sorry for her, as she appeared so lost and so miserable. *At least I am a married woman,* she thought, *a woman of experience, one capable of bearing the brunt of real hurt.* Surely Devlin had been Virginia's first lover. No wonder she was crushed. Had he rejected her now, too? "It is such an exceedingly pleasant day for this late in the year," she said. "Although I have heard that there will be rain before the week is out."

Virginia looked up, biting her lip. "I must beg your help, my lady," she whispered.

Elizabeth could not stand it. She reached out and took Virginia's hands in her own. "My dear, you know we are family. Given the circumstances, I had not really thought about it, but now, seeing you so saddened, it comes back to me. Of course I will help you if I can."

Virginia looked close to tears. "I must get home to Virginia," she said. "And I have no money for the fare. If you could but lend it to me, I promise I would pay you back."

Elizabeth did wish to help, but lending her any spare coin, when her funds were so strained, was out of the question. "What has happened, child?"

Virginia shook her head as if she could not speak. "I must go home."

Elizabeth hesitated, choosing her words with care. "And Devlin will not let you go? For he certainly can spare the fare for your passage."

Her face tightened. "I have run away, my lady, I have run away from him, and I must leave the country immediately, before he can possibly find me."

Her brows lifted and she was seized with rabid interest. "But did you not love him?"

She held herself proudly. "Yes."

"Has he abused you in some way?"

Her eyes widened. "Is it not abuse to be flaunted about the world as his whore?" she cried.

Her language took Elizabeth aback. "I have never understood his behavior," she said carefully.

Virginia stood. For one moment she stared. "It is not my place to explain to you his motivations—I refuse to get between your family and him. I only beg you to spare me the fare to return to America. I cannot go on this way!"

Elizabeth also stood. Clearly Virginia remained fond of Devlin, otherwise she would have no inhibitions about speaking of him and his aims. "So you still love him," she said.

Virginia shook her head in denial. "No. My heart is broken for the last time. There is only pain."

For one moment Elizabeth was so moved that she could not speak. She clasped Virginia's cheek. "Why? Why has he treated you so miserably?"

"When I am gone, you may surely ask him," Virginia said stubbornly.

"First myself and then you. And he lives at Waverly Hall. He almost killed Thomas. I would almost suspect he has a grudge against my family." She laughed a little then.

Virginia stared.

Her eyes widened in incredulity. "Is that the case?" she cried.

"You must ask him," Virginia said firmly. "Have you anything to spare me for my escape?"

"I so wish I could help you," Elizabeth said softly, still reeling from the possibility that all of Devlin's actions were the part of some vast grudge. In that case, his sharing her bed for six long years had nothing to do with love or desire, but with something else entirely. "But, my dear, we have nothing to spare."

Virginia seemed dismayed. "Would you at least send me back to London in a coach? I used the few shillings I had to get here."

That she could do. "Of course. So you will return to him after all?"

Virginia flinched. "Never!" she said.

"My lady?" The butler appeared with a tea cart.

As he wheeled it in, Elizabeth was almost relieved by the interruption. "Shall we have some tea?" She smiled. "Our chef also makes wonderful scones."

"I am afraid I must return to town immediately," Virginia said, making no move to sit.

Elizabeth decided that a hasty departure would be for the best. "Walden? Have my coach brought around and tell Jeffries that he will take Miss Hughes to London."

"Yes, my lady," Walden said, quickly leaving.

Elizabeth poured a cup of tea. "Are you certain you do not wish some tea before you leave?"

Virginia shook her head, moving to the window. She stared outside.

Elizabeth remarked her poor manners, sipping the tea herself. Yes, she was very fetching, but surely that was not why Devlin had made her his mistress. No, it had something to do with some kind of vendetta he held against her family. There was no other explanation.

Ten minutes later, Virginia was in the countess's coach. Wrapped in a cashmere shawl, Elizabeth waved as the coach rolled down the drive. Then she ceased smiling and hurried inside. "Walden, where is the earl?"

"He has taken a walk with the hounds," Walden replied.

That was good. "And William?"

"In the library, my lady."

Her heart raced. She despised William and sometimes she was even afraid of him, but there was no choice. She hurried through the house, purposefully not looking at the patches of peeling paint, the scarred tabletops or the cracked floors. The library door was closed; she hesitated and then walked in.

William sat at the desk with a quill in hand. He looked up, vastly displeased with the impolitic interruption.

"I must speak with you," she said, closing the door behind her.

His brows lifted. "Really? How odd," he said, standing. And his gaze moved over her in a sexually suggestive manner.

He made her want to vomit. She had not a doubt that if she were willing, he would bend her over that desk and do as he pleased. "Miss Hughes was just here."

His eyes widened. "What did she want?"

Elizabeth shrugged—she would never tell him anything without very carefully deciding whom it might aid and whom it might hurt. "What does O'Neill want with us?"

"In general, or specifically?" he asked coldly.

She did not understand him. "I think something odd is

afoot. First myself, now my niece. And then there is Waverly Hall. I also heard he wished to kill Thomas at the Carew ball. Can you explain this?"

William left his desk.

She stiffened as he approached.

"There is little to understand, now, is there...*Mother?* He tired of you and he chose a far prettier, far younger figure and face."

She felt her cheeks heat.

He stood an inch away. "He has asked for a ransom for Miss Hughes."

She was stunned. "What?"

"That's right. You see, my dear stepmother, it is all quite simple—and quite clever. He has kept her a prisoner, and when we refused to pay his ransom, he decided to destroy this family in reputation as he could not do so in finance."

Elizabeth was stunned. "She was never a real mistress...."

"Oh, he made her his mistress, all right. I do think that is obvious. But it had nothing to do with love, or even lust, so you can rest more easily. You lost only to revenge. You see, your dear husband murdered O'Neill's father years ago, and we have been paying the price ever since."

VIRGINIA CROUCHED IN THE TREES, shivering, as the drizzle turned to rain. She wished the fine weather in Hampshire had extended to London, but it had not—by the time she had reached town, rain threatened, and she was regretting not accepting the countess's offer of tea and cakes, as she had not eaten a thing all day. Even more so, she regretted the countess's state of finances. It had seemed clear that she was a compassionate woman and that she would have helped Virginia if she could have done so.

Virginia trembled with cold and felt faint from hunger.

She had had the coach drop her at the gated entrance to the de Warenne Mayfair home. Then, when the coach had turned back to return to Eastleigh Hall, she had climbed the iron-topped brick wall. Keeping to the shrubs and trees, she had crossed the lawns, but perhaps because of the inclement weather, she had seen no sign of anyone. It was late afternoon and she was exhausted. Tyrell de Warenne was her very last hope.

Please let him help me, she prayed.

She hoped to meet with him in secret and planned to wait for him to emerge from the house. And if he did not intend to go out that evening, due to the rain? She imagined that she would sleep in the stables and try to accost him the following morning. But God, what kind of plan was this? Her teeth were chattering from the cold and her hiding place—a stand of trees not far from one of the stables— was rapidly becoming useless. She felt like dashing to the stables now and finding a dry place to hide.

But she didn't dare move—she needed a good view of the house, she needed to speak with Tyrell tonight, if at all possible. Virginia did not know how long she waited in the wind and the rain before there was any activity. A groom appeared, leading a fancy bay from the stables. The rain had stopped although the skies remained dull, and even though it looked as if it might rain again before the night was through, the bay horse was tacked. Virginia did not know who was in residence, but she doubted that the earl would go out at this hour, alone and on horseback. She almost cried out in relief when she saw Tyrell striding down the front steps of the house, a dashing figure in his coat, britches and high boots, a dark cloak draped about his shoulders.

He strode toward the courtyard in front of the stables, taking the reins from the groom. As they spoke, Virginia stood, watching for a moment, wishing desperately that the interview was over and he had agreed to help her leave England. Her gaze moved back to the house, but no one else appeared. Her heart racing, she stepped out of the shadow of the trees and hurried toward him.

The groom was about to leave and Tyrell looked ready to mount. They both saw her at the same time; Tyrell's eyes widened. "Virginia?" He was incredulous.

She tried to smile, no easy task when she was trembling almost convulsively from the damp cold. "My lord, please, do wait! I desperately need to speak with you."

He shoved the reins at the groom, hurrying toward her. "What in God's name is this? You're frozen and soaking wet—how did you get here? Did you walk from Waverly Hall?" he cried.

He was clearly concerned. Virginia managed a smile. "I am only a little bit cold and slightly damp," she lied. "Please, my lord, I *desperately* need to discuss an *urgent* matter with you!"

"We can discuss anything that you wish, but first, you must come inside, get into some dry clothes and sit in front of a fire!" he exclaimed.

"No!" she cried, backing away as he took her arm.

"I beg your pardon?" He started, surprised, his dark gaze searching hers.

She swallowed. "I cannot go inside."

He stared carefully; his expression became grim. "Why ever not?"

She inhaled, and then she dared to trust him. "I have run away," she said hoarsely. "I have run away from Devlin and I beg you now to keep my secret and help me get to America."

VIRGINIA SAT IN THE LIBRARY before a blazing fire, wearing one of the countess's gowns, which was quite large on her, a blanket wrapped around her, while she sipped hot tea laced with whiskey. As it turned out, the earl and countess had left for a dinner party. As warmth finally seeped through her, chasing away the cold, she became aware of an exhaustion that was far more than physical—it seemed to emanate from her very heart, and maybe from her soul. Tyrell had already proved himself as gallant as a gentleman could be; she knew he would help her. Tomorrow she might be on her way across the ocean.

Devlin's gray eyes assailed her, not cold and remote, but blazing with anger. She had no doubt that, just then, he was furious with her.

She would never see him again.

Her heart lurched. Grief choked her. But this *was* what she wanted; to escape him forever, to never see him again—unless it was years from now, when she was married and truly in love with a fine, heroic man, and she would be so beautiful and so happy and Devlin would know just what he had lost.

Grief made it impossible to drink and she set her teacup aside.

She closed her eyes. *I am not going to go back to Waverly Hall; I can never hate him, but I do not love him, not anymore; I am going home.*

Her silent words, partly a declaration, partly a reminder, felt terribly hollow.

She sighed heavily and looked up.

Tyrell was pacing the room. He seemed grim. She was so tired she could not quite recall exactly what she had said to him when he had carried her into the house after finding her outside in the rain.

He paused before her. "Virginia?"

She clutched the arms of the chair, incapable of smiling. "Thank you for being so kind."

He did not smile or soften. "Send word to Devlin. If you have run away, he must be frantic by now."

"No!" She was wide awake now, adrenaline surging. "Trust me, he does not care—I am quite sure he is relieved!"

"You are bitter," he remarked, staring closely.

"I am not bitter." But her words felt so much like a lie.

"I don't understand. Father announced the news last night—wonderful news, I think."

"I am not marrying him," she gritted. And that image returned, of her in her wedding clothes, Devlin in his dress uniform beside her in an ancient church.

Never, she told herself with some panic.

"Why not?" Tyrell demanded.

"Why not?" she exclaimed. "The man abducted me, held me prisoner, demanded we live openly together—all for the sake of his obsession. And two nights ago he almost killed my cousin. Why not? I have given you four reasons why not, five if you count the fact that I am merely a pawn in his game of revenge."

"You are bitter and angry and I cannot blame you. He has treated you abominably, but he has agreed to marry you, and that is the just outcome, I think."

"Just for whom?" she cried. "For him? I think not—he has no wish to be shackled to me in marriage. Just for me? He doesn't love me! Not at all!" she cried. Then, trembling, she said, "I only wish to go home to my plantation."

He looked distraught. "I am afraid your anger gets the best of you. It is the only way to save your reputation, Virginia."

"I don't care about my reputation."

He was grim. "Then it is a good thing that I do, and that my father and stepmother also care." His tone softened. "We have all become quite fond of you, Virginia. And

Devlin is a very eligible bachelor. He must wed—and why not you?" He smiled. "You may be small, but your spirit is huge, and I happen to think there is more here than meets the eye. I think it is a good match."

She leapt to her feet. "It is not a good match! I do not want to spend my life with that man! In fact, I cannot bear to ever set eyes upon him again!" And if she left tomorrow as she planned, she would surely never see him again.

Oh, God, could she really do this? Somehow, a part of her could not imagine a life without Devlin O'Neill in it.

"And you expect me to do what? Hide you here? Send you to America? What is it that you think I can—or will— do?"

"I beg you, my lord, to loan me the sum of a transatlantic fare. I promise to repay you, though it may take some time." Their stares held for a pregnant moment.

He looked away. "And where do you go when you reach the United States? *If* you reach it—as we are at war with your country. And what do you do when you get there?"

"I am going to Sweet Briar—"

"It belongs to your uncle. And he has put it up for sale. For all we know, it has already been sold and you have no home to return to," he said, his eyes flashing. "This is madness, Virginia, sheer madness, and I cannot be a part of it."

"You deny me?" she cried, stunned.

He stared, his face set. "I am looking after you, Virginia. It is your best interest that I have in mind."

"No, it's not," she cried, furious and appalled. "You are my very last hope! Why can't you see? I will not marry that man, it is simply intolerable after all he has done!"

Devlin strode in. He swept his damp cloak behind his back and bowed briefly. "I am sorry you feel that way, madam," he said, his eyes flashing.

Her heart seemed to stop. In shock, she stared, and sensing danger, she backed up.

His face was so hard. The only emotion evident was anger. He now nodded at Tyrell. "I have had my men searching the streets of London for her. I should have guessed she would come to you. Thank you, Ty, for sending me word."

"You have many broken fences to mend," he said. "She is very angry with you, as she should be."

"I can see that," Devlin said, looking at Virginia again.

Virginia realized that while she had been bathing and changing clothes, Tyrell had sent word to Devlin. "You have betrayed me," she cried, shaking with anger now. "I thought you were my friend. I trusted you!"

"I am your friend," he said, his expression one of regret. "I sincerely think only of your best interest, and I think— I hope—in time that you will be thankful for what I did."

"You are not my friend," she whispered, still stunned by his treachery.

He bowed and left.

Devlin walked after him, but only to close the door and then face Virginia again. "What madness is this? Do you think to commit suicide?"

"No," she gritted, "I only think to avoid marriage to you!"

"By catching pneumonia and dying?" he demanded.

"You do not want this, either! Send me home, Devlin, and we will both be free!"

"I am afraid I have agreed to this union."

She swatted at her tears. "I can hardly comprehend why."

His face was taut, indicating some tension, but he did not hesitate. "They are right."

"They are right? The earl and countess are right? You now accept blame—and guilt—for your actions?"

"I do."

"You lie!" She advanced. "You have no guilt, no regrets!"

He was motionless. It was a long moment before he spoke and when he did, it was slowly, with the utmost care. "Actually, you are very wrong, Virginia. I do have guilt, and I have had so for some time. The other night at Lord Carew's made it impossible for me to deny it. I regret using you as I have."

She could no longer breathe. Was this the truth?

"I am sorry I brought you into this," he added grimly. "And now I will pay the price of having used you so callously. It is what an honorable man would do."

She was afraid to believe him—and she reminded herself that this change of heart had nothing to do with love. But it was a change of *heart*. It was evidence of a conscience, of a soul.

"I see I have dumbfounded you," he said with some self-derision. He walked past her toward the liquor bottles placed on a nearby table. "I am rather dumbfounded myself. A brandy should warm you far better than a cup of tea."

"The tea is laced with whiskey." She stared at him as he poured. She was stunned and she did not know what to think or what to feel. *He was sorry. He was genuinely sorry.* But what did it change? He had hurt her too many times. She knew if she married him, he would hurt her again and again. A conscience was not love. Behaving honorably was only that.

He faced her, a snifter in hand. "My mother is planning a wedding for the twelfth of December—two days before I set sail."

Her pulse began a heavy, rapid beat. "I saw your orders," she said stiffly.

He stared, his expression a mask devoid of emotion.

"You go to war against my country, my countrymen. What kind of marriage is that?"

"Yes, I do, and we shall make the best of it. We will hardly be the only couple with divided loyalties in this conflict."

She trembled, cold all over again. She knew she was losing—she had lost every single battle she had ever waged against this man. "I cannot marry you, Devlin. Not now, not ever."

He straightened.

"I mean it," she said nervously.

A terrible silence ensued. He looked at her for a long time with such a severe mask in place that it was impossible to tell what he was thinking or feeling—if, indeed, he felt anything. He set his glass carefully down. "But my regret is sincere. I am sorry for everything and I wish to make amends. I wish to save your reputation."

She felt like weeping. "Your regret comes too late!"

He looked at her, his gaze searching. "You did not always hate me."

She stiffened. "This is not about hatred. My letter was sincere. I do not hate you, Devlin, in spite of all that you have done."

"Then accept this marriage, for Tyrell is right—it is in your best interest."

"I want to go home," she heard herself say, almost pathetically.

He started.

How she wanted to weep. Her tone quavering, she took a deep breath and said, "I admit what we both now know— once I loved you, and I wanted you to love me in return. But you cannot offer me love, can you?"

His nostrils flared, and he shook his head. "No."

"No," she echoed, and it was impossible not to be bitter. "You offer me marriage now. I simply cannot accept. You see, you have hurt me for the last time," she said tersely. "If you wish to appease this new conscience of yours, then send me home, a free woman, at long last."

"I cannot."

"Of course you can. You are the most powerful and independent man I have ever met. Of course you can." She realized that she was crying.

He suddenly approached.

Virginia stiffened as he paused before her, his expression very severe.

"I will not sell Sweet Briar."

She froze. *"What?"* Had he just said what she thought he had?

"I will not sell Sweet Briar."

She felt faint. She must have reeled because he caught her. "You won't sell Sweet Briar? But...I do not understand."

"Sit down," he commanded, guiding her to a chair.

She was too stunned to refuse.

"I have purchased the plantation," he said. "I bought it to give to you in an effort to make amends for what I have done."

Virginia felt faint. She could hardly comprehend his words. He now owned her home?

"It will be your wedding present," he said softly. "A gift from me to you."

Part Three

The Bride

CHAPTER TWENTY-THREE

THE WEDDING WAS BUT days away.

Virginia had never felt more like a powerless pawn. With her wedding looming so near, it was impossible not to admit that if Devlin O'Neill loved her, just a little, she would be more than thrilled to be marrying him. But he didn't love her, not at all; until recently, his intention had been to send her home, done with her at last. It hurt still. And as for his grand gesture of buying Sweet Briar with the intention of giving it to her, that had become tainted by the suggestion of blackmail in his offer. It was to be a wedding gift—and Virginia did not have to ask him to know that if she refused to marry him there would be no gift at all. She could not be unhappy with his "gift," but she wished it had been offered with no consequent threats. And she would not refuse. Devlin was paying off the plantation's debts and in a few days, her home would belong to her, at last. She was marrying a man who frightened her, a man still bent on revenge, a man she continued to hopelessly love; the future was uncertain and shadowed with doubt. At least she would have a refuge if she ever needed one.

She took the safest possible course; she retreated into herself. She slept late and went to bed early. She immersed herself in books. She tried hard not to think, and when she did, she thought of Sweet Briar and how one day her children would inherit it. She kept her distance from

Devlin, knowing it would hurt to be near him, and that was an easy task. He spent most of his waking hours either at the *Defiance,* as she was in the final stages of being out-fitted for her tour, or at the Admiralty, being briefed upon the war. She suspected that he might be avoiding her, as well, and she could only surmise that he found the impending marriage more than distasteful. Most evenings he took his supper out, leaving her to dine alone in the huge, empty dining room. Upon crossing each other's paths, they both became polite, formal strangers, which relieved Virginia to no end, no matter how odd it was.

Mary de Warenne was another problem entirely. Virginia liked his mother and suspected that, had circumstances been different, they might have become deep and abiding friends. Now, however, his mother was busily and happily planning their small wedding. Virginia was constantly called on for Mary wished her to approve every detail, every decision. The wedding would be held at their Mayfair home in the old chapel there—fine. The wedding would be restricted to the immediate family—fine. The reception afterward would also be at Harmon House—fine. There would be salmon, pheasant, venison, and would French champagne be inappropriate? No, that was fine. And finally there was the matter of Virginia's gown.

Mary de Warenne's couturier was beside herself with enthusiasm. Virginia nodded at lace, at beads, at silk, at satin—she had no idea what the dress would be like and she did not care. Why couldn't they just plan the event, have her appear at the appointed hour and leave her entirely alone?

But Virginia could not be rude to Mary. The effort cost her dearly, but she was polite, friendly and, in general, quite amiable. The moment Mary left her though, Virginia would lock herself in her room, take huge calming breaths and, somehow, avoid the terrible need to cry.

It was noon. Virginia knew what day it was—she kept track of the days with the morbid fascination of a prisoner on his way to the guillotine. It was December 9—in three more days she would be walking down the aisle. Her stomach tightened at the thought, and it was a painful stabbing in her gut.

"Virginia?" Mary knocked on her door. "I have your gown! You must see it—may I come in?"

Virginia was seated by the window, staring out at the back lawns and the river. Her heart lurched and she stood. "Come in," she said.

Mary entered, a bulky, wrapped garment in her arms. "It is beautiful beyond words, and you must try it on!" She rushed over to Virginia and kissed her cheek. Her face was alight, her eyes sparkling, and she was a very beautiful woman, indeed.

"I don't really think I should try it on," Virginia said slowly, her heart beating uncomfortably now. She sensed it would be hard to maintain her composure if she tried on her wedding dress, but how to avoid doing so? What logic could she use?

"But what if it needs an alteration?" Mary exclaimed, already placing the garment on the bed and removing the brown wrapper. "Look! Just look!" she cried.

Virginia hugged herself, ill. Mary held up a white silk dress and Virginia had to look. Almost hypnotized, she saw a gown with a square neckline and long sleeves, covered with a layer of lace that was heavily beaded, the skirts impossibly full, the train elegant and long. She forced a smile; it felt sickly. "How beautiful," she whispered. How could this be happening? How?

She was on the verge of marrying Devlin—and he did not love her, not at all.

"You will be the most beautiful bride ever seen at Harmon House," Mary gushed. "Let me help you out of your clothes."

Virginia turned, giving Mary her back, facing the window. An elegant yacht had berthed at their dock and a number of sailors were tying the lines. She blinked back a tear, vaguely wondering who had arrived, as she did not recognize the vessel. A man leapt from the stern to the dock and the sight he made was terribly familiar.

Virginia froze.

He leapt over the stone path, ignoring it, and started swiftly up the lawn.

"Sean!" she cried. And thrilled, she threw open the window, waving. "Sean! Sean!"

He heard her, looked up, and he waved back.

VIRGINIA LEFT MARY BEHIND, racing downstairs at breakneck speed. As she skidded through the house and into the family salon, she vaguely realized that Devlin was in the library, speaking to someone. She had not realized he was home; it hardly made a difference. She flung open the terrace doors and raced outside.

Sean was bounding up the stone steps to the patio. He grinned at her.

"I am so glad to see you," she cried, and she rushed to him, throwing her arms around him and holding him hard.

She felt him tense in surprise, but Virginia felt so safe, so secure, so beloved that she did not care and she clung. Finally he patted her back, almost as if he felt awkward. "This is not the greeting I imagined," he murmured.

Virginia realized he did not hug her in return and she let him go, smiling up at him. "I am so happy you are here!"

His gray gaze wandered over her face.

She smiled again and touched his cheek. This time she did not speak.

He pulled away, clasping her hand gently. "You are going to make the groom jealous," he said tightly.

She glanced behind her and saw a curtain fall at the window. She faced him and shrugged. "I know that is not possible," she said.

He stared closely at her. "Are you all right?" he asked, clearly concerned.

That was her final undoing; she could not speak, and she shook her head.

"Come." He released her hand and pressed her back. "Let's take a turn about the gardens."

It was about to rain, but she nodded in assent.

Sean slipped his cloak off and placed it about her shoulders. "You are not a happy bride," he remarked as they went down the steps to the lawns.

"Oh, no one has told you?" How hysterical and bitter she sounded, she thought. "Devlin has decided to be honorable and save my sordid reputation, at long last."

He faced her, pausing. "You sound very angry."

"Sean!" Tears threatened. "I am more than angry—I am being forced into a loveless marriage with a man I cannot stand!"

He started and cursed. "I thought you were in love with him, Virginia. At Askeaton you had stars in your eyes."

"Do you see stars now?" she flung.

His mouth was tight. "No, I do not."

She tucked her arm in his and they started to walk again. "I tried to run away. But Tyrell betrayed me and called Devlin. He bought Sweet Briar and he has made it clear that if I marry him, the plantation will be my wedding gift."

Sean halted. "He has blackmailed you into this?" He was incredulous.

Virginia hesitated. "Not exactly. But the suggestion was clear—Sweet Briar is to be a wedding gift. If he wanted me to freely have it, he could simply sign the deed over now."

Sean stared and finally said, "Virginia, I heard you were living openly with him. I heard you were his mistress, and so it seemed to me that his finally marrying you was the right thing for him to do."

She hesitated. Because she had willingly enjoyed his bed after the terrible Carew ball, she could not tell Sean that they had played a deadly charade. Did Sean still love her? She knew he remained fond of her. Now she worried that he was more than fond of her and that she should not have involved him in her crisis. She finally said, "I don't want to marry him—but I also have no choice."

He tilted up her chin. "You loved him once. Can you genuinely claim that you do not love him now?"

She opened her mouth to deny it. No words came out.

And his reaction, a terrible darkening of his eyes, followed by the shadow of anguish, told her everything that she had to know. *His feelings had not changed.*

"My feelings do not matter," she finally said, hoarsely. "What matters is that he has hurt me time and again, and if we marry, he will somehow find a way to hurt me another time. I can no longer bear it, Sean, I can no longer bear his terrible indifference!"

Sean swallowed. Tightly, he said, "Virginia, I do not think he is indifferent. I know my brother. No one knows him as well as I. If he did not wish to marry you, nothing on earth could persuade him to do so, nothing and no one."

TOMORROW WAS HER wedding day.

It would soon be dawn. Virginia sat in a window seat, the sky outside a dusky blue-black. Sometime in the evening it had begun to rain, and the gentle rainfall silvered the curtain of night.

She stared at the falling rain. Virginia was trying to imagine the kind of woman she would be like if she had seen her father beheaded as a small child. There was no possible way to do so. She thought she might react like Sean, forgetting every detail.

But Devlin remembered everything. Unlike his brother, he had spent the past fourteen years plotting revenge against his father's murderer. She shivered, and not from the cold morning. That would make anyone heartless, she thought, but the man who had lain with her after the Carew ball had not been heartless, she was certain.

She had refused to reconsider that night again, but now, it was all she could think of.

She closed her eyes in turmoil. Tomorrow was her wedding. She could run away or she could stay; she could accept marriage to a cold, vengeful man who insisted he was heartless or she could have faith. Running away would probably fail, but having faith only promised a future of heartache, if the past were any consideration.

Virginia stood grimly. Her logic indicated that she had little choice but to stay and accept marriage to a heartless man, expecting nothing in return except Sweet Briar. How could she endure such a matrimonial state?

Virginia shivered again, chilled in her soul, watching the falling rain. Images of her parents, laughing, teasing, stealing a kiss or a touch when they thought no one was looking, assailed her then.

God, she and Devlin had hardly exchanged words since that awful day when he had almost blackmailed her into accepting their union. One thing was so clear. She could not endure a mechanical marriage to a man universally acclaimed as heartless; therefore, she must continue on, foolishly daring to hope she could somehow save his soul. Virginia realized the amount of courage she now needed to go forward to the altar.

And it was time for a civil conversation. It was time for

a truce. They certainly could not live this way after their marriage—or, at least, she could not—and more images of her parents came, full-force, bittersweet.

Her decision was made. She walked barefoot across the bedroom, Arthur happily following, filled with trepidation. She already knew Devlin had not come up to his bed in the adjacent room, so she went downstairs, certain she would find him at his desk in the library.

Virginia let the puppy out on the terrace before approaching the single room that was Devlin's sanctuary. The library door was open and she had been right. A huge fire blazed in the hearth and Devlin sat at his desk, a quill in hand, parchment before him. He looked up, startled.

She smiled and it felt very grim. *She was not giving up. She would try to be a real wife to him, no matter the courage it took.*

His gaze took in her white cotton and lace nightgown and her bare feet. "Virginia?"

"I thought we could speak—if you have the time," she added in a nervous rush.

"You will catch cold," he said, standing and laying the quill aside.

He had a night's growth of beard upon his jaw, his ruffled shirt was open at the throat and lower, and it was also rumpled. Virginia's heart skipped a beat or two. He looked dangerous, disreputable and terribly seductive.

She came into the room and went to stand before the fire, her back now to him. She felt his gaze upon her, dared not look back, and then heard him walk over to her. She finally glanced up at him; he glanced down at her. She saw that he held a throw in his hands. "May I?"

She nodded, her throat now constricted, and he settled the dark red wool rug over her shoulders. The fire was hot and she was considerably warmed.

"What is it you wish to speak about at five-thirty in the morning?" There was some dry amusement in his tone.

"Our marriage," she managed.

He nodded, his jaw tight, the light in his eyes flaring.

She hesitated. Her parents had based their marriage on the truth. "I debated running away again and decided against it."

He leaned on the mantel. "Go on."

"Therefore, my intention is to make the best of our situation."

"That is reasonable," he nodded.

"How shall we get along? Once, we were almost friends," she blurted, more nervous than before. She swallowed hard and reached for his hand. As she took it, he tensed and she felt it. "We can be friends. I am certain of it. I have been very angry these past weeks, but I have thought a great deal about this, and now I wish to start over. Tomorrow is our wedding day. What better foundation for a marriage than friendship?"

He simply stared as if mesmerized at her.

"Devlin?"

"Is this a ploy?" he asked carefully.

"No," she said quickly. "But I cannot be married to a man I cannot laugh with and speak with. I cannot be married to a man and bear his children if we cannot stroll in the park and ride horseback together and in general, engage in a pleasant camaraderie. We are going to share our lives, Devlin, and that is worthy of friendship."

For a moment he was silent. "I do believe you asked me for my friendship once and I failed you miserably, Virginia. It is very bold of you—and brave—to ask me yet again."

"But is it too much to ask?" she cried. "Are you saying you have no wish to be friends? That you only wish to share my bed and sit across from me at supper? That is not acceptable to me, Devlin," she warned.

He stared. "So this is the criteria for our marriage, then? Laughter, conversation, long walks and hacks across the countryside?"

With great dignity, she said, "I cannot live in a cold, barren union, Devlin. Surely you know me well enough now to know that."

"I doubt it will be cold or barren," he said swiftly.

"You are avoiding my question," she said as calmly as she could.

"Yes, I suppose I am." His jaw flexed. "You seem to think I am a gentleman of leisure, that I will be home and at your beck and call. I am a military man. Two days after our union I am going to war, Virginia, and my tour will last six months."

She felt crushed.

"But when I return," he said seriously, "we will take long walks and horseback rides, if that is what you wish. And if you say something amusing," he said, his gaze intent, "I will make every effort to laugh."

Relief overcame her. Her knees buckled. "Thank you, Devlin."

He smiled just a little and then he shook his head. "You remain unpredictable, Virginia."

"Then you shall not be bored," she replied. He was going to try to be a real husband to her! Her elation began, swiftly increasing. He wasn't willing, oh no, stubborn man that he was, but he had given in, he had conceded, he was going to *try*.

He smiled a little at her. "I do want you to know this. In this marriage, your every need will be met. I have already made it clear to my steward that you will lack for nothing, and if there is ever any problem, there is Adare to turn to, or Tyrell or Sean. And you have yet to meet Rex or Cliff, but they are as noble."

Some of her elation vanished. Her every need would not be met, not unless Sean was right and she was the woman who could save Devlin's soul. But she had won enough that day and she refused to dwell on that.

"Thank you, Devlin," she said. She smiled at him and turned to go. Her bare feet were numb from the cold stone floors.

"Virginia?" His tone had softened remarkably and she whirled.

"Now that I have had time to consider it, I am not displeased about our union. I think we will do well together, in the end." He smiled a little at her, his gaze searching.

Stunned, she met his gaze. His smile was small but genuine and it reached his gray eyes, and somehow, it stole her breath away.

He seemed to flush as if embarrassed with his small confession—or perhaps he was merely a bit warm from the fire.

Virginia turned away. She remained in terrible danger. One small smile, one soft look, and she was as hopeful as ever. To enter a union so one-sided, to love a man who refused to ever return her feelings, a man obstinately dedicated to hatred and revenge, was surely madness on her part. But then, the human heart knew no reason.

Virginia knew she would not give up on him, not ever.

THE WEDDING MARCH BEGAN.

Devlin felt his heart lurch and then it picked up a maddening beat. He stood before the altar in the chapel at Harmon House, his brother Sean acting as his best man. The only guests present were his family—Tyrell, Rex and Cliff stood in the front row with Mary and his stepsister, Eleanor, who had just returned from Bath. He turned, strangely breathless, and it was as if time had somehow become suspended.

Virginia was coming down the aisle, escorted by his stepfather.

He could only stare. And suddenly he was terrified of his bride, the most beautiful woman he had ever beheld, her violet eyes huge and bright and riveted upon him as she slowly approached. He could not breathe. He was about to be married and his life would never be the same.

The tumult in his heart increased. Terror ran rampant. He need not fall victim to her allure, he told himself in panic, nothing need really change. He had promised her long walks and country hacks and conversation, but in two days he was going to war, and it would be six months before he returned.

He was relieved; insanely, he was even more disappointed.

She was a vision in the glittering white gown, a sheer veil covering her face, her long hair braided with diamonds and curling riotously about her shoulders. He simply could not look away. There were so many memories. Virginia, standing at the rail of the *Americana,* aiming a pistol at his head. Virginia in his cabin, proud and defiant, demanding to know his intentions. Virginia at Askeaton, too lovely for words, offering him her body, beseeching his love with her eyes. Virginia that morning in her nightclothes, as slender as a child, offering him a truce and a real marriage if he dared accept it.

He did not deserve such a woman. He never had and he never would.

But it was too late to back out now! He closed his eyes, sweating. He would play her game, follow her rules. He would honor her, be her companion, her lover, father their children, but he needed neither joy nor love.

· Virginia paused at his side, while Edward moved away. She gazed up at him expectantly. He was too stunned to even offer her the smallest smile. Instead, he nodded at her. Appearing uncertain, she faced the priest.

Father McCarthy gestured and they both went down on their knees as the mass began.

Devlin heard not a word the priest said. Instead he was acutely aware of his bride, and as acutely aware of the opportunity being presented to him. He was at a crossroads. It was glaring at him. There were two directions his life could take.

Joy and love...or revenge and hate.

THE SMALL WEDDING PARTY had been removed to one of the salons at Harmon House. A long table had been set up with a buffet offering enough food for fifty, including a resplendent, multitiered wedding cake. Servants passed silver trays containing flutes of champagne and a small orchestra played from one corner of the room. Virginia remained stunned and she could not speak; in fact, other than to say, "I do," she had not said a word in hours. *She and Devlin were married. It had really come to pass.*

She blinked at her left hand where a simple gold band declared the fact. She was weak of knee, it was hard to breathe, and indeed, she almost felt faint.

She was married to the man who had abducted her from the high seas, who had held her hostage, who had flaunted her in society as his mistress, and who now, finally, had forced her to the altar. She could summon up no regret. But she wondered what the future held for them and foolishly prayed that all of her dreams might one day come true. She looked across the room.

In his full dress uniform, Devlin sipped a flute of champagne, surrounded by his stepbrothers. She had met Rex, the middle one, and Cliff, the youngest, a few hours before the wedding. Like Tyrell, both brothers were tall and dark of complexion. Rex was in the army and he wore his scarlet uniform, decorated with gold epaulets and numerous medals. Like Devlin, he was a captain, but his regiment was cavalry, and like Devlin, his aspect was a bit forbidding. She vaguely recalled that he had been wounded at Salamanca last year. As vaguely, she heard he had been in the Russian theater, having only returned home recently.

Cliff she knew little about. His hair was almost golden-brown, and he had a somewhat arrogant air. She had overheard something about his ships and the Caribbean, leading her to believe that he was a merchant of sorts. He did not appear to be a trader, but his rakish look also reminded her of Devlin. All three de Warenne brothers were dangerously attractive, each in their own way.

Devlin suddenly looked across the room at her and her heart stopped. They stared, neither one smiling.

Tonight was their wedding night. It felt like it had been an eternity since she had been in his arms and she was hollow inside at the prospect of lying with him.

A huge wave of desire threatened to make her faint. She looked at him as he stood there across the room, politely conversing with his stepbrothers, resplendent in his navy blue tailcoat and white britches, at once powerful and charismatic, at once seductive and dangerous. And he was now her husband.

"He is so handsome! I can't imagine having such a husband."

Virginia blinked and looked at a young girl perhaps two years her junior. The girl was terribly beautiful, with high cheekbones, amber eyes and dark blond hair that was almost the color of honey. She was smiling hopefully at Virginia.

"I am Eleanor de Warenne," she said with a graceful curtsy, her cheeks flushed. "Devlin's stepsister."

Virginia curtsied. "Forgive me," she managed, her eyes moving back to Devlin again. He was speaking with Cliff but his gaze veered instantly to her. The hollow feeling of immense desire increased. She needed to be in his arms now. She tried to smile at his stepsister. "How nice to finally meet you. Haven't you been in Bath this season?" She had vaguely heard that the de Warennes' daughter had spent the last season there as another young lady's companion.

Eleanor murmured an affirmative.

Virginia took a closer look at her. She was gazing at Sean, her cheeks far more pink than before.

Then Eleanor turned. "Are you nervous about your wedding night?" she asked quite directly.

Virginia was taken aback. But she was nervous, very nervous, if she dared be honest with herself. "Frankly, I am," she said softly. And she glanced at him again.

Sean suddenly stepped between them. "I see you have both, finally, met. Eleanor, if you think to lure Virginia into the topic of wedding nights, you are wrong." His tone was mild but his stare was not. Then he smiled at Virginia. "She is sixteen and certain subjects are not suitable for her ears."

Eleanor's smile vanished and she turned crimson. "I will be seventeen in three months," she cried. "I am not a barefoot child in pigtails anymore! I am a lady now—a lady with suitors—ask anyone in Bath." Lifting her skirts, she hurried away.

Sean sighed, staring after her for one moment, appearing oddly thoughtful. Then he handed Virginia a flute of champagne. "You look exhausted. Should I summon Devlin?"

Virginia smiled back, hesitating. If he summoned Devlin, they might find an excuse to leave. "Yes, that would be wonderful," she managed. It was hard to breathe.

Sean bowed and walked off, leaving Virginia alone. She took a sip of champagne, hoping to cool herself as she did so. Instead, the crowd in the room turned into a sea of faces.

And finally Virginia could not get any air at all. *I must sit down,* she thought. But before she could move to do so, the flute slipped from her fingers and crashed upon the floor.

Virginia looked down at the puddle of pale liquid, terribly surprised, and the puddle darkened and wavered in her vision. How odd, she began to think, as the entire room seemed to tilt and sway and finally darken, too.

I am going to faint, she thought.

"Virginia!" Devlin cried.

CHAPTER TWENTY-FOUR

HIS HEART FELT AS IF IT had stopped. He knelt over his bride, quickly seeking out her pulse. It was strong and steady. Relief crashed over him like a tidal wave; she had merely fainted.

Devlin gathered her in his arms, glancing up at his family, who surrounded him. "She has fainted. I think this day has been long enough." He swiftly stood. Virginia felt as light as a feather, and her weight always amazed him.

"She has been under too much duress," Mary whispered, her face ashen, her eyes filled with guilt. "Oh, dear, I should have never insisted on such a hasty wedding!"

"You are not to blame, dear," Edward said, putting his arm around her.

Devlin strode from the salon, Virginia limp in his arms. Sean reached his side and Devlin met his brother's eyes. They were grave and concerned.

"Shall I send up a maid with some salts?"

"She'll be fine," he said a bit curtly. He was very aware that his brother's feelings had not changed, just as he remained aware that Virginia truly should have married someone like Sean.

"Devlin!" His mother slipped salts into the pocket of his jacket. "She hasn't been eating well. She needs rest and nourishment."

He nodded and left the room.

And once he was alone with Virginia, bounding up the steps, he gazed at her face and his heart warmed inexplicably. She deserved Sean, or someone like Sean, but she was stuck with him. Suddenly he wanted to make it up to her.

Their suite had been filled with flowers and roses. Devlin laid her on the bed, which was turned down, just as she began to stir. He sat down at her hip and held the salts to her nostrils; she gasped, her eyes flying open.

For one moment, she stared. Then she started to sit up.

He clasped her shoulder and held her down. "Stay still for a moment," he said gently, an odd affection filling him, soft and tender. He was aware of the fact that the fear remained, but he had somehow managed to shove it aside. "You fainted."

She smiled a little. "I am so sorry. I don't faint."

He found his mouth curving. "All women faint."

"Not this one...until now."

He realized he still held her small shoulder, and that her diamond-encrusted hair brushed his fingers. He meant to remove his hand; somehow, he touched her face. "It has been a difficult day, I know. Virginia..." He stopped, unsure of what he wanted to say, but the warmth was filling his chest and he wanted to say something to her.

"What?" she whispered.

He hesitated. His mind raced but no coherent thoughts came, there was only the warmth, oddly tender and so surprisingly unfamiliar. "I will try to be a good husband."

Her eyes widened; she smiled. "I cannot ask for more than that," she said.

She was so beautiful, so original, so unique—and she was his. Devlin found himself leaning over her as the room around them blurred and disappeared, as the small noises coming from the guests downstairs and the wind outside faded and vanished. Time seemed to slow. Virginia did not move. She held his gaze until their lips brushed.

A harsh sound escaped from him. He caught her face in his hands and opened her lips gently. Slowly, gently, their mouths fused and their tongues tangled. He stroked his hand down her shoulder, her arm. Urgency slammed over him. The need to explode, then and there, caused him to begin to shake.

He exercised an impossible amount of restraint and he drew away from her. "I will let you rest," he said roughly, about to get up.

She seized his arm, her grip surprisingly strong. "No."

"Virginia," he began, sitting back down as she sat up. "You just fainted." He wanted to do the right thing now.

Her cheeks were pink, her pupils dilated. "I am fine," she insisted.

"We have a lifetime ahead—" he began.

She caught his shoulders, pressing her mouth to his, and there was nothing soft or gentle or controlled about her kiss. Her mouth moved insistently, her small tongue prodding, and when he did not respond, she nipped his lip.

He lost all self-restraint. He seized her, pushing her down, taking back the kiss, opening her and thrusting inside. He knew what was coming, and something vast, huge and hollow filled him—the sensation almost like standing in the path of a gale, knowing that when it came, he would be blown away. He held her hard, tightly, kissing her even more deeply, and the gale winds came.

Thought collapsed, and with its destruction, all logic was also gone. There was only feeling—a huge madness, part desire, part triumph and something else, something different, something never before felt, swelling impossibly, expanding inside, cresting upward, outward, consuming his body and his being.

Virginia was pawing his back frantically, making small, eager cries. He somehow found the tiny buttons on the back of her dress. "Hurry," she cried.

He simply could not speak. Emotion made it impossible. He could only pant and stare as he tore the dress away, chemise, corset and frilly drawers following. Devlin leapt to his feet.

She sat up, naked except for her garters and stockings and the diamonds in her hair. As he tore off his own clothes, she watched, her small breasts heaving, the tips pink and elongated. When he was naked, she held out her arms.

For one moment, he did not move, triumph washing over him, savage and barbaric and male. *This woman belonged to him. But hadn't he always known that—from the first moment he had ever seen her—when she had thought to assassinate him with a sniper shot?* And then he went to her.

He pushed her slowly down, smiling a little, and she smiled a little back. He spread her thighs and moved against her, and she gasped.

"Watch me," he whispered, a command, and he slowly began to fill her.

She moaned as he entered, and he found that it was him watching her now, as her eyes glazed, as her flush increased, and finally, when he was seated to the hilt, as her eyes widened with real surprise and profound pleasure. More triumph seared him, and with it, more love. Slowly he began to move.

Her eyes closed, she found his rhythm, and as one, they strained. Devlin held her in his arms, tighter and tighter still, fighting the need to explode, knowing now that this was what he would always need, forever and ever, and he kissed her cheek, her neck, her temple, as she whimpered and begged, clawing him. Then she gasped, eyes flying wide, and she cried, "I still love you!"

He stiffened, holding her as she began her climax, incredulous and disbelieving, and her words echoed. *I still love you.* And Devlin could no longer restrain himself, and holding her hard, convulsed into her body, time and again, the frantic chant *I still love you* a litany in his mind.

VIRGINIA BECAME AWARE of strong fingers easing along the side of her arm.

For one moment, as sleep slowly lifted, she was disoriented, and then she was awake.

She lay curled against Devlin—her husband—and he was stroking her arm. She tensed, recalling the wedding, the small family gathering afterward and his lovemaking. *He had been so gentle.*

Her eyes opened and she craned her neck to look up at him. Instantly she saw that he was staring at her, his expression soft and relaxed as she had never before seen it. In fact, the light in his eyes was just as soft, unguarded and warm. Her brows lifted.

He met her gaze and his face tightened and his lashes lowered, as if shielding himself from her scrutiny.

"I fell asleep," she whispered, shaken. Had she really seen that incredible light of warmth just then? Had he been looking at her that way while she slept? As if he loved her in return?

"Yes, you did," he said quietly, his hand now still on her arm. He smiled a little at her.

She sighed and lay her cheek on his chest. Oh, but she did like that—she could hear his powerful heart beating, slow and steady. She smiled and the love she felt for him washed over her. Trying not to love this man was simply impossible.

"How are you feeling?" he asked soberly.

"Wonderful." She looked up and grinned.

He smiled and amusement appeared in his eyes. "That is not what I meant. I was referring to the fact that you fainted."

"Oh, that!" She was dismissive. "I do feel wonderful."

"Perhaps you should eat something. I can have a tray sent up."

She smiled against his chest. Did she dare? Why not! "I am hungry," she murmured, "very hungry—but not for food."

He was still.

She glanced up.

"You are a minx," he said softly, but he was smiling.

"Am I?" she said, pleased by his remark. She kissed the muscle beneath her cheek, then slid her hand down his rib cage and his abdomen. She felt the muscles there tense.

She kissed his skin again and brushed her fingers over his manhood, which lay half-stiff upon his belly. She watched it grow with real interest and teased her fingertips over it again.

"You play with fire, little one," he murmured.

"Does this always happen so easily?" she had to ask as she began to explore both shape and texture.

There was no response.

Virginia closed her hand around him, and inside, she felt hugely hollow. She glanced slowly up.

He watched her, his face strained, his breathing harsh, uneven. He said, slowly, with effort, "If you do as you are doing, yes."

She smiled, pleased, and stroked his length. "And if I do this?"

"Then I do this," he growled, and she found herself lifted up above his body and held over his head, against the headboard. "What?" she began, and then his tongue swept over her.

Virginia held on to the headboard, gasping.

Clasping her buttocks in each hand, his tongue washed over her sex, swift and intent.

Virginia felt faint. "Oh, I can't manage," she gasped. "Do not stop now!"

He laughed as he tormented her, more deeply, more explicitly, than before.

Virginia felt her terrible climax begin and she grabbed his hand, squeezing it; he understood and before she knew it, he had pulled her down, and he was surging up into her; a moment later he had flipped her over and he was riding her hard.

She looked up into his beloved face and began to weep in pleasure. And he held her tightly, whispering, "Yes, my darling, yes."

DEVLIN SAT IN THE CHAIR BY the fire that barely blazed in the hearth, fully dressed in his naval uniform, his black hat on his knee. He stared at his bride.

Virginia slept deeply, a soft smile on her lovely face, a few diamonds still clinging to the masses of her curling hair. She lay on her side, her back bare where the hair revealed it, the covers pulled only to her waist. He had made love to her for two nights and the day in between, and he still wanted her again.

It was 5:02 a.m., December 14. In another fifty-eight minutes he would set sail for America. He did not want to leave his bride; he did not want to go.

He did not want to go.

He stood, hat in hand. What nonsense was this? What was happening to him? He was a warrior, it was all that he knew, and of course he wanted to go to war yet again.

She sighed in her sleep.

His heart ached suddenly, hugely, then. Good God, he

was going to miss her—he missed her already and he had yet to leave.

The ever-present fear, a monster lurking behind him, threatening his very life, came closer, reaching out. *What nonsense was this?* He had a war to attend. He might be married now, but his bride could not make him soft, she could not change his character or his choices. All the other emotions he had been feeling since their wedding, both soft and huge, were not for him. He was not in love. Love was not for him. Once he set sail, once he became a part of the wind and the sea, his legs braced firmly as he rode the deck of the *Defiance,* he would not be feeling like such a romantic fool and he would not miss her, not at all.

Which meant that it was time to go, now, before his foolish brooding unmanned him.

But the leave-taking was so hard.

And he thought of a hundred past bloody battles and a weariness claimed his soul—a weariness he could not deny.

Abruptly Devlin walked over to the bed. He made no move to wake her, but he stared at her angelic face, aware that he wished to memorize it. And for one moment, he thought about waking her.

But he did not. Her lure was too strong. Instead, he pulled the covers up to her shoulders. She sighed again in her sleep, and this time she smiled.

His heart lurched, aching within him.

The monster of fear came closer and seized him with a vengeance.

This woman was his *wife.* This marriage could change *everything.* He stared down at Virginia and realized that in spite of all logic in his heart he wished that he were not leaving.

Which meant that it was time to go. Abruptly Devlin

turned and left his sleeping bride, his strides hard and determined.

Later, his regret would be vast.

VIRGINIA DREAMED THAT Devlin was gone.

She was in a sweet, happy place, warm and beloved, and suddenly she was chilled to the bone. Suddenly she was not in her bed, but she stood on some sandy shore, watching the *Defiance* as it sailed away. Horrified, afraid, Virginia cried out.

She blinked and found herself awake, quite naked and sitting up in bed. "Devlin?" She realized she had had a nightmare and relief washed over her.

But as she threw off the blanket, she saw that she was alone. "Devlin?" She began to feel hollow inside and sick with apprehension. She slid to the floor, beginning to shiver. The bronze clock on one bureau said it was half-past five that morning.

It was December 14.

Devlin was due to set sail that morning.

But he could not have left yet, without saying goodbye! Tearing a blanket from the bed and wrapping it around her, Virginia rushed to the sitting room, but it was vacant. Horrified, she raced into the bathing room and grabbed her wrapper. She saw a bowl of soapy water and his wet shaving brush sitting on the vanity; in the act of belting the robe, she froze.

The horror of her nightmare returned.

Virginia ran to the armoire and threw it open, dressing as quickly as she could without help. Clad in a pale green dress, shoes and stockings in hand, she ran downstairs, barefoot.

A housemaid was passing through the hall. "Rosemary! Where is the Captain? Has he left?"

The maid appeared surprised by her question. "He left a few minutes ago, madam."

Virginia stood there, shoes and stockings dangling from her hands, stunned. He had left? He had left like that, without a word? But why hadn't he said goodbye?

"I need the carriage," she said sharply, her heart seeming quite wedged now in her chest, a painful, congealed lump. Acid burned. She sat down in a chair as the maid rushed out, pulling on her stockings and putting on her shoes.

So many memories assaulted her now—his smile, his soft laughter, the way he called her "little one" and "my darling," the light of amusement as it sparked his eyes, the blaze of lust, and his lovemaking, at times hard and rushed, at other times soft and gentle. She thought of how he had held her as she fell asleep in his arms. She recalled his declaration that he would be a good husband to her.

She brushed away her tears. Why hadn't he awoken her? Why hadn't he said goodbye?

Another terrible time came to mind, a time when she had been loved by him with both urgency and tenderness, only to find him cold and indifferent the next day.

She was ill, about to retch. There was no possible way that Devlin could retreat now to that other, horrid place, a cold and heartless place where he had once before lived. The thought was unbearable—it could not possibly happen again.

She had to find him. She had to say goodbye. And she had to see him smile tenderly at her one more time, to know that they had passed safely through a terrible storm and that the light of a bright, gentle new day awaited them on the other side.

She could not survive the next six months otherwise.

A half an hour later her coach raced through the shipyard, passing stored containers, loaded wagons, cranes and crates. Longshoremen, civilians and sailors were busy everywhere. Virginia strained to see out of her window, and when her coach paused a moment later, she almost catapulted out.

A huge ship she did not recognize faced her. Other ships lined the docks, but none were the *Defiance*. And one berth, in their midst, was terribly empty.

Her heart hurt her now. Virginia raised her hand to her eyes to shield them from the rising sun. She looked past the docks.

And she cried out.

She knew the *Defiance* by heart—she always would. Perhaps a hundred yards distant, it slowly eased out of the channel, heading into the open harbor.

And there was no mistaking the tall, gallant figure standing hatless on the quarterdeck.

Virginia ran.

Holding her skirts, she ran down one dock, waving frantically. "Devlin! Devlin!" she screamed.

But the ship continued to move away, toward the horizon, and he never turned once to look back.

Virginia's steps slowed and faltered.

She paused, out of breath, panting hard. He still didn't look back and he would never hear her; it was hopeless. She stopped at the very end of the dock, staring desperately after the departing ship.

It sailed into the harbor, and once there, the main sails were unfurled. They quickly billowed and the frigate picked up speed, now flying across the seas, now flying away.

Virginia watched it disappear.

DEVLIN STOOD ON THE quarterdeck, the oddest urge to look back at the retreating shipyard within him. It was his habit to stand at the helm and search the horizons ahead; still, he could not shake the need to look back, as if in doing so he might glance at his bride one last time.

"A fine day for sailing, Captain," Red said, his hands on the helm. His grin was stained and yellow.

"Yes, indeed." They had a fresh breeze of about eighteen or nineteen knots, causing the seas ahead to foam with dancing white horses. They would make good time today, and after being on land for so long, he should be thrilled with the departure. He was not. Finally, Devlin sighed and looked back.

But the shipyard was just a jumble of shapes and colors now. Then a flash of light from the deck below caught his eye. Devlin turned—as a seaman pointed a musket at him.

Time stood still. He knew an assassination attempt when he saw one and he knew he would die. And as he told himself to dive, sensing it was futile, he knew that the assassin had been sent by his mortal enemy, the Earl of Eastleigh.

And as the shot rang out, the ship lurched with a sudden gust of wind. Devlin was already diving across the bridge, a burning sensation along his upper arm.

He had just used up another life. And as he slid across the wood deck, savage anger filled him. The assassin had missed, but only because of the fresh breeze. Still on the deck, Devlin drew his pistol, shouting, "Seize that man!" He rolled to his side, quickly loading the gun, glancing in the direction of where he thought the assassin might be, and he was right. The man was frantically reloading.

From behind, Gus and another sailor were charging the assailant.

Devlin got to one knee as the assassin aimed again and almost simultaneously, they fired at each other.

The assailant was struck in the lower leg and he cried

out, falling. Devlin threw his pistol aside, drawing his saber, racing across the quarterdeck and leaping down to the main deck. "I want him alive," he shouted as Gus and the second sailor seized the wounded man.

He was struck over the head and his hands were shoved behind his back but he remained half-conscious, on his knees, bleeding all over the deck.

Devlin paused before him, filled with fury.

"Captain?" Gus cried, as more sailors encircled them. "How badly are you hurt?"

"It's a graze," he said grimly. With his boot, he kicked the assassin under his jaw, snapping his head back, hard enough to flip him onto his back but not hard enough to break his neck. Gasping in pain, the man stared up at him with wide wild eyes. "Mercy, Captain, sir! I only did what I was told to do! What I was paid to do! Have mercy, I beg you, I got a wife, three boys, all hungry, please—"

Devlin stepped on his chest with most of his weight.

Ribs cracked. The man screamed.

"Who sent you?"

Frantic eyes met his. "I don't know. He never said his name! Wait—"

Devlin stepped on him again.

"I suggest you think very carefully," Devlin said.

"He never told me his name," the man panted. "Wait!"

Devlin decreased the pressure of his foot. "Continue."

"But I know who he was! It was a lord, Captain, sir, a lord—I saw the coat of arms on the coach, and I asked, I asked who it was after he was gone!"

"Who was it?"

"Eastleigh, it was Lord Eastleigh, Captain. Please, please spare my life!"

Devlin coldly debated the request. "Put him in the brig. Have the ship's surgeon attend him."

"Aye, sir," Gus said.

Devlin turned away. He was inwardly shaken—and furious with himself. He had been mooning over his bride like a school-age boy, thinking about her bed, thinking about love and almost feeling joy, when he had a blood enemy to destroy. His behavior had almost cost him his life.

The reminder was a timely one. He was married now, but it changed nothing.

CHAPTER TWENTY-FIVE

HANNAH KNOCKED ON VIRGINIA'S door. "Mrs. O'Neill? It is Lady de Warenne, she is downstairs." The girl smiled uncertainly at her.

Virginia had returned from her failed attempt to say goodbye to Devlin and had instantly retreated to her rooms. Grief had overcome her and she had sought her bed, trying to tell herself that six months was not that long, and instead missing him more and more with every passing moment. Fear had warred with her confusion. What if he was injured, or worse, in the war he was soon to attend? And how could he go to war against her country? Fortunately, her exhaustion was so great that she had finally collapsed and fallen asleep.

She had awoken an hour ago, feeling more composed and somewhat refreshed. She had bathed and dressed, preparing to go downstairs and take a solitary dinner. She was pleased that her mother-in-law had called; she was so acutely aware of Devlin's absence and the house felt spectacularly empty.

She hurried downstairs and found Mary seated in one salon, sipping a cup of tea. The moment she saw Virginia she stood, her gaze searching.

All of Virginia's composure vanished. She stood there and felt the tears stream down her face.

"Oh, dear," Mary whispered, hurrying forward. "Whatever has happened, child?"

Virginia turned away. "Forgive me, I'm so sorry!" But this woman was too kind and she could not stop the tears, no matter how she choked.

As if she were Virginia's own mother, Mary embraced her. "Oh, I thought to find you happy today! Oh, please do not tell me he has behaved despicably to hurt you again!"

Virginia managed to shake her head. "No, no, he has done nothing wrong—I mean, he left this morning and did not say goodbye, but that is not why I am distraught. I miss him, Lady Adare, I miss him terribly and I do not know how I can survive the next six months until he returns!"

The two women stared. Virginia wiped her eyes, breathless and shaking. "I am so foolish, I know."

Mary cupped her face. "You are not foolish, you are in love, and that thrills me, my dear."

Virginia bit her lip, her heart daring to defy her and soar. "I *am* in love, my lady, more so than ever, I think."

Mary smiled, pleased. "Do not think too much of his hasty departure. Men can be such fools. I am sure he was trying to be kind by not waking you at dawn, or there was some other such nonsense in his mind. We will probably never know what he was thinking. And Devlin is not romantic, not in the least—but I do think he loves you. In fact, I am almost sure of it."

Virginia was seized with hope. "You think so?"

"He could barely keep his eyes off of you during the wedding ceremony. I never saw a man so mesmerized."

Virginia thrilled. "I think he may feel warmly toward me, too," she confessed. "But how will I get through the next six months?"

"Very easily," Mary said. "You shall move into Harmon House, as it is impossible for you to stay here alone. Rex will not leave for his next post until after the New Year, and Cliff is staying in town for the winter. And then there is

Eleanor. She is your sister now and the two of you should become acquainted before she returns to the Hinckleys at Bath." Mary smiled, her eyes sparkling. "There is simply no other alternative, my dear."

Virginia felt warmed to the bone. She dared to take the other woman's hand. "You are so kind, my lady. May I speak frankly?"

"Please do," Mary said, the twinkle remaining in her eyes.

"I already feel as if I am truly your daughter."

Mary hugged her, hard. "But you are, my dear, you are."

"WE SEEM TO HAVE CALLERS," Mary murmured wryly as they entered the grand foyer of Harmon House.

Giggles and laughter, all of it feminine and quite coy, sounded from one nearby salon. Virginia glanced at Mary in some surprise.

"There has been a parade of eager young women coming through this house ever since Rex and Cliff arrived." She gave Virginia a look. "Neither one are spoken for and they both have fine inheritances. But they are both randy sorts, and instead of taking these young women seriously, I do believe it has become a simple source of entertainment for them both, especially for Cliff."

Virginia glanced into the salon where they had held the wedding reception. Rex was darkly handsome in his army dress uniform, yet there was little correct about him—his posture was indolent and his dark eyes were distinctly bored as he listened to a plump blonde regale him with some chitchat. His gaze wandered repeatedly about the company and finally to the doorway where Virginia and Mary stood. His expression brightened as it settled on them and he slowly smiled.

Virginia felt certain that he had broken many hearts. She smiled in return and glanced at Cliff. He was not bored, oh no. A gorgeous brunette woman, quite older than the three young ladies present, had him in a corner, her heavily ringed hand on his arm. Cliff was leaning very close to her, quite intimately, as she whispered in his ear, obviously flirting. He might have been the youngest brother, but he seemed the most sardonic and the most jaded. Suddenly he realized that new company was present; he straightened without haste, and rather lazily took a single step back, putting a more appropriate distance between himself and the brunette.

Mary said, low, "That is Lady Arlette. She is widowed and *not* suitable for any of my sons."

"I dare say Cliff is rather fond of her."

Mary made a derisive sound. "He is fond of her bosom and her penchant for discreet affairs."

Virginia had to bite back her gasp of surprise. She glanced at Mary, whom she had never heard utter an unkind word.

Rex approached, bowing. "The lovely bride saves the day." He smiled warmly at her. "Has my ignoble and reckless brother taken to the high seas, then?"

Virginia recognized the warmth he felt for Devlin and she liked him very much. "Your noble and reliable brother has set sail, indeed."

He laughed. "But how could he leave such a lovely bride behind so quickly?" He gave her a look.

Did he dare flirt with her now? "My lord, I feel certain it was a most difficult matter."

He bent and took her arm, whispering, "I have no doubt. You must rescue me, little sister. I should go mad if I have to listen to another marriage-minded maid prattle on about my medals and my honor."

She looked up at his hard, handsome face. There was some annoyance in his eyes—and something dark she unfortunately recognized. "Will you walk with me?" she asked. "I long for a turn in the gardens." She wondered why he found female pursuit so distasteful and what ghosts haunted him.

He gave her a wink. "Of course." He kissed his mother's cheek. "I am escorting Virginia outside. You may think to rescue Cliff soon." With that, he tucked Virginia's arm in his and they crossed the room and stepped out onto the terrace. Once there, she felt his large body relax.

"Most men would love to be so chased," she said.

He smiled a little at her. "I am *not* most men."

"I doubt any man in this family is like most men." She thought of Devlin and her heart skipped.

He eyed her as they strolled down the steps and to the frosted lawns, following a stone path there. "That is very flattering...I think."

"I meant it as flattery," she said.

"Yes, I am aware of that. And how does it feel to be a married woman?"

Her heart skipped wildly again. "I haven't changed—but then again, I have changed completely. I suppose I make no sense."

He grinned. "None at all. You are not what I would have expected Devlin to land."

Her brows lifted. "Is that an insult?"

"No, it is flattery."

They both smiled.

"I expected him to one day settle for an heiress, the matter a strictly financial one. I never expected him to lose his heart to a little American orphan who once tried to assassinate him from the deck of a ship while he was seizing it."

For one moment, Virginia was swept turbulently back
in time. She paused. "How did you hear about that?"

"The other night we dragged him off to a club. A little
bachelor's farewell fête. He waxed rather eloquent when
prodded. An interesting beginning—and apparently, an
auspicious one, as well."

"I hated him on sight," she whispered.

"Did you?" He stared.

She smiled. "The truth?"

"If you dare." He was no longer smiling.

"I was so afraid I don't know what I thought or felt. But
I knew from that first moment that I had never met a man
like him before—and that I never would again."

Rex de Warenne grinned. "I am glad to hear it," he said.

THERE WERE TWO DINING rooms in Harmon House. The
family gathered in the smaller one for supper, a room with
gold paper on the walls, a huge chandelier above, a long
trestle table set with gold candlesticks, gilt flatware, gold-
and-white china and linen and lace. Mary and Edward sat
at opposite ends of the exquisitely set table, formally
dressed. Virginia found herself seated between Cliff and
Tyrell, with Eleanor, Rex and Sean across from them. The
conversation ran rampant around her, Eleanor conversing
across Sean with her mother, Tyrell and Edward discussing rents, Cliff and Rex the state of Napoleon's finances.
Virginia smiled happily to herself. Devlin had a wonderful family and she was a part of it. There was so much
warmth in the room that she could feel the affection
between everyone present, a vibrant, tangible thing.

She caught Sean looking at her and she smiled at him.
He smiled back and looked away, toying with the fish on
his plate. Eleanor suddenly said brightly to her, "I heard
you spent quite a bit of time at Askeaton when Devlin was

in London," she said. "Did you like it there? I think it is one of the most beautiful places in Ireland."

Virginia laid her fork down, smiling back. "I liked it very much. And I agree, Askeaton is beautiful."

"Is it as nice as your home in Virginia?"

"Yes." Virginia was touched briefly with wistful longing. "Sweet Briar is a wonderful place. But the riding trails are better at Askeaton." She smiled at Sean, remembering all the long country rides they had shared.

Eleanor glanced between them with confusion. "I forgot...while Devlin was away, you only had Sean for company."

Virginia became uncomfortable. She didn't know what to say.

Sean ignored the conversation, concentrating on his food.

"I haven't ridden about Askeaton in years," Cliff remarked languidly. Although he remained impossibly relaxed, Virginia knew he meant to rescue her from an uncomfortable moment. "Sean has some fine horses, does he not?"

She glanced at him. He was a bit unsettling even now, and she had little doubt that he was the kind of man to enjoy the favors of a notorious widow. But she was grateful he was redirecting the conversation. "Yes, he does. There are some fine horses at Askeaton. Especially Bayberry," she added, smiling as she recalled the brave little filly.

Sean finally looked at her. "She is yours," he said suddenly. "Please accept her as my wedding present."

Virginia was so overcome she could not speak.

Eleanor looked back and forth between them, her expression stunned. "But you bred her! And you're giving her to Virginia?"

Sean glanced at her. "Virginia loves the horse."

Eleanor was suddenly standing. "Excuse me, I seem to have a terrible migraine." She hurried from the room.

Virginia blinked. *What was that?*

Sean sighed. "I forgot...she was there the day the filly foaled. She helped me bring her into the world." He stood, appearing grim. "Excuse me." He walked out.

Edward looked perplexed. "Mary, what is going on? Why is Eleanor upset?"

Mary began to smile. "I do think your daughter is growing up."

Tyrell said thoughtfully, "What a strange turn. Eleanor has spent her life provoking Sean, from the time she could walk. Her favorite game used to be 'ambush'—she would assault him when he would least expect it. Her favorite weapons were sticks and stones." He started to grin, shaking his head.

"Indeed. She is now jealous of Virginia," Rex said smoothly, and he saluted Virginia with his wineglass before sipping.

Virginia began to protest.

Cliff said calmly, "Sean needs to kiss her. That will solve one matter—while creating a few new ones." And he laughed, leaning back in his chair.

"That is enough!" Mary de Warenne cried. "Benson, the next course, thank you."

THE DAYS PASSED SLOWLY, but without a dull moment. Virginia rode in the early mornings with one brother or another, although never with Sean. She made afternoon calls with Mary and Eleanor, or stayed home to rescue Rex from the various ladies calling upon him and Cliff. It was clear that Cliff was having an affair with the widowed Lady Arlette, as they were not very discreet. Cliff reminded her very much of Devlin now, as he did not seem to care about his rather notorious reputation.

Evenings were either a family affair or spent on the town. Virginia found herself swiftly reintroduced into society by the powerful de Warenne family. There were dinner parties, charities and balls. Escorted as she was by either the Earl of Adare and his wife or the three strapping de Warenne brothers and Sean, she became a favorite, fawned over and admired by all. She only once bumped into William Hughes and his wife, and polite greetings were cursorily exchanged.

She met the other de Warennes and learned a little of the family's history. The family's founding father had fought with William the Conqueror. Once a landless Norman, he had married a wealthy Saxon heiress and eventually had been awarded an earldom. One of his descendants had journeyed to Ireland to obtain lands and titles there, the result being the Adare branch of the family. The original Northumberland branch of the family had become too powerful for any king to bear. Apparently those lands and titles had been forfeit in a deadly rebellion centuries ago. Afterward, some of the de Warennes had become wealthy merchants; a few had managed to win back some small estates, while others had emigrated to America to make brand-new fortunes. It was a most interesting family that she had married into.

And Virginia never stopped missing Devlin. There was no word from him. She followed news of the war avidly, aware that every tidbit was months old. The biggest news was the defeat of the USS *Vixen* by the HMS *Southampton,* and for a week, everywhere Virginia went, Londoners rejoiced. She could not share their enthusiasm and her loyalties were painfully torn and divided.

"I will kill him if he doesn't write you," Sean told her in late January.

"I can't imagine how a naval captain can post a letter,"

Virginia replied. She missed him so much that there were days when it hurt. One letter was all she would need to endure their separation. She counted the days until June. He had promised her he would be back by the middle of that month.

"Our naval ships go back and forth between America and Britain all the time to resupply," he said. "There is no excuse."

"He is in a war, Sean," she said quietly.

He smiled a little at her. "I am going back to Askeaton, I have been away too long. But you are in good hands now, I feel certain. Everyone loves you, Virginia. You have truly become a sister here."

Virginia warmed with real pleasure. "I love your family, Sean. I actually feel as if I belong here."

"You do," he said firmly. "And you do know that if you ever have a problem, you can turn to any of us. I will come running in an instant, but Tyrell, Rex and Cliff would do the same."

"I think I know that," she said, meaning it. While Rex and especially Cliff intimidated her somewhat, she had little doubt they would rush to defend her honor if ever the need arose.

He hesitated. "You and Eleanor have become friends. I'm glad. She's so young..." He trailed off.

"Of course we are friends. She is my new sister," Virginia said softly. "And every time you look at me she watches us like a hawk."

He seemed very surprised and he made a face. "What? I don't think so." Then he kissed her cheek. "I want you to promise me that you will not hesitate if in need. You have a real family now, and no one here lacks courage, loyalty or purpose."

"I doubt I will need to call out the de Warenne cavalry," she teased.

He laughed, the sound warm.

Virginia knew then that his heart had healed and she was happy for him.

CHAPTER TWENTY-SIX

January 1, 1813
Dear Virginia,
The New Year has come and I hope this missive finds you in good health and good spirits. How do you fare at Waverly Hall? I assume by now that you have become fast friends with my mother, and I hope you will not hesitate to ask her for anything you may be lacking. I also hope that my brothers have not overwhelmed you with their various characters. How has the winter been? It has been freezing cold as we sail the Atlantic, but that is to be expected. We now approach the coast of New Jersey, having seen little action thus far. We turned back a single American merchantman, the *Southern Belle,* although we seized a French privateer, which I have sent to Newfoundland to be outfitted there. The men are in good spirits, although growing bored, as they are not used to such inactivity, and they remain eager to engage the enemy. I have a new ship's surgeon, Paul White, a gentleman I think you would find erudite and amusing should you ever meet. He plays the violin and brought his instrument with him, providing the men with many hours of entertainment.

Please give my regards to my family. I wish you happy New Year.
Yours truly,
Devlin O'Neill

VIRGINIA RECEIVED DEVLIN'S LETTER on the fifth of February. She was so excited she flew to her room to tear open the sealed parchment. Her heart slammed in her chest as she read it quickly, and then she read it again, more slowly. She wished he had written that he missed her and could not wait to come home. But Devlin had never been comfortable with intimacy in person, so why would he be so in a letter, especially one written at sea, to his bride, their very first exchange since their wedding night?

Virginia sighed and gave up. She was happy that he had taken the time to write to her and had made the effort to get the letter to her at all. And he had asked her several questions, so clearly he wished for a reply.

February 5, 1813
Dear Devlin,
I was so pleased to receive your letter and even more pleased to learn that all is well with you and your crew. I have become good friends with both your mother and Eleanor; in fact, the very day you left your mother insisted I move into Harmon House, which I have done. I have become very fond of your entire family! Alas, Rex has returned to duty, Cliff will soon sail off to Martinique (I did not realize he had a sugar plantation there!) and Sean has returned to Askeaton, so suddenly the house is so empty and so forlorn. Tyrell remains, but I only see him in passing, as he seems preoccupied with his own affairs. Your mother and stepfather remain in good

health. Soon Eleanor leaves for Bath to rejoin the Hinckleys, although there is some controversy over whether she should be allowed to go. I do wish she would stay, as I enjoy the time we spend together.

We missed you at Christmastime. That eve we had a splendid family celebration. Your mother arranged a spectacular meal with enough to feed a regiment. Eleanor and Sean fought, as usual, over her returning to Bath, where apparently she has far too many suitors for a young lady of her age (at least, in Sean's opinion). Cliff invited the widowed Lady Arlette to join us, much to your mother's dismay. Have you ever met her? She is an amazing beauty, and quite fond of Cliff. The men spent quite a bit of time discussing the change in Napoleon's fortunes, the state of Europe and what a peace might be like there. Everyone kindly avoided the subject of the American war, I suspect in deference to me. After supper Rex caught me under the mistletoe, but his kiss was a brotherly one. Sean was so angry with Eleanor that he walked out on us all, but I do not know why or what happened.

Your family has been so wonderful. Your mother gave me a lovely locket with your portrait inside and I have come to treasure it. I received a shawl from Eleanor, gloves, chocolate and a fan from your brothers, and a book from Sean. The book is a history of Ireland and it is fascinating. He also gave me Bayberry as a wedding gift and she is here now, for Sean sent her down. I ride every morning, rain or shine.

I should love to meet your new ship's surgeon as he sounds like an agreeable man. I still have fond memories of Jack Harvey. Have you ever heard of him since he left your ship?

I have given your regards to your family. I wish you good health and good cheer. May God keep you and your men safe.

Your loving wife,

Virginia

Virginia knew that it might be months before she received a reply—the navy had told her that—but by the second week of March she was disappointed that she had not heard from him. In two more days it would be her birthday. She foolishly wished that Devlin could be home to share it with her.

"Do not despair," Mary said, her arm around her. It was a gray, windy day and the windows rattled. "You will hear from him again, I have no doubt."

Virginia smiled at her. "I do hope so." She touched her belly, an unconscious gesture. She was beginning to think that she was pregnant. She hadn't had her monthly since Devlin had left, and she was stunned by the possibility that she might be with Devlin's child, as well as both thrilled and afraid. She dearly wished to have Devlin's child, even if she hadn't expected to become pregnant so quickly. But would Devlin be as pleased? Every man wished for a son, but their relationship remained a new and fragile thing and it was too soon for it to be tested in any way. He might not be ready to see their child come into this world. And if that were so, she could not really blame him.

A horse's clopping hooves could just be heard from outside, in spite of the wind and the rattling glass panes. "Maybe it's the post," Virginia cried. His last letter had been conveyed to the house by a postal rider and Virginia suddenly hoped that the rider was bringing her another one. She rushed to the window and looked out—and her heart seemed to stop.

The rider leaping from his mount wore a navy-blue cloak over his blue naval jacket, a black felt officer's hat upon his head. The moment she glimpsed him, even before he turned, she knew and she cried out.

"What is it?" Mary murmured.

It was Devlin, and Virginia could not answer.

He turned, his cloak swirling about his shoulders, his white britches and high boots mud-splashed. He strode toward the house and Virginia gripped the windowsill, breathless and faint. *He had come home.*

The door was flung open. Devlin took one step across the threshold and froze as he saw her.

She could not even smile. Their gazes locked and she could only stare, failing utterly to breathe.

She loved him so much that it hurt.

His gray eyes blazed. "Virginia." He swept off his hat and bowed.

She curtsied. "We...we did not expect you...so soon."

He smiled a little. "I decided to chase an American merchantman across the ocean."

Her eyes widened. "How...how utterly convenient."

And he smiled. "I thought so."

Was he trying to tell her that he had chased a ship across the ocean merely as an excuse so he could come home to see her? As her mind raced with the notion, he approached and kissed her cheek. She closed her eyes, her cheeks flaming, hollow with needing him now. He turned and murmured a greeting to Mary.

"You wonderful man," Mary said, hugging him. Then, smiling, she said, "I have a call to make, in spite of the weather. Edward is not home," she added significantly. She turned and left the front hall.

Virginia bit her lip, her fingers curling into her palms. Devlin handed his cloak and hat to a servant. "I received your letter," he said, his gaze moving over her face as if he were making an inspection of her features.

"I hope it brought you some warm comfort on a cold Atlantic night," she managed.

"Indeed, it did." His smile flashed, brief and strained. "Although I might behead Rex, for I doubt the kiss was a brotherly one."

Virginia flushed, as it hadn't been all that chaste, although Rex had heartily apologized afterward.

"I thought so," Devlin said, appearing vastly annoyed, his silver eyes flashing.

"He is the worst flirt," she said, and then she amended, "with me, at least. He seems to despise all other ladies."

"I do not want to talk about my brother," Devlin said roughly.

The servant had left the hall and they were entirely alone. "Neither do I," Virginia whispered. Tears moistened her eyes. "I am so glad you have come home."

He hesitated, as if he wished to speak.

She did not move.

Then he grimaced and walked over to her, his hands closing over her arms. "I am glad to be here, too," he said as roughly as before.

She swallowed and dared to say, "I have missed you, Devlin."

His expression tightened. He pulled her close and covered her mouth with his.

She cried out, clinging, and in his embrace, she felt warm and loved—safe. His mouth was voracious and Virginia kissed him back as frantically, thrilled when she felt his arousal against her hip.

Suddenly he lifted her into his arms. "Where is your room?" he demanded.

She held on to him tightly. "Devlin, we are in your parents' house!"

"I don't give a damn and I cannot wait another minute to be with you." He pounded up the stairs with her in his arms. His eyes blazed as he said, "I thought that once I was back at sea I would be free. But I was wrong."

She blinked. What did he mean?

"I could not stop thinking about you, Virginia." He seemed grim. "You have haunted my every waking moment. You have haunted my dreams."

She was thrilled. She smiled and said softly, "Then we are even, I think."

His eyes widened as he reached the landing. "Which room?"

Her entire body was already enflamed at the inevitability of what was to be. "The third door on the right," she managed.

He pushed it open with his shoulder and carried her to the bed. He set her down and sat beside her, silent for one moment. "You are more beautiful than ever," he said thickly, touching her cheek. "I expected you to be pale in the midst of winter—your face blooms like a flower, instead."

She hesitated, about to blurt out her suspicion that she was with child, but she thought the better of it. She wasn't quite certain and the moment was perfect; she was afraid to ruin it. "I'm not blooming, I am flushing, Devlin," she said.

He laughed, his hands now deftly undoing the buttons on the back of her dress. "You have never been more beautiful," he said, sliding the dress down to her waist. His eyes widened with appreciation at the sight of her breasts, caressed by the sheer linen of her chemise, now fuller than before and swelling out of her corset. "And you have bloomed, Virginia," he murmured.

"Impudent man," Virginia retorted, no easy feat when utterly breathless and hot.

He tugged her chemise over her head, tossing it aside. "I will show you impudence, madam," he said, and he wrapped a hard arm around her, lowering his head to her bosom.

He nuzzled her voluptuousness, then lipped her nipple. Virginia was very sensitive and she almost swooned from the released flood of desire.

"I do not want to hurt you," he gasped, releasing her and taking her hand and guiding it to his loins. Virginia cried out at his heat and hardness, at the throbbing against her palm. "But I have little patience this day."

"You do not hurt me," she whispered. "Please, hurry!"

He suddenly sat, eyes ablaze, quickly pulling her dress off. Virginia watched him as he removed her drawers and she knew she had never seen him more desperately in need. When she was clad only in her corset and stockings, he palmed her sex.

Triumph flared in his eyes, on his face. "Spread your legs," he said, and as she instantly obeyed, he leaned over her, rubbing his cheek there.

Virginia cried out, overcome with pleasure and excitement. Her body had changed in many ways and maybe their separation had something to do with it, but she knew she would fly into the blue-black heavens in another instant. "Hurry," she cried hoarsely.

His mouth moved over her, thorough and slow, his tongue insistent, a probe.

Virginia began to shatter, crying out, clawing his shoulders.

"Oh, little one, wait for me," he gasped, and suddenly she felt his massive length sliding deeply into her.

But it was too late and she wept with the greatest pleasure she had ever known.

He surged more deeply, crying out hoarsely, instantly spilling himself into her, his huge body racked with pleasure, convulsing over her. When he was done, he moved to his side, pulling her close.

Virginia smiled as she came back to the earth and their bed, turning onto her side, her cheek against his hard chest. He held her tightly there, kissing her temple repeatedly. His kisses were not all that gentle. She instantly realized that he remained huge and hard, ready to take her all over again.

She kissed his chest another time and boldly held him in her hand. "What is this?" She was sly.

He laughed, the sound raw. "I think you know."

"And if I have forgotten?"

He grinned wickedly. "Then I shall have to remind you, darling." And he rolled her over, swiftly entering her at the very same time.

VIRGINIA SAT BEFORE HER dressing mirror, fully dressed, pinning up her coiled hair. Devlin's reflection appeared in the mirror as he moved onto the threshold of the dressing room. He was also fully dressed, but in civilian clothes. Virginia felt herself blush.

It was the following morning and they remained at Harmon House. The only reason that they were not in bed was because she had insisted they go downstairs before they irrevocably scandalized the entire household. In the mirror, Devlin smiled at her and came forward, pausing behind her.

Virginia tucked the last hairpin into her coiffure. "I very much feel like a wife today," she said softly.

He placed his hands on her shoulders. "I should hope you still feel like a bride."

She watched herself blush. "A very happy bride," she breathed.

He leaned down and kissed the bare nape of her neck. "And a satisfied one, I hope." It was not a question.

She turned around on her stool. "You know just how satisfied I am."

"You are such a bold minx," he said with a laugh.

She stood and found herself in the circle of his arms. "And it pleases you, I hope?"

He hesitated. "I am very pleased, Virginia."

Her heart burst into song. Did that mean what she thought it did—could it mean more? Did it mean he was coming to love her—just a little?

He reached into the interior breast pocket of his coat. "I have something for you," he began.

Her eyes widened with surprise as he produced a jeweler's velvet box. "What is this?"

"It's your birthday present."

Her heart stopped. Trembling, she met his steady gaze. "But...you know it's my birthday?"

"Tomorrow, is it not?" He smiled slightly. "All of nineteen, a true woman of the world," he said, his tone teasing.

She smiled, wanting to cry with happiness. "How...how did you know?"

"I made it my business to know. Open it," he said gently.

"Shouldn't I wait until tomorrow?"

"I am sure you will be deluged with gifts tomorrow, as I have no doubt my mother has planned some kind of extravaganza for you."

"No, I asked her for a small family affair. Rex is back in Spain and Sean at Askeaton, so it will be but two-thirds of our family." She wished they could all be present. She lifted the box lid.

Virginia gasped at the sight of a gorgeous amethyst pendant encrusted with diamonds. "This is beautiful, Devlin!" she cried.

"I ordered it made for you before I set sail," he said with a small, pleased smile. "I wanted something to match your eyes."

"Devlin?" She was clinging to his arms. "This is the best birthday I have ever had. Thank you. Thank you for the necklace and thank you for coming home!"

He hesitated. "I had to come home. Happy birthday, Virginia."

LATER THAT DAY, VIRGINIA heard hearty male laughter and recognized Devlin's rich tones. She paused outside of the salon, smiling to herself. Her husband sounded happy, indeed. She was thrilled to hear him laughing with his brothers. She was about to step into the salon when Tyrell spoke.

"And the war?" Tyrell asked. "I've heard rumors that we'll be attacking the entire Chesapeake Bay."

Virginia stiffened, her smile vanishing, drawing back out of sight. What was this? Until that precise moment she had refused to dwell on the fact that he had just returned from a war with her own country. Since his arrival home, she had not asked him a single detail of his tour of duty and he had not volunteered a single fact. She strained to hear, her heart racing madly with distress and fear.

"I'm afraid I can't discuss classified matters, Ty." Devlin's voice had an odd edge to it. "I just received my new orders, however. The war is escalating."

Virginia's heart sank. In the time he had been gone, there had been the news of the defeat of the *Vixen* and some talk of a blockade of the Chesapeake, which was where her own home was located. But that had been all, and it had been convenient to forget the fact that Devlin was in a war being waged against her country and her kin. What did Devlin now mean? And what was the rumor Tyrell referred to? Suddenly she was afraid for Tillie and Frank and everyone at Sweet Briar. But surely the British would not roam about the Virginia countryside, doing battle there! And if he had just received new orders, was he already preparing to leave, when he had only come home yesterday?

She was dismayed, and unconsciously, she touched her belly. What if she was pregnant? They were finally falling in love, they had a future to share. There was simply no place now for a war—any war—in their lives. And especially not one against her homeland.

Virginia hesitated and then darted past the open doors of the salon and into the library. It was late afternoon and the draperies were open, so soft daylight filled the room. But even from the threshold, she could see the papers on his desk.

Her heart lurched, and even knowing that she should not look at a classified document, she hurried to it. The papers there did not interest her, though, and she opened the center drawer. Instantly she found what she was looking for.

Her heart slammed to a stop. Any sense of composure vanished. Trembling, she seized the parchment and read.

Lord Admiral St. John to Sir Captain Devlin O'Neill
Waverly Hall
Greenwich
March 18, 1813
Sir Captain O'Neill,
Pleased be advised of the following. Your orders are to proceed by March 24 to the Chesapeake Bay,

where you shall report to Admiral Sir George Cockburn. In conjunction with Admiral Cockburn, you are to destroy any and all American warships, including those in port. You shall destroy all depots suspected of harboring possible American supplies, including those on land, and any farms or factories involved in the government supply effort; you shall all make every effort to effect the utter ruination of the American coastal trade. You are accorded complete discretion as to the means necessary to carry out the above orders; aiding and abetting runaway slaves is highly suggested, especially to guide marines through the American countryside. While efforts are to be made to avoid harmful intercourse with American noncombatants, any suspicion of direct involvement on the part of such American civilians is to be deemed a serious military threat and you are therefore to act accordingly.

The Right Honorable Lord Admiral St. John
The Admiralty
13 Brook Street
West Square

Virginia went into shock.

"Virginia?"

She looked up, trembling, and saw Devlin in the doorway. She flinched, but somehow she managed to return the letter to its original position in the drawer. Her heart now slammed, hurting her terribly. *He was to destroy American ships, including those in the harbor. He was to take his marines onto American soil and destroy farms, factories and depots. He was to encourage runaway slaves, using them as spies and guides. Oh, God. These were terrible orders, indeed!*

"What are you doing?" he asked, as still as a statue.

She had had no idea of the extent of his orders. How could he participate in such death and destruction when he was married to her? How many American lives would be lost because of his efforts? She swallowed, staring at him. She was chilled to the bone—no, she was chilled to her very soul. "I overheard you and Tyrell," she said unsteadily.

His gaze sharp, he walked toward her slowly, his face that impersonal mask she had hoped to never again see. His gaze slid over the desk—so did hers. He looked up—so did she. Quietly he said, "Did you read my orders?"

"Yes," she whispered, wondering if she were ashen. For she felt terribly faint. She swallowed hard and cried, "Don't go! I need you here! Resign. Resign your commission. Don't go back to war—I can't bear it."

He hesitated, his eyes widening. "Only cowards refuse their duty, Virginia."

"The world knows you are no coward! My God, you have proved yourself a hundred times over, at least!" It was hard to think clearly, she was so shocked by the content of his orders and the devastation he was to wage against her countrymen.

"Virginia," he said, his gaze searching, "I'm a naval captain. You knew that when we married. I am sorry our countries are at war, truly sorry, but this war will pass."

"After how much death? After how much destruction?" And she cried before she could stop herself, "How many Americans have died already because of you, Devlin?"

His gaze widened and he became rigid. "I do not know."

"I think you do." She did not wish to attack him and she knew that was what she was doing. She hurried around his desk and paused before him. "We have been happy together, at last. This war will come between us."

His face was strained. "Only if you let it. Damn it, you shouldn't have read my orders."

"No, I shouldn't have. Devlin, please! Do not go to war against my country!"

He made a harsh sound. "You are distressed, and rightly so. Again, do not let the war come between us. This I ask of you."

She was silent. And she was ill.

He reached for her hand.

She allowed him to take it. "All right. I won't let it come between us," she said, desperately hoping that it was possible to do as he asked.

The mask slipped away and she saw that he was relieved.

VIRGINIA HAD TO TAKE A SEAT. She was moved beyond words, moved almost to tears. The salon was filled with warmth and laughter, and as she sat, she inhaled deeply, looking around the room, smiling.

It was the evening of her birthday, perhaps five o'clock. A fire blazed in the hearth beneath the handsome carved mantel there, where Edward stood with Tyrell, Cliff, Devlin and Sean. The men sipped champagne and chatted quietly, occasionally laughing at one or another remark. Devlin had never been more splendid or handsome, clad in his civilian clothes. He sensed her gaze and half turned, smiling at her. Virginia smiled back, suddenly filled with desire.

She was trying to do as Devlin had asked. It was an extreme effort, but she refused to think about the war. Every time she did, she turned her thoughts to another matter, determined to cherish the time they had left together. The fact that he had been given such terrible orders could not change how she felt about him; she simply loved him too much. And he was right. She must not let the war come between them—especially because she had had her pregnancy confirmed that morning.

She had secretly gone to see a doctor, with only Mary aware of the appointment. Her baby was due the following October.

She smiled and touched her abdomen. She would tell Devlin the news before he left. Her heart skipped and she glanced at him. She prayed he would be pleased.

She also prayed she would not be a widow when she gave birth to their child the following fall, and she worried about the war yet again. If only he did not have to go!

"I wonder if anyone will love me enough one day to match a necklace to my eyes," Eleanor said.

Virginia glanced at Eleanor, who sat with Mary on the moss-green sofa near her chair, a half a dozen opened boxes at their feet. Eleanor and Mary were admiring the necklace that Devlin had given her, which she was wearing.

"Your time will come," Mary murmured. "This necklace suits Virginia perfectly. It truly accentuates the unusual color of her eyes." Mary shared an intimate glance with Virginia and Virginia knew she was thinking about the baby.

"I sense a secret," Devlin murmured, his tone soft and seductive.

And that was when the Earl of Eastleigh walked into the room.

VIRGINIA REMAINED IN SHOCK. She was barely able to comprehend his presence as he bowed; nor could she hear the butler, pale and distressed, as he tried to apologize for the intrusion. What could he want? What was her uncle doing there? And then Devlin started forward.

Virginia's heart lurched with fear as it struck her that Devlin might think to kill Eastleigh for this incident. But both Tyrell and Cliff gripped his shoulders, restraining him. A frightening mask had slipped over his face.

Edward quickly blocked his entrance. "Eastleigh, you are not welcome here."

"Adare," Eastleigh said, his pale blue eyes ice cold. "But surely the lack of an invitation to my niece's birthday was an unfortunate oversight—as was the lack of an invitation to her wedding. I have only come to wish Virginia a most fortuitous birthday. I have even brought her a gift." He turned and gestured at his servant who held a large wrapped parcel.

Devlin shook off his brothers and strode forward, his eyes cold. "Well, well," he said, "the man I had hoped to see. And how is it that you do not seem surprised to see *me,* my lord?"

The two men locked stares. Eastleigh's teeth bared in a parody of a smile. "Why would I be surprised to see you present at your wife's birthday? I had heard you returned, O'Neill. Oh, congratulations on your most advantageous marriage." Suddenly he looked at Virginia and inclined his head. "Congratulations, my dear."

A chill went up her spine. Virginia watched the two men, both reeking of enmity and hatred, and she despaired. If she did not miss her guess something terrible was about to happen. Could she somehow diffuse the situation? She stepped swiftly forward. "Thank you, Uncle. How kind of you to call."

Devlin gripped her arm, silencing her before she could go on. "Save your false words for a foolish man," he said coldly. "My stepfather is correct. You are not welcome here. But before I escort you out, I do have one question. Do you not want to know what fate befell your assassin?"

Virginia gasped. Assassin? What was Devlin speaking of? In confusion and dismay, she stared at him. But he did not seem to be aware of her presence now.

"Assassin?" Eastleigh laughed. "I know of no assassin.

Did someone try to murder you, O'Neill?" He laughed again. "Why think it was me? You have more enemies than can be counted, and we both know it."

Devlin leaned closer, smiling, and it was chilling. "Your assassin failed. But I suggest you watch your back, Eastleigh, as two can play this new game."

Virginia cried out. No one seemed to hear.

"Is that a threat? Have you decided to murder me now? Is my destitution not enough?" He smiled. "Perhaps *your* back needs watching, O'Neill, not mine." He turned and bowed at Virginia. "I do hope you enjoy your birthday gift." He left.

Virginia simply stared after him as Devlin turned, his expression so hard and ruthless it was frightening. She was vaguely aware of Edward rushing to comfort Mary, as she was close to tears. When Eastleigh was out of sight, his footsteps no longer falling, she turned. The room was now filled with an icy tension.

"I'll get rid of that," Tyrell said, lifting the wrapped parcel.

"No!" Devlin strode over and tore the brown waxed paper apart. A painting was beneath.

Virginia could hardly breathe. She was also beginning to feel faint. "What is it?"

Devlin made a rough sound. "Get rid of it. Burn it," he said.

"Stop!" Virginia ran forward and shoved past him. Then she cried out.

The painting was a beautiful portrait of her parents, painted eighteen years ago, her mother lovely and breathtaking, her father proud and handsome. An infant was in their arms—a babe that could only be Virginia. But they were standing in front of a house that Virginia recognized with stunning dismay. It was Eastleigh Hall. And the Earl of Eastleigh stood with them, younger, more vital, less overweight and as proud and overbearing as ever. The meaning of his gift was unmistakable.

She was a Hughes and the earl's niece and nothing could ever change that fact—not even her marriage to Devlin.

"I'll get rid of it," Tyrell repeated grimly, glancing at Virginia. She nodded numbly and he took the canvas and left.

"Mary is going to lie down," Edward said, pausing with her at the door. "Eleanor, come."

Mary smiled apologetically, her eyes moist with tears. "I'm sorry. This evening has not been what I planned..."

Virginia gripped her hands. "It's all right," she whispered. "It was wonderful, really."

As they left Cliff went over to Devlin. "Don't let him provoke you," he said.

Devlin didn't respond, staring furiously out the window at the dusky night.

Cliff turned to Virginia. "Are you all right?"

She nodded her head in the affirmative, but it was a lie. "Perhaps you should leave us," she managed.

He hesitated, glancing back at his brother, but then he nodded and went out.

She and Devlin were alone. He remained at the window now, and it was as if he was unaware that she remained in the room. She looked at his rigid shoulders and back. She could feel his hatred. Worse, she knew he was planning some terrible deed now.

She was ill.

Trembling, she walked up to him. "He tried to assassinate you?" she asked.

He finally glanced at her. "I'm sorry you had to learn of it. It doesn't matter. He failed."

"Of course it matters!" she cried.

"Virginia, I survived the foolish attempt."

"This time!" She knew she was hysterical, but she was

so afraid now for Devlin that she could not think straight. And she was even more afraid for their child. "But what about next time?"

"He is not my first enemy to wish me dead—or attempt to do it, either," Devlin said grimly, reaching for her hand.

She jerked it free and backed away, hugging herself. "This has gone too far! You started this and look at what has happened—you are now in jeopardy!"

Anger blazed. "I did not start this, my dear, he started this fifteen years ago!"

"And that makes it right?"

He was flushed. "I am not in any real jeopardy, Virginia," he warned. "I have been living by my wits for a long time now. No hired thug shall bring me down."

Virginia wanted to weep. So this was how they would live? With Devlin hounding Eastleigh, and Eastleigh hiring assassins to kill him in return? And what would happen when the baby was born? Would she one day find an assassin in her room, too? What if Eastleigh took his hatred of Devlin out on their child?

She inhaled but she could not breathe. She could not live this way.

Devlin turned abruptly back to the window, clearly angry with her. Virginia turned as abruptly and hurried out of the salon, beginning to cry. She found herself next door in the library. It was filled with Devlin's powerful and masculine presence, but she needed no reminder to know how much she loved him.

If she told him about the child, would he change his ways?

Surely he would be able to see that they could not bring their child into a world filled with hatred and revenge.

She was so afraid.

DEVLIN STARED OUT OF THE window but saw nothing but blackness. He was shaking with rage and could not stop, but there was a hollow feeling in his chest. He understood the feeling—it was dread. Although he hadn't turned, he was well aware that Virginia was distressed and that she had run from the room and him.

Did she finally see him as the man he really was? A man filled with ice-cold blood and a heart of hate?

The past few days had seemed like a fairy tale or a dream. He had not recognized the man who laughed and smiled so frequently and who thought of little other than his wife. He had tasted happiness; he had even felt the glimmer of joy. The feelings had been unfamiliar and strange, at once frightening yet oddly welcome, too. For the first time in his life, he felt cherished, and more important, for the first time in his life he knew he was not alone.

And now Virginia was upset and afraid. The most courageous woman he had ever met wanted love and laughter, not war and hate. He had seen the truth in her eyes a moment ago. She had just run from him, and if he dared face his own truth, he was terrified that he would lose her now, when he had only just found her.

He knew he did not deserve such a life. He knew it was a dream, and he would one day open his eyes to find it all gone—the joy, the peace, Virginia.

He reminded himself that he was a soldier first and last, that he knew only a life of constant battle, constant war. He had married her intending to change nothing, and in the few days they had been together *everything* had changed—almost. She had shown him a different kind of life, and a part of him desperately wanted to seize it. But that other part of him felt stronger, more ruthless and more dedicated to revenge than ever. That part of him knew he must finish Eastleigh once and for all and finally allow his father peace.

He had never been more torn. Inhaling harshly, he started after his bride. He could not allow her to weep over her damned uncle in the other room.

Devlin paused on the threshold of the library. Virginia stood by his desk, gripping it as if for support. Tears streaked her face when she turned to meet his gaze.

He wanted to take those tears away, but he made no move to do so, as if his body refused to obey his mind. "I am sorry your uncle had to ruin your birthday, Virginia," Devlin said cautiously.

She wet her lips, the knuckles on her hands turning white. It was a moment before she spoke, and then, she did so hoarsely. "Devlin? These past few days have been wonderful, have they not?"

He started, wondering what this tack meant. "Yes, they have." Wariness filled him now.

She forced a smile. "Isn't it time to forgive and forget? Isn't it time to think about all that we have—all that we could have? A wonderful future awaits us—"

"You go too far," he warned abruptly. Did she think to deter him now? He was not a man to be led around by his bride as if a puppet on a string!

She stiffened. "You haven't heard me out."

"There is nothing to discuss. Not on the subject of Eastleigh. That battle must be waged—and it must be finished, Virginia, to my satisfaction."

She stared at him with her huge, moist eyes, impossibly pale.

He wished he had spoken in a softer, less masterful tone. "He wanted to distress you," he began, but she interrupted.

"Devlin, there is something I haven't told you."

His heart lurched. He did not like her tone or expression. What terrible news did she wish to impart? And he retreated instantly, closing his expression as if she were his worst adversary and not his beautiful bride. "Do tell," he said formally.

She clung to the desk. "I am having our baby."

For one moment, he felt that he must have hallucinated. His heart raced. *"What?"*

"And I beg you," she said hoarsely, "to promise me a life of peace and happiness. To promise *us* that life!"

He jerked, barely able to comprehend what she had told him. *She was with child.* But how? When? His mind raced, calculated. Their child must have been conceived after their marriage in December. Dear God, he was going to be a father—it was too soon!

And Eastleigh's mocking expression as he had stood in Adare's salon just a moment ago filled his mind.

"I beg you to give up your need for murder and revenge!" She began to cry. "I can't bring our child into such a life! Don't you see? We are about to become a family, and I need you to choose."

Once again, it was a moment before he understood her. He was shaking and his knees felt weak and all he could think of was the baby and the fact that he had a ruthless enemy in the world. He stared at her as she wept. Choose? She wanted him to choose? And the ugliest comprehension came.

He inhaled, becoming rigid with anger. "Don't do this, Virginia," he warned. There could be no choice to make! Not yet, not now!

"You must choose!" she cried, trembling wildly.

"Don't ask this of me," he commanded as if on the quarterdeck of his ship. And he felt everything begin to slip away, fading then and there, the joy, the love, the fear...

"You must choose," she whispered. "I will not bequeath

a life of hatred to our child. I will not put our child in jeopardy. Choose, Devlin. Choose us—the baby and me!"

But he could not choose. He simply could not. And he felt his heart disappear, vanishing into nothingness. And with its disappearance, all emotion congealed into ice and was gone.

"Don't!" she begged. And she ran forward. "Don't turn away from me now! Not after all we have shared—not when I am carrying your child!" And she seized his hand and placed it on her abdomen.

He stared at her small, still-flat belly, but there was only emptiness now. No joy, no love, just the dispassionate nature his enemy had left him with when he was ten years old.

"You can have us—or you can have your revenge. But you can't have both!"

He dropped his hand and turned away. "I am sorry," he said, "but you knew my nature when you married me."

She cried out.

CHAPTER TWENTY-SEVEN

VIRGINIA REMAINED IN BED for the entire day, afflicted with a huge migraine and a malaise of the soul. She did not weep. She was too frozen with fear to do so.

She had the baby to consider now. Her unborn child had become her priority. It had been one thing for her to manage a relationship with Devlin, to somehow survive his ruthless obsession and his hard heart, but dear God, what kind of father would Devlin be?

If only she did not love him still...but she did, and she always would.

Virginia did not know what to do, and Devlin was leaving for his tour of duty—for his damnable war—in three more days.

Now she faced the closed bedroom door, dressed for supper. She had not seen him even once since their argument yesterday. He had chosen not to share their room or their bed last night and she had avoided him as well. What should she do? She had no appetite, but that was not the issue. He remained her husband and the child within her womb would always be his. But she no longer wished to compromise herself for the sake of their marriage, for the sake of being with him. It felt as if their marriage was turning to ashes before her very eyes.

Virginia opened the door and went downstairs, trembling nervously, her face stiff with tension and trying desperately to appear natural.

To her surprise and dismay, once in the entry hall she heard male voices that she recognized. Tyrell and Cliff were with him, apparently having a drink before supper. She liked both brothers but now prayed they did not intend to stay and dine with them. Virginia slowly approached the salon. Its double doors were wide open and she saw all three men seated causally there, glasses of wine in hand.

Tyrell and Cliff saw her almost at once and came instantly to their feet. Devlin also stood, but more slowly, and he did not quite look at her. His brothers bowed, but in turn, their smiles faded as she came forward and she knew her distress was clear.

"Good evening," she said, holding her head high.

"Virginia, you are as lovely as always," Cliff murmured, but he had lowered his lashes over his blue eyes, a clear indication that he was merely being gallant.

She thanked him. "I hope you will be staying for supper," she said, aware she was being as dishonest as him.

Cliff looked up, and then he and Tyrell exchanged glances. "I think we have other arrangements," he said.

"I'm afraid that is the case," Tyrell said. He then glanced somewhat darkly at Devlin, who stood as still as a statue. "Take care of your wife," he said, and with a nod at Virginia, he and Cliff set their wineglasses down and walked out.

Alone at last with her husband, Virginia tensed.

He faced her, his expression that mask she knew so well and so hated, and he held out his arm. "I believe supper is being served, Madam," he said.

She flinched. "You never call me 'madam,'" she somehow managed.

His shoulders, already ramrod stiff, tightened even

more. "I am not trying to offend you," he said as if she were a stranger, not his wife.

"Don't do this," she breathed.

His face closed impossibly. "I hardly know of what you speak." He gestured toward the hall. "Shall we?" And without waiting for a reply, he took her arm in his.

She recoiled. Was this how it would now be? A polite mockery of a marriage? A cold and formal relationship, at once tense and strained? "I only asked you to give up hatred, Devlin, for the sake of your child," she whispered through stiff lips.

He started forward as if he had not heard her—clearly pretending that he had not.

But she refused to follow, tearing her arm from his.

He stopped and faced her. "Are we going in to dine?" he asked.

She hugged herself. "Not like this, never like this."

He inclined his head. "Then I am going out," he said.

She started in surprise.

"Madam? I believe I will join my brothers at White's." He nodded at her and abruptly walked out.

She stared after him in shock.

And that night, he did not return.

DAWN ARRIVED, DARK and grim.

Devlin had spent the past two days out of the house. He did not sleep at home, either, and Virginia learned from a servant that he was sleeping on his ship. At least, she thought, he had not gone to another woman.

But their marriage was over and she knew it. There did not seem to be any possibility of saving it.

Her depression knew no bounds. Her world had become dark and black. She could not sleep at night, nor could she get out of bed in the morning. She had no appetite, never mind the child growing inside of her womb. She wept frequently and ignored Hannah's worried glances.

Now, clad in a lavender robe, she stared at her pale, listless expression in the mirror of her dressing room. She had hardly slept last night, as had become the norm, but she had somehow roused herself from her bed, knowing that Devlin would soon set sail. She knew the tides would be high in another hour or so, for she had asked Hannah to check for her yesterday. But Devlin had slept yet again on the *Defiance*. She assumed he was going to set sail for his war without coming to say goodbye. He had broken her heart before, but never like this.

I simply cannot go on this way, she thought as she stared at her impossibly pale reflection.

A knock sounded on her door. She turned, making no reply, wondering what her maid wanted at this unholy hour.

The door opened and from her boudoir she saw Devlin in full dress, his black felt hat in hand, standing on the threshold of the bedroom. She felt her eyes widen and she trembled with surprise.

His expression was hard, but his nostrils were flared and tinged with red—from the cold, she thought. "I see I did not wake you." His gaze quickly took in her untidy appearance. "I set sail within the hour and I have come to take my leave."

She wanted to beg him to love her again, the way he had before. She wanted to tell him that she could live with his need for revenge, if it meant so much to him. But she did not speak because she could not. She did not move; she did not breathe.

His jaw hardened; his eyes darkened. "How are you, madam?"

She wanted to scream, I am dying inside, moment by

moment and minute by minute. But she simply stared. Then, finally, she managed, "As well as can be expected."

"How is the child?" he demanded sharply.

She inhaled and fought for some composure now. "Fine, I believe."

He nodded, grinding down his jaw, and it was a long moment before he spoke, as if he had something to say that he was struggling with.

And she prayed.

But she was wrong. He merely said, "I will return in six months, I think. God keep you, Virginia." And he bowed and turned and left.

She wanted to run after him and tell him to stay safe. But her damnable body simply would not move.

Oh, God. He would go away like this? And what if she never saw him again? What if this was the war that took his life?

Virginia ran to the window. Outside, she saw him striding toward his coach. She struggled to unlatch the panes of heavy glass and heave them open. He was already inside the carriage. Panting from the exertion, she stuck her head outside. The coach began to roll away. "Devlin! God speed," she cried.

But she had no idea if he heard her.

LATER THAT DAY, VIRGINIA stood in a salon in Harmon House, wringing her hands nervously. Devlin's departure had been a stunning blow—and she knew what she must do now.

Cliff entered the room, his stride long but unhurried, his manner as indolent. "Virginia? You wish to see me?" he asked with mild surprise.

She nodded, then wet her lips and said, "Could you close the doors?"

More surprise flickered in his sky-blue eyes. Cliff turned and closed the double doors. "This is very odd," he said, moving toward her. He held out a chair. "Please."

"I would rather stand," she whispered, filled with desperation now.

"What is wrong?" he asked, his gaze intent and searching.

She did not avoid it. "I am with child," she said. He started. "I am with child and I must go home to Sweet Briar, where I was born, and bear my child there."

His expression was one of astonishment.

"You have a fleet of ships!" she cried. "Surely one of them will disembark for an American port? Please, my lord, I can pay for my fare, and I beg you to let me find a berth on that ship!"

He was clearly shocked. "Are you running away from my brother?"

She stiffened. That was not quite the case, but she had no delusions. She doubted they would ever recover what they had so briefly had. Still, her goal was not to leave her husband. She simply had to go home. Her country was at war, Sweet Briar was being threatened, and she must bear her child there, where she would not be alone.

"Virginia—" his tone became kind "—I cannot aid you in such a feat." Clearly he had taken her silence for an affirmative.

She inhaled harshly and sat down. Then she covered her face with her hands. "I love your brother," she whispered, not looking up. "And I always will. But it was one thing for me to bear the brunt of his obsession with the Earl of Eastleigh." She glanced at Cliff and held his gaze. "I have begged him to give up his revenge for the sake of his child. He will not. I must think about our babe now. *Our child comes first.*"

Cliff was grim. "Of course I agree with you. I agree that Devlin must end his obsession—but I am doubtful that he can."

"He can't," she whispered, fighting her tears. "He has made that clear. And he is gone now, gone to war against my country, maybe even against my home. I am not staying here, Cliff. If you do not help me, I will find another way, another ship. I am going home to have my child, and if the war dares come near Sweet Briar, I will defend my land, even if I must defend it against Devlin. I have no choice now."

Cliff stared, his eyes wide and thoughtful. It was a long moment before he spoke. And when he did, he sighed. "I know you will do exactly as you have said. I would rather escort you safely to Sweet Briar than see you on some ship that founders or is attacked. I was setting sail next week for Martinique—I have acquired a sugar plantation there. I will take you home first."

She cried out in abject relief.

"But I will not keep this a secret," he warned.

She began to protest.

"No!" His blue eyes flashed. "You are my brother's wife. He has every right to know where you are—especially as you are with child. I will take you to Sweet Briar, Virginia, but I will also tell Devlin what I have done."

Virginia knew better than to argue. At least she would be escorted safely to her home. She took his large, rough hands in her own. "Thank you, Cliff. Thank you."

He was grim.

IT WAS NOW THE MIDDLE OF MAY. The transatlantic crossing had been a slow and difficult one, with several storms and disadvantageous winds slowing Cliff's schooner down. It had also been a dangerous journey. Cliff, who captained the ship, had ordered a twenty-four-hour lookout for any warships, friend or foe. Twice they had evaded American ships; once, the *Amelie* had even flown the Stars and Stripes in order to provide cover when a pursuit had begun. Cliff had given her his cabin, a luxuriously appointed affair, but otherwise, he had kept his distance, at once formal and polite. That had been fine with Virginia. Her spirits were bleak and she had not wanted anyone to confide in. All in all, the journey had been long and dismal and she was relieved to see its end.

Virginia had one arm around Arthur, who shared the back seat of the open carriage she had hired in Norfolk. With her other hand, she held on to the carriage door as they bounced down the rutted driveway, her home rising in real glory before her. She almost expected to see her mother running out of the front door, waving madly at her and crying with joy; she almost imagined her father on horseback, riding in from one of the fields. She smiled tearfully, for the house remained such a splendid sight, tall and stately and oh, so welcoming. She had come home after all this time, and her smile was her first since leaving Britain, Somehow, she would bear Devlin's child alone and everything would be all right.

She smiled still, even though more tears fell. To even think of Devlin brought crushing heartache. Instead, she gazed at the fields, which had yet to be planted, as it was too early in the year. She could see that the soil was in the process of being burned, which sterilized it before the transplanting of the seedling plants, and her heart leapt for the first time in a long time. Suddenly she was eager to walk the fields and inspect them for fungus, rot and other seedbed disease. She was as eager to inspect the crop of seedlings, protected by a thin layer of mulch, so she could calculate the crop they might harvest at the end of the

summer. She did not expect much, not with the plantation
having been up for sale for most of the past year. But Sweet
Briar was now debt-free, so she could borrow money to get
them through next winter if she had to. And there had been
plenty of rain—she could tell by the thickness of the grass
on the lawns and the abundance of the flowering gardens.

Excitement rippled through her, like the cool, fresh air
that came after a hot summer storm.

She inhaled deeply then. The salty-sweet, thick Virginia
air was like an elixir; her stomach, long since settled,
growled with hunger for the first time in months.

A thin, tall, familiar figure appeared on the porch.
Virginia really smiled and she waved at Tillie as the
carriage halted in front of the house. *She could do this.
Before, she had secretly doubted her strength, but now she
knew Sweet Briar would save both her and the baby.*

"Do come in for a meal before you drive all the way
back to Norfolk, Ned," Virginia told the driver, a man she
had known most of her life.

"Thank you kindly, Miss Virginia—I mean, Mrs.
O'Neill," he said, tipping his felt hat at her.

"Down, Arthur," she said softly, and the big dog
bounded to the ground, wagging his tail enthusiastically.

Tillie had not moved. She appeared immobilized as she
stared toward Virginia in shock.

Virginia climbed down. "Tillie!" And the seed of happiness began to take root.

Tillie screamed. "Virginia! Virginia, it's you!" Skirts
lifted, she flew down the porch steps. Virginia ran to meet
her and they embraced halfway.

"I haven't heard from you since I got your letter in
February," Tillie cried, pulling away and clasping
Virginia's face. Virginia had written her about her marriage
and Devlin's wedding gift of the plantation. "You didn't

tell me you were coming home—why didn't you tell me you were coming home? And why are you as white as a ghost—and so skinny?"

Virginia hugged her again. "There was no time to write since then," she whispered.

"And you're alone? I mean, other than that dog?" Tillie put her arm around her. She stiffened in surprise, for Virginia's cloak had hidden the protrusion of her tummy. "You with child? Honey, you got pregnant so soon?"

Virginia nodded, suddenly incapable of speech. Their gazes locked.

Tillie stared and her brows lifted in confusion. "What's wrong?"

Virginia swallowed hard. "My marriage is over, Tillie, and I am here to stay."

VIRGINIA BUSIED HERSELF with running Sweet Briar, never mind that Tillie scolded her to no end for doing so in her condition. The seedlings were transplanted the last week of May, and it looked as if they had enough plants for an abundant crop. Far to the north in Canada, the British fort of York had fallen to the American troops, and as word of the hugely significant victory traveled about the countryside, her neighbors rejoiced. Still, the toll had been huge, due to an explosion of the garrison's magazine. One county newspaper claimed that more than three hundred Americans were killed in the explosion, twice as many losses as the British had in their defeat.

Virginia did not want to hear about the war, but it was impossible to avoid now that she was home. There was constant fighting in the Canadian Territory. Even more distressing, four Sweet Briar slaves had run away, as had dozens in the rest of the county. Rumor had it they were encouraged by the redcoats, and that they were even fighting for them. There were also terrible shortages of the most basic foodstuffs—sugar was exorbitantly priced at more than $20 a hundredweight in Richmond and Baltimore, almost triple what it had once been. Flour had risen to $4.50 a barrel in Richmond, and Virginia heard it was five times that in New York. Everywhere she went, the hottest topic was the cost of essential food items that no one could now afford. There was no sugar at Sweet Briar and Tillie's jams were sour.

Toward the end of May, Virginia began to feel unwell. It was just a slight lightness in her head and some difficulty breathing, but it was enough to make her feel faint. She worried that she might actually black out if she did not rest. Tillie scolded her endlessly and refused to let her out of the house. Virginia complied, afraid she knew the real reason for her sudden illness. The day before, at church, she had heard that the *Defiance* was hovering off the coast of Maryland with another British frigate, the *Honor,* hoping to do battle with any American warship brave enough to come out of the Chesapeake Bay.

Virginia had done her best to make it appear that she had forgotten about Devlin and her failed marriage. In the month since her return home, she was careful to never mention him, not even to Tillie. But the truth was that she thought about him every day, fear for his safety warring with the grief that had claimed her soul. And the worst part of it was that it was so painfully clear they were on opposite sides of the same war.

It was a warm and humid day. Virginia had asked her foreman, MacGregor, to meet her in the study so they could go over the plantation's ledgers. Arthur was sleeping on the floor near her desk, panting heavily, and Virginia was fanning herself and standing by the window when she saw Frank riding up to the house at a frantic pace.

She was seized with dread. She ran outside, where it was even hotter and more muggy. Perspiration made her face shine and her skin sticky. "Frank?"

His expression taut, he dismounted and hurried up the porch. "Miz Virginia?"

"What is it? What has happened?"

He hesitated.

And somehow she knew. Her heart lurched with a sickening fear. "It's Devlin, isn't it?" There were no secrets at Sweet Briar.

"He gone an' sent the *Honor* away. But it was a trap, Miz Virginia. The *Independence* sailed out, thinking she could get by him, but she couldn't. He sailed right up to us an' started firing when the two ships were about to collide. Our troops done lost control of the *Independence* and the redcoats boarded her—all in fifteen minutes."

Virginia clung to Frank's arm. Devlin had seized one of the American navy's greatest battleships. "Did he destroy her?" she managed numbly. Her head felt light again and her heart raced so swiftly that she could not breathe.

Frank shook his head. "He's sailin' her north, maybe to Halifax, as a prize."

She nodded, still feeling ill enough to faint, hanging on to Frank's solid arm. *Devlin had been so close by. And damn it, she missed him so terribly that she ached for him, night and day, even as he fought and destroyed her own people.* She must work harder, she decided abruptly, for that was the only way to keep her mind from such treacherous thoughts, the only way to keep her heart whole and beating. "Of course—how foolish of me." She wet her lips and tried to slow down her breathing, to no avail. "How many died?"

"I heard half the crew, maybe a hundred sailors."

Virginia made a sound.

"Ma'am? It's worse. There's all kinds of talk in town, talk of an invasion."

Alarm stiffened her spine. "An invasion here?"

"They say them Brits will invade Norfolk real soon—and we be too close to town, Miz Virginia, if you ask me."

Virginia turned toward the house, her heart beating so quickly now that she was becoming alarmed. She rubbed her chest. Sweat beaded on her brow. "I need some lemonade. Would you like some, Frank?" Would the troops come this way, burning and looting as they had done farther south and farther north? Would Devlin participate in the invasion? Were Sweet Briar and her people in danger? They had put together a small arsenal, in case they ever needed to defend the plantation. But Virginia prayed it would not come to that, for she knew they could not win an engagement with any British troops.

"Miz Virginia, I don't like the idea of us bein' so close to Norfolk!" He was afraid and it showed.

She must be calm and strong now, for the sake of Frank and all the people at Sweet Briar who relied upon her. Instead of going into the house for a cool drink, Virginia sat down in a wood rocking chair on the porch and vainly tried to fan herself. "Frank, we're eight miles from the city. Even if they are dastardly enough to invade our small town, we will be safe where we are—our militia and the army will never let them get this far." But it was a lie. The army would have their hands full with an invasion and Virginia knew many who served in the militia by name—they were young boys and old men.

Virginia knew that she could not let Frank see her fear. So she smiled at him. "Could you get me a glass of Tillie's lemonade?"

He hesitated, then finally his expression relaxed. He nodded, tipped his cap and walked into the house.

Her smile vanished. Virginia gripped the arms of her wood rocker, staring out at her beloved fields. It had been bad enough hearing the war news from her frightened neighbors for the past two months and suffering distinct shortages because of the blockade, but still, somehow the war had seemed distant. Now, with the news of Devlin's triumph just off the coast and the rumor of an imminent invasion, the war had become a very real and close threat.

She closed her eyes and was struck instantly with the strongest feeling that she would see Devlin again—soon.

VIRGINIA NEVER SLEPT SOUNDLY. In fact, sleep had become the enemy, for her dreams were filled with pain and heartache. She was always in Devlin's arms, happy and well loved, only to have him turn coldly upon her and walk away. Sometimes she would chase after him as he left, begging him to stay. At other times, he had their child in his arms and she could not even get her voice to work to scream at him to give her baby back.

She awoke now from just such a horrible nightmare, her body covered with sweat, her heart beating frantically. As Virginia sat up in the shadowy bedroom, panting and sobbing, she told herself it was just a dream. She touched her belly to reassure herself; their child was still there, inside her tummy. She lay back down, holding her belly, waiting for her breathing to return to normal, for her pounding heart to subside. It was a very hot and cloying night, and although her windows were open, there was no breeze.

Arthur, who slept on the bed at her feet, suddenly jumped to the floor, growling.

Virginia wiped her forehead with an edge of her sleeveless nightgown, alarmed.

The dog ran to the window, putting both paws on the sill, and growled menacingly again.

Virginia stiffened, now filled with fear. He had become a fine watchdog, but at this hour, no one should be about. She quickly lit a candle and hurried to stand with him at the window. She stared into the night, but it was black and still. Arthur growled long and low once more.

And then Virginia heard the riders approaching.

Fear consumed her.

Arthur barked.

"Quiet," she cried, and as she stared out into the night she saw a flickering torchlight.

Talk of invasion remained...but the British invaded by day, not by night.

Still, no one roamed about the countryside at night. It was far too dangerous.

Virginia returned to her bed and took a pistol from under the pillow. Her hands were shaking badly and it took her a moment to load it. In the hall she met Tillie and Frank as they came upstairs. and Frank carried a hunting rifle. Both were wide-eyed. "Riders coming," Tillie whispered.

"I know, I saw," Virginia whispered back. "Do you know how many there are?"

"I seen four or five," Frank said, low.

For one moment, standing there on the landing at the top of the stairs, they all stared at one another in the gloom, trying to decide what to do.

And they heard a number of horses halting in front of the house.

Virginia flinched, facing Tillie, when someone began knocking on the front door.

"Maybe we should hide?" Tillie whispered.

But Virginia almost swooned with relief. "The British do not knock," she said. "I'll go answer it."

Tillie seized her. "And honest folk don't come out at this hour!"

She was right. "Stay behind me in the shadows. Frank, don't hesitate to use that rifle if it sounds like our visitors have a nasty business in mind."

Whoever had come calling at the midnight hour was pounding again on the door. Virginia went slowly downstairs, filled with trepidation, followed by both slaves. At her side, Arthur growled, his hackles up.

Virginia hurried to the door, her heart slamming with alarm and fear. "One moment," she said, putting the candle down. The baby chose that moment to deliver his first kick, a solid and strange blow, and she hesitated, stunned. But she had no moment to dwell on this strange miracle, as the person outside banged again, three times. Keeping the pistol in the folds of her nightgown, her finger found the trigger. She opened the door a crack.

A man stood there and even in the darkness, she knew. She was paralyzed. Arthur was not. He rushed forward, wagging his tail with excitement, his entire body writhing with happiness.

"Get down," Devlin said, pushing inside, as the dog leapt up on him. He closed the door behind him.

The dog sat, his tail thumping on the floor, grinning at him.

Virginia began to shake. In spite of everything, Devlin's cold, gray eyes were the best thing she had ever seen. "Do you always open the door for strangers?" he said.

She wet her lips, briefly incapable of speech. She whispered, "Enemy soldiers do not knock."

He inclined his head, accepting her statement, and his gaze slid over her belly.

She wanted to seize his hand and place it on their child, but she did not. Too well, she suddenly recalled the last time he had touched her that way.

"How are you, madam?" he asked softly.

Virginia realized that she was trembling wildly. Why had he come? Had he risked his life merely to see her? "We are fine, the child and I," she managed. She was so stunned she could barely think straight, but there was a seed of hope flaring within her now.

He studied every inch of her face. "Cliff told me you were here. I almost killed him for what he did—until I realized that you would have found another ship on which to come. Instead, I had to thank him for keeping you and the child safe. This is madness, Virginia."

She had wrapped her arms around herself, because what she really wanted to do was to wrap her arms around him. "I was born here, Devlin. Our child will be born here, too."

He was not pleased. "The war is close. I've risked the lives of four good men to call at this hour," he said swiftly now. "I have come to tell you to stay at Sweet Briar for the next week. And I mean it, Virginia. Do not leave this plantation," he warned.

Something terrible was about to happen and he knew what that was. "Why?"

"I am afraid I cannot tell you why, but Sweet Briar will be spared."

She bit her lip hard, causing it to bleed. "And why..." It was so hard to speak. "And why would my home be spared?"

"Because I have demanded that it be spared," he ground out.

She nodded, having expected him to say that, pleased. But her fear was greater than any pleasure now. "Is it Norfolk? Will they invade the town?"

"You know I cannot give you any details."

She nodded, briefly closing her eyes. *Could he not take her in his arms, just this single time?* "One week?"

"Maybe more. It will depend on factors I cannot control."

He watched her closely. "You will know when it is safe to leave the plantation."

She leaned heavily against the wall. She felt certain an invasion of Norfolk was imminent. She must warn the town. Despair crashed over her. If only the damned war would end. Maybe then they would have a chance—but even so, the subject of his revenge still stood in their way.

He hesitated. "Virginia, I want your promise, your word, that you will obey me this one single time. Your life and the child's may depend on it."

She knew he was about to leave. Her despair grew. "Yes... Devlin?"

He was grim. "We must go."

"Do you wish to rest...here?" She wct her lips, wishing he would stay.

"I cannot. The county is crawling with scouts."

She nodded, seized with anguish.

"I have to go," he repeated harshly, their eyes colliding. His expression was filled with anguish, too, or at least she thought so. He quickly looked away as if to compose himself, before facing her one more time. "I have one question for you."

She wanted to beg him yet again not to leave her, for her nightmare was now coming true. But she did no such thing. The sane part of her knew he must leave, and swiftly, for if he and his men were captured they would all be imprisoned, or worse. She inhaled. "Please."

"Have you left me?"

She stared, stunned. Of course she had, though not by choice. Everything had changed since she had arrived on American soil—and nothing had changed, nothing at all. Virginia did not hesitate. She did not have to think about her answer; her heart answered for her. "No."

His expression tightened. And before she knew it, he

swept her into his arms, hard, and up against his chest, his mouth seizing hers.

Virginia cried out as their mouths fused. In his powerful embrace, she felt safe—and she knew then that he loved her. Frantically they kissed, again and again, the war outside a burning fuse set to explode at any moment.

He pulled away, nodded at her, and went out the door.

For one moment, she did not move, stunned and tearful. Then she ran after him but paused on the porch, clinging to the rail, as he strode to his mount. "Stay safe, Devlin," she said thickly as he swung up into the saddle.

His stead pranced, sensing a gallop at hand. Devlin controlled the beast, turning it to face her. He nodded at her. "Do as you have promised," he said.

"I promise," she breathed.

He stared for one more moment, and then he wheeled the bay and galloped off, his men flying with him. She was vaguely aware of Tillie coming to stand beside her, putting her arm around her. They stood there for a long time, staring blindly out into the night after Devlin and his men.

CHAPTER TWENTY-EIGHT

THE ATTACK ON NORFOLK quickly failed. Although the British began an attack both by land and by sea, apparently with heavy reinforcements, a huge summer storm prevented the landing of half of their marines and those that succeeded were decimated by the heavy artillery fire of the American regulars. Within two hours, the British forces withdrew

The news of the American victory rapidly swept through the county and reached Sweet Briar by the end of the day. Once again, Virginia was not quite well. She sat in the kitchen as Tillie prepared a light supper of fried greens, ham and eggs, fanning herself. It was a very warm day, but that was not why she could not seem to breathe properly and she knew it. She was also light-headed, enough so that she saw dancing lights in the room and her heart raced and pounded uncomfortably. When Frank came in, beaming, to impart the news of their triumph, she could not breathe at all.

As he began to speak— "Turned tail and ran, cowards, all of 'em" —her world grayed and began undulating and she began to fall.

"Frank, help her," Tillie screamed.

Virginia fought the blackness and she fought for air. Images of Devlin as she had last seen him assailed her as she clawed someone's arms. Her last thought was she needed her husband, and then the blackness came.

She awoke slowly in her bed, stripped down to her chemise and drawers, with an ice compress on her throbbing head. Tillie sat beside her, her eyes huge with fear. Virginia tested her lungs and found she could breathe normally and she inhaled hard. Relief assailed her. Then she smiled. "Tillie. The baby. He kicked again." It was true. Just before she had passed out, she had felt her child kick.

Tillie did not smile. "You need to see a doctor. You swooned and hit your head on the floor! I sent Frank to go get Doc Barnes." Her tone meant she would tolerate only compliance.

Virginia closed her eyes. These attacks where she felt faint, her heart beating so hard that it hurt her, were becoming more and more frequent. She was afraid. This time she had fainted and hit her head—what if this happened yet again? She looked at Tillie. "I agree with you. I need a doctor. Something is wrong. I'm afraid for the baby, Tillie."

Tillie stood, looking ferocious. "I know what is wrong! You need your husband home, that's what's wrong. He broke your heart and now you're sick because of it! How dare he treat you so! How can he war against *us?*" she cried.

Virginia did not know how to respond, because she had to wonder if Tillie was right. It almost seemed that whenever she heard word of him or his actions, or some war news that might involve him, she could not breathe and she felt faint. It was as if her anxiety over where her husband was and what he was doing was simply too much for her to bear. And seeing him so briefly last week— being in his arms one more time—made her love him more than ever. It made their separation hurt more than ever, too. Virginia desperately yearned for the future. Just as desperately, she feared what that day might bring.

But when Doc Barnes visited the next day, he insisted it was exhaustion combined with her pregnancy and the strain of the war. "A small woman like you needs a man at home to run things," he said, snapping closed his satchel. "I heard all about that husband of yours, fighting for the enemy! No good can come of a divided marriage, missy. I feel right in telling you that, as I've known you since you were born."

Still in bed and feeling somewhat better, Virginia smiled at him. "So what do you suggest?"

"Get your man to throw down his arms and come home," Barnes challenged. Although close to sixty, with shocking white hair, he stood as straight as an arrow.

"We are estranged," Virginia said softly.

"As if I don't know! Whole county knows! You stay in bed if you don't want to lose that baby." With that last bit of abrupt advice, he walked out.

Virginia looked at Tillie. "It's late June. The baby won't be born until sometime in October. I can't stay in bed for three or four months!"

"You may have to, whether you like it or not." Tillie hesitated. "I think we should tell the captain how ill you are."

Virginia froze. Then she said, "I'm not ill. And Devlin has enough to worry about."

"He should know," Tillie said stubbornly.

Very grim, Virginia patted her bed and Arthur leapt up, sprawling his length down beside her. She stroked him, seeking comfort. "I want to see another doctor, Tillie. That's what we should do." Surely she would not have to stay in bed for months on end. Surely everything was all right.

Tillie sighed. "You are still as stubborn as a mule."

Virginia watched her walk out, sinking back against the

pillows, her arm around Arthur. A part of her desperately wished to do as Tillie wanted, but Devlin had enough on his mind. Besides, they were separated—and she was proud. But he had come once to see her. Maybe he would come again.

HAMPTON WAS A SMALL, sleepy town compared to the bustling port and commercial center of Norfolk. Several days later, Virginia was feeling well enough to make the short trip there; Frank drove the buggy and Tillie sat in the back seat with her, both of them dressed in their best day gowns, bonnets and pelisses. Virginia hadn't had another attack since the other day. And it was a truly pleasant summer day, warm but not humid. In fact, the sky was a robin's-egg blue, with hardly a cloud to mar it. "We're an hour early," Virginia commented.

"Better than an hour late," Tillie said. "Do you want to walk a bit before we go see Dr. Niles?"

"Why not?" Virginia smiled a little. Maybe a stroll through the quiet town would help her to get her mind off of Devlin. His strange midnight visit had given her so much to think about and so much hope.

They alighted from the carriage not far from a pawnshop. "Should I wait here?" Frank asked.

"Why don't you go get our flour while we walk? Meet us in two hours at Dr. Niles's," Virginia said. They had ordered one single sack last week and Tillie'd promised she'd make a pie.

Frank nodded and drove the buggy off.

Virginia smiled at Tillie as they paused before the shop window. Displayed were a gold watch, a pretty silver locket, two fine cameos and filigreed earrings with topaz stones. The earrings would be lovely on Tillie. Virginia was about to suggest they step inside when she heard an explosion.

It was terribly close by and Virginia instantly tensed with fear and dread. Surely this was a blast from someone's furnace or oven, or maybe even the ordnance belonging to the militia!

"What was that?" Tillie asked warily, pale beneath her dark complexion.

"I don't know," Virginia said. In truth, she was afraid it was not an innocent explosion. Virginia grabbed Tillie's hand and they ran down the block and around the corner, which afforded them a view of the inlet and, just beyond it, the Chesapeake Bay.

Her heart stopped.

"Dear God," Tillie whispered.

Virginia stared in horror. Two huge ships had cruised into the inlet and were dangerously close to the shore. Dozens of rowboats, all loaded with scarlet marines, were being launched. And as she stared, paralyzed, both ships fired broadsides directly at the town.

They screamed and ducked. A house down the block was struck. Windows behind them shattered.

Virginia and Tillie looked at each other and shrank against the wall of a building. "We're being attacked," Tillie exclaimed.

Virginia was in disbelief.

Suddenly a troop of militia came running toward them from farther down the block. The men wore their blue-and-gray uniforms, all homemade, and carried muskets, pistols and the occasional sword. More cannons were fired from the two ships and the first battery of rowed boats was almost upon the shore. Virginia stared at the closest frigate. She knew the *Defiance* from any distance, any angle. It was Devlin.

Tillie leapt up and ran to the passing militiamen. "What's happening?" she cried, seizing the arm of one of the men.

Blond, dirty and blue-eyed, no more than eighteen, he paused, grim. "They're attacking the town. It's O'Neill and Cockburn. They must be a thousand strong and we have only militia to defend the town!" He shook Tillie off and ran after his regiment.

Virginia came to stand beside her, faint now with horror and fear. She turned to stare at the shore as the first line of attacking British marines leapt from their craft. There was no Virginia militia to greet them. Another broadside sounded; Tillie and Virginia ducked and ran to the closest building for shelter. Crouching there, they saw smoke billowing from the northern edge of town, where apparently a fire or fires had started. More broadsides exploded.

"We have to find Frank and get home," Tillie said fiercely.

She was right. But Virginia did not move, thinking about Devlin standing on the quarterdeck of the *Defiance,* commanding his men, ordering them to attack her town, her people, Tillie and herself.

The baby kicked and she soothed him with her palm.

But she was sick, and it was not the illness that had been afflicting her these past few months. How had their marriage—their love—come to this terrible moment?

"Virginia, let's go," Tillie said, gripping her arm.

Virginia took one last look at the strip of beach, but to her amazement and utter dismay, still no militia appeared to stop the invaders. Hundreds of redcoats were running up the beach and would soon reach the town. She turned away, beginning to tremble with fear. "Let's go," she said hoarsely.

Holding hands, they lifted their skirts and ran down the block and around the corner. The moment they did so, they skidded to a stop.

Hundreds of British soldiers, including some cavalry,

were rushing down the street, muskets blasting, sabers raised. The militia who were charging to meet them formed a pathetic resistance, a mere handful of men. Aghast, Virginia could not move, watching the massacre taking place before her very eyes. One by one, every single American militiaman was slain in the matter of a moment. Virginia had never seen so much blood and death. She gagged, clutching her belly, vaguely aware of the tears streaming down her face.

Devlin was a part of this.

Virginia turned and retched.

Tillie held her, whispering urgently, "We need to go! There's more on the way!"

Virginia's heart pounded with sickening force. She turned and fled back the way they had come, her arm in Tillie's, and when they turned the corner they paused, facing each other in real fear. Virginia wondered if her eyes were as wide and horrified as Tillie's. "They must have planned a second assault from the rear—they must have landed other troops farther up the inlet," Virginia whispered, trembling.

"How do we get out of here? We cannot leave Frank," Tillie cried.

Virginia did not know how they were going to get out of the town. "Come," she whispered. They could hardly stay where they were, so close to that terrible battle, and as they ran down the block, a building behind them exploded, then burst into flames. They turned onto another street and then leapt back against a brick house. A hundred British troops were fighting some dozen militiamen with muskets blazing and swords clanging. Within moments, not a militiaman was left standing and a river of blood ran through the street.

Virginia choked on bile.

Tillie was sobbing, but soundlessly.

The redcoats hadn't seen them as they stood huddled in a doorway, the mounted officers ordering the infantry to regroup. Their predicament had become crystal clear.

The town was overrun. Hampton would fall. It would be a massacre. How in God's name would they escape? Could they even survive?

"Virginia," Tillie said tersely, poking her with an elbow.

Virginia followed her gaze and froze in abject horror at the sight of a mounted officer wearing the blue coat of the British navy.

"Over there," a British army officer shouted.

Virginia jerked and saw a man stepping out of his stable. She knew him well—it was the Hampton blacksmith, John Ames, holding his hunting rifle. As he lifted it, a dozen muskets blasted and he fell.

A woman screamed. She came running out of the stable, screaming still, and Virginia shouted, "No, Martha!" to his wife, but it was too late. Martha flung herself down on her husband's body as Virginia saw a marine aim his musket at her. The British soldier fired and hit the woman, clearly killing her. Virginia could not move, stunned.

Tillie had taken Virginia's hand. "They're murdering innocent people," she said hoarsely. "We've got to go."

Virginia turned, her heart lurching with dread, seeking out the naval officer in blue. Instantly she found him. She cried out.

"What is it?"

It was Thomas Hughes.

She stared at him across the street, a battlefield of the wounded and the dead, and a chill went down her spine.

What was he doing there? As far as she knew, his career had been spent in the offices of the Admiralty in London. But she could not think about him now.

Because Tillie was dragging her away and shouting at her to run. Virginia realized that they had been seen—and a dozen marines had turned their way.

As they started firing, she and Tillie ran.

"JESUS CHRIST," DEVLIN CRIED, sitting astride the horse he had summarily taken from a civilian.

The town was an inferno. The dead and the dying littered the streets, both militia and civilians, women and children. The attacking forces had been two thousand strong, to ensure a decisive and swift victory after the humiliation of Norfolk. Devlin had seen soldiers go berserk and burn, rape, loot and murder before, but he had not expected to see the terrible plunder he was now witnessing. Word had quickly reached him aboard the *Defiance* that the British marines were out of hand—mostly fueled on by the French who fought with them, prisoners of war who had enlisted to avoid their confinement. Yet he doubted all the blame lay with the Frenchmen in their ranks—he suspected Cockburn had encouraged the carnage, damn his black soul to the fires of hell.

Even now, a group of marines, mostly inebriated, were destroying a shop, the nearby buildings entirely in flames, a dead woman and child in the middle of the street.

"Lieutenant," he shouted in fury to one of the British officers.

The officer rode up to him. "Yes, sir?"

"Stop those men and arrest them all," he ordered. And he was thinking of his wife.

"But, sir!" The young officer was wide-eyed.

"Shoot them if you have to!" he said grimly. "All troops are to return to their respective commands. Our work is done here. We have clearly won." Inside, he was sick, a sickness that reached his soul.

But he shoved it aside. The battle might be over, but there remained much work to be done. He spurred his mount into a canter, determined to inspect the town. But inspection was a real impossibility. British troops ran amok everywhere. As he turned the corner he discovered two more of his troops in the act of raping a woman, surrounded by a dozen cheering men. Seized with fury, Devlin did not pause. He unsheathed his sword and charged the men. Instantly several turned and fled, the others backing away. The woman scrambled to her feet and ran.

"Stand at attention," he snapped, the urge to strike them all down wild and huge. They stared at him with wide, fearful eyes. "There is to be no more plunder, no rape, no looting. Report to your respective commands."

The men stood down. "Aye, sir," one said, his eyes popping.

He spurred his mount on, thinking of Virginia again. This was her home—the town was close enough to Sweet Briar that she must frequent it often—and he hated what he and the British had done. At least she was spared the sight of this, he thought grimly, and he thanked God for that.

But it did not seem as if the town could be saved. Half of it would be ashes by nightfall, and he was afraid to count the American dead. Not for the first time, he was silently grateful that Virginia was safe and sound at Sweet Briar.

As always, regret and grief warred in his chest.

Dusk began. The battle was over except for a few isolated incidents; most of the troops had been brought back under control. Devlin dismounted to inspect one scene, where dozens of militia and civilians lay dead or dying in the street, the British medics already present and tending to their own. "What is the tally so far?" he asked, weary beyond words.

"Our losses are few, sir," a young doctor said. He was covered in soot and blood, as was Devlin, though he hadn't realized it until that moment. "But I'm afraid the Americans have suffered in the hundreds."

"How many hundreds?" he asked, a movement catching his eye. There would be hell to pay for this day.

"Three, four, five, it's impossible to say just now."

Devlin narrowed his eyes. He knew that man lurking across the street, did he not? And then Devlin recognized the slave, having seen him once before, at night, hiding in the front hall at Sweet Briar. He strode across the bloody street, avoiding tramping upon the bodies there. "You, man, wait!"

The black man turned and began to run.

"Damn it, halt! Halt before I fire," he roared, the threat an idle one.

The man froze, hands lifting in the air.

Devlin hurried to him. "Turn around. I will not hurt you," he said. The man obeyed. "You're from Sweet Briar."

He nodded, eyes wide with both fear and recognition. "An' you be Miz Virginia's husband. The captain," he said.

He now nodded, a sudden, terrible inkling beginning. "She is safe, is she not? She did obey me when I told her to stay at the plantation?"

The man's eyes filled with tears. "No, sir!" he cried. "She done come to town to see a doctor, as she's been poorly for some time now, and then the fighting began and I don't know where she is!"

Devlin's world tilted wildly. And for the first time in his life he knew horror.

"She is here?" he shouted. "My wife is here, in this town, now, today?" he cried.

The man nodded.

"Where?" he gasped, seized with a fear he had never before experienced. Had she been wounded? Raped? Was she even alive? How could she have survived this terrible battle? "Where did you last see her?" He realized he was shaking the man.

"I'll show you, sir," the man cried.

Together they ran through the burning town. It seemed to take hours to arrive at a shop that had its display window broken, the entire interior looted, but Devlin knew it had taken mere minutes. "I left 'em here to shop for a bit, before goin' to the doctor," Frank said on a sob.

Devlin went cold inside, and slowly, his hand on his sword, he looked around.

Dead littered the streets. A few shops and homes burned. Dusk was deepening. There were stars tonight, stars and the beginning of a full moon. He felt helpless then.

If she's dead I will die, he thought. *And I will kill whoever was responsible.*

But he was responsible, wasn't he?

For if it weren't for his damned obsession with the Earl of Eastleigh and his refusal to put revenge aside, she would be safely at Waverly Hall, not here in this hellhole of blood and death.

"Help me find her," he said.

"I THINK IT'S SAFE TO GO," Virginia said hoarsely. They had spent the entire day hiding in the attic of someone's home. From a tiny window there, they had seen death, destruction, murder and rape. They had seen vicious brutality, unspeakable carnage and mass mayhem. They had seen so much blood and it flecked and stained their faces, hands and clothes. Once, troops had entered and searched the house, but had not bothered with the attic where they hid, faint with fear. Miraculously, the house had somehow been spared, when half of the town surrounding them seemed to be burning still.

Virginia was shaking uncontrollably, as was Tillie. She remained in a numb state of fear and terror. Still, she thought about Devlin. He might be ruthless, but she was sure, as she had never been so sure of anything, that he would never condone what had been done that day.

She looked at Tillie. Her long, curly hair had come down to hang wildly about her shoulders. Blood smeared her pelisse, her dress was torn and muddy, and her eyes were wide and wild. Virginia knew she must look as frightful, as terrified, as her friend. "Shall we try to go?" she whispered raggedly. Her heart continued to beat hard and fast, uncomfortable in her chest. Every time the house creaked, she flinched and whirled, raising the musket she had taken from a dead man, expecting to confront a British soldier on the attic's threshold and prepared to fire first.

Tillie nodded, looking frightened and uncertain.

The street below was empty, although two buildings still burned. They crept through the house and slipped outside, holding their guns so tightly their knuckles were white. It remained hard to breathe, because of the fear, because of the smoke, and because of the stench of death. The night was starry and lit by a full moon.

Virginia fought tears. "So many have died, and for what? Free trade? Land in Canada? For what?" she cried, shaking wildly.

Voices could be heard, drunken, leering, approaching.

"Hush," Tillie said hoarsely. "You hush until we are safe at home."

Breathless with renewed fear, Virginia leaned close and whispered, "We have to find Frank."

Tillie's eyes suddenly overflowed with tears. "We both know he can't be alive."

Virginia didn't want to believe it. But Tillie was probably right. They started down the street at a quick pace, Virginia determined to ignore the aching in her belly. She had been fighting mild cramps all day and the baby had been kicking.

Please hang on, she silently told her unborn baby. *Just a little longer and we will be safe at home.*

She ran alongside Tillie, wishing Devlin might appear and safely spirit her away, then tell her that he was wrong, he was sorry, that he still loved her and he always would and that they would make their marriage right.

They turned the corner and came face-to-face with five dangerous, bloody, red-coated men.

They whirled to run the other way.

A man suddenly blocked their path, his sword raised.

Instinctively Virginia raised the musket, finding the trigger, aiming at him. Then she saw the navy-blue jacket, the gold buttons and epaulets. She saw the clear gray eyes, the hard face. She began to shake and her musket waffled wildly.

"Virginia," Devlin said harshly. "Put the musket down." He lowered his sword.

Devlin. She had been praying for him to come and he was there. Stunned, she started to lower the gun. "Devlin," she whispered, suddenly flooded with relief. And she was an instant away from moving into his arms.

But his expression changed. His eyes went wide and his sword was raised. "Virginia," he shouted in warning.

And in that instant, she felt the hostile presence behind her. But before she could react, she was seized from behind. As she twisted, she met glazed eyes, a toothless grin and saw the man's scarlet coat. Other marines were with him and one held a fiercely struggling Tillie.

"Got me a nice whore," the man laughed, his breath foul with rotten teeth and whiskey.

"Devlin!" Virginia cried, trying hopelessly to break free

of the marine's grasp. And suddenly his grip eased and the marine howled in pain, hot liquid spraying over her. Dumbfounded, she saw that the hand still attached to her breast was severed from the marine's arm. As dumbfounded, he stared at his armless shoulder.

A saber whistled and the marine's head disappeared.

Virginia stumbled away, gagging, as the armless, headless body collapsed at her feet. She turned to see Devlin assault the other marine, his face frightening in its fury. As he landed blow after blow, she went down on her hands and knees, crawling away as fast as she could, somehow realizing that Devlin was insane with rage. Now, nearly paralyzed with terror, she turned from the ground and saw four dead marines not far from where she knelt. Devlin was viciously attacking the last soldier, clearly intent on murdering him, too. Suddenly Tillie was beside her on the ground, but she had eyes only for Devlin, wide and aghast.

A voice whispered in the night. *"O'Neill."*

It was soft, taunting. Virginia knew that voice and knew the threat and she desperately wanted to warn Devlin. But the earth had tilted wildly and she had to hold on tight. Somehow, as her world spun around, she managed to look up. And the last thing she saw was Thomas Hughes standing behind Devlin, smiling as he raised his musket and aimed it at his head. And the last thing she heard was his gun being fired.

CHAPTER TWENTY-NINE

HER DREAM WAS A TERRIBLE ONE; soldiers were everywhere, killing one another, and Devlin stood on the other side of a wall of fire, shouting for her, but she dared not run to him, for to do so would mean being burned. Desperate, she held out her arms; between them, the fire roared. "Devlin!" she wept.

"It's all right."

Virginia gasped, her eyes flying open, certain he had spoken, and as sleep instantly fled, she recognized her bedroom at Sweet Briar. She was there in her own bed. She turned her head, whispering, "Devlin?" She needed him so—she had never needed him more.

Tillie gripped her hand and stroked her forehead. "You're awake," she said softly.

Virginia blinked, a terrible dismay beginning. "Is...is Devlin here?"

"No, honey, he is not."

And she lay back against the pillows, closing her eyes, seared with ghastly recollections of the battle of Hampton. And suddenly she could see Thomas Hughes pointing a gun at the back of Devlin's head. *Devlin had been there. He had come to her rescue when soldiers had seized her from behind. He had been enraged as she had never before seen him, murdering one soldier after another. And then Thomas Hughes had appeared, raising his pistol, pointing it at the back of Devlin's head.*

And she had heard the shot, hadn't she?

"Where's Devlin?" she cried, her heart beating frantically, filled with fear. "Please, God, tell me he's all right!"

"Doc Barnes gave me some laudanum. Here, let me give you some," Tillie began, holding a cup of tea laced with the drug.

Virginia struck her hand away, the cup and saucer falling to the floor. *"Where is Devlin?"*

More tears fell down Tillie's face. "He went mad when he saw those men grab you. He killed them both, then went after the man holding me. He killed him, too. I never saw so much rage, honey, and he did it all in a single moment," Tillie whispered.

She seized Tillie's wrist. *"Is he alive?"*

The tears became a flood. "I don't know," Tillie wept. "Someone shot him from behind—and I didn't see anymore—I had you to take away!"

Virginia somehow sat up. Her heart pounded with sickening force. The baby chose that moment to kick. She clutched her belly, trying to calm herself for the child's sake, but it was impossible. *Devlin could not be dead.* "It was Tom Hughes," she said hoarsely, in horror. "I saw him, I saw him shoot Devlin from behind. He wanted to murder him in cold blood!" And she began, finally, to cry.

Was this how Devlin's obsession with his father's murderer would end? With his own murder, as well?

Virginia closed her eyes and tried to breathe. She demanded composure and self-control of herself. Grief and fear would not serve her now. If Devlin were alive, she had to find him; she had to find him even if he were dead. But he could not be dead!

"Help me get dressed," she said, and threw her legs over the bed.

"You're supposed to stay in bed until the child is born," Tillie shouted at her.

"My husband may be dead," Virginia said quietly. She stood, holding on to the bed for support. Grief and fear continued to rack her, but she fought them both. How calm she sounded. "You can come with me or you can stay here. But I am going to find my husband, one way or the other."

IT WAS A BRIGHT, HOT AFTERNOON and the town stank of death. Buzzards flew in the skies overhead, circling with deadly intent. The British were gone, of course, and the inlet and bay were blandly vacant except for a bobbing fishing ship. The American army had arrived and had set up a makeshift fort with a prison camp and field hospital on the perimeter of town.

Virginia was weak with fear and exhaustion and she walked with Tillie holding her under one arm. Frank trailed behind them, ever vigilant, as if expecting the hordes of British to descend upon them once again. A soldier at the camp's gates had pointed out Captain Lewis, the camp's commander, and she approached him now slowly from behind. She continued to hang on to her composure with every ounce of strength she had left, as it was all she had.

She burned with determination now. She would find Devlin, and she would find him alive.

But she was so afraid, because she knew Tom Hughes had shot him with murder in his mind.

Lewis was in a fierce conversation with several officers, all of whom turned and strode swiftly off as Virginia paused before him. He was not much older than she was, with bright blond hair and blue eyes, his cheeks sunburned, and his expression turned weary as he faced her. "Let me guess," he said heavily. "You are missing a husband, brother or father. Here's the list. It is incomplete."

Virginia accepted a sheaf of papers he lifted from the table he was apparently using as a field desk. "My husband is a British officer, sir. Perhaps you would know if he were captured or killed." She remained amazed at her calm tone. She felt as if she floated outside of her body, completely detached, watching a magnificent performance.

For she dared not feel.

If she felt, she would come apart, she would become crazed, and she would never be able to locate Devlin.

The stakes were so high.

His brows lifted and his eyes showed some interest now.

"His name is Captain Devlin O'Neill." She held her head with pride.

His jaw tightened. "O'Neill? The captain of the *Defiance?* The one who did this?" He gestured toward the hospital just beyond them, a sea of tents, with the wounded lying on pallets and blankets, bloody, bandaged, moaning and crying for help. A few doctors and staff were trying to attend to the hundreds needing attention.

"My husband would never condone such an attack."

"No?" His jaw was hard, his skepticism obvious. "I have not seen his name on either list."

She glanced down. One page was for the dead, another for the wounded. "You said these lists are incomplete?"

"They are."

"And what about prisoners of war?"

He made a mocking sound. "There are only two dozen."

She swallowed. "I'd like to tour the dead, the wounded and the prisoners, Captain."

He shrugged. "If you find O'Neill in our control, I shall be a very happy man." He turned. "Sergeant Ames! Escort Mrs. O'Neill to the morgue, then allow her to tour the hospital and the prisoners of war."

A burly, grizzled man came running. "Yes, sir." He saluted. "This way, ma'am."

Virginia followed with Tillie still holding her arm, the sergeant shortening his stride to accommodate her slower steps. "The hospital's right here," he said, "morgue's just outside of camp. 'Course, it ain't really a morgue, but it's what we call it."

"I am looking for a British naval officer," she said as they crossed over toward the field hospital.

"Mostly Americans here. Shouldn't be too hard to find someone British—and in blue," he said. He did not seem at all curious that her husband was British and Virginia was thankful for that small boon.

Fifteen minutes later, Virginia was exceedingly ill but certain Devlin was not among the wounded at Hampton. As if reading her thoughts, Tillie said, "He's not here, Sergeant. Can we see the prisoners?"

He nodded and led them back into the center of the camp. "Morgue's just over there," he said, pointing.

Virginia saw where he indicated. Rows of bodies were neatly laid out, each covered with sheets. She stopped in her tracks. "I can't do this," she said, choking. Her self-control was about to disintegrate.

"I can go. I can identify the captain," Frank said quickly.

"Bless you," Virginia whispered.

He returned a half an hour later, looking green beneath his dark skin. "I looked at everyone," he said roughly. "Only one bluecoat there, but I looked at 'em all. He ain't among the dead, Miz Virginia."

Virginia had been sitting on a chair the sergeant had kindly provided her with. She felt the tears begin. "Thank God," she whispered. She fought for the composure that had thus far served her so well, trembling hard with the effort. He wasn't among the wounded here and he wasn't among the dead. There was hope and she clung to it. Even if she and Devlin never reconciled, she would never complain—not if he was alive.

"Come this way, ma'am," the sergeant said rather kindly.

At the far end of the camp, a small stockade had been erected. Virginia was allowed to enter with Sergeant Ames, who spoke with the camp's warden. She only half listened, her gaze scanning the two dozen assembled men. Half were in red coats, the other half in their shirts. Not a single blue coat was among them.

"If we had Captain O'Neill here, I would know it," the warden said. "I know these men by name."

Virginia turned away. If he wasn't dead, wounded or a prisoner of war, did that mean he was back on the *Defiance?* She trembled with relief. Maybe Tillie had been wrong. Maybe the shot had missed him and maybe he hadn't been seized after all.

"Virginia?" A familiar male voice called.

She slowly started to turn, stunned.

"Virginia Hughes? Is that you?"

One of the prisoners, his wrists shackled, was approaching. Her eyes widened as she recognized him. It was Jack Harvey, the man who had once been the ship's surgeon on the *Defiance.* "Mr. Harvey!" she cried, rushing forward.

He smiled at her as if glad to see her. "You are a sight for sore eyes, Miss Hughes."

"Mr. Harvey, are you all right? Have you survived that terrible battle?"

"I am unhurt—and I have tried to offer my services numerous times to the Americans, but no one wishes to avail themselves of my medical expertise." His dark eyes were now bleak.

She turned. "Warden! This man is a fine doctor as well

as a surgeon! He must be allowed to help attend the wounded!"

The warden just grunted.

Sergeant Ames came to life. "I'll speak with Captain Lewis," he said. "We need every doctor we can get."

Harvey smiled wanly at Virginia. She smiled back and squeezed his hand.

He said, "What are you doing here, Miss Hughes?"

She was grim. "It is Mrs. O'Neill now, Mr. Harvey."

His eyes widened in real surprise. Then he shook his head, smiling just a little. "And so it all begins to make sense. I had never seen Devlin so agitated, not by anyone or anything, as he was by you."

She gripped his hand with her free one. "Have you see Devlin? I heard he was shot! I am desperately trying to find him—I am praying he is alive." And she inhaled hard, seeking to keep hold of the last shreds of her composure.

Harvey hesitated.

And Virginia saw from his eyes that he knew something. "What is it! What is it that you know and are afraid to tell me?"

"I heard he was arrested, Virginia. Arrested by Admiral Cockburn himself. Apparently he went berserk and killed his own troops." Harvey winced. "It makes no sense and obviously cannot be true, but that is the rumor around here."

"He's been arrested?" she gasped, though she rejoiced because he was alive. "Where would they send him? Where would he be?"

"I heard he's in the brig—on the *Defiance*," Jack Harvey said.

"I'M AFRAID YOU'LL LIVE, Captain," Paul White, his ship's most recent surgeon, grinned.

Devlin was shirtless, seated on the narrow pallet behind bars in the tiny cell that was his own brig. White had just finished bandaging his right shoulder, which hurt like hell, but he did not give a damn. He knew the wound was not a serious one. Fortunately, his senses honed by a dozen years of battle, he had felt the attacker behind him and had turned just in time. If he had not, he would now be dead, murdered by Tom Hughes.

He knew with every fiber of his being that Hughes had followed him to this war to assassinate him. He did not care.

Because this last battle had reduced his life to one thing, and one thing only: his wife. He kept seeing Virginia as she turned the corner and came face-to-face with him, her visage pale with exhaustion and marred with blood, her eyes huge with fear, the fear of a hunted animal. He kept seeing her as she aimed her musket at him, her hands shaking wildly. He kept seeing her as she was assaulted by those soldiers, her belly swollen with his child. And even now, the memory was enough to terrify him.

If he lost her, he could not bear it. If he lost her, he knew he would never recover from his grief.

Once, long ago, powerless and afraid, he had watched the redcoats murder his father. Yesterday he had seen Virginia being assaulted by the British marines, and for one moment, it had been as if he were a child of ten again. For one moment, the fear and horror had unmanned him and he had been powerless again, watching the woman he loved being assaulted, about to be raped and slain.

But the paralysis gripping him had only been for an instant—because he was not that ten-year-old boy anymore: he was a powerful man, a captain and commander. And then the rage had come, a rage that knew no bounds. To save Virginia, he would have murdered every redcoat in Hampton if that was what had to be done.

Devlin closed his eyes, trembling. But Virginia had not been raped, she had not been slain, and dear God, no man had been as foolish as he had been. He had sacrificed her love and their marriage for his damned revenge. He had given thanks to a God he had stopped praying to long ago a hundred times in the past twenty-four hours, and he could not be grateful enough that Virginia was alive. Before he had been arrested, he had seen Frank and Tillie carry her safely away.

He cradled his face in his hands. He desperately needed his wife. He needed her forgiveness and he needed her love and this last battle had shown him that.

His life had been one of death and hate. No more. He was choosing joy and love—if Virginia would forgive him and take him back.

"Do you want some grog for the pain, sir?"

Devlin looked at the ship's surgeon. There was so much pain, but it was in his heart, and he knew the grog would not ease it. Only Virginia could ease it, if she agreed to return to him, if she could forgive him and if she would love him again, just a little. "No."

A movement sounded. It was the hatch being opened. Both men watched as a pair of very shiny boots came into view, descending the ladder, followed by short thighs encased in bright white britches, a blue jacket, gold buttons, numerous medals and two gold epaulets. Admiral Cockburn faced Devlin and Paul White, as a junior officer descended behind him. It was Thomas Hughes.

Devlin looked at Eastleigh's son and with some surprise realized that he felt no anger, no rage. He felt nothing at all except an odd indifference—and the intense urge to find his wife.

"How's Devlin?" Cockburn asked White.

"Got a real sore shoulder, sir, and a right fine lump on

the head, but he should be able to resume duties in a few days. I mean, if he weren't in the brig," White amended, flushing.

Devlin slowly stood, reaching for his bloodstained shirt, aware of everyone's eyes upon him. How odd this indifference was, how odd and such a relief. Finally, he was done.

And he felt himself smile as he turned to face Cockburn and Hughes, buttoning up his shirt. *He was choosing joy and love.*

As Devlin turned, he happened to glance at Hughes. The man's hostile eyes widened in confusion and surprise when their gazes met. Devlin looked away. He was impatient now to get on with his life, but he had some loose ends to tidy up—he owed Virginia and their unborn child that.

"Release him," Cockburn said.

"But, sir," Hughes began in protest. "He murdered British troops!"

Devlin said not a word as he stepped out of the cell, followed by White.

"We'll speak on deck," Cockburn said firmly, turning and going aloft first. Ignoring Hughes, who stared, Devlin followed the admiral up to the main deck, where the breeze was gentle, the seas soft, the skies bright and blue. In fact, they had never been brighter or bluer.

He smiled and in his mind's eye he saw Virginia, her expression bright, forgiving him, wanting him, and his heart quickened. Devlin quickly took in his surroundings. He instantly recognized where they were—just outside the mouth of the Chesapeake, perhaps a mile from the Virginia shore. The day looked to remain pleasant and he did not feel any stronger wind coming. He saw they were tacking south at three or four knots. He could be at Sweet Briar within two hours. He could not wait.

"I am being released?" he asked as Tom Hughes joined them.

"Yes, you are. Unfortunate events occur in battle, my boy, and I'll be damned if I am losing my best captain over some bloody frogs. Besides, any man would have acted as you did to protect his wife."

Hughes seemed to choke.

"It was a stunning triumph," the admiral continued. "I will make full reference to the part played by your marines and the *Defiance*. A good job, Captain, a very good job, indeed." Cockburn smiled at him.

Devlin did not want to discuss the terrible battle of Hampton. He chafed to leave. Instead, he faced his commanding officer. "I am resigning my commission, Admiral."

Cockburn gaped. So did Tom Hughes at his side. *"What?"* the admiral cried.

Devlin smiled. "I do believe you heard me," he said. "Excuse me. I am going home." Leaving both men staring in disbelief, he strode to his cabin, something light and joyful unfurling in his chest, like a ready sail in a fresh breeze.

He knew nothing about joy and love but surely Virginia could teach him. For she knew enough about those things for the both of them.

And he laughed.

Then, still smiling, he sat and quickly penned the resignation, blew it dry and folded it, then sealed it with wax. He returned to the deck outside, handing the notice of his resignation to Cockburn. "I would recommend turning the command of the *Defiance* over to Red Barlow," he said.

Cockburn was livid. "If I didn't know better, I would call you a coward, sir." He signaled his men, indicating that he wished to be taken to his flagship, stalking off.

Devlin shrugged, not perturbed. Then he turned and faced an incredulous Tom Hughes. "I have something for you," he said mildly.

"Is this a trick? If so, it is exceedingly clever," Hughes accused, stiff with alarm and watching Devlin's hands as if he expected to be assaulted with a dagger.

"My tricks are done. The game is over," Devlin said, "and I am wasting time. Here." He handed another parchment to Hughes, written while in the brig earlier that day.

Hughes was wary. "What is this?"

"A deed," Devlin said, and took a deep breath of the sweet Virginia air. It felt different, tasted different, smelled different—it was somehow clean and fresh.

"I have no use for Sweet Briar!"

"The deed is to Waverly Hall. I don't want it. It's yours." Hughes gaped.

Devlin gestured to a seaman who came running. "I am going ashore," he said. "Prepare a dinghy." And his heart raced as he thought of seeing Virginia again.

"Aye, sir!" The sailor ran off, barking orders.

"You are returning Waverly Hall to us?" Hughes had followed him to the railing of the ship. He was clearly in disbelief.

"Yes, I am."

"I don't understand."

"It doesn't matter." He stared at the sandy beach and the forest beyond, thinking of Virginia again.

"It matters!" Tom Hughes cried. Then he lowered his voice. "My father murdered your father. You have committed your entire life to revenge. You have stolen our home, bedded my stepmother, made a mistress out of my cousin, beaten me to a near pulp and I almost murdered you the other day! So it does matter!"

Devlin didn't even bother to look at him, for the dinghy

he had requested was being lowered into the swells and his heart raced with excitement. "I no longer want revenge," he said. "I want something else."

VIRGINIA FELT BEATEN. The buggy paused before the house and she was so tired she just sat there, staring at the white columns on the porch and the pink roses growing up against the railing. At least Devlin was not among the dead left at Hampton.

But he was a prisoner now, a prisoner of his own people.

Tillie patted her arm. "We'll send a letter to Admiral Cockburn right away. You're his wife. The admiral has to tell you how he is and where he is," she said firmly.

Tears filled Virginia's eyes. "He was protecting me. He only killed those soldiers to protect me. Surely if I tell that to Admiral Cockburn, he will let Devlin go."

"First we have to write him," Tillie said as firmly. And suddenly she stiffened.

Virginia saw her surprise and turned back to the house, following her gaze. And standing there on the porch in a simple shirt, britches and high boots, was the most welcome sight she had ever seen. She cried out, incapable of movement, as Devlin came slowly down the porch steps, his gaze upon her, intense and unwavering.

"Devlin," she managed, beyond relief.

He came to the buggy and clasped her hands. His face was strained with emotion, his eyes wide with anxiety. "Thank God you're all right," he said roughly.

Virginia could not speak. She was stunned—for his eyes were also shining with *tears*.

He smiled a little and cupped her cheek. "I have never known so much fear, Virginia, as when I found Frank in town and he said you were there...." He could not continue. He choked.

Virginia watched in amazement as tears rolled down his cheeks. "You're crying," she whispered, shocked. She felt certain that this man had not cried since he was a small boy, watching his father die.

He nodded, still unable to speak, and the tears continued to slide down his sun-bronzed cheeks. He opened the carriage door to help her out, but he pulled her into his arms instead. He held her hard against his tall, powerful body. "You almost died, Virginia. It was my fault. Because of my damned need for revenge, you could have died yesterday in Hampton. Everything that you have suffered, you have suffered because of me and my revenge. *I am sorry. I am so sorry.* But a mere apology is not enough."

She touched his damp cheek as more tears fell. "Devlin, I cannot regret anything we have shared!" And somehow, it was true. She loved him so much that she treasured every memory, both the good and the bad, the bitter and the sweet.

He shook his head. "We both know that you are being kind, and I do not deserve your kindness." He hesitated and beneath her hands, his body trembled. "When I saw that marine attack you, I went mad with rage, I was truly mad— I was ready to kill every redcoat in my path. I have never been so blinded with rage—except when I saw Tom Hughes assaulting you at the ball. I felt the same murderous intent then—because I love you, Virginia," he said.

She went still. Her heart beat hard. She trembled wildly. How she had yearned to hear these words from him, and now, finally, after so much loss and grief, after so much time, so much pain, her time had come. "You love me?" she whispered, dazed. And elation began.

He nodded, smiling through his tears. "In truth, I have loved you for a very long time, from almost the beginning, when we first met. I was so afraid, Virginia—I was so afraid of you. I was afraid to choose love and joy, because I only knew revenge and hate."

"And now?" she managed, stunned.

"I am still afraid, but the pain of our separation has been too much to bear. I cannot stand to be apart from you," he said simply. "Can you teach me how to live with joy, Virginia? Can you teach me how to love?"

Virginia was amazed. The pain was in his gaze. It was the same pain she herself had withstood for so long, for the very same reasons. "I can teach you all those things, Devlin," she whispered. "Does this mean...what I think it does?" She was afraid to hope.

He nodded soberly, another tear sliding down his cheek. "You asked me to choose, and I made the wrong choice. I know that now. So I am choosing you and our child, Virginia."

She cried out and he held her hard, for a very long time. When he spoke again, it was in a rough whisper. "It's over. Never again. I gave Hughes the deed to Waverly Hall. It's truly over, darling."

She wept against his chest, tears of joy and happiness.

"I was going to ask you for your forgiveness," he said roughly. "But I will not ask that because I do not deserve it. But I will do anything that you ask of me, anything, even though nothing that I can do could possibly make up for what you have been through." He looked down at her and their eyes met. His were shining with love, but the fear was there, too. "Will you return to me? As my wife?"

She smiled and cupped his cheek. "I never left you, Devlin, not in my heart. You have had my heart from those first few days when you took me hostage aboard the *Defiance.*"

He hesitated. "I love you, Virginia, and I know I cannot live without you. I know that now."

She was thrilled. She clasped his hands and held them to her chest. "And you already have my forgiveness, Devlin. I cannot blame you for choosing a life of hatred and revenge, given what happened to your father."

He nodded. "It's time to let Gerald rest in peace—and I want peace, Virginia, I need peace the way I need you."

Virginia laughed, thrilled. "So we will start over?"

"Yes," he said softly, kissing each of her hands tenderly in turn. Then he gave her a significant look. "I resigned my commission."

She could only gape, stunned.

He smiled slowly at her, then took a deep, cleansing breath and stepped to her side. They gazed together at the handsome brick plantation home and the fields beyond, rippling and green with the summer's new crops. "Sweet Briar is doing well," he said quietly, his gaze moving over the rolling fields as if he were inspecting one of his ships, and then he looked down at her, taking her hand. His smile was warm and loving. "I think we should divide our time. Half of the year here, the other half at Askeaton."

"You would stay here for half of every year?" she cried in surprise.

"Would that please you, my darling?" And he smiled more broadly.

"Very much," she whispered. With Devlin at her side, she knew they would make Sweet Briar prosper. They would harvest its fields of tobacco and fill its halls with children. But she loved Askeaton, too, for in her many months there as his hostage, she had come to think of the manor as her home. They would make his ancestral home prosper, too, and more important, those dark and ancient halls would soon be filled with love and laughter and as many of Devlin's children as she could bear. Her heart pounding in excitement, she took his hand. "This pleases me very much."

"Then I am pleased." He took her in his arms and kissed her forehead tenderly. "I missed you terribly, Virginia. From this day forward, I will fulfill your every wish."

She smiled up at him and had to laugh. "I do doubt that, somehow...Captain."

"I mean it," he said, with such fervor that she laughed again.

"Then it is my wish that we go inside so I can introduce everyone to my husband."

He bowed, sending her a seductive look, leaving her in no doubt as to what he wished to do—and soon. "After you, my darling."

She took his hand and, smiling, they went inside, the new master of Sweet Briar and his wife. Now there was simply too much joy to bear and, finally, the future beckoned, shining and bright.

Virginia could not wait.

AUTHOR'S NOTE

Dear Reader,
As always, when I am writing a "more historical" historical romance, I try to blend as much fact as possible with fiction. While many Americans are blissfully unaware of the War of 1812, most of us, myself included, are absolutely ignorant as to the reasons for the war, the extent of the actual fighting, the loss of lives and the war's duration. Some of the reasons for the war I have suggested—internal politics were as significant as fear of British domination, free trade, impressments and the agrarian agenda to expand into Canada. Loss of life was terrible, and the war was really under way by 1811, although the Chesapeake Affair was in 1807! The war did not end until February 1815, although a peace was concluded the previous December.

All battles alluded to in *The Prize* are historical fact. Devlin's fifteen-minute victory over the USS *Independence* is wholly based on the exploits of Captain Philip Broke of the *Shannon,* who sent his sister ship away, lured the *Chesapeake* out of Boston harbor and demolished her in fifteen minutes. Fortunately, the British failed to carry out their invasion of Norfolk, Virginia; as unfortunately, the massacre at Hampton and some of the atrocities I have described were committed and were even worse.

I have loosely based the naval career of Devlin O'Neill on that of Thomas Cochrane, the eldest son of a Scottish earl, his family an old and distinguished one without means. He was one of the greatest British fighting naval captains ever, a man at once notorious for his exploits at sea in battle and for his unorthodox strategies and his innovative naval thinking. He was also well-known for his insubordination and lack of respect for the admirals ranked above him. In the middle of his career he became a radical M.P.—a fervent champion of the poor and the oppressed. I am not the first to base my fictional hero upon his life; the hero of Patrick O'Brien's bestselling seafaring series is also based on the life of this truly amazing man.

As many of you may already know, Devlin is a descendant of Liam O'Neill and Katherine FitzGerald *(The Game),* while the Earl of Adare and his sons are descendants of Rolfe de Warenne *(The Conqueror).* I feel sure that most of you must be asking how Liam's family lost their land and fortune, and how the de Warennes wound up in Ireland. The history of England and Ireland from the Conquest to the Regency is one of extreme political turbulence and the rise and fall of family dynasties. The British conquest of Ireland happened over centuries, in stages. Fortune-hunting landless younger sons fought in Ireland for the Crown, and were rewarded for their triumphs with land taken from the original Celtic kings and noblemen, who were defeated and then dispossessed. Many of these Norman and English settlers became as Celtic as their native forebears in the earlier years. During Queen Elizabeth's reign, the final subjugation and colonization of Ireland was completed—by the time of her death, very few Catholic Irish lords owned their ancestral lands, most of it being in the hands of the Anglo Protestant interlopers. Some of these lords intermarried with the original Celtic families; most preferred to wed into a British family. Being Irish and Protestant was second class, being Irish and Catholic far worse. It had now become criminal to be a Catholic.

Clearly one of Rolfe's grandsons sought his fortune in Ireland, establishing the de Warenne dynasty there. Clearly the O'Neills fought one rebellion too many against their English overlords, resulting in their dispossession. And as for Devlin being Catholic (Liam was Protestant), his great ancestress Katherine FitzGerald was also Catholic.

I hope you have enjoyed *The Prize*. After writing contemporary romance for several years, I have found it a real joy to write about a bygone time when men were really men and women dared to try to tame them. Frankly, it was a blast! I have discovered that there is no genre I prefer writing more—telling Devlin and Virginia's story was like coming home. I hope to continue writing about these two extraordinary families. The second book in this saga, which I am currently about to complete, is *The Masquerade*, Tyrell's story. It will be published in the fall of 2005.

Please visit my Web site at www.brendajoyce.com. I visit my message boards frequently and will answer your questions there. If you need to catch up on the O'Neills and de Warennes, you can find all my novels listed under Novels, including *The Game, The Conqueror* and *Promise of the Rose*.

I look forward to hearing from you.

Happy reading, always,

Brenda Joyce

From *New York Times* bestselling author

Gena Showalter

Enter a mythical world
of dragons, demons and nymphs...
Enter a world of dark seduction
and powerful magic...
Enter Atlantis....

Catch these thrilling tales in a bookstore near you!

THE NYMPH KING • Available now!

HEART OF THE DRAGON • Available January 2009

JEWEL OF ATLANTIS • Available February 2009

THE VAMPIRE'S BRIDE • Available March 2009

"Lots of danger and sexy passion give lucky readers a
spicy taste of adventure and romance."
—*Romantic Times BOOKreviews*
on *Heart of the Dragon*

REQUEST YOUR FREE BOOKS!

2 FREE NOVELS FROM THE ROMANCE/SUSPENSE COLLECTION PLUS 2 FREE GIFTS!

YES! Please send me 2 FREE novels from the Romance/Suspense Collection and my 2 FREE gifts (gifts are worth about $10). After receiving them, if I don't wish to receive any more books, I can return the shipping statement marked "cancel." If I don't cancel, I will receive 4 brand-new novels every month and be billed just $5.49 per book in the U.S. or $5.99 per book in Canada, plus 25¢ shipping and handling per book plus applicable taxes, if any*. That's a savings of at least 20% off the cover price! I understand that accepting the 2 free books and gifts places me under no obligation to buy anything. I can always return a shipment and cancel at any time. Even if I never buy another book from the Reader Service, the two free books and gifts are mine to keep forever.

185 MDN EF5Y   385 MDN EF6C

Name _____ (PLEASE PRINT)

Address _____ Apt. #

City _____ State/Prov. _____ Zip/Postal Code

Signature (if under 18, a parent or guardian must sign)

Mail to **The Reader Service:**
IN U.S.A.: P.O. Box 1867, Buffalo, NY 14240-1867
IN CANADA: P.O. Box 609, Fort Erie, Ontario L2A 5X3

Not valid to current subscribers to the Romance Collection,
the Suspense Collection or the Romance/Suspense Collection.

Want to try two free books from another line?
Call 1-800-873-8635 or visit www.morefreebooks.com.

* Terms and prices subject to change without notice. N.Y. residents add applicable sales tax. Canadian residents will be charged applicable provincial taxes and GST. Offer not valid in Quebec. This offer is limited to one order per household. All orders subject to approval. Credit or debit balances in a customer's account(s) may be offset by any other outstanding balance owed by or to the customer. Please allow 4 to 6 weeks for delivery. Offer available while quantities last.

Your Privacy: Harlequin is committed to protecting your privacy. Our Privacy Policy is available online at www.eHarlequin.com or upon request from the Reader Service. From time to time we make our lists of customers available to reputable third parties who may have a product or service of interest to you. If you would prefer we not share your name and address, please check here. ☐

BOB08R

BRENDA JOYCE

HQN™

We *are* romance™

www.HQNBooks.com   PHBJ0109BL